Northern Wars

Quentin Black

Cover design by : Golden Rivet

https://golden-rivet.com/

An Outlaw's Reprieve – A Connor Reed Novella – For **FREE**

Click here for Free E-Book

DEDICATION

To Holly,

You knew I needed you before I had anything
to offer you.

ACKNOWLEDGEMENTS

To Jay Gardiner, Lee Barret and Sam Laird for your encouragement and support.

To the Evolution of Combat MMA promotions and Blur Tattoo.

Golden-Rivet for the cover design and promotional video.

To Ian Butlin and 'Big' Andy Butlin for their technical advice.

<u>Special Thanks</u> to fellow Royal Marine, Jake Olafsen, author of *Wearing the Green Beret*.

And Chris Searle for his in-depth and polishing critiques.

AUTHOR'S NOTE

Any specific terms and phrases have been highlighted in italics and can be found in the glossary.

RYDER FAMILY TREE

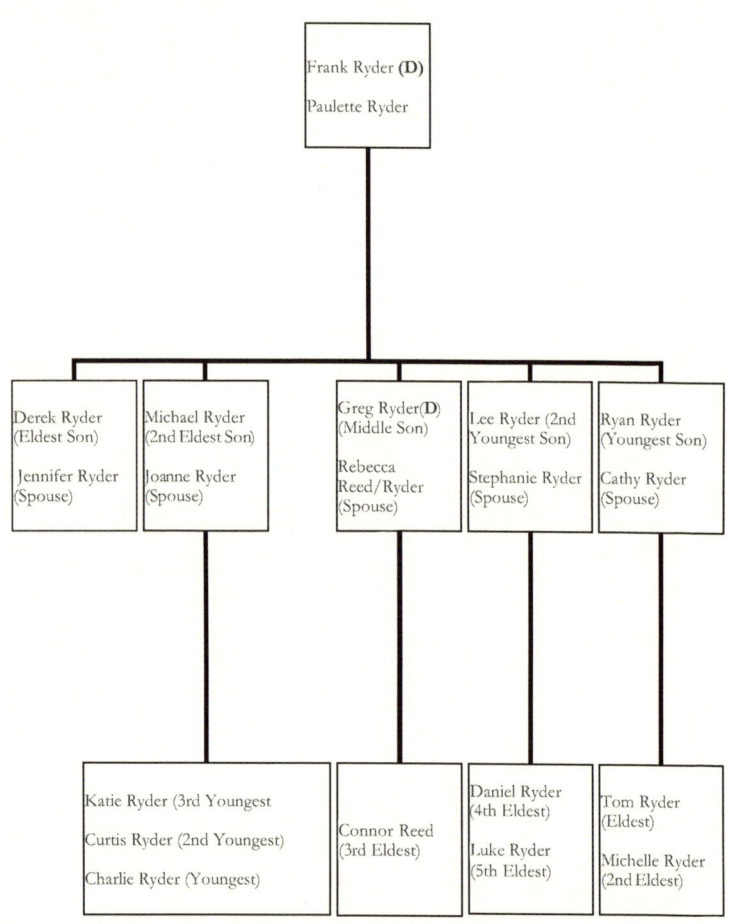

Frank Ryder **(D)**

Paulette Ryder

Derek Ryder
(Eldest Son)

Jennifer Ryder
(Spouse)

Michael Ryder
(2nd Eldest Son)

Joanne Ryder
(Spouse)

Greg Ryder**(D)**
(Middle Son)

Rebecca
Reed/Ryder
(Spouse)

Lee Ryder (2nd
Youngest Son)

Stephanie Ryder
(Spouse)

Ryan Ryder
(Youngest Son)

Cathy Ryder
(Spouse)

Katie Ryder (3rd Youngest

Curtis Ryder (2nd Youngest)

Charlie Ryder (Youngest)

Connor Reed
(3rd Eldest)

Daniel Ryder
(4th Eldest)

Luke Ryder
(5th Eldest)

Tom Ryder
(Eldest)

Michelle Ryder
(2nd Eldest)

"Out of every one hundred men, ten should not even be there, eighty are just targets, nine are the real fighters, and we are lucky to have them, for they make the battle. Ah, but the one, one is a warrior, and he will bring the others back."

Heraclitus, Greek philosopher

1

Connor knew that to simply deny his hate would be futile. He would have to focus on his actions so the intense emotion would observe from the background, rather than interfering with what he had to do. As unfit and inept at one-on-one unarmed combat he suspected his uncle might be, his father's older brother was still a big, strong man with adrenaline-wide eyes.

In the after-hours quiet of The Buxton Arms, he and cousins Tom—older than him—Luke and the twins Curtis and Charlie had formed a loose semi-circle facing their uncle and head of the Ryder crime family, Derek.

A copy of a three-hundred-year-old picture of a tavern scene hung on the wall behind Derek, with one of the card-playing, beer-supping men in it looking out at the spectacle that was about to unfold.

The corpse of Brendan Chappel, an associate of Derek's, lay to one side. They had asphyxiated him with a plastic bag.

Connor held a pistol aimed at Derek and said, "Tom, play the recording. The first voice is a corrupt copper named Stephen Mahon."

The recording began to play from Tom's phone.

Mahon—*They can't come back to* (garbled) *live to tell this tale.*

Derek—*The money I am giving them pair is plenty. Besides, where are they going* (garbled)—*can't stay in Bradford. Aziz would have them torn up.*

Mahon—*How you going to get him into the moors without him telling anyone? If even one person knows you have asked him there, they'll know you're behind it.*

Derek—*If I ask my brother to come alone and not tell anyone, he won't—all that 'a man is only as good as his word', the pious cunt. It'll be bang, bang. I'll take over, and you'll get paid more.*

Mahon—*Think anyone will suspect?*

Derek—*What? That I had my brother killed? Nah—I'll make sure people's eyes look over to Bradford.*

The recording clicked off. It was the third time he had heard it, except this time, the tremor did not reach his hands.

Derek's panic-streaked voice cut through, "That has been fucking doctored by Aziz."

He was referring to Bradford's most notorious crime lord.

"How did you know Aziz gave it to me?" Connor answered.

Derek spluttered, "Cos, cos he's had it in for me, hasn't he?"

"Luke, go check if that fat cunt is carrying anything."

He 'castled' the rear sights with the foresight of the pistol evenly on Derek's centre mass.

His younger cousin, a naughty boxer both gloved and bare-knuckle, kept his eyes open as he frisked the big, steroid-jacked underworld boss.

"He's clean."

Connor tilted his head, and Luke made his way back. He fully unloaded the pistol before stripping it and throwing each separate part to his cousins.

He lifted his sleeves, his jean bottoms and then his T-shirt.

"I am unarmed. If you beat me," he said to Derek, "we'll pretend your murder of my dad didn't happen. You'll walk out, still head of the family. But you will not leave here without us fighting."

The breathing of the former patriarch of the family came out raggedly, and Connor steadied his own.

Knowing his uncle had zero expertise wrestling or fighting on the ground, he did not concern himself with getting taken down—but anyone could get lucky with a punch.

Jab, feints, don't rush in.

He felt the stirrings in his diaphragm of a dark excitement and reminded himself to focus.

Derek eventually stepped forward.

His reaction to Connor's feint was more of a flinch than a defensive block. Connor's first landed punch was a jab to the face. More followed, from different angles—jabs to the body, screw jabs, double jabs. He easily evaded Derek's telegraphed punches. Each of the younger man's jabs sounded like a piece of defrosted steak slapping onto a chopping board.

A left hook axed into Derek's liver, and the former Royal Marine's foot-sweep sent him crashing. He rolled into a crouch, sucking for breath.

Connor sniggered. "You never could fight. All show and no go."

He caught a flash of defiance in the eyes when he eventually rose. Derek rushed at him, throwing wild punches, sometimes starting from his hip, following Connor with them, who—though always in range—ducked, swayed and stepped around the flailing. When he did not throw back, Derek's already porous defence became non-existent.

A mighty right hand fired off Derek's jaw, snapping his head around with cartoonish force. He fell like a log. He lay on his back, his eyes unblinking, only the heaving of his chest showing he was still alive.

"Get up, you fat cunt," said Connor, allowing his anger to step closer.

"Please. It was…complicated."

"Jealous brother wanted control. A yellow school bus passenger could pull his tongue off the window and explain that one."

"There was—stuff with our Jennifer, and—he wasn't the Messiah everyone makes out."

"Did he rape her?"

"What?"

"Did. He. Rape. Her."

"No, but—"

"Then shut the fuck up," Connor said and held out his hand. Tom stepped forward and placed Connor's commando dagger into his palm.

Derek scuttled backwards, but as he attempted to stand Connor's toecap found his mouth. Derek roiled back, spitting out blood-laced shards of teeth like broken mints.

The sobs came.

"Please don't kill me—I know it's rich to ask but please."

"You think I'd kill my grandparents' son?" answered Connor.

"I…I…I had your dad murd—"

"Yeh, that's what yoooou did. But there are certain things you can't come back from, and murdering family is one of them. Besides, you could die in a traffic accident. Or get stabbed by some chav you've been bullying. No," said Connor, pointing the blade at him for emphasis, "you'll walk out of here and leave for good. Not just Leeds, but the North of England. If you so much as set foot in West Yorkshire again, or set up shop anywhere north of Birmingham or south of Newcastle, I'll take it as an act of war on my family, and you'll die—and if there is a Judgement Day, I'll tell God why."

After a moment, Derek's voice tremored the question, "Why do you have the knife?"

Connor smirked. "You didn't think you were going to get off that easy, did you? Lads, pin him and hold his head steady."

Derek's surges came to nothing under their collective grip. Tom's knees pinched his head like a vice.

As Luke clamped his palm over the blood-smeared mouth, Connor said, "Take your hand away, mate, no one is going to hear but us. And I want to remember the sound."

As Connor began carving into the forehead, the agonising roars bounced off the walls in a cruel symphony. Both he and Derek took gasping breaths throughout the ordeal—but Connor's were punctuating his own laugher.

2

Three months later.

Connor stood with Tom in the car park overlooking the bleak reservoir. Dawn crept from behind the horizon, turning Saddleworth Moor from black to the darkest of blues. The cold air stroked his face in the eerie quiet.

Tom said, rubbing his hands together, "The whole point of meeting this early was so as not to attract attention. Where is he?"

They were waiting for a notorious Liverpudlian criminal enforcer.

Connor shrugged against his dark blue sweater. "He'll still be fucked off that we made him come out this far, this early. It's a play for dominance. If he's not here in five, we'll fuck off. Speaking of attracting attention, why did you rock up in that Scooby Doo Mystery Machine?"

He was referring to the rusted 1972 Volkswagen T2 Camper parked next to the pub.

"Taking it down to Sheffield after this to sell it."

"Surely it'd barely be worth your fuel money."

"That's going twenty-five grand, mate. It's a done deal."

"That heap of shit? Fuck off," Connor exclaimed.

"Who do you think knows more about automobiles, you or me?"

"You," Connor conceded to his mechanic elder cousin. "Why, though? Looks like something Fred Flintstone would drive—or run, or whatever he did."

"It's the split-screen, patina windows, and that it's a classic—don't ask. Anyway, I thought you'd have got a motorbike by now?"

Connor smiled; his cousin must have eyes and ears all over Leeds. "Who told you?"

"The gaffer at the test centre comes in for his car repairs. He said you took their crash course. Thought you'd be riding around like Arnie off *Terminator 2*."

"Well, I am built like him," he said. "To be honest, mate, I'd rather have the licence and rent them out on occasion. If I bought one outright, I'd have to fuck around maintaining and insuring it."

"You'll end up buying one. What bikes do you like the look of?"

"I like the look of some of the Triumphs—especially that Thunderbird Storm. British company too."

"Made in Thailand," said Tom, with his hands thrust into his black Puffa jacket. "And those Thunderbird Storms are fucking beasts. I am telling ya, you won't enjoy riding it as a beginner cos you'll keep thinking you're going to die every time you pick up speed."

"What are you suggesting then?"

"I know a guy in Wakey who sells Royal Enfield bikes. He's got some of those new Interceptor 650s in…gorgeous bikes and probably better for you seeing as the only bikes you've been on are the scramblers we used to ride as lads, and the one at the test centre."

"Chicks' bikes, aren't they?"

"Why do you say they are chicks' bikes?" Tom frowned. "Cos you've seen girls sat on 'em on Instagram? They're proper bikes from a manufacturer that has been chucking out bikes longer than anyone—1901."

"I'll think about it," replied Connor. He felt a pleasant nostalgia remembering how his Uncle Ryan—Tom's Dad— used to take them to a disused quarry between Halifax and Keighley called the Flappits as young teenagers.

A Range Rover appeared in the distance and meandered down to them, zipping Connor into a demeanour of professionalism.

The Range Rover parked, and out of the passenger side stepped a man, taller than average, with a tanned face full of grooves and angles on account of his leanness. He wore jeans, and an oatmeal crew-neck sweater under a Parka. His light brown hair was shaved high up the sides and swept to one side.

Connor could see the Range Rover was laden with men.

Marty McKinley stepped towards them with a, "Fuck me, la, it's freezing, we going inside or what?"

"There's no need," said Tom. "This won't take long."

Marty nodded. "Mr Ellis understands there's 'ad to be some time for things to settle now Derek is off the scene and youse 'av had a reshuffle. Your Uncle Michael and Lee are out of the clink now and we heard good things—that you've massively grown your businesses, so fair's fair now. Derek had our money dropped off in cash in Liverpool at—"

"That's not happening any more," said Connor, flatly.

He met McKinley's stare with his own as Tom said, "We might be open to a business arrangement."

McKinley broke a moment of silence with, "I might have to discuss it with my lads in the Rover, and they might have to discuss it with youse."

"Of course," said Connor. "That's why we picked this place. So any 'discussions' won't have any witnesses."

Connor saw a flicker in McKinley's eyes and knew he was fighting the urge to look around. Instead, he said, "Mr Ellis isn't going to be happy. Sure youse want to go down this road?"

"We're sure," Tom replied.

"Look, I know youse aren't plazzy gangsters but youse two—your family—are still way over your head. This ain't *Emmerdale Farm*—this is a man who has been running things in the North since Ian Rush was still a boss striker."

"We're aware of Harry Ellis's CV," interjected Connor. "Now, you can either take the message to him, or you can get the lads in the Range Rover out to help you with negotiations. We'd prefer you didn't as it'll take time and energy filling the holes in."

McKinley's eyebrows compressed. "Not sure why you're being so aggy, la."

"I think you know the reason—"

"Nah, I don't, why don't—"

"But let's not cry over spilt milk. You take the message to Mr Ellis that there's no more protection money or whatever you rinsed our cretin of an uncle for. If he wants to discuss future business proposals, then we'll be all ears, but as of now, we don't have any with you."

McKinley said, "All right. I'll tell him. He won't like it but knows business is business. One of those things."

With that, he backed away, got into the Range Rover and Connor remained poised until it drove off.

The sun crested the hills just as the vehicle disappeared behind them.

"About what we expected," said Tom. "What's that look for?"

"It wasn't what he said that bothered me. It was what he didn't say."

"Meaning?"

"He never asked about our leptin-resistant cunt of an uncle, Derek—not what happened, not where he is, nothing. Over five years of a steady revenue stream for them and there wasn't one question asked."

"Maybe he's not bothered what's happened to Derek as long as he gets the money. Maybe he thought there was no point in asking."

"Or he might know what's happened to Derek and where he is because he's sheltering him. And, in exchange, he'll be singing like a choirboy regarding our businesses. You were right to hide some of it from him."

"What you thinking?"

"I am thinking we're going to have to put everyone on standby now. There's no telling what Harry Ellis's reaction is going to be. The way McKinley was all 'nicey, nicey' at the end bothered me too."

"How come?"

"*'Humble words and increased preparations are signs the enemy is about to attack'*, according to Sun Tzu. Didn't you say you heard they've had an uptick in arms?"

"So I've heard," said Tom. "What does it mean to be leptin-resistant?"

19

"Leptin is a hormone that tells your brain you are full."

"A bookworm's way of calling someone fat?"

"Yeh," answered Connor. "When does Luke get back from Thailand?"

"On Monday. That's if he hasn't been arrested or murdered or whatever the fuck he'll have got himself into."

"Why? Has he said something?"

"No, but it's just him, isn't it, always getting himself in mither. Stupid too, he could get to the top—whether it's in our game or boxing—he's going to ruin it all if he's not careful."

Connor shook his hands out. "I stopped getting frustrated with how others live their lives a while ago—how hard is it to change something about yourself you don't like? Let's hope he gets it together soon."

3

At the head of the table of thirteen, in a room that combined historical art with a smart-box projector and gel foam lumbar support seats, Oso Xhelli's forehead lined with disdain while looking at the images on the elevated screen. Now a few years past his sixtieth birthday and having risen to the top of the Albanian mafia, he told the ensemble before him, "Times will change, character will always remain timeless."

He meant it; some men were happy to play with smooth rocks that lay on the surface than dig for diamonds. Those whose social media pages he was now looking at were such men—posing with wads of cash, gold-plated AKs, whorish women and big, fast cars.

He smoothed his moustache and beard; the white raced through the grey, as it did his hair. Although there were hints of it receding, it still hung to his shoulders. His voice gravelled in the Gheg dialect of the northern Albanian hills.

"These are the type of men who might talk to the authorities if faced with prison here. But in England, they are sent to holiday camps."

Oso was the Krye—'boss'— of his family clan. His was one of fifteen clans controlling the organised crime in Albania. The men present were his executive committee, minus a couple of absentees.

However, the men on the screen were young men of Albanian heritage, making their names the wrong way. And he pitied them—they would never rise to the heights because even if they ever had the right focus in the first place, they had lost it in the haze of pleasures and addiction that notoriety in a large city could bring. Oso's father told him, *Take moments to smell the meadow's wildflowers as you pass through, but don't sleep in it—you might never wake again.*

It was in observing the loud and brash criminals that Oso was thankful for the many degrees of separation between himself and these 'internet gangsters'.

Andrei Faja asked him, "Would you like them to be punished?"

Faja was his clan's Mik—a title meaning 'friend' who acted as a liaison to members and had the responsibility of coordinating unit activities. With Xhelli's underboss away on business in Shijak, Andrei was this committee's most senior member, after himself.

Though the youngest Mik in the Mafia Shqiptare—the term used for the real Albanian mafia— being in his late twenties, he commanded respect throughout the organisation. Oso noted how his mannerisms and appearance could change from one encounter to the next; the dark hair could be dishevelled or slicked back like a Hollywood actor. His frame could give off the appearance of rugged masculinity or hint at frailty. It was Faja's dark eyes that could be truly chameleon— he had seen them convey childlike curiosity, absorptive concentration, wry amusement and terrifying authority. Andrei's father had been more transparent.

Three principles kept the true Albanian mafia steadfast: a flat hierarchal structure based on honour, family and marriage for its inner circle, an acceptance of outsiders for one-off jobs or secondary roles and, finally, disciplinary action against any deviation from their rules.

"They are of secondary importance at this time. I want a close eye kept on them, Andrei, but at this time the encroachment of certain competitors needs to be addressed."

Raymond Van Der Saar, a Dutch drug lord, had been expanding to the point of cutting into the Tirana clan's bottom line. So, at Oso's request, Andrei had sent a family associate to Amsterdam to form a business link.

The offer had been rebuffed.

Van Der Saar had strict guidelines on the limit of the cutting of his product, and the reply had been, "*Due to your organisation's size and many working parts, you cannot guarantee adherence to my wishes.*"

Oso found the Dutchman's attitude churlish, but he was a businessman—*would the expense of war with Van Der Saar cost more than the gain?*

He was also a figurehead in an organisation that valued honour above all else. For Van Der Saar to dismiss his emissary out of hand without even a counter-offer was a demonstration of disrespect—and it could not go uncorrected.

"What would you have me do, Krye?" asked Andrei.

Oso smoothed the suit lapels over his tired but trim torso. "Gain every morsel of intelligence you can on Mr Van Der Saar's operation. Manufacturing, transport, distribution. I want to know who his business associates are and how many soldiers he can bring to bear. And I want to know who his friends and, especially, who his family are. Be as quiet as possible—even if it means the progress is slow. As time passes, fear of our potential wrath will wither within him. When you are done, I should know how he makes love and what he likes to eat. Understand?"

"I understand, my Krye."

Connor sat with his laptop at a quarter past five in the morning. He made it a priority to study for at least an hour each day.

A few years ago, Bruce McQuillan had recruited him into a black operations unit named The Chameleon Project for which he would be forever grateful. It had given him a focus for the mass of burning energy within. A purpose that not only stimulated him mentally, quenched a thirst for danger but was additionally altruistic.

Bruce had explained to him that "*the remit of The Project is to protect British citizens from the threat of organised crime and terrorism that could cause irreversible damage before the judicial system had a hope of preventing them.*"

Connor had completed a mission in Ukraine months back. Before he could escape back to the UK, it had been necessary for him to lay low and stay with a friend of

23

McQuillan's from 'the old days'. The charismatic and entertaining Yuri Kozlov had regaled him with stories over superb whisky on his porch overlooking the moon-puddled river. The Yorkshireman remembered something the ruthless Ukrainian had imparted to him.

"Do you realise why you have become his preferred agent after such a short space of time?"

"Because I come from a criminal family and can move within these worlds."

The multimillionaire sighed a quiet laugh and asked, "How much do you know about ancient Greece?"

"A reasonable amount. Read Steven Pressfield's *Gates of Fire* and thought it was fucking superb."

"Ahh, yes, Pressfield. Have you read his book *The Tides of War*, about the Peloponnesian War between Athens and Sparta?"

"Not yet."

"I will not spoil it all. But there is a passage where the difference between the two is described. The Athenian mindset is one of *thrasytes*—what you British would translate as an ambitious boldness. The Spartan mindset was one of *andreia*—a manly braving of enduring what must be endured and doing what must be done. The reason why you're the one he calls upon is because he sees both in you. But remember, it is a man's andreia that gives out before his thrasytes, and you must guard against this every day."

It had resonated with Connor. So in maintaining his andreia, the agent would wake early and review and absorb whatever Jaime—The Chameleon Project's tech genius—sent him on current events and players pertinent to his role as an agent. After that, he would learn a few phrases of Dutch and Polish. Finally, he would pick a random topic.

The caffeine from the black coffee beside him began to take effect, the owner of the Ilkley Air BnB—he continually switched locations—had good taste in ground beans. Though he enjoyed this lifestyle of constantly moving, he knew he would need a permanent residence one day.

His phone alerted him to a WhatsApp call coming through—it was his younger cousin, Luke.

He answered the call. "What's up? Thought you weren't back until tonight?"

"I am but I'm in the shit."

Connor took a breath. "What is it?"

"I went to a brothel last night."

"Shemale? Scrapping?"

"No. I didn't bag up. The taxi driver was chuckling—the gist was there's been an outbreak of HIV in there."

"You've got time. Tom told me the hotel you're in. I'll send you the location of a clinic out there—go straight there, they'll give you a course of PEP, they'll—"

"What's PEP?"

"Post-exposure prophylaxis—it's a nerd's term for a course of antiretroviral medicine. You'll feel sick and you'll have to take them for a week, which serves you right."

"I thought you had to take it for a month?"

"You'll be getting a new formula that hit the market only a couple of months ago."

"Am I paying in cash or—"

"I'll pay for them—you can square up with me when you're back. Luckily, you'll have caught it within seventy-two hours, you absolute fucking div."

There were a few moments' silence and then, "It's not just that—Candice is meant to be picking me up from the airport."

"So?"

"She's booked a hotel."

"Tell her there's a change of plan, that the family needs you on business."

"Connor, I can't avoid her for a week, and then she's going to want to know why I aren't fucking her—we never used condoms before. I can't start now or she'll click on."

"I thought she was a fuck-buddy, not your bird?"

"She is, but she's one I want to keep."

Connor thought for a moment. "Right, listen. When I end this call, I am going to be sorting out your medicine. Call a taxi and then call this Candice. Tell her you got wasted last night and ended up with a Leeds United tattoo, but the taxi driver told you there was an outbreak of HIV in that parlour. You've had to book into a clinic and it's delayed your flight by a day. I'll pick you up from the airport—we'll go around to a parlour, and you'll get a tattoo—it'll be a naff one, anything too nice and people might suspect. Understand?"

After a few moments Luke said, "You're a genius."

"I am disappointed in you, Luke. A lack of self-discipline leads to unreliability. I thought you'd have seen enough of an example of that even in our own family," answered Connor before ending the call.

Derek Ryder sat on the balcony warmed by the Tenerife sun. He averted his eyes from the circular tea stains in his mug to watch the seemingly carefree holidaymakers, with their families and friends. And felt intense resentment towards them.

The fantasy he was merely taking a well-earned holiday comforted him. Almost three months ago, he had arrived in the 'more Spanish part of the island' and could only bear the truth of his situation for short periods. He rolled his tongue around his new veneers, resenting them even though he had contemplated having them before the smashing of his teeth.

His entire world had collapsed, and the scar on his forehead had been a constant reminder.

His nephews had pinned him to the floor and formed a vice around his head. The son of the brother he had murdered sat on his chest, scoring a blade into his forehead. The tearing of the flesh, unzipping the blood rivulets into his eyes and the scolding of Connor's laughter at his screaming were still all too much to bear.

What hurt the most was when he was released Connor had thrown him a tea towel to stem the bleeding and, with a "Go on, fuck off", shooed him away like the local newsagent had when Derek was eleven years old and got caught reading magazines he had not saved the money for. The stripping of his power and exiling him from *his* city had banished him into the cold of irrelevancy.

The apartment belonged to a gangster associate, who previously owned a piece of the once lucrative time-share racket. Now he had African, Indian and Chinese street dealers along the strips under the pretence of selling sunglasses, watches and handbags, and there were even hair braiders. Then came the offers of coke to the drunken holidaymakers. He had been coming on holiday here for seven years and got to know the operation—more so in the last year or two, as he had been leaving Jennifer at home in the face of her reluctance to come with him. It was bizarre, the more successful he became the more she drew away from him. Not that she genuinely loved him anyway—she had never looked at him *that* way—and Derek knew she was capable of it.

He sneered—they had all worshipped Connor's father, Greg, but they did not know what he knew.

He felt drained and after this morning's failed attempt at masturbation, he realised he had not 'jabbed up' for almost four weeks.

The keys rattling in the door startled him, and he whipped around.

"Gave you a fright there, la?" said Marty McKinley.

To say he oversaw some of the most feared gangsters on the island, there was nothing to the Scouser—light frame, hollow cheeks, but eyes bright with health. With his tanned skin, short of leathery, the sides of his head were shaved so high that any shorter and he would have a Mohawk.

"Forgot you 'ad keys," he replied.

"Not good that, kidda. Can't stay in 'ere, moping. You need to get a foothold back over there. 'Ere," McKinley said, throwing him a brown paper bag. "Go do what you need to do, an' we'll talk. There's some blow in there too."

Derek opened it to find a syringe, a small bag of white powder and a bottle labelled 'Trenbolone acetate'.

"How come the bag's this small?" he asked.

"One, don't be an ungrateful cunt, you've had that on tab," said McKinley, the edge in his voice shrinking Derek.

27

"And two, cos no matter how big the bag was, it would just fly up your nose in twenty-four hours, big lad."

Derek's inclination was to protest but it was the truth.

McKinley clicked his fingers. "Fuck off to the bathroom and do what you got to do; we've got things to discuss."

Derek felt his ire rise, for years no man had ever ordered him around. But as he looked into the eyes of his derisive benefactor, he realised his fall from the top of the pecking order had taken his self-esteem with it.

He creaked to his feet and sloped to the bathroom. The old hand decided to jab up first—when he did, he began to feel better. He knew this had to be a placebo as Trenbolone took at least two to three days to take effect. Next, the coke. He had not had it in a while, and the strong snort soon bathed his brain in a focused, serene numbness.

He came back out feeling a little like his old self. Perching on the sofa, he asked, "OK, what were we talking about?"

"My boss wants the revenue we were getting when you were in charge up there, la."

"I don't even know who's in charge there now."

"I think the guy that's carved chow mein in Chinese into ya forehead would be the first choice."

Derek's embarrassment burnt a hole through his high.

"What do you want from me?"

"What I need to know is everything about your family up there. See, the boss says gaining intel is key. Because it'll strengthen our negotiations or give us a better idea of how to 'convince' them if they refuse to play ball."

"What do I get out of this?"

McKinley brought his face level. "Kidda, you'll have us to back ya mission to reclaim the throne."

"Not sure if any of the family would 'av me back up there."

"Look after those that look after you, fuck off those that fuck off you. You don't owe any of 'em."

"I know. What I mean is, I can't be the Don again without local backing. And—"

"Don't kid a kidda, you have scallies who'd welcome you back if you show strength again. And nothing screams a 'bad la' more than a bloke who'd kill any fucker for revenge. Even his own family."

4

Kathryn Bainbridge stared at Salvador Dali's picture of a rose floating in the blue sky above a desolate landscape. It hung on her otherwise sparse office wall and she focused on her breath. She had a long career of dealing with the stress of policing, and the image had helped on occasion.

She had joined *the Met* during the late eighties, an unforgiving policing environment for any rookie copper, let alone a woman. From the beginning, she had shut down any flirtations with colleagues and knew it had hampered her short-term popularity as a result. However, she had witnessed a score of WPCs throwing away their careers amid one kind of extra-marital liaison or another. Kathryn had kept her focus on work throughout it all.

She transferred to Liverpool on promotion to Sergeant to begin her Detective training. In her first two years, there had been several times where she had felt policing in the port city could have capsized her resolve.

In the wake of the Hillsborough disaster, a large part of the city's populous felt the police were an institution complicit in a cover-up. Unemployment had compounded this distaste into a hate for law enforcement even among non-criminal elements in the communities.

Even the Liverpudlian officers struggled to decipher the way of speaking amongst its underworld members, and she found it especially difficult in the beginning.

The fluidity of the criminal partnerships there—including some unusual cross-cultural alliances— made identifying hierarchies a constant challenge.

She had been there when Premiership football combined with cheap airfare to make 'the travelling Scouser'. Entrepreneurial Liverpudlian criminals began to form links on the continent and then beyond.

She could see now how that phase in her career had been the making of it. Her hard work against the tide of challenges taught her strategies, disciplined her, made her more emotionally resilient and helped her gain the begrudging respect of her northern colleagues. It had been noticed and led to her selection for a task force set up to bring down some of the bigger fish.

And the biggest of these fish had been one Curtis Warren. The mixed-raced drug trafficker had been Interpol's Number One target despite him being listed on the *Sunday Times* rich list as a property developer. His vision, energy, audacity, powers of manipulation and photographic memory combined into an extreme competence that had proven impossible to crack for a host of law enforcement agencies at home and on the continent.

One night, she and her friend were enjoying a particularly delicious bottle of wine; so good her friend commented, "*God, this is gorgeous—you sure there aren't drugs in this?*" The comment clicked a piece into place. Through her urging, the wine at Warren's Bulgarian vineyard was tested— the wine had cocaine suspended in it, ready for shipment to the Netherlands, then on to Liverpool. The discovery had been only one of the many nails driven into the drug lord's coffin. Holland's Brigade *Speciale Beveiligingsopdrachten* conducted a raid on Warren's Netherlands villa and other properties and found £125 million in illegal drugs and weaponry—but the right people noticed her contribution. Warren's conviction ignited her fast track promotion, and things were never as overwhelming as those early days in Liverpool—until now.

Her mobile rang, and she answered. "Speak of the devil. I was just looking at your picture."

"Is it helping?" came the clear, confident Scottish voice of Bruce McQuillan.

"Yes, I think so," she said, still smiling. "I'd ask what you need, but most of your calls are about helping me."

"In helping you I help myself, Kathryn."

"I am sure the favours you've done for me far outstrip the ones I have done for you."

"That's the police mentality in you. As long as bad people are stopped from doing bad things then I do not care who gets the credit."

They don't make men like this often.

"You know I feel the same."

"I know, and that's why on this occasion, it'll be you helping me—can we meet so I can pick your brains?"

"When and where?"

"I can fit in around you."

"You far from Bloomsbury?"

"The British Museum it is then."

Surprise jolted her. "Oh my, you're good."

George Follet smiled as Connor Reed entered his sun-patched, white-matted dojo, complete with a small octagon cage. He knew this day would come.

He had been fighting all his life. Now in his mid-forties, he remembered as a child, smaller than his classmates, feeling scared and vulnerable. It was this vulnerability that had led him to learn how to fight.

Except, as a ten-year-old son to a single mother who did not drive, the nearest boxing club was too far for him to walk and be back at a reasonable hour. However, the Oakwood catch wrestling club—the only real one in London—was a mere five-minute walk. The older Follet could see now the training would have been considered 'brutal' today, especially for a young lad. However, he also could see that such hard schooling in such an effective system during his formative years had anchored him throughout his fight career. At first glance, many mistook it for NoGi jiu-jitsu but there were differences in the approaches.

Under his Lancastrian coach, a highly respected, wizened, cane-supported former champion from the old school, he learnt to take them down, keep them down, stay on top, get them pinned and submitted. George knew the old man would be rolling in his grave at some high-level BJJ competitors' recourse of 'pulling guard'—sitting to begin a match.

The proper term for the submission wrestling art was 'catch as catch can' and as such, did not rely on the 'position before submission' mantra of Brazilian jiu-jitsu which emphasised securing a pin before attempting a choke, strangle or joint lock. Instead, combatants were encouraged to snatch whatever limb was available.

Another difference was a real catch wrestler was encouraged to cause pain to an opponent in order to force them into giving up position or an arm, or a leg, or exposing the throat, in a way that would cause affront to some practitioners of the 'gentle art'.

George went on to train in a plethora of different arts, including Brazilian jiu-jitsu—which had developed his ability to fight with his back to the floor—and competed at the highest level in MMA in Japan in the late nineties, early noughties.

Almost six years ago, he had been approached by a tall, lean Scotsman with a proposition—a £1,500 per month retainer to train the people he sent him. He was to assess their abilities, give them things to work on and monitor their progress on the sporadic occasions they dropped in.

Although they all improved, and most developed fighting skills way beyond an average civilian, none had forced him out of third gear in sparring.

Except one.

Connor Reed had been checking in with him for nearly three years now. He was already a superb and well-rounded fighter when he first came. George used his vast experience to identify and exploit flaws in his game and thus far came out on top during their sparring sessions. The gap had been closing, with George having to dig deep to defeat the younger man the last time they had gone at it. As a result, it had lit a fire within him to train and study harder.

If the agent had been his student day in, day out, he would not have engaged him in such hard sparring each time, but he needed to assess his progress quickly and so their sessions always began with tough rounds.

They warmed up in front of one another. He wore a pair of mid-thigh, black grappling shorts, and Connor white and grey Vale Tudo shorts. Both sported thin leather MMA gloves.

Because Follet was not supposed to pry into the backgrounds of students Bruce McQuillan sent him, a lot of the times the conversation centred on Connor picking his brains on his opinion of MMA history, characters and ideas.

"Can I ask you, if you're prepping me to be an unarmed combat demon ninja, why do we focus so much on submission wrestling?"

"For lots of reasons, but you're planning on being able to defend yourself into an advanced age, aren't you?"

"Of course. If I am half as good as you when I am in my sixties I'll be happy."

George hid a smile, *cheeky bastard*, before asking him, "Well, who would you prefer to fight—sixty-year-old Lyoto Machida or a sixty-year-old Rickson Gracie?"

"Machida."

"Why?"

"Because striking relies on reflexes, which diminish with age. Grappling is more a feel."

"Exactly."

"So," Connor began, "who's the best jiu-jitsu practitioner in your opinion?"

"It's not a black-and-white answer. Sport jiu-jitsu looks very different from MMA jiu-jitsu. The differences between Gi and NoGi have gotten wider."

"Who was the name that came to mind when I asked that?"

"You said jiu-jitsu, not submission grappling, so Damian Maia came to mind."

"Maia? I've seen a clip of Marcelo Garcia handling him in training?"

"Marcelo is better in a straight grappling match. But Damian Maia has to contend with some of the world's best mixed martial artists trying to punch, knee, kick and elbow him into oblivion. He had to adapt by becoming a superb MMA wrestler so he could take fighters into his world, quite a thing to learn when striking is involved, especially at the age he is. You understand the difference?"

"Would your answer have been different if I'd have said submission grappling?"

George said, "We'll talk about this another time. You ready?"

"Yeh, I'm ready."

"We'll set the timer—twenty minutes straight through."

They stepped into the deliberately small thirteen-foot cage.

Connor assimilated this new information—*twenty minutes straight, he wants me to shoot my bolt so he can punish me later*. He remained confident, stamina had never been his shortfall, and he knew not to expend his energy needlessly.

The ten-second countdown chimed, signalling the beginning of the round; Connor reminded himself—*feints and angles*.

He took the centre. He feinted and rolled to his right. Last time, he had managed to edge the veteran while they were both stood striking. George would look to take him down, and unless in the unlikely event Connor knocked the savvy old hand out, he would eventually succeed. Unless Connor did something unexpected.

George knew to be wary. Closing the distance on such a proficient and hard puncher always carried its risks. The younger man would look to slide around him and work the jab. George knew he would not commit to anything else in the beginning, seeking to make him over-commit so he could exploit openings.

The more experienced man parried the first few jabs and sought to feint him out of position. One thing that seemed to disturb the Yorkshireman in past sessions had been George's scything low kicks—but before he could get any off, he found himself *checking* some of his opponent's.

He shot for a single leg takedown after one of the kicks but found a quick sprawl of his opponent shooting his legs back, thwarting it. As he stood to punch, a head smashed into his stomach and the back of his knees got knifed from behind by his opponents' hands—*good fucking lad*.

He was taken down on an angle by the driving 'double leg'.

His hand clamped onto Connor's neck and shoulder curve, fighting his hips back. He fired short palm strikes into the face with the other. His arm shot inside Connor's arm as he raised it to protect his face. Before George could get his feet in on the inside of Connor's thighs—his *butterfly hooks*—in order to elevate him, the younger man stood up, and after blocking a kick aimed to his head, George did the same.

Connor shot for his legs again, but George sprawled with his arms lowered. He registered it was a feint a split second before partially riding the right hand to his jaw.

It sent his legs skating out from under him but mercifully he was still conscious. His left foot shot up to control the space between him and his vastly improved student. His other foot hooked inside and around the back of Connor's knee to prevent him from darting past his jiu-jitsu *guard*.

As the younger man grabbed the foot on his hip, George pulled it to the mat. With his opponent in a lower position, George sprang up, whipping his arm around the head for a guillotine choke.

Connor cleared his legs, and George, fearing being caught in a *Von Flue choke* by his opponent's driving shoulder, spun his hips out and away.

They both scrambled back to standing.

Feints and shifts of angle by both punctuated the swift exchanges of strikes.

George kept alert as he stepped into the storm of the younger man's striking ability. He blocked, parried, slipped

36

what he could and rode the sting out of the rest. Imperceptible though it might be to an onlooker, he could feel his student's edge in the standing striking.

The fight veteran feinted a double leg, before firing a jab—parried—then fully committing to the actual double leg. His hands found purchase around the back of the knees, and he drove with all his might before 'cutting the corner' and tipping Connor over.

George adhered to his mantra of maintaining the top position and punished the former Royal Marine with heavy pressure and strikes. He dug his elbows and knees into the soft tissue to cause enough pain so his prey would shift position.

Finally, he passed to full mount and with the roles switched, took full advantage to rain down shots. His quarry seemed to relax his guard a fraction, and George reared up to deliver a huge punch. He found himself bucked forward under the Herculean Bridge, and Connor slipped out.

A fraction too slow in the ensuing scramble, the Yorkshireman took his back—the first time anyone had in years. Anticipating a rear-naked choke, he found himself caught in an *ushiro-sankaku-jime*—rear triangle.

He knew he was about to be choked unconscious by his own student, and he knew his refusal to submit was a fool's gold. Still, he could not bring himself to tap. He found himself in the floaty dimension just before unconsciousness would snatch him.

The buzzer sounded, the choke immediately released, and his scramble to regain composure had begun.

They sat quietly for a minute, both regaining their breath and George feeling a little nauseous.

It passed and he turned to look at Connor. "Martial arts—real martial arts—are about developing yourself as a man. And you have come on leaps and bounds since the first sessions. A few seconds later, you'd have choked me out."

"The match was set for a time limit. You got the better of that."

"Put it this way, I'd rather have been you than me at the end. You can stop being modest."

"I have an outstanding teacher," Connor replied. "And you've taught me a bit too, I suppose."

George laughed. "Cheeky bastard."

5

Tom Ryder felt a warmth watching his uncle Lee behind The Buxton Arms bar. Despite his high-energy manner, he never came across as overbearing, and male and female punters alike warmed to him.

He saw Lee look up from serving and announce, "There he is. My son with the fastest fists in the West."

Tom turned to see his cousin, Luke—looking a little pale and gaunt—walk in.

"Hiya, Dad, can I get an orange juice?"

Tom and Lee laughed before Lee said, "A week in Thailand 'as turned 'im from 'Cool Hand Luke' to 'Alcohol makes me puke'."

Luke sat next to Tom with his drink and his dad went back to talking to the customers.

"Here, just got sent this," said Luke, opening his phone. He played a video clip showing two burly men facing one another over a compact standing table, encircled by a crowd. One lined up his palm against the other's face, who stood stoically still. The impact, sound and the resultant knockout jolted Tom.

"What the fuck is that?"

Luke laughed. "Russian slapping championships. Mad fuckers, aren't they?"

"That lad who just got decked looks a similar colour to yer'sen," said Tom.

"These pills are wiping me out. Just another day, though."

"HIV would have wiped you out permanently. What the fuck were you thinking, shagging out there without wrapping up."

"I wasn't—thinking, I mean."

"Yeh, that's your problem."

A look of contriteness appeared on his younger cousin's face. "I know. I'm sorry."

Tom exhaled through his nose. "It's done now."

After a few moments, Luke said, "Suits my dad being behind the bar, doesn't it?"

"Yeh, he's a natural."

"Thanks for doing this for him. I'm not sure what 'straight' work he'd have got with his record. Probably being a driver or summat, which would have depressed him."

"You don't ever have to thank me for looking after our family," Tom replied.

"Well, that's another thing, Tom. Michael is going to speak to you about collecting a debt for him down south. While inside, an independent letting agent looked after some student flats he owned outright in North London. Looks like he's just been pocketing the rent."

"Why didn't Michael mention it before?"

"This agent bullshitted him, said everything was fine. After Michael got out, he asked for the back rent—minus the letting fees, but the bloke just fucked him off—told him he couldn't find tenants, but he didn't want to worry him. Gave him an insulting amount. He knows Michael's on probation for a long time, thinks he'll just forget about it."

"How much is it?"

"About 15K."

"I see."

"Just throwing it out there, if you wanted to come down with me. We can have a night out down there," said Luke.

Tom shook his head. "We don't go in for that 'door-knocking' debt collecting now—not in large cities like that."

"What do you mean?"

"Almost every major city's naughty club south of us is divided into three—white, black and brown. They stick fairly rigid to that, there are sideways deals and a few multi-cultural gangs but that's basically it."

"So, what's that got to do with not collecting that debt for Uncle Mike?"

"Because, in the major cities like London, Manchester, Birmingham, Bristol, Liverpool and all that, I have at least a telephone number of someone who can go and collect for me—be it a white, black or brown problem."

"Fucking hell. What have you got them under?"

"Don't ever have those numbers stored on a phone. If the police catch hold of it and see a who's who of UK gangsters it'll make them excited."

"How do you remember all the numbers then?"

"Connor taught me a technique. You change numbers to objects or animals that are shaped like the numbers. Like a swan for two, or the sail of a boat for a four, an' that. Then you do a story in your head linking them, so for a number like 8732 you'd imagine the person making a snowman, which gets its head cut off by a boomerang, which then attaches to a giant magnet before a swan smashes the magnet. The more stupid and mental it is, the better."

"Sounds like fuckin' graft."

"It is. I had to write them down as shapes on paper but with the last three digits jumbled up at first. Then I got better and better, and now they are all in my head, cos I tell you what graft is."

"What?"

"Prison."

Luke nodded. "Where is Connor now?"

"His favourite city."

Connor wiped his hands on his jeans to get rid of the clamminess of his palms amid the Dutch crowd's excited chatter inside the large hall. Rayella Scott, his fourteen-year-old quasi-sister, now stood across the ring from a similarly aged girl for her first Muay Thai match abroad.

Her brother Liam had been Connor's childhood best friend and they went on to serve in the Royal Marines. During an operational tour, Liam lost his life in a suicide bombing in Afghanistan. Rayella and her family felt like an extension of his own.

Watching her now, he thought it remarkable, as she only had been competing shy of eighteen months; prolifically though, sometimes three weekends on the bounce, often against heavier girls, travelling all over the country. She had dropped a couple of decisions early and Connor feared she would lose heart. She surprised and lifted him with her ferocious response—a maniacal increase in her efforts and focus. She beat those girls mercilessly in rematches, and soon found it difficult to get fights. And, because of that, the offer came in to fight another promising girl here in Amsterdam. As he felt the butterflies, he thought back to what he had said when she had asked his opinion on whether she should take it—*There's no growth in comfort.*

He had meant it, and still did, but now his Mr Negative began his whispers—*What if she gets fucked up? Her confidence destroyed?*

He countered it—*Then she'll learn from it. Real confidence is based on a knowledge of your character, not on how things turn out.*

He looked approvingly at her shadow boxing—he saw a glimpse of her deceased brother doing an identical routine before his boxing matches. Connor had often similarly supported him ringside, as they had boxed for the same club as young teenagers.

Of the few hundred people in attendance, he felt sure only he was there to support her.

Being a junior bout, no elbows were permitted, but knees, kicks and punches were. The duration was set at five one-minute-thirty-seconds rounds.

He felt a rise in anticipation as they were brought together for the referee's instructions.

Back to their corners and the bell sounded. There was not the traditional Thai music—Sarama—played, instead just the whoops, gasps, applause and shouts from the crowd.

The chants of "Femki, Femki, Femki" reverberated around the walls, emphasising the support for the home fighter. Femki attacked Rayella, who seemed content to block, slip and check her opponent's strikes.

That's it, feel her out first.

Rayella disengaged and skipped away, to the derision of the crowd. When Femki rushed her, a teep—front push kick—took advantage of her lack of balance to send her to the floor. Connor saw the change of expression in the Dutch girl's face and knew the next minute would be pivotal.

As he expected, she powered into attacking Rayella, and as he hoped, Rayella covered up before hitting back with well-placed counters.

The bell sounded, and Femki's punch landed after it. Rayella's riposte was a harder one, and within seconds the referee and respective corner teams had to separate them.

Savage that bitch, Rayella—he thought, realising he was enjoying himself. Under the lights, steam rose off both girls.

Connor guessed Femki had a telling-off in the corner as she seemed to regain her composure. The next two rounds saw superb and varied kickboxing from both girls which the knowledgeable Dutch crowd appreciated.

Beforehand, Connor had endeavoured to restrain himself from shouting instructions; he did not want to disrespect her world-class corner and knew how too much information could overload a fighter.

Nevertheless, he now felt obliged to shout, "Rayella, don't let them rob you!"

She looked at him and gave him a nod.

The bell sounded, and Rayella increased her work rate while maintaining her technique. Connor smiled—he could see the other girl struggling. Her low kicks thudded into Femki's legs, and her straight punches seemed to both frustrate and sting the Dutch girl.

The crowd roared as Femki fought back, leading to a furious exchange.

At the final bell, the two fell into an embrace and the crowd roared their approval.

The voice behind him said, "I honestly think she has won, Connor. The blonde-haired girl."

Connor turned, feigning nonchalance in the presence of Raymond Van Der Saar. "I hope the judges see it that way. Still, she performed, and that's all that counts."

"I think she'll be OK," replied one of Holland's richest crime bosses.

Connor caught something in Van Der Saar's voice and understood. "You knew all along about my ties to her and her family?"

"I put two and two together."

Connor beamed at the announcement of the verdict—Rayella had won a close decision. Her beam matched his as she waved her glove at him before her corner team corralled her in celebration.

"Would she have won anyway?"

"I only ensured fairness."

The security around Van Der Saar was invisible to the average civilian, but Connor picked them out after a scan.

"I thought we weren't meeting until tomorrow?"

"The business meeting is tomorrow, I thought we could celebrate?"

"I am taking Rayella out now, and I—"

"The invitation naturally extends to her, as she's the reason we celebrate."

Van Der Saar must have caught the flash of reticence on Connor's face as he quickly followed with, "But I understand if you are not comfortable mixing business with family."

Connor was not comfortable—he never wanted Rayella near this precarious world of his. Still, Van Der Saar was a friend, and Connor knew his security would be both high-level and unobtrusive. "She's fourteen—no strippers or Es—maybe when she's fifteen."

"You have a dangerous sense of humour." Van Der Saar laughed. "A limousine is waiting outside."

Twat, thought Connor, *he knew I'd cave.*

Kathryn had wandered the British Museum for around ten minutes. Bruce McQuillan told her he would find her. She looked around and considered calling him but was enjoying the respite from talking shop. She stopped to look at The Gweagal shield behind its glass casing—*so it's over this they are arguing?* It reminded her of a burnt bread loaf.

"Thought you'd appreciate some time to yourself." His voice came from behind her.

She stiffened a little from the surprise. "Are you a mind reader as well as a bloody ninja?"

Bruce laughed, then gestured to the shield. "What's this?"

"Saw an article in *The Guardian* regarding it recently."

"I'll guess it revolved around it being stolen from its indigenous people by imperialistic Britain, probably a couple of hundred years ago. And how it should be returned?"

"How do you know that from what I just said?"

"Detective work."

"What do you think?"

"Does being nostalgic to the point of anger about things belonging to a generation that not even your grandparents remember sound healthy to you?"

"It's part of the Aboriginal culture. It should stay in a Sydney museum."

"Agreed. But if a man must ask for something more than once or twice, then it was never his in the first place," said Bruce. "Besides, just take a pack of teabags and a football shirt back and we're even."

She hummed a laugh before saying, "Listen, Bruce, I don't how you did it, but thank you for helping me with the DeWalt case. Seeing that depraved, twisted bastard being locked up was one of the most satisfying days of my life— even if thirty years wasn't long enough."

"Let's take a walk," he said, leading them off to a quieter part of the museum. "What makes you think I had anything to do with that?"

Alexander DeWalt had hidden behind anonymous online accounts on the dark web, coercing men, women and young teenagers into taking degrading pictures of themselves before blackmailing them into other more extreme behaviours. He would share images of these acts to various 'Hurtcore' sites, and at least two girls had committed suicide as a result. The mental damage to other victims had been horrendous, and the National Crime Agency had, along with a few other agencies, an immense struggle to pin down the culprit.

"Because the evidence came through to me anonymously around four days after it had been discussed in your presence."

"I am not confirming anything, Kathryn, but you'll never have to thank me for helping you protect the vulnerable from evil."

What a man.

He turned to her. "What's been bothering you?"

She sighed, then admonished herself—*you're not a victim.*

"It's challenging," she began. "The NCA has absorbed parts of other policing agencies and taken on their roles, but only inherited half its subsidy, we're chronically underfunded. The attrition rate of good people is high—we can't pay them enough. And the docket of serious cases is piling up: North Korean cyber-attacks, fentanyl is on the rise again, Eastern European slave traffickers, historic sexual abuse cases. They are proving difficult to prioritise."

"If I asked you which threat you considered the most serious, what is the first that would come to mind?"

"Organised crime from the Western Balkans."

"A politically correct term for the Albanian mafia."

She gave him a sighing smile. "There's intelligence to suggest the clan heads in Tirana and Shkodra fear their UK revenue will slow in the wake of BREXIT, and so are going to capitalise before the tightening of border restrictions. And the scary thing is, it's said they have obtained massive amounts of fentanyl. We've had relatively small batches hit our shores before and already cause havoc."

She saw him stare at one of the pieces of artwork for a few seconds while waiting for a gaggle to pass them.

"How reliable is the intelligence?"

"It's been difficult sifting through the credible and unreliable. Their security's so tight there's a distinct lack of informants among their ranks—a criminal honour code very few dare break."

"The Albanians, especially those from the north, follow a set of traditional laws named the Kanun. Within it, to give one's 'Besa' is a blood oath to that person or organisation. An estimated 2,000 Jews were sheltered and protected by Muslim Albanians during World War II."

"Is there anything you don't know?" she asked playfully.

When he simply smiled, she continued with, "This same code of honour makes accurate intelligence of their criminals extremely difficult, and their ruthlessness is unparalleled in Europe. Some of the cases I have worked involved horrific events."

"I've heard the comparison to the Italian mafia before they became civilised."

"I am not sure the Italians were ever like this," she said. "We are working with our Dutch counterparts. They are bracing for war between the Albanians and some of their white, old guard Godfathers. It's not going to be pretty."

"I'll see what influence I can exert over the situation."

"All right," she said cautiously. "Well, I better be getting to work then."

6

Andrei Faja thanked the angels of fortune as he watched Van
Der Saar through the crowd from the far side of the hall. One
of his strengths was the ordinariness of how he could make
himself look—average height and build, his dark hair cut into
a dishevelled but not overly unkempt style. His face was
neither memorably handsome nor ugly, with a few days' facial
hair but no more than that. His white and grey-lined patterned
shirt, with jeans neither too flash nor too low-rent.

On arriving in Amsterdam, Andrei had decided to
familiarise himself with some of Van Der Saar's businesses to
get a feel for the man. Companies meant employees—people
who might have access to the crime lord. He decided to begin
at one of the kickboxing promotions he heard Van Der Saar
funded.

The Albanian had anticipated a drawn-out scouting
mission, and so felt pleased to have eyes on the Dutch drug
czar on only his third day in.

He did not recognise the man he was talking to, and the
way they were conversing caught his attention. The sandy-
haired man with blue eyes spoke over his shoulder with the
powerful crime boss—that would rule out him being an
underling. He could not hear or lip-read what was being said,
but he recognised camaraderie when he saw it.

It looked like he had found his first person who would
have access to Van Der Saar.

Kevin Kellings walked into The Black Swan to the quietening
of voices and averted eyes. If his nineteen-stone frame, shaven
head and goatee did not cause the reaction, it was because his
reputation as one of Newcastle's biggest gangsters did.

"Pint," he said to the young barman, who was new, and
before he could open his mouth the barmaid answered his
question with,

"Stella, pet. He's on a tab."

The barman nodded. Kellings was not on any tab, he simply did not pay. He remained perched heavily on the bar stool, though one of the booths would have been more comfortable for his frame—he liked being able to command the room. He gulped his pint and thought about the events of last week.

Brendan Chappel, his 'enforcer' had gone behind Kellings's back with the former 'Godfather' of Leeds Derek Ryder—*he was fuckin' plastic too*.

A few months ago, Derek had invited Kellings and Brendan down to a pub in Leeds—told him he was going to make an example of his nephew Tom. "I need a hand in case anyone gets lairy," had been the Yorkshireman's words.

Instead, the son of the deceased Greg Ryder—Connor—had shown up with a pistol.

The Ryder cousins had suffocated Brendan with a drawstring plastic bag as he and Derek looked on in shock. Kellings found it hard to look into the eyes of Connor—he could not remember a man frightening him like that, especially one who could not be much more than thirteen stone—*then again, a fucking piece pointed at you would do that*.

However, Connor let Kellings go—with a recording of Chappel and Derek Ryder discussing future deals while referencing that Chappel had handled the beating of Ryan Ryder and robbed him of the thousands in cash he had in the car—money Kellings never even got a taste of.

He still did not yet know what had happened to Derek, and Derek's phone had gone straight to voicemail.

On the drive back to Newcastle, immediately after he had listened to the recording, he felt relief they had let him go. Over time, he felt a thorn grow into his brain—they did not respect him enough to ask for his permission to kill Chappel, probably thinking he was not worthy if his own lackey would dare go behind his back. And Kellings had always been used to respect, ever since infant school.

He looked up but no one made eye contact with him, and he drained his pint. He stood, as the bottom of the glass clinked on the bar. He turned, wishing the young barman would call out for payment—but he did not.

The smell of fish and chips drifted on the night air, convincing him of its promise. He crossed the road and entered the shop.

Again, he was frustrated—there was no queue.

"What will it be bab?" sang the twenty-something blonde girl—*probably bonny on a night out.*

"Fish 'n' chips."

"Salt 'n' vinegar?"

He nodded. "Howay, am clamming."

The abrupt tone dulled her beaming expression. She scooped the chips onto the paper before nestling the fish beside them. He watched her anointing the meal with vinegar.

"Fuckin' do it again," he growled.

Her face drained, but her voice held steady. "What's the matter?"

"I said yes to 'Salt 'n' vinegar'. I didn't say yes to 'Vinegar 'n' salt', or ya deaf?"

Her voice rose. "Jus' cos ye in a fettle, doesn't—"

"It's all right, Marcy. Make a cup of tea in the back and I'll sort Mr Kellings's order out," interjected the greying owner. His look closed her mouth before she could protest. She sulked off into the back of the shop.

Kellings did not know this man, who had his fish and chips salted then splashed with vinegar and wrapped within seconds.

"No charge," he said as he handed over the parcel.

"I fucking know there isn't, man," said Kellings, as he picked out a plastic fork and left, the bruising of his ego left by Connor Reed not even remotely soothed.

Connor had always admired Van Der Saar's taste in restaurants and bars. When Rayella had stated she would like pizza as her post-victory meal, Van Der Saar had declared he would take them to the best place in Holland. Rayella's head coach, Kelly Jensen, had great popularity in Amsterdam, and

Connor sensed both he and his assistant trainer were grateful of his offer to take Rayella out for the night—*get knee-deep in prostitutes and coke, lads.*

Glass formed the three sides of the exterior of the inside dining area, looking out onto the car park encircled by forestry. The hum of chatter floated around the attentive waiting staff, as the cream lighting glinted off spotless glasses.

As Connor, Rayella, Van Der Saar and two of his security team entered, a female voice called out excitedly in Dutch. A handsome woman Connor guessed to be in her early fifties, wearing a willowy, light blue suit stood to greet him. The exchanges between them were too quick for the Yorkshireman to decipher fully, but he gathered they were friends, had not seen one another for a long time and she was inviting them to join the group spread along four tables.

Within a minute Connor sat with a group of three others to the left of Van Der Saar's table, with Rayella seated in front of the Dutchman. The party they had joined were made up of smartly outfitted men and beautifully dressed women. These were members of the famous Applestone Philharmonic Orchestra—Connor had to google how famous.

Connor leant forward and Rayella mirrored him to hear. He said, "I'm not sure they will sell pizza in a place like this."

"Nonsense," said Van Der Saar, whose hearing Connor had underestimated. "She will have the best pizza in Holland—for whatever that's worth."

The Chameleon Project agent joined in with the others chuckling at the joke, as his eyes made subtle scans of the restaurant, assessing threats or shadows. The checklist of indicators taught to him in his agent training had morphed into instinct through time and repetition. A man around his mid-twenties, with wavy brown hair and a beard, but a shorter trimmed moustache, sat alone on an outside table, nursing a beer. He wore a shirt and corduroy trousers, perhaps waiting on a date.

Connor appreciated that despite his and Rayella's appearance—smart casual, not formal elegant—almost all the esteemed ensemble made them feel welcome. He wore a denim shirt with the sleeves rolled up, darker stylish jeans and brown ankle boots. Rayella, a grey cashmere top and black trouser pants.

Seated in front of him was a gentleman in his sixties, with a bald pate and grey and white beard. To his right at the end of the table was a twenty-something blonde girl with wide eyes and a shy smile. To Connor's immediate left was a woman he thought startlingly attractive, with her jet-black hair cascading in curls to her shoulders, framing a face that transformed from pretty to beautiful when she smiled. A Japanese-style button-up to the throat with a skirt wrapped around the hourglass figure cracked a capsule of dopamine in his brain.

Earlier, Van Der Saar had presented them all, using their full names. His tone of voice held particular reverence when introducing hers, so Connor had excused himself on the pretence of making a phone call and when outside googled Monique Bayer—the Italian-Austrian was one of Europe's premier violinists. The fussing of the waiting staff over her now made more sense.

He had quickly googled what he reasonably could on orchestras and used a memory technique drilled into him during his agent training.

Van Der Saar regaled Rayella and his side of the table with a story which elicited her genuine laughter.

Connor began to make conversation with the three on his side; the blonde—Sara Aerts—responded shyly, Monique with a reserved warmth, and the elder of the three curtly. Their English was impeccable.

Connor believed everyone had something interesting or useful to tell, and he could have a conversation with anyone. However, he also knew sometimes the juice was not worth the squeeze, and suspected concertmaster Mark Heukels considered him beneath him.

Rayella asked, "So it's a philharmonic orchestra not a symphony orchestra?"

He just about caught Heukels' snort of derision, and Connor replied, "'Philharmonic' is a specific term like

Applestone Philharmonic Orchestra, whereas 'symphony' is a more general term, so all philharmonic orchestras are symphony orchestras, but not all symphony orchestras are philharmonic."

Rayella tilted her head before waggling it forward with the teasing question, "What do you know about orchestras, Connor?"

He mirrored her head movement and said, "You can ask me and find out."

A quiet descended on the table.

Rayella began, "OK…ahem…what is a chamber orchestra?"

The smiling woman beside her must have been educating her while Connor had been in conversation with his trio.

"A small orchestra, typically less than fifty. For example, orchestras performing baroque or classical tend to be smaller than those playing a romantic music repertoire such as the symphonies of Johannes Brahms," he replied, with an amplified aristocratic accent.

"Has he made that up?" Rayella asked the woman beside her.

"No, he hasn't," she answered with a small laugh.

"OK," said Rayella, turning her attention back to him. "What is a concertmaster?"

He replied in his normal voice, "A concertmaster is what Mr Heukels, here is. He is the leader of the violin section, a prodigious title which takes years and years of hard, persistent practice—hence his stoic demeanour."

With that, Connor exaggeratedly mimicked Heukels' haughty demeanour and the rest of the tables burst into laughter. The elderly gentleman's brow furrowed, and Connor saw a trace of a smile. He also felt Monique's hand on his upper arm, seemingly in appreciation of his imitation; before she ran it down the rest of his arm.

"What's a concerto then?" asked Rayella, when people had settled.

"It's where one player sits or stands at the front and plays with the rest of the orchestra following him or her—they get paid that much they can afford outfits custom-designed by Phoebe Rocha."

Monique gasped. "How did you know? The label isn't visible!"

"I took it out of your wardrobe last night as you slept."

She beckoned him closer so the others could not hear. "I have better outfits than this."

The next hour passed with Connor and Monique hogging one another's attention. He reminded himself that men's antennas were tuned to sexualise the conversation with attractive members of the opposite sex—it was not the case for women.

Connor made sure to check on Rayella often, but she seemed to be in her element charming and being charmed by various members of the party. He was pleased as she could be shy around strangers.

"So what is it you do, Mr Reed?" Monique asked him.

"I design biscuits."

"You design biscuits?" she said disbelievingly.

"Are you familiar with the Veress French chocolate biscuit?"

"Oh my, you designed that?"

"No, I just presumed it," he said, touching her side with his fingers and controlling the breakout of a smirk.

"Ooohhh, you take a risk there, Mr Reed. Though, I imagine you're adept at taking them," she said, her eyes indicating she had not taken offence. It occurred to him, with the reverence people had for her within the circles she kept, that his playful teasing was probably refreshing to her.

"I'd rather regret something I've done, than something I haven't. Unless it's detrimental to good people of course."

"How long have you had this philosophy?"

"It isn't my overriding philosophy but as soon as I realised that life—and youth—are short, and regret is a bad thing."

Her lips pursed at this. They talked for another ten minutes before Monique announced, "I am going to freshen up."

As she stood, her finger ran over the back of his neck. Rayella seemed enthralled with a Van Der Saar story about Thai boxing great Raymond Dekkers. She was such a fan of the deceased Muay Thai legend that she had named her Jack Russel Dekkers.

He counted thirty seconds and then followed Monique. She came out of the women's restroom just in time to prevent his waiting from turning into loitering.

"Fancy seeing you here," she said.

"Well, I'm always obliged to give good restaurants good reviews, but I can't do that without a thorough inspection of the disabled bathroom—the quality of which gives me an indication of the management's nature."

She mirrored his smile before shifting and blowing out her exhale. She peered down the empty corridor.

"An interesting theory. I didn't see anyone obviously disabled, so your inspection wouldn't interfere with anyone's needs."

"Quite. Still, two make the process quicker than one."

She tilted her head, looking at a spot behind him before locking eyes with him. Without speaking, she opened the door to the disabled restroom and walked in.

7

Harold—'Harry'—Ellis, listened quietly to Marty McKinley. They sat in his office within one of his businesses—a vehicle wrapping shop in the small town of Prescot, Liverpool. He looked on through the window at the tense expression of one of the lads as he lifted the door off a black McLaren 675LT.

"That lad probably looks at cars like that, like a plumber looks at a boiler, eh?" remarked McKinley, after he turned to see what Ellis was looking at.

"He'll be a lot more nervous—thousands of pounds worth of potential damage there. Although, I am the forgiving type."

McKinley sniggered.

Ellis was not the fighter he had once been, but was still powerful and, at first glance, intimidating to most. His black hair had thinned a little on top, but remained thick on the sides, as was the beard around his mouth, though trimmed on the cheeks, adding contours to his face—according to his esteemed barber. He was now almost four stone lighter than in his powerlifting heyday but had not lost that much strength, considering. Back then, his father, since deceased, called him 'Bluto', half in jest, half in pride. Now, at first and second glance, he resembled the successful white-collar businessman he was. This was by his design; the intimidating aura had suited him when navigating, and bludgeoning, through the Liverpool underworld at street and nightclub security level but could prove a hindrance on the golf courses and country clubs in the stratosphere of the elite white-collar. Still, the eyes never lied, as his father told him, and he could beam the darkness out of them like an evil Cyclops when he needed to.

"Did they give a reason for their attitude to our proposal?" asked Ellis.

"Nah, but I reckon they were ground off that the legal counsel Caris provided didn't get their Uncle Michael off."

"They thought they could have done better?"

McKinley simply shrugged.

In truth, Ellis never liked Caris; the man was slimy and had tried *geggin'in* when he should not. But he was excellent at what he did—supplying legal protection for the Liverpool cartel—but there were others. He had only met him once, and caught a vibe off him. Ellis had used emissaries for over two decades now for dealing with any 'dirty' business; back in the day, if the coppers came to him looking for the pull, he knew whose families to go after. Another reason he chose the likes of Caris was if anything went to court, it would be easier for his barrister to tear them to shreds on the stand.

"So," Ellis said, almost to himself. "They think they'd be better off going their own way?"

Despite Liverpool only having seventy-five thousand or so more people than Leeds, Ellis knew what everyone in their world knew—that their Liverpool-centred criminal underworld was miles ahead in terms of connections, know-how and ruthlessness. Leeds' crime was controlled by the gypsies, a couple of security firms, a few bad lads from Chappel Town, and the Ryder family. The Scouse crime network was layers deeper, with its tentacles reaching all over the world.

However, he also knew the Ryders had expanded into the larger West Yorkshire Urban Area which included some medium-sized cities.

"Maybe. They have international connections now—doing really well. Since that *stedhead* has gone from the top spot, they are probably raking it in."

A few moments of silence passed.

"This is what you're going to do, Marty," began Ellis, before giving his instructions.

Monique's lips felt soft despite the passion with which she kissed him. Her tongue slid into his mouth as his hands snatched up her skirt, dragging it up her legs.

She took her mouth from his and began to gently bite his face and neck.

Her perfume mixed with her sweet breath, and his cock ached with its hardness. He pressed her back to the wall, his palms curving over her tight backside, before tearing her knickers to one side. He stroked her pussy and it thrilled him she had not shaved—*she didn't expect to get fucked tonight. Or maybe she prefers it.*

His fingers delved as her hand gripped his cock. She moaned, and his fingers slid easily inside her slick pussy. His finger fucking made her bury her face into his neck and shoulder, her make-up smearing on him. His hands scrabbled to release himself fully before driving into her. He cut off her guttural moan by clamping his palm over her mouth.

Amid his relentless pounding, his middle finger pressed into her arsehole and he felt her excitement wet his lower abdomen. Connor felt the rush of his orgasm—*fuck, fuck, fuck, not this quick.*

He continued thrusting as he felt his cum torn from him—*come on, stay hard.*

Finally, when he could feel himself about to wilt, he buried his head into her throat to mimic the orgasm he had already achieved.

They stayed locked together for a few long moments.

She gave him a playful slap. "That's for climaxing too quickly and thinking I wouldn't notice."

Slowly they disentangled themselves as he laughed.

"You always laugh at good sex?" she asked, as he washed his hands.

"No," he replied. "At the thought of some guy outside in a wheelchair, desperately trying not to wet himself and giving you the evils."

"The evils?"

"The evil eye," he clarified and demonstrated.

"He would be giving it to you too?"

"Yeh, but I wouldn't be bothered."

She smirked, before opening her handbag. She took out some baby wipes and removed most of the make-up on his collar. She used a fresh one to wipe her pussy.

She gave him a light kiss on the lips and said, "You go first. I have to make myself look respectable again."

"Yeh." He winked. "Look respectable."

She gave him a playful slap. He kissed her but deliberately broke it off before he got aroused again.

Like ripping off a plaster, he brazenly walked out to a thankfully empty corridor. Making his way back, he realised he would feel self-conscious around Rayella now he smelt of sex.

Those thoughts vanished as he walked back into the restaurant. Everyone was still where he left them—everyone including the smartly dressed man, still nursing his beer. If Connor had been stood up for this long, he would have left. Maybe he was simply enjoying a drink on his own. It was still disconcerting to Connor—not many people got dressed up, came to an establishment like this to drink alone. If he was a watcher, then who was he watching? Van Der Saar or him?

He fought his anxiety and urge to admonish himself over bringing Rayella—neither was going to help. He had two options: leave Rayella under Van Der Saar's protection and go, so if it was him being watched then Rayella would be safe. He dismissed the option. It was more likely that Van Der Saar was being watched, and if on the off-chance he was being primed for an ambush from any half-decent outfit, it would involve guns.

If I leave now, it'll make Monique feel like a slag. He shook his head at the ridiculousness of his thoughts.

The realisation came that he was still standing when Monique's fingertips brushed his sides on her way to taking her seat.

Rayella looked at him, and he hid his concern behind a surreptitious V-sign. He could see her frustration at not being able to return it. He took out his phone and sent her a message before sitting.

Give it a min, and then tell everyone you're tired, including me.

He stuffed it back into his pocket and sat, giving Monique a sly stroke at the back of her knee. He made conversation with her, under the Heukels' arch—and Sara's curious—gazes.

After a few minutes, he could hear Rayella announcing her tiredness.

"Come on then," he said. "Let's get you back. I'm just going to order a coffee to take out, then we'll go."

He went to the bar, and within a few minutes had steaming black coffee in an expensive-looking, flowery-decorated, plastic flask.

When he returned to the table, the members of the orchestra voiced their commiserations, congratulations and good luck for the future. As he stood, Monique looked at him strangely, and in reply he ran the fingers he once had inside her under his nose. Her tongue pushed into her cheek to stifle her laugh.

He patted Rayella between her shoulder blades as they made their exit. The breeze hit them, picking up her blonde hair as they walked in and out of the pools of light cast by the long drive's lamps. Expensive cars were parked in a line to their left.

His eyes flickered around without him moving his head.

"How come you sent me that message then? Thought you were trying to get in there with Kim Kardashian's older sister?"

"She tried kissing me in the corridor on the way to the toilets, but I'd only engage in that sort of behaviour with a woman I was married to—I found it offensive, that's why we left."

She laughed. "Whatever! Like you'd have a chance with her."

A smile appeared on his lips. He kept it there despite it wanting to die as he noticed in one of the car's side mirrors—the 'watcher' emerging from around the corner.

Ryan grinned as he watched his two brothers bickering from opposite sides of the bar. Like most of the males in the Ryder family, they loved boxing—and Michael and Lee loved arguing about it.

"Wash your mouth out," exclaimed Michael. "Marvin Hagler is still to this day underrated. Even Manny Steward said he was the greatest middleweight he saw."

"That 'underrated' tag has been thrown around so much that he's now 'overrated', in my opinion."

"Southpaw. Iron jaw. Hard punch. Great boxing skills. Always in condition. They shut 'im out of the title for so long that John Kennedy's Senator of a brother, Ted, had to step in. The only loss he didn't avenge was to Ray Leonard, and that shouldn't have been a loss, and—"

"Wait. Wait. Wait. That's my point—Ray Leonard had been off for three years and fought once in five. He was a blown-up welterweight. It shouldn't have been close, Hagler should hav—"

"He insisted on twelve rounds because he knew he couldn't handle the 'real' fifteen-round distance with Marvellous Marvin."

Ryan thought one of the reasons Michael liked these interactions with Lee was he found it refreshing to have someone so vehemently disagree with him.

"Then how did Roberto Duran take him the 'real' distance then? Cunt was a former lightweight and a fifty-seven-year-old!"

Ryan snorted beer at his younger brother's animated exaggeration of the Latin boxer's age. His surgically repaired jaw hurt, but it was worth it. And when Michael laughed too, Ryan realised how much he had missed this—the family being together.

Michael turned to Ryan. "Educate this dingbat, will ya, Ryan? Hagler let him off."

Ryan was about to speak when Lee interjected.

"Let him off? Duran was ahead after thirteen rounds. And Hagler's best win was against Hearns—another welterweight—"

"The hardest hitting welterweight ever—"

"A welterweight. And Hagler never moved up to fight Michael Spinks, did he?"

"You get points for disciplining yourself to keep at your fighting weight. Not to blow up."

"Then you've lost more points than a malting hedgehog."

All three burst into laughter.

The shunting open of the pub's door jolted Ryan out of his warm cloud. The revolver floated under the balaclava before snapping the air with gunfire amid the screams.

The bullets pummelled Michael forward as Ryan dived off his stool and scrambled behind the bar with Lee. Spirits and shards of glass rained on them as bottles exploded.

The shots ceased and Ryan thought he could make out the door opening. After a few moments, the murmurs and whimpers began. Ryan picked up a broken piece of mirror, crept on his knees to the corner and gingerly angled it around the bar. The gunman had disappeared.

He scooted around to see his brother frothing red foam as he bathed in his own blood.

Lee swung past Ryan and they knelt either side of their elder brother.

Ryan pulled out his phone and called for an ambulance. Lee was now clasping Michael's hands.

"That's them on their way," said Ryan.

"Hey," Michael croaked, the blood sliding down the side of his mouth like a tap not fully turned off.

"What is it, Mike?" asked Lee.

"Hagler did beat Ray Leonard," he said with a frothy chuckle.

His eyes stilled before his head slumped.

The ambulance would not be necessary.

8

Bekim felt glad the target and the blonde girl had decided to leave. He did not know how much longer he could watch the display of pomposity of the diners. The way they dressed, spoke, what they ate and drank, spoke of lives without real hardship—or danger. He had been admitted access to the 'drinks only' section of the restaurant after paying the hundred-euro fee to do so. Luckily, he was wearing a collared shirt and pressed trousers.

Andrei had given him his instructions: mark the stranger with ash-blonde hair Van Der Saar had been talking to at the party, ambush him for interrogation. He had messaged Andrei that the blonde girl who had been fighting in the ring earlier was with him, and the reply came back—**Use her to make him sing.**

The nature of the relationship between the man and girl was not apparent to Bekim. He seemed too young to be her father—possible maybe—but unlikely. And she appeared under the age of consent in Holland—sixteen, though perhaps legal in his native Albania which was thirteen. Maybe an older brother. They did seem to have similar-coloured hair, though his was darker.

Bekim knew he was not a danger—the man walked without any awareness of his surroundings, laughing and joking with the girl. As the pair turned the corner, Bekim ran forward to close the gap without being seen. Before he turned the corner, he had got close enough to hear they were not Dutch but British. Bekim knew these things from his time in London. They spoke more like the people from that television programme—something Street. 'Northern Monkeys' he had heard the London English call people from the north.

He turned the corner, close but not so he could be heard in his soft-soled shoes. There were a few other walkers too. He saw the pair again turn a corner, this time into what looked like an alleyway. He jogged to close the gap, not knowing if the alley split off.

As he rounded it, the shock slapped his face before the wet, scalding pain did. He cried out. His feet were swept from beneath him. He landed with a thud.

The last thing he saw before his consciousness shattered through the back of his head and all over the pavement was a foot descending on his face.

Connor sat by Rayella in the Uber car. He had ordered one to take them to the other side of the city, to get them off the street and keep them moving until he chose the best course of action.

He checked his phone and found four missed calls from Tom and a message imploring him to call back. He compartmentalised it—he had to focus on the task at hand.

Fear threatened to freeze Connor's insides in a way he had not felt as an adult. He had dealt with the emotion all his life and held a mastery over it. From fights at school, matches in multiple combat sports, operational tours, navigating a judicial system with the loss of his liberty on the line, through to combating the powerful and malevolent where the safety of thousands and perhaps millions of lives were on the line. And he always followed the same drill: work out the best way to prevent what you fear from happening—barring avoidance—and focus your energy on it.

This was different—he had put Rayella in danger, and he had been aware of this at the time; putting the feelings of a business acquaintance he liked and respected above the possible threat to her.

Crying about it isn't going to help her. Think.

He could not risk having her with him when picking up his things from the hotel. If they—whoever 'they' were—had traced him there then he would be exposing her to further danger. In fact, the less she was around him, the better. He could get the driver to drop her at the hotel on her own, but then he could not physically protect her.

"You still got the key card to your hotel room? Haven't dropped it?"

Rayella peeled it out of her pocket.

He took out his phone and called Van Der Saar's 'secretary'.

"Yes?" answered the voice in lightly accented English.

"I need to speak to him," Connor replied.

Within thirty seconds Van Der Saar's voice came on the line. "Yes, my friend?"—they did not use names on the phone.

Connor gave him a concise rundown of the events since leaving the restaurant—omitting he removed his follower's trousers and was now in possession of his phone—and what he now required.

"Do not be troubled. I will send three of my best to be with you at a distance—they will not attract attention."

"I'll WhatsApp the location."

He leaned over to the driver, holding out a fistful of Euros. "Take me to Oosterdoksstraat."

The driver looked at the money.

Rayella peered up at him, her eyes devoid of fear. "Who was that guy, Connor?"

"Not sure yet," he said. "A messy drinker though."

"Funny," she said. "What's gonna happen now?"

Connor briefly debated with himself how much to tell her, before deciding on the truth. Keeping his voice lowered, he said, "The man who invited us to that meal was Raymond Van Der Saar—the most influential crime lord in Holland. And—"

"I thought he was the conductor?"

"The only thing he conducts is the production and distribution of illegal pharmaceuticals throughout Europe."

"So, that's how you know him."

Now he knew for sure she knew about the criminal side of his life.

"Yes," he answered. "I don't know if 'Trouserless' followed us because we were with Van Der Saar, or if he was following me. Van Der Saar is going to arrange for a few of his guys to watch over us until we get back to the UK."

Connor took a moment to look at his phone and saw Luke had attempted to call several times too.

Several sensations pierced through the fog of Bekim's slumber and dragged him back into wakefulness, the scorching of his face barely overriding the throbbing on the back of his head, and the cold over his legs and groin.

He painfully craned his neck forward, and the shock splashed over him as he saw his nakedness from the waist down. He looked around quickly—no one. A huge metal bin shielded him.

Then the realisation struck him through his embarrassment, as he frantically looked around and patted himself—his phone and wallet were missing.

He knew what this meant—a severe punishment, at least. Not only had he lost the target and had his dignity stripped, worse still he had compromised security. Andrei's work number was on there, and he had not deleted the messages as he had been told to.

He opened the bin; no trousers. He grabbed a cardboard box and fashioned it around himself. Now he had to make it back to the hotel, somehow partially clothed.

In their Amsterdam hotel, Andrei looked at Bekim like a man who has stained his shirt with coffee—annoyed but with only himself to blame. Back in Albania, he had been conflicted whether to bring the enthusiastic young *ushtar*—soldier. He was unproven, but how could one gain experience if denied the opportunity. In the end, he had decided to bring him for any menial work—and to be a decoy. At the same time, Andrei and his more experienced and professional team observed Van Der Saar from a concealed position.

Andrei had presumed the man with dark blonde hair and the teenage girl with the brighter blonde hair were simply civilians who Van Der Saar had invited on account of his love of Thai boxing. And Andrei cursed inside—he could always spot dangerous men, in any setting, so how did this one escape his attention? When the man and the girl got up to leave, Andrei had sent Bekim to follow in case they were good friends of Van Der Saar's and could be of use at another time. His error presented itself in the form of Bekim, a layer of skin peeled from around his mouth and left cheek, wearing a skirt fashioned from a bin liner.

Bekim sat on the bed, and though his shaking on initially seeing Andrei had subsided, he fidgeted.

"What happened?" Andrei asked, conversing in Gheg dialect Albanian.

"I followed them from a distance. But they kept turning corners, so I walked faster. There was a gang of men. Must have been an ambush. I fought and fought but they overpowered me. They removed my trousers and burnt my face while I was unconsciousness."

Disappointing—thought Andrei. That Bekim would receive punishment was a given, but Andrei would have taken a forgiving attitude in the face of Bekim's inexperienced zeal.

That was before he lied to him—an act of cowardice and disrespect. Bekim's hands were free of the abrasions, and his shirt of the rips, to indicate a wild fight had taken place.

Andrei had assessed what had happened within the first few seconds of seeing Bekim; that the target had surprised Bekim with the coffee to the face, probably knocked him out with a single punch to the jaw—there were no marks on Bekim's face apart from the burn.

Andrei remembered a ferocious beating he had received from his father when he was ten years old. His father had missed much of Andrei's childhood, languishing in an Italian prison. He was a stranger to Andrei when he had first arrived. Once, Andrei had stolen a bracelet from an inner-city jewellery store in Shkodër. He had done this several times as an *nxënës*—apprentice—in the gang he was in, and it was his responsibility to hide the stolen goods until they found a buyer. His description had been circulated, and the police arrived at his door. He maintained his silence. A cursory search yielded nothing, and they left. They had not checked the inside of the dog's cushion.

However, when his father asked him, Andrei's denial of the crime was met with a punch in the face, followed by being pinned and slapped with horrific force several times, before a blow to the stomach winded him. In the desperation to recover his breath, he had not felt the kicks to the legs until afterwards. The bracelet appeared in his father's hand.

He had to take a couple of days off school. On the second day, his father entered his room, and Andrei stared defiantly despite his pain. His father held up a conciliatory hand before sitting on the bed.

He remembered the words now, "*I am not angry you stole, not angry you kept silent to the police, or that I had to pay them to leave. I am angry you lied. A lie says, 'I am too scared to tell the truth', and that is an admittance of cowardice, and cowards cannot be trusted, and in our world trust— especially amongst 'our' kind— means everything, Andrei. Do you understand?*"

He had carried the harsh lesson with him all this time. Though his father had forgiven that little boy back then, Bekim was of the age to have long known better.

"You have lost the phone, Bekim, and that cannot go unpunished—you understand?"

Bekim's tremors gave hints of returning. "Yes."

"Remove your shirt and lay on your front," said Andrei, spotting the relief in Bekim's eyes as Andrei began to remove his belt—Bekim was no stranger to a whipping.

He lay down but turned at the sound of the masking tape being peeled off.

Andrei answered Bekim's eyes with, "It is a hotel. Cannot risk you crying out and drawing attention. Close your mouth tight."

It looked like Bekim was going to speak, but instead he nodded. Andrei knelt over him and applied the tape. When he had finished, he punched his arm around Bekim's throat, gripped his own bicep and pushed the flat of his palm on the back of Bekim's head. He splayed his feet wide and pressed his pelvis into the lower back as a counter to Bekim's wild thrashing rolling him off.

The sheer desperation freed Bekim's hands enough to claw at Andrei's clamp-like arms in futility. The muffled screams and seal-like snorts died seconds before he did.

9

Connor sat in the lobby of Rayella's hotel, waiting for her to pack her things together. He had told her coaches she was leaving early and the first Eurostar back to the UK was due in a couple of hours.

A few months back, Bruce McQuillan—the head of The Chameleon Project and his boss—had given him direct access to Jaime—The Chameleon Project's cyber-technician—for emergencies only. McQuillan's attention was spread much further than when Connor had first begun working for him, and so made him memorise a number and series of e-mail addresses for contact with Jaime in an emergency.

Over an hour ago, after a series of concise messages left in the 'drafts' box of an e-mail account, Connor sent Jaime the number, the IMEI, make and model, and all the numbers on it beginning with the contacted ones first.

His hope was it was a local gang that either he or Van Der Saar could quietly deal with. He told himself—*whoever it is, you'll put one foot in front of the other until it's done.*

His phone buzzed.

"Yes," he answered, as calmly as possible—Jaime had invented a voice stress analysis for calls and Connor did not want to set the Peruvian's paranoia off.

"The phone was bought in Tirana a week ago, and so were the phones of the contact numbers found on it. They went dark around two hours after your contact with the phone's owner."

Connor guessed that when the shadow had reported back to his team, they ditched their phones as a security measure.

"I would suggest," said Jaime in his much improved and now near-perfect English, "this man is Albanian mafia. This is bad—their reach is huge, and they are not scared of the Italian or Russian mafias, or Interpol, no one."

"Yeah, I know. I have seen *Taken*."

"This is not funny, Connor."

"You hear me fucking laughing?" he replied irritably. He caught himself—*Jaime is entitled to his anxiety, and don't take your own out on him.* "I apologise. Does the boss know?"

"Not yet, I will update him. He will contact you."

The call ended, and Connor centred his breathing. He had heard some of the horror stories regarding the Albanians' ruthlessness, and maybe some were just that—stories. However, he could not bank on that, so now he had to assume whoever he was dealing with would not care about harming a fourteen-year-old girl.

His phone rang—it was Tom and he answered this time.

Andrei had killed Bekim in the confidence he could solve the issue of detection after the fact. It was now after four o'clock in the morning.

He had chosen strangulation so DNA would be less of an issue.

Andrei had learnt the adage of thinking unconventionally to solve problems a long time ago and had an intuitive knowledge of human psychology. He remembered in his studying of English as a youth the proverb 'you can't see the wood for the trees'; he came to realise this meant a person could get so caught up in the detail they miss the big picture. But it was easier to make people miss details with distraction.

Cutting up the body before walking out with it in duffel bags was not an option, no matter how thorough the cleaning method was. It was too high-risk and laborious. He had a crew of six men, not including Bekim, dotted around between this and a hotel opposite.

He considered the problem from different angles and tried to think of a better way. After half an hour, with no better options coming to mind, he dialled several numbers and gave his instructions.

The first soldier arrived at the room after six minutes, the rest following at irregular intervals. Within eleven minutes

71

they were all there—and he wanted them to see exactly how Bekim had died.

"OK. You are a drunken party and tasked to get this one—your lovable but no good friend—from the embrace of a whore back to his wife. Egzon, you will put him on your back, backpack style due to his drunken stupor—keep his head on the shoulder opposite the one the receptionist can see. The rest of you be a loud, drunk annoyance—but no more than that. You want her glad to see you leave quickly but not cause so much a disturbance she decides to call the police—understand?"

They nodded in unison.

"Veli, take Egzon and the rental car and drop the body off at the location that will appear on your phone once you have left. It is thirty minutes away—do not speed. Simply hand over the body to the man with the surgical mask on—he will not ask questions and you will not ask any either. Understand?"

Veli answered, "Of course, Andrei."

"Everyone will begin to return to the hotel after one hour—in singles and pairs, and quietly. We will leave from 10.30 onwards. Then you will destroy your phones at the earliest opportunity. Go now."

The hulking Egzon draped Bekim's dead arms around his neck like a scarf. They left, acting the alcohol-infused rabble, making noise until it receded.

Andrei, wherever he was, always strived to have specific measures in place for the unforeseen—quick access to cash, arms, off-the-books medical care and body disposal.

Ingenuity could only jump so far—the gap had to be narrowed by proper planning.

He turned and opened his laptop and then the Google search engine. He cursed that he had not remembered the names of the Thai boxers announced eight hours before—he had not seen the connection.

He typed in English—*British Teen female Thai boxer defeats Dutch girl at the Sky Factory nightclub*—before hitting Enter.

Connor sat cross-legged on the hotel bed in Leeds city centre. He had been using hotels for a long time—too long. His mum's home in Roundhay had been sold with her emigrating to Australia, and Connor's feet had not touched the ground since being recruited into The Chameleon Project. Bruce had offered to set him up wherever he wanted but he had declined for the time being.

The knock at the door broke through his attempt at organising his thoughts. Though fully expecting his cousins, he still stepped to one side of the door and called out, "Who is it?"

"Tom and Luke."

They entered, and he hugged them both before asking Luke, "How you feeling?"

"Finished the course yesterday. Feel a bit rinsed out. What's happened hasn't helped."

Connor asked Tom, "What exactly did happen?"

"Masked gunmen. Uncle Ryan and Uncle Lee were with him. I don't know if they were targeting him specifically, or if they were happy to get any of them, or just the pub in general."

"Where's Uncle Ryan and Uncle Lee now?"

"At Gran's last time I heard," answered Luke.

"What about the twins?"

"With their mam," said Tom. "They'll be *cabbaged* for a while."

Connor made them all a coffee. He sat on the edge of the bed while Luke and Tom leaned on the table.

"I expected some type of reaction," said Connor. "But I didn't think Ellis's first move would be a hit straight off the bat. More a squeeze on our businesses first—the ones he might know about."

"Same," said Tom, sipping his coffee.

"Why Uncle Mike?" asked Luke. "Why didn't they try and take one of you two out?"

"Maybe they thought he was the real decision-maker," said Connor. "Or maybe Ellis had a tip-off three Ryder men were in The Buxton Arms and saw it like a pool player sees a ball hanging over the pocket. What do you want to do, Tom?"

"We can't put everyone in our businesses on lockdown, we need to keep the cash flow going. All I can do is to preach watchfulness until we get this sorted out—and no one is to go anywhere without telling everyone else first. I'll get our Charlie to make a group just for the family on the Bat phones, and the messages will be deleted on reading. You got any ideas?"

The male members of the Ryder family each had a second encrypted Encro phone, which they would only use for sensitive messages involving their criminal enterprises that could not be referred to in any sort of code. Otherwise, they used WhatsApp and deleted messages upon reading.

Connor said, "Getting it sorted out means going on the offensive, but we can't just rush in without intelligence. I've got a card I am going to play."

Tom gave him a subtle look and Connor telepathically thanked him for not asking.

"When you going to see Gran?" asked Luke.

Connor felt a jolt of guilt at the question. "Soon. She'll have plenty of people fussing around now, anyway."

"Don't do that, Connor," said Tom, looking at him.

"Do what?"

"Make an excuse to delay it. Everyone knows it's you she wants to see."

Connor nodded. "I'll go and see her. When she's on her own."

"She fucks everyone off in the evening, says it's because she wants to watch *Corrie* but did the same to me last Tuesday. I know it's not on, not on a Tuesday," said Luke. "Why does she have to be on her own for you to go, anyway? You going to rob her?"

"No," said Connor. "It's because I reckon the grief of Uncle Mike's death combined with the fact Grandad has been gone a long time makes this the ideal opportunity to fuck her."

His two cousins' laugh-blended groans made him smile, before Tom said, "Fuck me, is there any depths you won't go to?"

10

In his air-conditioned office, Robert Caris felt satisfaction as he read the report of Michael Ryder's death. He had been made aware of the family's disgruntlement at his handling of Michael Ryder's legal case that saw him imprisoned.

However, with Derek Ryder torn from his position as head of the family, he had lost his business up there and might never get it back now after the murder of the new boss. Some of his clients included members of the Liverpool cartel, big-name firms in Manchester and beyond, and so the Leeds faction was always relatively small change to him. Still, he was aware of the concept of maximal profitability in any given situation.

He looked at himself in the full-length mirror on the side of the combined filing cabinet/inside coat hanger. He decided to loosen his dusty pink tie as it was bulging his chin-fat out. He grimaced, his eyes—his best features he had been told—had sunk into his face as he had put on weight.

He had tried; joined weight loss groups, bought supplements, had a calorie counting monitor, hired a personal trainer. He would make progress for a couple of weeks, but this sedentary lifestyle and the almost constant schmoozing in restaurants made it much too difficult. His gastric band surgery was due in a few weeks and that would be that—the perks of success. The poor had to sweat and deny themselves.

A part of him was glad he would not have to deal with the Yorkite criminals in any capacity—they were beneath him, and more than Scouse slang, their 'Yersens', 'Reights' and 'Ey up' made him cringe.

He was safe—protected by the most ruthless UK cartel. He had heard rumours of the exploits of Connor Reed but decided to treat them as exactly that—rumours. Besides, they would be finished now, and would not have the funds to afford him anyway.

Derek felt the scar burn hotter on his forehead now.

Over seven hours ago he had been stood in Tenerife's airport—the first time, bar visiting the apartment complex's gym and the dentist, that he had been out in public. McKinley had assigned him a gofer when he had first arrived. Since coming to the island, a dressing covered the wound; but now the Japanese mark was on full display. Though he had not seen anyone oriental yet, people did not have to know what it said to stare in shock, judgement and pity.

He now sat with Marty McKinley in a reception room of a vast vehicle wrapping shop in the small Merseyside town of Prescot. Through the glass partitions, he looked on at the luxury cars having their bodywork coated with plastic vinyl and seethed with a cold bitterness. His own Jaguar lay in Leeds, under Jennifer's name. Since he had left, Derek had heard from her twice—he had been holed up and isolated in an apartment in Tenerife watching a cycle of DVDs—while she had been bathing in the extravagances he had provided.

He had not felt like this—this…insignificant since Greg had been alive. A memory tormented him, from when Greg was around seven years old and Derek ten. They were playing in the back garden, shooting the ball at their jumpers-for-posts goal.

Michael, between Greg and Derek in age, stood his turn as the keeper. Their father, Frank, was fixing his motorcycle in front of the garage beside the 'pitch'.

Derek, initially blasé about tackling his younger brother, found himself getting increasingly embarrassed as Greg ran rings around him. The burning in his face arrived when Michael began to chortle, 'Go on, Greg, nice one, lad.'

And when Derek caught his dad watching on approvingly at Greg's skill, Derek snapped and shoved Greg over. His head snapped in the direction of his father's 'Oi!'

That was when he felt the angry fists of Greg thwacking into his face. Such was the shock that he had been momentarily unable to defend himself. Frank had rushed over and separated them, before giving them both a dressing-down on the importance of family.

A seed rooted itself in Derek, as the feeling of being 'saved' from his sparrow-like younger brother was exacerbated by Michael's insistence he had been. Although his dad would never say it, Greg was his favourite. What was worse was as Greg got past the age of fifteen, it was Greg the brothers— even Michael—looked up to.

When a gang of thugs had hospitalised Frank as he stood up to their abusive behaviour towards the bar staff and a group of young girls in his local, it set the embers of Derek's resentment ablaze. Resentment, because when Greg led the Ryder brothers in a storm of vengeance, Derek ended up in hospital himself from a retaliatory gunshot. With his clavicle shattered, he was helpless as the brothers committed acts of revenge that took them from being civilians to the most feared family in Leeds, with Greg at the helm.

Worse was to come.

The change in body language of the workers of the wrapping shop snapped him back to the present—a straightening of their backs, a little more urgency in their work.

Harry Ellis had walked in.

Derek had never met the man before, as Marty had always acted as a go-between for the loose amalgamation of Scouse crime lords the police still referred to as 'the Liverpool cartel'.

He was not as big as Derek thought he would be—but he walked with an authority. He stopped and spoke a few words with every worker he passed. Derek felt himself straighten up.

As Ellis opened the glass door, Derek stood and felt his scar scorch. Ellis held eye contact as he extended his hand.

"Derek Ryder, great to meet you, finally."

The words kindled a pleasant feeling in Derek. "Likewise, Harry."

"Marty, do me a favour, can you grab Mr Ryder a coffee—how do you have it, Derek?"

"White, two sugars. Cheers."

"No problem, boss," said Marty.

When he had left, Harry turned to him. "What's it been? Seven years since we became business partners, and this is the first time we've met."

"It is, that's right."

"Come on, let's go through to my office."

As they went through, the first thing Derek noticed was a framed action shot of two boxers amid an exchange. There were two signatures on it. When they had both sat either side of the desk, Ellis said, "Firstly, Derek, I know what you must be thinking—but hand on heart, I did not order your brother Michael to be grounded. It's not my style."

"McKinley's also said that to me. You don't have to hide 'owt from me—he was a blackleg anyway."

"Blackleg?"

"It was a saying for those who wouldn't join the strikes—a traitorous bastard."

"Fair enough, but I am telling the truth."

Derek knew he was lying, but instead of pressing, pointed to the picture and asked, "What match is that from?"

"That is Shea Neary and Andy Holligan in a proper blue-collar war that. People say yer could hear the crowd's roar for miles. I was gutted when Neary stopped Holligan— I'd done a bit with Andy as a lad down at Rotunda ABC. Julio Cesar Chavez had mangled 'im, but that was Chavez—greatest Mexican boxer ever. Thought Holligan would have Neary. You've got an excellent featherweight in Leeds now, haven't yer?"

Derek said, "I wouldn't know, to be honest."

"Bad form that, men like us should know who the people doing good out of our city are."

Derek felt a brush of a sting at the words. "I haven't been keeping up lately."

"As long you still got breath, Des, then it isn't over. Besides, we want you up there—a city like that needs a strong hand."

Derek's heart soared at this. "What do I need to do?"

"What we want to avoid is a long, drawn-out war that'll bring it on top of us. But like dominos, if we can subdue the main domino then the rest will fall."

"Which domino would that be?"

"The one that took a skiv to you. Marty tells me he's the one that started off this mutiny."

"He doesn't stay in Leeds much though. And it's not just him we have to mind—it's Thomas too."

Ellis took a few moments to respond. "Well, we might use one to draw out the other. Once we have you back running things we can talk business. We'll do the heavy lifting, but we'll need your help."

"How?"

"McKinley will fill you in on the details," he said, as Derek's coffee arrived. "I have to go now."

They stood and shook hands before Ellis departed. McKinley took his seat when he left. "I need to know everything about your family's operations—everything. And I want to know about the extended family—for leverage."

Derek had an uneasy feeling at the words 'extended family' and 'leverage'. Then he remembered the nights they had enjoyed at his expense—the buffet spreads he paid for, the bar tabs he had taken care of and the entertainment he had sorted for christenings, weddings, karaoke nights, birthdays and Christmases. And not one of them had messaged him.

"Whatever you need."

Connor braced himself as he pushed the iron poppy doorbell—he breathed deeply and hid his nerves the best he could. The moments of waiting seemed to draw out like a blade. Finally, the door opened to reveal an elderly woman— back still straight—with shoulder-length hair, grey at the roots simmering into a fawn brown. Her left eye was slightly clouded and a tiny bit offset.

"Hiya, Gran."

She scrunched her eyes. "Don't you be 'Hiya, Gran'ing' me. You've not been around in weeks, Connor Ryder. Takes one of my sons dying to get you round?"

His Grandma Paulette was the only person he would not dare correct regarding using his real surname 'Reed'.

"I know. There's no excuse."

"Well, come in, instead of faffing around."

As he stepped through the door, he fell into her embrace. His grandmother had always displayed composure despite turbulent events. However, as time went on—and especially after his grandad's and dad's death, this morphed into a stoicism earning her the nickname of 'Thatcher' from his cousin, Tom.

Connor could tell by the tightness of the hug she was hurting.

He looked around the kitchen and was heartened to see it as clean and tidy as always. Even the fridge magnets of all the children, grandchildren and great-grandchildren were aligned and in age order.

Despite the neatness of everything, the room was an array of bright colours—a red kettle, green chopping boards, yellow cutlery.

She let him go. "What do you want to eat and drink?"

"I am fine, Gran."

"Why do we have to go through this bloody rigmarole every time? You know you're going to get watered and fed coming here."

"Can't you just give me money instead?"

She flicked his ear. "What you having? Do you want a butty?"

"A black coffee. And an apple with a knife to peel it with—surely you can't mess that up in your old age."

"Everyone likes my cooking."

"Come on, Gran, if you served the shepherd's pie you gave me last time at 'The Last Supper', I think Jesus would have betrayed himself."

She scowled and gave him a light tap in the face with the back of her hand. "Go into the living room. Sit in your grandfather's chair."

Connor looked at her strangely—she never let anyone sit in his chair.

"I can't sit in his chair, Gran."

"You bloody will—get in there."

Taken aback, he slid into the living room. The warm colours of peach and cream made up the room. This made the corner sofa unit of leopard print stand out even more. His chair sat next to the sofa unit—simple brown leather with a coffee table to the right of it. He remembered once, as an eight-year-old, being at a family party. Afterwards, his grandad had put on a documentary about tigers hunting humans.

He remembered the pride he felt when his grandad said, "Connor, come sit here."

He gestured by his feet. As they had watched the footage of an Amur tiger, his grandad whispered, "One-on-one, it would kill any lion that."

"Really? A lion?"

"Stronger and heavier. They can fight off their hind legs better. Brainier too. They've been known to copy the calls of an Asian bear to attract and kill them."

"They kill bears?" exclaimed Connor.

"Yeh, Asian bears are small ones not like grizzlies, but Siberian tigers literally eat bears for breakfast."

"I want to be a tiger then."

His grandad laughed. "It's better to be a lion—tigers are loners, but lions come in a team—they'd kill a tiger because tigers won't help other tigers. You understand what I am telling you?"

The memory reminded him of a documentary he had seen regarding a coalition of brutal lions named The Mapogos. They ruthlessly took over a massive territory of the Sabi Sands in South Africa.

His gran snapped him out of his reverie as she brought in his coffee and apple.

"What you staring off into space for? You on drugs?"

"Why? Did you want some?"

She tutted. "You daft bat. Come on, sit down."

As the seat came up to embrace and support him, he felt a strange belonging. She sat on the leopard-skin sofa opposite. "I should have thrown this settee out. You know, even back then, other men—especially ones living a life like us—would give their wives an allowance. Your grandad used to give me all his money, and I'd divvy it all out on the bills, shopping, savings pot. That's why we had this house paid off early, holidays and investments. But now and then, he'd have to have something no matter what I said, like this bloody sofa—wildlife mad he was."

"I just thought that—when I was staring off into space. He'd put those programmes on, and all the family had to watch."

A melancholic smile appeared. "I sometimes put them on if I've nowt to do."

"He's been gone a while, Gran—ever thought about meeting someone else? You wouldn't even necessarily have to go in for surgery—there are some amazing things they can do with Botox, fillers and make-up nowadays."

"You're not too old to have your arse tanned, Connor."

He snorted a laugh and she continued, "It would have to be a very special man to take your grandad's place, and no woman gets two of them in this life—I was lucky to have him."

Connor felt his heart both swell and get heavier—
Imagine having a woman say that about you.

He looked at her. "I am going to get our family out of this lifestyle, Gran."

She looked at him with a frown. "That was your dad's problem."

His expression matched hers. "He didn't get the family out in time?"

She shook her head. "That he even thought he could. You see, that's when he took his eye off the ball—started dreaming of this fantasy life of legitimate businesses, of the family being straight goers. And that's what killed him—and

80

like dominos, this family went under and now Michael is dead."

"I haven't talked to you about Derek yet, Gran—"

"I already know about Derek. Weeks and weeks and weeks ago he calls up, snivelling, saying you had the wrong end of the stick abart him having something to do with our Greg's passing. Asking me to have a word with you. You know what I did?"

"What?"

"Hung up on him. He thinks I was born yesterday."

"So, you don't believe him?"

"Of course not. I've known you all since you were all hours old—seen you all grown up, seen you all before you could hide the badness you didn't want people to see. Though you were such a sweet child—there was a change in you later, about seven or eight."

"I can't have him back around here, Gran, even to visit you—"

"I don't want him to visit. I don't care ever to see him again."

"Then what do you want?"

She put her cup down and leaned forward. "Do you know why I let you sit there?"

"Go on."

"Because you're the head of this family now."

"Gran, Tom's the head of the family."

"Connor, if this is a business then Tom would be one of those operations managers, but you would be the CEO. Guess who said that."

"Who?"

"He did."

"He said that?"

"Do you need your lugs cleaning? Yes. He visits me a little more than you, you know."

Connor took the admonishment with a chin jut. "Tell me how I can make it up to you then, Gran."

Paulette picked up her cup, smoothed her skirt and said, "I want you to give up this daydream that you lot are going to ride off into the sunset all with your 'legitimate' businesses. And I want you to deal with these people who are attacking our family in any way you have to—no, I want you to deal with them in a way that people will think twice about just sauntering into one of our pubs and killing one of us. You understand what I am saying?"

Connor took a moment to respond—he had never heard his gran talk like this.

"You sure you're not just saying this because it's so soon after Uncle Michael's death?"

She stood as if she had not heard him. "Thomas says that you've passed your motorcycle licence test?"

"That's right. I haven't got a bike yet. I might never get one, might just rent while I am on holiday."

Again, she did not acknowledge what he said, and instead commanded, "Follow me."

Connor did so as she led him outside and into the garage. She switched the light on to reveal the enclosure as pristine as he remembered it—the tools hung from nails on the hardwood at the back, bordered by chalk outlines. Miniature plastic drawers with an assortment of nails, screws, washers and bolts. A welding mask and MIG welder neatly placed to one side. The nose of her car pushed near the entrance.

Connor knew what was underneath the dust cover before she told him. She pulled it off to reveal a black motorcycle that looked to Connor like a cross between a sports bike and a cruiser. It had a single headlamp with 'Triumph' written on the fuel tank and 'Speed Triple' along the seat.

"This is your grandad's last bike. The only one he bought new, funnily enough, the day the Queen Mother had her hip replacement when she was ninety-five. I told him that was what was going to happen to him if he came off it, but he wouldn't listen. Anyway, if you insist on riding one, then you may as well have it—it's only collecting dust."

"I don't know what to say, Gran," he said, surprised. "But maybe you can stop putting pound coins in my birthday cards now."

She smiled before a sad look came over her face.

"What is it?"

"What I was saying earlier, it isn't because our Michael is dead—I've felt like this for a long time. I want you to stop whoever these heathens are running roughshod over us. I want you to bring this family together again."

He met her eyes. "All right, Gran."

11

Andrei sat on the Eurostar, studying the geography and crime statistics of the North of England. He had ingested the alertness-enhancing drug Modafinil and stacked it with choline to erase the headache. The Mafioso used the drug sparingly, but he had not had much sleep and needed to absorb what information he could efficiently.

He had decided to make the journey to the UK alone. Travelling to an isle of over six million CCTV cameras with an entourage could attract the wrong attention. He could not be fully aware of the advancements of facial recognition technology, and keeping his face constantly shielded could prove nigh impossible.

Being the Mik of the most notorious Albanian mafia clan meant he could call upon soldiers in most capital cities in Europe and more than a few elsewhere in the world.

There was a dual purpose to his visit. He had to assess and rearrange the structure of the Albanian mafia affiliates in London and the other major cities.

Besides, Andrei's passion in life was to solve problems. This—combined with his aloof nature—had led to more than one of his fellow students in his time at the Polytechnic University of Tirana referring to him as being on a lower rung of the autism spectrum.

Unlike most of the Mafiosi within Albanian organised crime, Andrei did not have any living family in or associated with Mafia Shqiptare—his father had died not long after Andrei had begun his engineering degree in Tirana. It had been in the final year that he became embroiled and eventually seduced by the organisation. But practicality infused with creativity remained embedded within him; sometimes he would even act first, such was his confidence in solving any difficulties afterwards.

The complications with the Shqiptare's associate group—the Hellbanianz—in London had been festering for years. England's capital was not only over fifteen hundred miles away from Tirana and the Godfathers but had many more opportunities and distractions. Some criminals forgot, or perhaps never understood, that the goal was sustainable profitability and not the need to be seen as cash-rich and dangerous.

This had to be solved now. Andrei had convinced the bosses back home that in the confusion of BREXIT they could take advantage if they instilled discipline in the men there.

With London having so many culturally diverse gangs competing over the same lucrative pie, the Shqiptare needed men capable of extreme violence to protect and oil the workings of the operations. Such men also needed to understand business sustainability. Drug money was easy money and made convincing the young Albanian gangsters of the importance in keeping accounts, laundering, fostering the right business and personal relationships and staying under the radar exceptionally difficult.

But he would find a way.

Robert Caris floated in the state between wakefulness and unconsciousness. He did most nights, before awaking fully to relieve his bladder. This felt different—instead of waking from a terrifying dream, the legal fixer woke into one.

He surfaced awake to a sight more chilling than any nightmare he remembered having—Connor Reed.

The fright fired his torso upright, but a bracelet snapped against his wrist and he was handcuffed to his headboard. He let out an involuntary sob as his moist eyes settled on the barrel of a pistol.

After a few moments, his rigor mortis thawed. Wild-eyed, his mind computed Jade, his young half American, half Thai wife sat on the chair from his study, now placed beside the bed. She breathlessly clung to the front of her black, silk nightie.

His mouth opened with his brain lagging a second or two behind. "I'll…I'll pay it, whatever you need. How did you get in here? Did you—"

The force of the backhanded slap pummelled shock into his system.

"Shut up, Robert."

Reed turned and motioned for Jade to stand. The twenty-two-year-old obeyed. Reed said to her, "I won't hurt you unless you give me a reason to—like trying to snatch the gun, raising any type of alarm or trying to escape, do you understand?"

She nodded. Even through his fear, Caris could see she was scared—but he could also see something else in her eyes. He noticed their iron on the bedside cabinet, plugged in but not switched on.

"Say it," commanded Reed.

"You won't hurt me unless I give you reason."

"That's right," said Reed. "Now stand up, so I can sit and chat with your husband."

She stood and Reed took her place.

"Come and sit on my lap, no sense you having to stand too."

She paused for a few moments, before smoothing the back of her nightie and bending her knees. Reed's hand planted on her back to stop her, and he said, "You can remain standing if you prefer. I don't want to force you into anything you don't want to do."

Time seemed to slow as the young, dark blonde Yorkshireman bared his teeth at her. Incredulity shook Caris as she sat on Connor's lap.

"Try and keep still, it's difficult to act scary with a hard-on," he said, and with that, he raised his knees to tip her back onto him.

She giggled—*you fucking bitch*.

Connor began, "Now, Robert. My family has a perfectly good reason to be upset with you."

Robert took a deep breath. "I defended Michael Ryder to the best of my ability and—"

The spite in Reed's voice cut him off along with the pointing of the pistol. "Don't talk fucking wet. The CPS solicitor said—and I am paraphrasing—'Caris was like a member of the prosecution. Evidence not submitted, documents not reviewed, no plea bargain, no fight. Just a hollow and rudimentary display of a defence'. I have read the documents, so don't insult my intelligence."

"Please," said Caris, the desperation choking him. "I wouldn't lie."

A low laugh breezed through Reed.

"Tell me, Jade," he said, bumping her with his legs again. "You know him better than anyone. Does he tell lies?"

Caris focused in on Reed's fingers stroking small circles on the inside of his wife's thigh. Her nightie had parted at the bottom, and his fingers danced just above her knee.

Caris saw her bite her lip before she croaked, "Yes, he does tell lies."

"Of course he does, babe."

Caris wanted to stop him, but his tongue would not utter a protest.

"Now, you being a supposed man of law, you know the difference between retributive justice we have in the UK, and the restorative system they have in other parts of the world— you know: 'You ran over my daughter, now I want two camels from you', that type of sketch."

Caris mumbled, "Yes."

"Now, there's no way I am leaving tonight without justice being served, Robert. That isn't an option. But you do have a choice, the restorative approach or the retributive."

"Wha—what specifically? Not going to pick if I don't know."

Reed squeezed Jade's thigh to make her look at him and saying, "Go switch the iron on, Sugar Lips."

She paused momentarily, before giving Caris the briefest of glances and obeying. The orange light shone like an evil eye.

Reed said to him, as Jade sat back on his lap, "You have until the iron light clicks off before I decide for you."

The words burst from Caris. "Restorative—restorative, for Christ's sake, please."

"It's up to your wife, isn't it? Because, if she agrees to fuck me while my phone films it, that would constitute restorative justice, wouldn't it?"

Reed looked at Jade. "Obviously it's you and your husband's call, but yes—I will allow you to put some make-up on and do your hair—not that anyone else would see it— 'revenge porn' is illegal now, ask your legal-eagle husband."

Caris felt a knot of rage as he watched his wife simply nod her understanding.

"Now, an example of retributive justice would be to iron your wrinkled pyjamas—while you are still wearing them. So, what do you say, Robert? I'm excited, I have to tell you— not sure which I would prefer to do more."

"Please, there must be another way," pleaded Caris.

"You have ten seconds to decide."

"Restorative, restorative," he cried.

"Well, that's your vote. It's up to delectable Jade here."

Time scored like a knife across the inside of his stomach, waiting for her answer.

12

Jade looked at her husband with contempt—*he didn't even have the decency to take five seconds to decide.* Not that she expected anything else. She had grown to despise him anyway.

She could not believe how she had let herself become star-struck by him. She had been twenty-one when they had first met. Her year's travelling after college had stretched to eighteen months, during which she had completed an online legal secretary's diploma. On arriving back in Liverpool, she slid straight into a position at Caris's practice.

She could see even at the time what a cliché it was—her older, powerful, rich boss taking her out, the gifts and eventually exotic holidays. Though she mostly fell in love with the lifestyle, she was fond of him; he could be smart, adoring and amusing.

Then it began—the paranoid fits of insecure rage, the horrible words, the childlike sobs when she threatened to leave and the cycle repeating itself when he had had a drink.

That was the man she was looking at as she fought the urge to grind on the rock-hard cock of the man whose lap she sat on. He had come in, taken control and was...dangerous but cheeky. He did not speak like he was one of Robert's usual clients, not just that he was not Liverpudlian but because he sounded more intelligent.

She shivered as his lips brushed the back of her neck, before she felt his fingers slide to a gentle grip of her throat and jaw. He leant her back on himself, and she felt her excitement. Expecting a kiss, he whispered so as Robert could not hear, "I won't burn him really if you decide you don't want sex. I just wanted to see what he'd do."

She took a moment before whispering back, "So you don't want to?"

He turned her head, and they began kissing. She ground herself on him, feeling his stubble and her tongue dabbed his.

She became aware of Robert quietly sobbing before Connor broke away and said, "He's going to end up putting me off—mind out so I can deal with this. Unless you get some kinky thrill out of his reactions to watching you?"

She shook her head. Within three minutes, Robert's wrists and ankles were tied by his clothing from the wardrobe to the chair she and Connor had been sat on. His mouth was stuffed with his socks from the laundry basket and wrapped by her nightie belt. Connor then tipped Robert over and placed him to the back of the cavernous room facing away from the bed.

Connor set his phone in an upright position on the bedside cabinet, and the light shone out of it. His pistol sat behind it as a makeshift prop stand.

As he turned to face her, she became aware of her wide-open nightdress, of her breathing—and the wetness of her pussy.

He walked to her, his fingers tracing the inside of her thighs before saying playfully, "Undress me then, wench, I haven't got all night."

She smiled at his cheekiness and complied. She admired the contours of his hard, muscled body—her fingertips dancing on the Superman logo tattoo on his haired chest. She sank to her knees, undoing his belt with now trembling fingers. She gasped, revealing him, and did not need the gentle insistence of his fingers in her hair to take him in her mouth. After initially struggling, she found her rhythm, breathing deeply through her nose. Soon her drool dripped onto the carpet as he hit the back of her throat. He pulled her head back and oxygen vacuumed back into her grateful lungs. She stood with his grip, and they kissed again, his wet cock pressing into her stomach.

His hands found her backside, gripping, spreading and his fingers pressing. She squealed in delight as she sailed into the air onto the bed. His strong hands gripped the back of her thighs, and his mouth fell on her pussy. She could feel his teeth as his tongue lashed her cunt before shocking her by probing her arsehole.

After a time, she could not take any more, and her hands found his face to drag him to her. He complied, his hardness brushing her thighs. One hand pinned her leg back, his other, gripped her hair. He kissed her hard before slipping inside her.

She cried out and he began to fuck her like they were animals. He switched his hands, forcing the tip of his finger into her arsehole as his other hand clamped her moaning mouth. He stilled himself as she came, soaking them and the bed.

Before her climax had entirely ebbed away, her legs were on his shoulders and he pounded her with a fury. He reached deeper than anyone she had been with and had never felt this possessed before. On seeing the veins banging out from his throat and his seed bursting within her, she came again.

Finally, he slid from her. She lay watching him catch his breath as he sat on the edge of the bed.

After a few moments he said, "Can you do me a favour?"

"Yes," she said without hesitancy.

"Can you say, 'Me love you long time, baby'?"

"What?" she exclaimed with amused incredulity.

"I am joking," he said. "I think I've got the timing of this question mixed up but are you on the pill?"

"Yes, been taking it in secret."

She became aware of Robert's muffled sob at her admission.

Connor laughed before saying, "That's fucking harsh. Still, you'll have to empty, as it were."

She felt almost disappointed before crunching into a sitting position.

His hand reached out and rested on her thigh before he continued, "Except not in the toilet. You're gonna empty on his face as I film it. If that's OK?"

She blinked a few times before saying, "Ahem…if that's what you want."

"It is, but I won't make you do it if you're uncomfortable."

She thought for a moment before nodding her consent.

He beckoned her closer before kissing her. She began to melt into him before he broke off and whispered in her ear, "What's the safe code?"

Her heart beat harder for a moment—*surely this was too far a betrayal?*

He continued, his voice barely audible, "You can have half the money and leave him."

She whispered back, "Just because you made me cum twice, don't think I am stupid."

"Well…you did marry him."

She mirrored his smile. "True."

Connor walked over to the bedside cabinet and clicked the light off before tapping his phone's screen and peering into it for a few seconds.

"I look amazing—you could work on some of your sex faces," he said, winking at her.

She laughed—*how is he doing this?*

Her adrenaline soared as he took the weapon and walked towards her. When stood over her, he flipped it around in his hand and held it out to her.

"You can always shoot me if I refuse to co-operate."

She stared at the barrel for a moment before—keeping her voice low—saying, "I'll do it—both. The code is 030364—his birthday."

"Thank you," he said. "Now chop, chop. Pill or no pill, you'll end up a single mum if you keep it for much longer."

"I don't think it works like that but OK."

She clenched as she walked over with Connor following behind. She felt butterflies—like she was about to let a snake bite her steel-gloved hand.

Robert looked pitiful with his tear-stained face. Her mouth fell open as she noticed the tent at the front of his pyjamas.

She met Connor's eyes and he remarked, "Each to their own, eh."

He then reached out to smooth her hair and in an exaggerated aristocratic accent said, "You look fabulous, darling, please do perform."

Then the phone was held up and the light back on.

Nervous energy coursed through her as she squatted over her husband's face. His gagged protests did not seem as ferocious as she would have expected.

She relaxed, and it came pouring out of her. She could not see Robert's face but was reminded of an ice cream dispenser. Connor held his stomach as his torso shook in silent laughter.

When she had finished, the flick of his head moved her to the side.

Connor knelt, loosening the gag before saying, "Listen here, Robert, your corruption led to my uncle's incarceration, so count your lucky stars it's just a sex video starring your missus and me, and my cum on your face—you never know, you might now find yourself imbued with a sense of masculinity."

Jade watched Robert trying to wipe away Connor's sliding seed with his shoulder. Connor laughed and continued, "You'll be my informant, Robert—except there won't be any sort of text floating around, I'll call on you when I need information—or the videos I have will go through the WhatsApp network quicker than Bill Cosby through a narcolepsy clinic."

Connor turned to her and said, "What's his date of birth, hun?"

"Ahem, why?" she replied, surprising herself with her acting ability. She realised he was asking her so he could feign he had guessed that would be the safe's code, and her husband would be none the wiser that she had already told him.

"So I can send him a card."

"Err, the third of March."

"Year?"

"Don't tell him!" exclaimed Robert but falling silent with the tip of the gun pressed into his left eye.

"Year? Before his brains splatter over this Persian rug."

"It'll be 1964."

The man laughed. "Your date of birth, eh, Robert. Narcissism is one thing, a lack of imagination is another."

"Please, just leave, I'll—"

The man's boot whipped away the rest of the sentence along with his consciousness.

13

Ciara Robson did not let her self-consciousness show as she stood at the focal point of the seated semi-circle. She stood in her suit, surrounded by the white and light grey of the sterile room.

It was not that these seventeen people constituted the UK's most influential think-tank on foreign policy; she was confident of her knowledge and presentation of the intricacies of Russian-Ukrainian relations. And she knew she could beat all but one of them in a fight or a physical challenge. Or that she thought her gender or appearance would detract from what she had to say.

It was Bruce McQuillan's presence on the panel that had both surprised and sharpened her focus. He was her boss in the world of black operations, although to the rest of the ensemble, she was a freelance journalist.

He remained silent as she fielded questions for twenty minutes at the end.

The session broke and he approached her. "Superb presentation."

"I wasn't expecting you here," she said, running a pair of fingers through her short, silvery-blonde hair.

"I frequently attend these things. I was pleased to see your name on the docket."

"The information would have been redundant to you, surely."

Much of what she had learnt had been on a mission in Ukraine aiding Connor in the rescue of a British national and the aversion of war between Russia and much of the Islamic world. She had given him a thorough debrief already.

"There were a few pieces I took away from this," he said. "It was good to observe this side of your skill set."

She kept the welling of pride off her face and said, "Thank you. I appreciate it."

He lowered his voice. "I have a tasking for you, one that doesn't require you to board a plane."

Connor sat in the modern church amongst the other mourners. He kept the hyper-awareness off his face. The inside smelled faintly of wood polish, perfume and tears. Most of the Ryder women sat in the front row. Though Connor knew they were crying, he could not hear it—his grandmother's stoicism shamed them to silence.

Tom had taken over the funeral arrangements, and Connor was thankful. Seemingly a thousand decisions needed making in the immediate aftermath.

Tom sat to his left and Luke to his right. Curtis and Charlie sat with their grieving mother, Joanne, and elder sister, Kate, and her boyfriend.

"Why the fuck is Kate's boyfriend sat in the front row?" asked Luke.

"Chill out," said Tom. "You're getting mardy about where people are sat? The div probably doesn't know where he should sit. Or Kate'll have asked him, to make a point."

Connor added, "Besides, he has enough on his plate with the state of his teeth—looks like his tongue's in jail."

Luke laughed and it reverberated against the roof of his closed mouth and he ducked his head. Connor put his hand on his neck to feign comforting him to the people who turned to glance at them.

Connor whispered, "Keep a sad and straight face, and sit up."

As Luke did so, Connor thought he could detect the faint smell of alcohol. He chose not to say anything. Instead he asked, "Where's Dan?" referring to Luke's elder brother—though he was younger than Connor and Tom. He had been living and working in London for years as a 'straight goer'.

"He's had to stay with Angela. She had a proper bad episode with her Crohns," said Luke, referring to Dan's wife. "She's in hospital. It's horrendous, mate. Don't say 'owt but

96

it's eaten through…ahem…what's that bit between the vagina and arsehole?"

"The chinrest?" Connor replied.

For the second time, Luke had to duck down and clamp his mouth. Tom craned his neck down to hide his smile as he shook his head.

"Either of you two heard anything about our problem?" asked Connor.

Tom answered, "Ellis always has some form of security around him at all times. And McKinley is always on the move. Apparently, their houses are like Fort Knox."

"You spoke to Aziz yet?"

"He's in Pakistan at the moment."

Luke said, "If Aziz is half Jamaican as well as being half Pakistani, why wouldn't he go over to the Caribbean for a holiday?"

"It'll be a business trip," said Tom.

Connor caught sight of his aunt Cathy—Tom's Mum, sat by his gran, turn and a sneer appear on her face. He turned to see that Jennifer—Derek's wife—had arrived.

"Fuck," whispered Luke. "It's gonna kick off."

Before Connor could attempt to defuse the situation, he heard his grandma's voice, loud and insistent, call out, "Come sit by me, Jennifer."

Connor admired his auntie's dignified walk under the familial stares. He, Tom and Luke returned her smile in unison before she sat by their gran.

"See, no one fucks with Thatcher, do they?" observed Tom. "By the way, did you go and see her?"

"Course I did."

"Did she give you a speech on not retaliating and that, Connor?" asked Luke.

"The opposite."

"No way," Luke exclaimed.

"So that's what she meant," murmured Tom, and without being prompted, he continued, "She said that I was to support you in whatever way I could. I said, 'What if Connor wants to kill every other gangster in the country?' and she said, 'Then you will help him to do that'."

Luke asked, "What about Charlie and Curtis?"

Connor looked at Tom. "You know them in this game better than me."

"They're inexperienced. The pair of 'em will be het up now. We'll keep them out of this as much as we can."

"What's the crack with 'em in relation to our business, so to speak? I'm not fully up to speed."

Tom sawed his moustache with his fingers and said, "Charlie over time might become the most valuable member of our family. He's a bit of a computer nerd, and it was him who got us into crypto-currency and came with me when we did the deal with the Latvians. He might not be much of a scrapper, but some of his ideas have helped massively. Curtis is...he's different."

After a few moments Connor looked at Tom. "Don't keep me in suspense. Different how?"

As Tom took a breath to answer, Connor felt Luke's hand on his wrist, "Tom means he's a stupid, insecure fuck who Tom is constantly having mares with."

"Is it true?" Connor asked.

Tom gave him a resigned expression. "Yeh."

Connor said, "All right, what we need are allies. We can't do this on our own. Aziz is away at the moment. Any ideas, Tom?"

"Yeh, I know someone that might be able to help."

Just then the minister appeared out front and the talking ceased.

Andrei could tell from the body language of Enver Alsanni that he thought he had the better hand. Not that Andrei could not see why; Alsanni, slouched behind the corner table in the restaurant—Vendi Special—was surrounded by five of his henchmen. The bottles of wine on shelves skirting the room looked down on them all.

"What is this? Negotiation? Check on us?" asked Alsanni with barely veiled derision. Though of Albanian heritage having lived there until the age of twelve, the London-based gangster, and the Hellbanianz cartel of which he was a key player, were affiliated to but not Mafia Shqiptare, who supplied them. However, because Hellbanianz could not obtain the quality of product that the Mafia Shqiptare provided, they gave the outward appearance of respect and cooperation.

That Alsanni had chosen to address Andrei in English spoke volumes to the Mik of his loyalty to his mother country—though Andrei conceded—Alsanni had lived in the Western capital since he was twelve.

He had not even offered Andrei a meal in the restaurant.

"I am here to make you aware of the concerns people have back home," replied Andrei, his perfect English momentarily splashing surprise on the six-foot-two-inch gangster's face.

The mask of arrogance returned. "What concerns? You are paid in full, on time, every time by my man."

"You are angering the authorities of this country unnecessarily?"

"Slinging half the drugs in London will do that," he sniggered, to the Hyena-like cackles of his men.

"I said unnecessarily."

The laughter stopped in time with Alsanni's tightened expression. "Go on, then. How?"

"The social media, displaying the cash, the exotic cars, the declarations of violence, the using of drugs—and some of this is within a prison cell."

"What can I say? It helps recruit 'youngers' and besides, if you've got it, flaunt it."

The cackles sounded again.

"One of your members has been talking to the media— I remember one line of 'I sold a grenade for seventeen pounds the other day—they may as well be grapes to me'."

"Seventeen pounds is a pretty expensive grape, yes?"

99

More guffaws.

Andrei smiled. "It is not true, as I will show you."

He raised his palms facing Alsanni before slowly reaching underneath the dark cardigan he wore. He pulled the pin out before revealing the grenade.

Alsanni recoiled into his chair with the collective gasp. One of the henchmen pulled a pistol and levelled it at Andrei—he could see in the mirror opposite that the rest had followed suit, all except one by the bar.

Andrei mimicked their previous chortles. "Very good, young one, shoot me and we all die."

He rested his grenade-filled fist on the table before standing.

"Drop it," one barked.

"A poor choice of words."

"Look, put the pin back in the pineapple and we can talk as men," said Alsanni, a ripple in his voice.

"We are going to talk, Enver," said Andrei, before addressing the man who had first drawn his pistol. "Young one, behind you is a waitress's notepad and pen. I want to show your leader something—please pass them to me."

The man hesitated, his eyes flickering before complying. Andrei ambled around the back of a flinching Alsanni.

"Relax, Enver. I want to rest the pad on your shoulder, keep still."

As he perched the pad, he addressed the room, holding up the grenade. "Now this is a HE fragmentation grenade with a delay of two seconds from the moment my fingers release the fly-off lever. Remember that before making any sudden movements, yes?"

He had lied—it was more like four seconds.

There were nervous glances and subtle nods. He held up the biro. "Have you heard the term that 'the pen is mightier than the sword'?"

The nods were a little more perceptible.

"Let me prove it to you."

He twirled the pen in his fingers until the point protruded from the bottom of his fist. It pierced Alsanni's brain through the eye like a fencing sword wielded by a Viking. The room recoiled. The shock hit Alsanni with catatonia. Andrei gripped Alsanni's thick black hair, before using his head to smash the biro off the table further into the brain.

He held up the head by his hair to reveal the socket of his eye turned to a mix of pulp and plastic shards. He let go and Alsanni's lifeless vessel thudded onto the floor.

"Put your guns down now," he ordered. After a few moments, they did so in a ripple.

"Which one of you is Arben Tinaj?"

"I am," said a dark-haired, flint-eyed man—the one who had not drawn a pistol on the reveal of the grenade.

"I have done my research—easy enough given the loose tongues of your members. You are now the leader," Andrei said, reaching into his pocket, skimming masks of nerves on the faces of the others. He took out a card and frisbee'd it into Arben's snatching hand.

"This is my card. You understand what I require before we continue with our business arrangement?"

Arben said, "No social media. No talking out of the organisation."

"Very good," said Andrei, meaning it. "We have big plans in store for our operation here. Your friend here let the person he was pretending to be hold him back from what he could have been. Do not make the same mistake."

Charlie drove the red Honda Civic Type R down the A1 as his brother answered messages on his phone. Eventually, he put it away and said, "You sure about this? I mean, not telling Tom?"

Curtis answered, "The whole family treats us like kids. When Connor left the Marines he fucked off around Europe and down south, and everyone thinks he's a hero—which I admit he is—but do you think he asked for permission? Fuck no. We have to make some of our own moves like."

"Those moves don't have to involve guns and violence. It's like Tom said, it's what the hoodrats do to make a name for themselves and it attracts attention—and it's not as if they make big money."

Curtis guffawed. "Like Connor and Tom haven't used guns and violence? Am not a boffin like you. And we aren't gonna use them unless we see the opportunity to take or to defend our'sens."

Charlie slowed and pulled up to the used car pitch in Doncaster. One of their money laundering schemes involved paying cash to certain independent dealerships for heavily discounted cars and inflated part-exchange, which Tom would then sell on for a profit.

Because they had been running errands like this for Tom for a few years they knew his preference—*"Jap cars first, Korean second, German third. Run anything else by me."*

The two Ryder twins were familiar faces around several West Yorkshire garages, and enjoyed the banter with the various dealerships.

John Stratton owned this particular one, and Charlie remembered the ribbing they both received on first meeting him a few years ago—*"Leeds version of the Kray twins, eh? Which one takes it up the aarrrsssseeee then?"* He remembered his more sensitive older brother—by eight minutes—being a little put out at the time.

Now, they both rolled with the abuse and gave it back harder.

The quiet of the forecourt echoed the time past six o'clock as they walked through it. The dregs of the remaining staff were getting into their cars.

Inside, Stratton was sat close to some customers, a young couple. A former Donny bouncer in the nineties, Stratton was now in his fifties, his black, slicked-back hair had tints of grey throughout. Above-average height, he still seemed strong across the chest and shoulders, but carried 'a bit of timber' around his midriff.

As the twins entered Charlie heard him going through a speech that he had heard more than once.

102

"Look, those online valuations presume the car is in pristine condition—yours is in good condition. But there are scuff marks on the driver's side door, the front tyres, especially on the driver's side, as I reckon there's only been one person in the car a lot of the time, and they'll need replacing in a few months. The miles on the clock are more than you put into the thing. Look, we're reasonable here, we can maybe do something with the finance, and I'll see about a free warranty, but I can't part-exchange your car for more, I'm afraid."

"So…ahem…" began the lad, "if it breaks down we can just bring it back?"

"As long as it's nothing to do with the wear and tear, then you can bring it back, no drama," Stratton replied, flanked by framed awards on the desk for 'Best Small Business' and 'Top Sales Branch'.

Charlie knew almost any fault on a car could be argued as wear and tear. Tom had taught him and his brother the golden rules to buying cars— *"Plead poverty, umm and arrr over finance—when they knock it down tell them you've squared a loan, and right at the end, tell them you have a car to part-exchange."*

Still, Charlie did not feel as sorry for the young couple as he once would have. Connor had pointed out it was the profitable companies that were the most reliable, and a company did not become profitable by being poor at sales.

Another five minutes passed, and the couple were enthusiastically signing the documents and thanking Stratton on a car deal that Charlie knew they could have had for well over a grand less. They drove off with smiles.

"That's how you do it, fellas. I make coin, and they are happy as Larry. Remember, it isn't the deal they get, it's the deal they think they get."

Curtis jutted his chin up and down. "The way of the world, John."

"Way of the world. Eh, come here," he said, and for the first time hugged the twins. "Sorry about your old man. He was a proper bloke."

They voiced their thanks and John added, "Take a seat, lads," indicating to the chairs the couple had vacated. He flipped the sign on the door to Closed.

"Coffee?"

They gave him their order.

Once they had all seated with their drinks, Charlie asked, "Business good then?"

"Yeh, seems to be, luv. Opened another pitch up on Barnsley road. We need a couple of young car washers."

"Let me guess," said Curtis. "We'd have to do it in our underwear while you 'inspected' our technique?"

"Even if I was a poofta, you two fuglies would be safe. Fuck me, if Michael Jackson babysat you both as kids, he'd have made you sleep in your own room."

Curtis and Charlie just laughed.

"How come you pair wanted to see me all hush-hush?"

The twins looked at one another before Curtis replied, "We're after those things that go bang."

Stratton frowned. "Why didn't you want your Tom to know?"

"He has enough on his plate," answered Charlie.

The lines in his head deepened before he said, "Nah, you're going to have to do better than that, lads. You get caught with what you asked for, Thomas is going to ask where you've got 'em from, then he's going to want to know why that person didn't let 'im know."

"We won't tell him. What's he going to do? Waterboard his own cousins?"

"You know as well as I do, he isn't daft. He'll guess it was me."

Curtis took his hand from his mouth. "We'll tell him we got them off Baz Sherman years ago."

Baz Sherman was a Huddersfield drug dealer who vanished four months ago, his disappearance still unsolved.

Stratton raised his eyebrow. "What if Sherman turns up and says otherwise?"

"He won't," answered Curtis.

"I see," said Stratton, stroking his jaw. "Thomas might still find out you've come to see me, so we need an alibi. I have a Suzuki Sx4 S-Cross in—fifteen plates. Got the paperwork here."

Always the salesman.

Curtis gave them a cursory glance. "You had it serviced and valeted?"

"Course I have. That's why Al's in. He's downstairs in the bays. I have some 'tools' down there we can discuss. You got enough readies?"

"There's a case in the car," said Curtis.

"Go down and see Al. Giz your cups and I'll be down in a minute."

Charlie smiled—*OCD gimp.*

The twins made their way down into the garage lot. It was open plan, facing the side of a massive fenced off warehouse.

"Al," Curtis called out when he was nowhere to be seen.

"Must be in the toilet," said Charlie. "The Suzuki's over there."

They rounded the corner to find Al lying prostrate, bleeding from the head. As Curtis rushed to his aid, Charlie's instinct made him spin around.

A flash of a baseball bat short-circuited his brain.

14

Charlie began to feel before he saw. The pain in his cheekbone and the top of his jaw dragged him closer to consciousness with every pulse.

He had enough about him not to open his eyes immediately. He knew he was in a chair and he could not feel any restraints.

"He's come round," said the Scouse voice.

The slap came as a painful surprise, opening his eyes to the reflection of himself battered and bleeding. Only when noticing his head was up and the reflection slumped, he realised it was his brother.

The man stood to his right was Kevin Kellings, one of Newcastle's most fearsome gangsters, whose enforcer Tom killed in front of Kellings in The Buxton Arms. There were three other men, two bald and hulking, with another looking like a cross between one of those punk rockers from the seventies and a fighter at a weigh-in.

"Remember me, Marra?" Kellings grinned.

Charlie didn't answer, instead said, "Where's Stratton?"

Kellings chuckled, before grabbing the top of Charlie's head. Before he could turn it, Charlie jumped up, smacking the hand off to the words of, "Get off me, you fat cunt."

The punch felt like an upturned baseball bat smashed into his stomach. He fell back into the chair with his lungs clawing for breath.

"It won't ever feel that good again if you keep misbehaving, kidda," said the hollow-cheeked Liverpudlian, before pointing behind him. "Yer friend is over here, see."

Charlie looked to see John Stratton on the floor, bound and gagged like Al on the other side.

He knew if he spoke, fear would tremor his voice.

"See, la," began the Scouser, clearly the one in charge. "Your family dropped a proper clanger. All they had to do was toe the line and show some respect. Instead, you all got it

106

into your heads you were some kind of Colombian cartel calling the shots. But you ain't—hang about, I think your bro wants to ask a question."

Curtis began to stir with a groan, before a blood drool stretched from his mouth onto his shirt.

"Guess not—now as you can see, ya both have had your beatings," said the hollow-cheeked man. "Your starters. Now he's awake it's time for the main course."

The man walked over to behind his brother, before pulling a silenced gun and holding it to Curtis's head.

"The bossman," he began. "He's one of those gays you defo couldn't refer to as a 'faggot', ya get me. A bit of a pervert with it too—so I've heard, obviously."

He began to laugh, seemingly to himself though the others grinned. He continued, "He says if you suck your brother's cock then the pair of you get to live. If not, then you can meet yer old man early."

Charlie's rage-laced scream of "Mother Fuck—" was cut off by a punch. He was then seized by the men and dragged over to his brother. Panic, anger and revulsion coursing through him, he fought against the straitjacket of hands— Brendan Chappel's death flashed in his brain.

"Struggle all you want, la, just means ya both die if you don't do it," said the Scouser, filming the scene on his phone.

He saw the point and stilled. As soon as he did, Curtis rasped, "Don't even think about it, you daft knobhead. I'd rather fucking die."

With that Curtis bolted upright, ramming the chair into the Scouser, knocking him back. As Curtis turned, Charlie stood only to see his brother's body snap sideways to a 'phuft' sound.

Curtis fell in slow motion. When he hit the floor, Charlie went berserk—punching, kicking, scratching before falling under an avalanche of blows.

It suddenly stopped and his ear canals reopened to, "One's enough, let him live to tell the others. Let's go."

Footsteps petered away, and he dragged himself over to his brother.

He somehow knew he was not dead; even as Curtis's head rolled in its blood under his shaking, Charlie knew. He pushed his middle and index finger into the side of his brother's windpipe—his heart soared—a beat.

He thought for a minute—*there's a phone upstairs*.

Tom drove as fast as he dared. Charlie cradled Curtis's head in his lap, the bleeding mercifully slowed by the gauze he had applied. Stratton was injury-free as was Al the mechanic when he regained consciousness.

Tom was in a quandary—if he took Curtis to an NHS hospital, then the police would be informed due to it being a gunshot wound. When Tom had arrived on the scene, he used the military medic kit given to him by Connor, which included an Asherman chest seal. Mercifully, the external bleeding had appeared to stop, but Curtis was barely conscious.

He took out his phone and keyed in a memorised number.

"Yeh?" said the voice.

"It's 'T' from Leeds. Is he there?"

"Hang on."

In less than twenty seconds, Zain Aziz's voice came on. "Hi."

"I have a problem," said Tom, listening out for what Bradford's most influential crime lord's response would be.

"I am here to solve it."

Tom felt relief mix with his urgency. "One of ours has been hit in the chest with one of those things that go bang. I can't take him to an NHS hospital."

"Drop him off at Strathmore Private Hospital. There'll be someone waiting for you at the back entrance. What are you driving?"

"A blue Nissan Skyline."

"No one goes in with him, you understand?"

"Yeh, I understand."

The line went dead.

He called back to the twins, "Should be about twenty-five minutes."

A groan was the reply.

"So Kevin Kellings organised this?"

Charlie replied, "He was there but it was this skinny Scouser who was in charge."

"Tell me what happened while it's still fresh in your head."

"Got there, Stratton was serving this couple. He finished up, and we had a chat, then—"

"What did you chat about?"

"About a Suzuki he had."

"Then what?"

"Told us the car was downstairs as it'd had a service and valet. We went down and saw Al on the deck. That's when I got banged out. When I came to, I was in a chair surrounded by these goons with Curtis in the chair opposite. The skinny Scouser sparks up, saying we took a liberty an' that. Then the sick fucker said 'is boss said we could live if one of us sucked off the other. That's when Curtis kicked off, and the geezer blasted 'im."

"He said his boss said it?"

"Yeh, said—wait, that's it—said his boss was gay and a pervert. He had his phone out to film it."

When Tom was quiet for a minute, Charlie asked, "Why? Do you know who it is?"

Tom blew out and said, "The skinny guy is Marty McKinley. He's the right-hand man of Harry Ellis—one of Liverpool's 'Old and Bold' Godfathers. We reckon Derek might have run to McKinley for sanctuary."

"That must be how he knew about Stratton's place."

"Maybe."

"So this Harry Ellis wants to kill us all then?"

"Obviously not, or you'd be dead."

"Have you ever met him?" asked Charlie.

Tom had a flashback to his twelve-year-old self, being in the car as his uncles Greg and Michael had been outside of it conversing with a group of men from Liverpool, in a lay-by overlooking the M62 motorway. At the time, gang violence in Manchester had reached the point where one had fired on the funeral of a rival gang associate they had murdered. With ongoing gang warfare affecting the drugs trade, the Liverpool cartel began looking to diversify their distribution networks. Tom also remembered there was a similarly aged kid in a car owned by one of the men—a tactic to safeguard against the potential use of firearms.

"I've sort of been in his presence but not actually met him."

They got to Strathmore with the greenery surrounding it resembling more a country park than a hospital. As Tom drove around to the back, three men in white coats stood ready with a gurney. They came to assist as soon as Tom stopped. Levering Curtis onto the stretcher, one barked, "What's his blood type?"

"O Pos," answered Charlie.

"What's his full name and his doctor?"

"Curtis Michael Ryder. Doctor Lewis at Birstall Medical."

"What are your contact numbers?"

Once Charlie and Tom gave them to him, he left with a, "We'll handle it from here. Update you as soon as we are able."

Charlie turned to Tom, his face ashen. "Do you think he'll be OK?"

"I think he'll live," said Tom quietly. "If he was gonna go, he'd have gone by now—but the bleeding has packed in. That said, sepsis is always a snake but he's in the best hands now."

After a few moments, Tom noticed the colour come back to Charlie's face a little, as he said, "He'll be carrying on with the story of 'how I got shot in the chest and survived' until he does one day peg it."

Connor walked the Amsterdam street, keeping his head still but eyes moving. Bicycles zipped by, unperturbed by the erratic motor vehicles beside them.

He knew his skills of compartmentalisation exceeded that of most people. Still, being perhaps the most influential member of his family and an agent for The Chameleon Project had its unique challenges.

Tom had told him about what had happened to Curtis. Connor had anticipated his family would have to go to war on the street one day—but the Ryder family still lacked a sure footing with regards to cash flow and soldiers.

And now McQuillan had requested a meeting—which meant a mission briefing.

It had been a while since Connor had met Bruce in person. With both their profiles now raised—Bruce's within the intelligence community and his within the UK and European underworld—extra caution had to be taken with face-to-face meetings.

They met in a café bar in the suburbs of Amsterdam. The Scotsman seemed the same, exuding relaxed alertness.

He stood to greet Connor as he walked in and surprised him with a pat on the arm as they shook hands.

"I am sorry about your uncle. And your cousin."

"Thanks."

They sat, and the hovering waitress came over. Connor ordered them both a black coffee in Dutch.

"How well can you speak it now?"

"Enough to hold a stilted conversation if I am leading it," Connor answered. "Hey, can you speak Gaelic?"

"It's not 'Gaylick'—that's a homosexual with an ice cream, it's pronounced 'Gar-lic'. And, no, only a few words."

"I see."

"George tells me you almost had him the other day," said Bruce.

"Tyson almost banged out Buster Douglas for a full count in the eighth round, but he didn't."

"It shows your improvement, which was the point."

"Or his age."

"Trust me, the others still get a skelping," said Bruce, referring to the other agents of The Chameleon Project. Agents Connor had not seen in a year; others he had never met, not that there were many.

"I am surprised to be meeting you. Were you just in town?"

Bruce shook his head. "No. I came over when Jaime briefed me. Seems you've stumbled on something that was on the agenda."

"OK."

"Tell me what you know about the Albanian mafia."

Bruce would always assess his current knowledge before getting into any specifics.

"I know they've been expanding at a rapid clip—Europe, both Americas, Middle East and Asia. Arms, drugs and human trafficking. I keep hearing different things about their structure—some say they are regimented with a definite hierarchy in place, and some say it's a collection of vicious gangs out of Albania or with members with Albanian heritage. In any case, apparently they are fucking brutal. We don't see a right lot of them in the North of England, but Louis says he tries to give them a wide berth if he can."

Louis was Connor's friend who headed the notorious Southwark Union Gang—the SUG—an amalgamation of black south-east London crews.

"The question of their structure is complicated, but there is one. There are fifteen family clans—or Fares—that control all the organised crime out of Albania and beyond. Some of these clans are more powerful than others—the ones out of Tirana and Shkodra being the most influential. Each family has an executive committee known as a 'Bajrak' who select a high-ranking member from each street 'unit' to represent that unit. It's presided over by a 'Krye'—a boss who selects an underboss named a 'Kryetar'. Roger so far?"

Connor understood 'roger so far' meant Bruce wanted him to repeat the information back to him in his own way. This technique helps with absorption.

"Roger. Fifteen fares in Albania, strongest ones in the capital Tirana and Shkodra in the north. Bajraks are committees made up of high-ranking members headed by a Krye and his Kryetar."

"These clans—the higher-performing ones—blend traditional characteristics like honour, rigid discipline and 'endogmatic closure'—a fancy term for—"

"A reliance on intermarriage and family ties."

"Correct. Blended with transnationality and adapting modern business practices. And you're right; it's underpinned by a willingness to escalate violence rarely seen on this side of the Atlantic."

"So, this mega-structured entity has a bedrock of honour and discipline, and not just a collection of bloodthirsty gangs—reminds me of a Keyser Soze saying, 'The greatest trick the devil ever pulled was convincing the world he didn't exist'."

"Yes."

"So, what's the situation then?"

"With BREXIT approaching, intelligence suggests these Godfathers are looking to flood the UK with fentanyl and maybe even carfentanyl."

"That's not very nice."

"It isn't. Until now cannabis grown in Albania has been their staple, and cocaine from South America. But they fear borders tightening after the UK leaves Europe and want to make a killing now. Not only with the drug trafficking, but with all crime—fraud, robbery of all kinds, extortion. And in the immediate aftermath of BREXIT, it could prove catastrophic. We need to disrupt this."

"How?"

"The NCA and police in general are overstretched, and the judicial system would not be able to cope even if they weren't. There isn't time to be reactive to this. We have to go on the offensive."

"Why can't SIS and SF go over and start dissolving the issue?"

"They can't cultivate reliable local assets for information as someone is always a cousin of someone who is Albanian mafia, and they can pay more for information than even our treasury. A pair of SIS agents were captured, presumed tortured before being chopped up and dumped in Lake Shkodër. The media isn't aware, but SIS pulled all their other agents, not knowing if there had been a leak at Vauxhall Cross."

Connor blew and said, "You think the Mafia Shqiptare could have infiltrated SIS?"

"It's possible."

"So, what do you want me to do? Go over there and make business contacts, transport their drugs and destroy them before UK city centres look like zombie apocalypses?"

"There's no time for that. I need you to go over and start a war. We need them to turn on one another, make them so preoccupied they lose sight of their UK objective."

Connor was quiet for a moment. "I have an issue developing at home. In order—"

"Your family has become embroiled in a conflict with adversaries in Liverpool."

"That's right. And the odds aren't looking in our favour at the moment."

"Which begs the question, was there anything you could have done to prevent yourselves becoming embroiled in it?"

Connor took a breath. "Harry Ellis had been rinsing our family for years because Derek was weak. We made a stand and fucked him off—we can't grow the operation and become a serious player if we're paying someone else the majority. We left the door open to negotiation—we'd thought he'd either go for it or at the most put the squeeze on us financially. I didn't expect this type of response. War with them might have happened eventually."

"Why would it have happened eventually?"

"My instinct tells me Derek reached out to them to have my dad murdered. In return, they squeezed Derek with the threat of exposing him."

Connor saw lines briefly appear in Bruce's forehead. "Is emotion clouding your judgement? It sounds like an *Advance to Contact*."

The former Marine said, "Confrontation of some kind was always going to happen unless we rolled over, which would set a dangerous precedent."

"What are you asking for?"

"You and I both know the main reason I am an asset to you is I can move in the underworld in a way other—maybe even technically better—operators can't. That ability disappears if I can't win this war with Harry Ellis and whoever else. I am asking for time so I can clasp my hands around this."

Bruce sipped his coffee. "How long do you need?"

"Not long. I just need to take out some of the key players and put a plan in place to contain the fallout."

"Harry Ellis makes a lot of people a lot of money," said Bruce. "And you know yourself that is one of the keys of surviving in that world. The Ryder family don't yet. And they are going to come for you and your family—and maybe not just the male members."

"You've looked into it already?"

"Of course I have. The first thing you need to do is to get the women away from Leeds. Harry Ellis has been involved in this world longer than anyone in your family— longer than you have been alive, and there's a reason he's still thriving."

"Do you think they know about Rayella?"

"Does your Uncle Derek know?"

"Fuck."

"Maybe she and her family win an impromptu cruise holiday? Jaime will e-mail you the details. You book them on board together, but you receive news at the last moment, calling you away."

Connor was stunned for a moment. "You already knew."

"And you need someone who knows the city, someone who can move around there—that's one place you can't, not now."

"Ciara?"

Bruce nodded, "She's back in Liverpool, doing the groundwork."

"How to fuck did you anticipate all this?"

"By doing what you should have done. Took a step back and worked out all the possible scenarios and mentally followed them through. Practise, and you'll get quicker in time. Because you now don't have the luxury of winging it, you're the 'go-to' guy for both your family and me. Your ability to think clearly, deeply and laterally will be critical—to strategise, to make contingencies."

"What are you saying?"

"What I am saying is that as my profile increases within the government and civil service, I'll need to delegate more to you. Jaime knows this too."

Connor asked, "What if I die?"

"That would be nature's way of letting me know you're not the right man...person...for the job."

15

Ciara felt a warmth on sitting into the leather-backed seat. The Berry and Rye had always been one of her favourite bars. The Vodka Spritz danced on her tongue. She admired the dreamlike painting of a man with blue-tinted skin matching his waistcoat but contrasting with his red shirt.

Ciara spent her youth bouncing around various locations including Germany and Cyprus, with her father being a career soldier until his death. However, she had spent a significant amount of time in Crosby, in the north of Merseyside.

She knew her way around geographically, but she did not have any underworld contacts. However, her journalistic credentials did not require fabrication. Despite her working as an agent for Bruce McQuillan, several of her articles had made national papers and respected online periodicals.

This enabled her to visit the hotspots Bruce assigned to her without the need to memorise elaborate *legends*.

Also, criminals or former criminals generally liked to publicise any legitimate enterprises they might be involved in—especially charities—to prop up the façade of being 'a straight goer'.

She watched the patrons of the bar as he entered. Most did not react, but a few did; a subtle bowing of the head and surreptitious whispering.

She stood to greet him. "Mr Ellis, a pleasure to meet you."

His grey suit trousers went well with the egg-shell shirt.

"The pleasure is all mine and all that. You can call me Harry."

"Ciara," she replied, as they shook hands. His were softer than she imagined. Then again, there was not much heavy lifting once a man reached this stratosphere of crime.

"You have good taste," he said, gesturing to her choice of meeting place.

"I think so. Can I buy you a drink?"

"It'll be a long time before I let a woman buy me a drink. You might find that sexist, I am sure. You want another of what you've had?"

"We'll just call you old school rather than sexist, and yes, please."

She noticed the young barman attempted to serve Ellis as soon as he reached the bar, as well as Ellis's pointing gesture that he serve the people waiting first. Ellis came back with her Vodka Spritz and Pale Ale for himself that she had not known they served.

"You've spent a lot of time here, haven't you?"

"You must have the ears of an owl." She smiled. "We lived in Crosby for a number of years."

"Ahh, the posh end of town, eh. It's debatable whether or not you're a Scouser or a *Woolyback*."

He had a disarming charm about him, she thought.

"Seems there are more posh ends in Liverpool now than when I was a child," she said.

"There's been a lot of development since I was a scally but there are still its deprived areas, the same as any city."

"I would suggest you wouldn't have to go much bigger than a village to have a good part and a bad part."

"There you go," he said. "The government might throw money our way now and then, but it's Liverpool's people who have turned the city around."

"That was one of the questions I was going to ask you—is it my imagination or is it that some Liverpudlians don't consider themselves English, just Scouse?"

"There is an element of that."

"I've heard some don't support the English football team they feel so strongly about it."

"There's a lot of things the people of Liverpool can get aggravated about with how the government and the media have treated us."

"Can you educate me?"

"Educate you? Or give you material to write about?"

"Can't it be both?"

118

He gulped his drink before answering, "First of all, this is a city of immigrants, and I am not just talking about the Irish, which you'll already know—being a good journalist—is my background. Liverpool has both the oldest Chinese and African communities in Britain. But yes, this goes back over a hundred and fifty years, when starving Irishmen crossed the sea and settled here and the English spat on them."

Ciara smiled. "I sense your history lesson is a way of you not talking about the present."

Ellis took a moment before answering with, "Well, let's put Hillsborough aside—which I shouldn't do but let's. I remember a time, back in the Thatcher-era, where it was stated in the Commons that Liverpool was beyond saving economically. And now look at us. Tory governments will always see us as thick Celts, and this sidling up to the Democratic Unionist Party is a slap in the face to many in the city."

"Playing the devil's advocate, I think that was more or less a necessity—"

"It doesn't change the sentiment."

"So, you're telling me Liverpool has this sense of independence because of the persecution by the government?"

"Look, I am not sitting here playing the 'Woe is me' Scouser. I have done plenty of naughty things, of which I am sure you're aware, and there's plenty of unreformed characters about the place. But yes, there'll always be an anti-establishment feeling in the city."

"Which brings us on to your initiatives within the local communities."

Ellis's eyes settled on her. "It was you who requested this interview—or at least your editor did. I apologise if endeavours to give back to my city isn't salacious enough for you."

"I am an independent journalist. I can't imagine the PR company you employ approving of your meeting with me, so I am grateful. I wasn't aware my questions were salacious."

"Perhaps it's my distrust of journalists in general. If you aren't the type to put entertainment in front of the truth, then I hope you accept my apologies."

"Apology accepted."

They both smiled before Ellis asked, "So, what did you want to know?"

"I wanted to know a little about the sports sessions run out of your gyms throughout the city. I believe they have been serving the purpose of relieving mental health issues for various affected groups."

"So, you're aware these schemes are subsidised by the NHS, which has since threatened to cut off our funding?"

"I am."

"Then you could forgive my paranoia of seeing the headlines of 'Gangster Harry Ellis uses taxpayers' money for front businesses', or something like that."

"Is that the truth?"

"No, though the headline would no doubt sell better."

She gave an exasperated sigh. "I thought we went over this?"

"I know."

"Well, in the interest of fair play, how about I attend one of these sessions, talk with the participants."

"I am surprised, and you are more than welcome to stop by. How about you schedule in with my PA and—"

"Oh no, you see, I am allowed to be suspicious too. You might fill the class with paid actors."

He returned her smile. "Feel free to drop in on any session you like, whenever you like."

16

Van Der Saar wandered around the Van Gogh museum in a lazy awe of the great artist's talent. He stood in front of the 'Starry Night Wolf' canvas and allowed himself to be enveloped by it. The dark wolf stood on a jutting rock, howling at the moon-bright sky with the simmering red and orange of the dying sun below. However, at the same time the painting seemed to also depict shoals of swirling fish.

He began to lament on how he got to this place in life—it had not been his intention when he started on this journey. The Dutchman's ruthlessness had been born out of necessity, not his nature. As the years went by, he became accustomed to the point of near feeling—'near' as part of him liked the power of it. It was a part he kept an eye on; he had seen plenty in this business fall by the wayside when they let their ego control them.

He also understood that with power came the limitations of certain freedoms—like visiting art galleries without armed security. They blended into the background so an undiscerning citizen would not be able to spot them, but every visit needed coordinating. Not that he was likely to be assassinated in broad daylight in public, but it was not an impossibility.

He had survived gangland wars before; most recently with the Moroccan crime element in Holland. That had been difficult, but he knew the Albanians were a different level entirely. Their sphere of influence was as deep as it was broad. Their cunning and ruthlessness had few equals.

People had warned him that to deny them was insane, but Van Der Saar knew the truth—to capitulate would be worse. The initial encroachment on his business under the guise of a partnership would escalate. Eventually, he would become their puppet and his product cut for greater profit.

He turned in search of the next masterpiece to admire when a bolt jolted his heart on seeing the dark-skinned man reach into his jacket. Van Der Saar used his long legs to step quickly around him like a bull would a cape. Before the snub-nosed pistol could be angled towards him, the aggressor was slammed against the wall and received a crushing knee to the balls from Rayen, one of Van Der Saar's security staff.

The other visitors resembled a gasping, diverting shoal of fish.

Van Der Saar spied the angle of the security camera before closing in and whispering, "Take his gun and any ID—quickly."

Rayen's deft hands slid both into his possession. The museum's security arrived.

When Van Der Saar saw the flash of nerves in their eyes, he congenially said, "I apologise on behalf of my overzealous security staff. If the gentleman wishes to press charges, I will bear witness."

The two anxious-looking protectors looked expectantly at the ashen man sat on the floor.

"Sir, do you wish to take this further?"

The shake of the man's head surprised Van Der Saar—he did not expect him to understand Dutch

Van Der Saar pulled out his smartphone phone, saying, "I wish for his answer to be recorded should he change his mind at a later date."

He did not expect consent to be given, but it afforded the opportunity to surreptitiously take pictures of him.

The man held his hand up to deny his permission, but the Dutch Czar already had what he wanted.

"Never mind, I am sure you two gentlemen will remember if he chooses to come forward at a later date."

"Absolutely Mr…ahem…. sir."

Van Der Saar hid his relief. Not only had he escaped death, but he had also avoided unwanted police attention.

As he walked away under the shadow of his security team, the laces of incongruity knotted in his head. If this was the Albanian mafia, why would they use an amateur to assassinate him? He accepted the attempt might have been successful had he not turned in that moment. Still, they had killers within their midst much more capable.

Then it dawned on him—that the man inside, now with the ability to father children temporarily compromised, would have been a man in the Albanians' debt. It was a testing salvo. If it had succeeded, then they could have carved up his empire easily. If he would have been injured or even the gun discovered, then he would have been embroiled in a legal case hampering his freedom of movement. He understood now—whoever he was dealing with was not only daring and ruthless but dangerously cerebral.

Bruce walked, enjoying the sea air of the Italian port of Bari. The late-night ferry to the Albanian city of Durres was still a few hours away. The sun had just disappeared leaving a simmering orange layer between the city's street lamps and the darkening blue sky.

Though Bruce had the official title of Security Services Liaison officer, he did not 'report' to anyone as such. He and Miles Parker—the SIS Chief—had come to an arrangement a few years back to bring him 'in from the cold'. They agreed he could still run his unit, but the Scotsman had to be present at key meetings between principal UK security agencies to act as an advisor. Other than that, he would check in on occasion but that would be that. Parker had offered to put Bruce forward to be his successor, but the former SAS soldier had always refused—he had not come up through the official SIS ranks, and his past would be dug into.

With his phone switched off and his planning done, the pleasant chatter of Italian voices and moon glints on the sea had a meditative effect. He thought himself lucky despite fighting wicked men and organisations for three decades and never seeing a lull in the malevolent waves. He had never fallen victim to nihilism. He knew his calling was to provide a balance and justice.

He also knew about cycles, and even he would have to be replaced.

He thought of Reed, of how he had developed over the time he had known him; how his audacity had been reinforced by forethought and that he seemed a natural leader.

The Romano-Ferguson bar caught McQuillan's eye. It seemed busier than the others, and both the Italian and Scottish flags hung from the rafters. He walked in, careful not to knock anyone with his shoulder bag. He smiled at the scene before him of an olive-skinned barman, with a black moustache curled at the edges, using a dishcloth to clean the heavy glass pint mug.

"La birra della casa, per favore,"—*the house beer, please*, said Bruce.

"Ovviamente,"—*of course*, replied the barman.

As the barman poured his drink, he spoke to another customer in English flecked with a Scottish dialect. When he returned with his pint, Bruce said, "Apologies, I thought you were Italian."

The barman smiled. "I am. Father is Scottish. I thought you were Italian—a pale one maybe, maybe a wop from the north."

"Fifteen hundred miles further north than you thought, maybe."

"Glasgow, huh?"

"Aye."

"My father was from Stirling."

"How much do I owe you?"

"Your money is no good," said the barman, with a dismissive gesture with his hand.

"Thank you."

"What brings you here then?"

"Business," said Bruce, taking a sip. "Where's ye old man now?"

"He works in a Roma," answered the barman with the Italian inflexion coming out in his voice. "He built this bar and restaurant with my mother from the floor up. My father the businessman and my mother the chef—both truly great at what they do. My father builds links with Scottish whisky distilleries and brings it down here, my mother cooks fine Italian food."

"So, how did their moving to Rome come about?"

"My father and mother are passionate about the blending of their two cultures—I am the perfect example," he said, before laughing uproariously.

Bruce smiled. "So they decided to expand?"

"Yes, well, more people, more opportunity, but they still wanted this—the original—to be kept going."

"So, they made you the protégé."

"Yes, my sister and me. My parents trained us the best they could and then left for Rome, leaving me with the bar and restaurant. They checked in on me from time to time, but eventually left me to it. And it has continued to flourish."

"I can see that," said Bruce, taking another swig. "Where's your sister?"

"Well, it was my sister who was meant to run this place. But she got caught up in Milan. She now runs her own business there. Sometimes the unexpected works out."

Bruce remained quiet for a moment before finishing his beer. He shook the man's hand. "Thank you for the chat."

Tom stood with Connor in the Dyer Street coach station watching most of the womenfolk of their family set off for Southampton. They were heading for a two-week cruise.

"Am impressed you managed this. Convincing them to ditch work. Convincing their bosses it's OK," said Tom.

"Amazing what you can do when eighty grand falls into your lap," replied Connor, still waving.

"Falls laundered into your lap, I hope."

"Naturally."

Tom did not want to press his cousin—if he wanted to tell him, he would. Instead, he said, "See you didn't manage to convince Gran."

"I doubt Darren Brown could convince her to do something she didn't want to do."

"Aunt Jennifer?"

"I haven't been to see her after the frosty reception she got at our Michael's wake, it was only because of Gran that Joanne didn't start."

"What about Rayella? Derek knows how close you are."

"Harry Ellis knows better than to harm a fourteen-year-old girl."

"It's up to you," said Tom. "Funny how McKinley and Kellings got around the back and down the stairs of John Stratton's garage undetected, isn't it? And how they were there at the time the twins came."

Connor gave a cynical smile. "Let's not take it personally, probably been made an offer he couldn't refuse. He isn't a priority at the moment."

"I know," said Tom. "But he'll be getting dealt with eventually—he's known us since we were nippers."

As they turned to walk back to the car, the coach peeled out of the station. Connor asked, "Where's Luke?"

"At a bird's house in Ashton-under-Lyne."

Connor shook his head. "I bet it's not a girl he knows well—he's susceptible to a honeytrap—oldest trick in the book."

"I know," answered Tom, as the coach disappeared out of sight. "By the way, I've let these guys we're going to meet know you're coming too."

Connor said in an Irish gypsy parodying accent, "He didn't say 'no one brings more than two fellas unless they're trying to say something without tarrking right baiy'?"

"No. He actually seemed pleased you're coming to meet him."

17

Luke sat in the back of the Range Rover while Tom drove. He looked out onto the housing and industrial estates either side of the M60 motorway. Connor was in the front passenger seat. They were making their way back from Ashton-under-Lyne where they had collected him from a girl's house he had met drinking the previous night. Connor had messaged him while he was on his third drink, telling him they had a meeting the next day and he had to be sharp—he cut the night short, and she offered for him to stay over—like he knew she would.

"Is there anything to eat in here?" asked Luke.

"You had nothing to eat?" said Connor, with concern tainting his voice.

"There's some Space Raiders in the glovebox," said Tom.

"Fucking hell, Tom," said Connor, getting them out and tossing them to Luke. "Poor man's Monster Munch then."

"Or maybe Monster Munch are over-priced Space Raiders."

"You'll spend thousands and thousands on a mansion to host drug-fuelled orgies but skimp on crisps. Bet those sunglasses are Roy Bons."

Before Tom could answer, Luke piped up, "Aren't you scared those NCA coppers and CPS will level a UWO against that mansion, Tom?"

Unexplained Wealth Orders had recently come into effect, where if the target could not explain the source of their wealth, the National Crime Agency could have assets seized under the High Court.

"It's called laundering. A bloke is either smart with money or not. The mansion is an asset and buying shit purely because of its name only is a loser's move. Besides, the athlete in the back shouldn't be drinking and eating shite anyway."

"I was on the Gin and Slimlines all night."

127

"Must have had a few of them, you look as rough as a bear's arse," commented Tom.

"That bird had her kids dropped off at their gran's at seven in the bastard morning—all four of 'em by three different dads," said Luke, rubbing his temples. "Get this, last night she says, 'Am not like that, you're gonna hav' to work for it', and am like, 'I bet you a gram I don't'."

Three men burst into laughter. When it died down Connor said, "Having nothing is better than having trans fats. We'll get breakfast on the way."

Luke folded the top of the packet and handed it back to Connor who said, "I don't know why you've turned to this bare-knuckle lark, you're going to get your looks marred."

"I'd rather be fuck ugly than brain-dead. Birds like a few scars anyway—think I am arsed about looking like one of those pansy reality TV stars?"

Tom said, "I think you're puddled if you think there's no punchy bare-knuckle boxers."

"There's not as many as with gloved boxers. You have to place your shots more, hit with the first two knuckles, or you'd cripple your hands catching the top of their swede. And a boxing glove adds weight to the punches."

Tom asked Connor, "Have you ever done anything bare-knuckle?"

Luke saw Connor rub his jaw before answering, "I had a Vale Tudo match back in the Ukraine which was bare-knuckle. My hands did chaff afterwards."

"No way," exclaimed Luke in surprise but not disbelief. "That's mental. So, you know what a buzz it is. The nearest thing to being a modern-day gladiator—apart from the dying at the end bit."

"Not for nothing," Connor replied, "but gladiators rarely fought to the death—it wouldn't have been financially viable."

"Do you have to ruin every film I like with your facts?" said Tom. Luke smiled.

"There's no money in it, Luke, and it's an even shorter career than gloved boxing," said Connor. "You'd have been best off going pro boxing."

"That's where you're wrong. BKB is getting more popular and sanctioned now. They had a massive show in Sheffield last weekend. I could be the Daddy of this as it gets bigger and bigger. Like you said, I am good-looking and talented, aren't I? Promotors looking to expand will get behind me. My style is well suited to it—I've always been elusive and a good banger."

Connor's head seemed to tilt before saying, "I never thought about it like that."

Tom looked at Luke in the rear-view mirror. "How is it different from boxing with gloves—like the training and how you fight?"

"The distance is different as the padding on the gloves adds a bit. I keep my hands open to catch punches. Got to place them more, like I say. Can't just shell up defensively like Winky Wright, as not having gloves leaves gaps. And I keep my combinations to two-three punches, so I am accurate. I don't spar often but when I do, I use the MMA gloves just to get the distance down. I do a bit of Greco-Roman wrestling over the wrong side of the Pennines, helps me in the clinches."

"Fuck me, you've been serious about this a while— thought it was something you were doing for a thrill and extra coin."

"Nah, Connor, I am going to be BKB's first superstar in this country, make it legitimate like that *The Ultimate Fighter* series did to MMA."

"Yeh, but you're from a family of gangsters. Sponsors won't want to touch you?"

"Who gives a fuck? Ronnie O'Sullivan is the biggest star in snooker and his dad was in the nick for an eighteen stretch—Tyson Fury's dad was in the nick too."

"Listen, Luke, don't be letting these gypsies know you do bare-knuckle cos they'll jump all over it," said Tom.

"Not arsed—they'll probably know anyway."

"Fuck's sake." Tom sighed.

"We buying a caravan with no wheels?" chortled Luke.

When Connor sniggered, Tom said, "These aren't Pavee—they're Roma gypsies and proud *Loiners.*"

"What's Pavee?" asked Luke.

"It's what gypsies call Irish travellers," answered Connor, before he asked Tom, "Where they staying now? Down Gildersome?"

The question reminded Luke that Connor had not spent a lot of time in Leeds ever since he had left for the Marines well over a decade ago.

"Not these gypsies, and it was causing aggro them staying on these campsites with holidaymakers, so Leeds council have come up with this scheme. They've picked out nine sites dotted all over Leeds that are awaiting redevelopment, an' said they can stop there for twenty-eight days at a time without being evicted—they have to sign a 'good behaviour' contract."

"What's to stop every gypsy and his horse rocking up?"

"Can't have more than nine caravans on at a time on 'em. Council provide the skips and Portaloos, can't use a site more than once a year."

"Who's the geezer we're meant to be meeting?"

"Hughie Birtle—fucking savage back in his day, think he's knocking on sixty now—"

"Big bloke who looks like he's come out of the fifties with the slacks, teddy boy haircut and the 'Johnny aged five' tattoos?" asked Connor.

"That's him," answered Tom.

"Yeh, I remember being in the car when my dad met him once."

"That's the thing—at first, he got a monk on when I told him there would be three of us, but like I said, when I said it was you he seemed all for it. Not sure whether that's a good thing or not."

"Did he have any dealings with Derek?"

"Not that I know of, but who knows."

Luke felt the air expand in his chest. "So, we could be just driving up to get *brayed* or worse by a wild bunch of pikeys?"

Connor replied, "The term 'pikey' is what these Romani gypsies use for non-gypsy travellers."

Tom tilted his head and said, "Fuck me, just go on *The Chase* and have done with it."

Ellis and McKinley were sat across from one another in his office in the vehicle wrapping shop.

The older man said, "I am away in Ireland until Sunday. I need you at the port on Saturday. The Arabs are sending a set of foals—worth millions these, so treat their delivery as such. And in six weeks I am sending you over with one of the horse trainers to look after him."

"What's the crack with these horses, Harry? If I am going over there anyway, I didn't want to be looking a divvy."

Harry frowned. "These guys have their champion stallions—sires the horse people call them—go through all these mares. I buy foals and have them sent over here before they are chipped or anything."

"Chipped?"

"Microchipped. They are making it so every horse is chipped," answered Harry. "Then I send them to horse breeders that are in my pocket. Then we have them chipped, making out their parents are a pair with fuck all in terms of racing pedigree—they have to be the same breed, mind—and so when they are entered into races the odds on them winning are low."

"I see," said McKinley, knowingly. "Not to be nosey but I thought you were pulling away from being naughty?"

"I have my reasons, but this will be the last time."

"I see," answered McKinley, stroking his jaw. "Anything else to it?"

"I get paid from the breeder—cos he has had his sub-par foal swapped out for champion stock and makes him look sparkling. That foal goes back to the Arabs, by the way, which is how I get a discount cos they sell it on making out it's the champion one. Then me and mine get rich off the bets we put on it, and finally I get paid when it's eventually put out to stud—you see?"

McKinley laughed. "Now I know why you are where you are."

Connor looked out the car window over Saddleworth Moor and wondered how many bodies were buried there. In addition to the Moors Murders by Myra Hindley and Ian Brady, he had heard stories of the victims of gangland murders ending up under the ground on the desolate heath.

They had finished their service station breakfasts and were drinking coffee—his elder cousin having voiced his resentment at the prices—when Tom received the text that the meeting with Hughie Birtle was in a scrapyard near Luddenfoot on the outskirts of Halifax. It had come just in time to slip onto the A672 scenic road.

Connor knew he needed allies in the North. Louis and the SUG were all the way down in London, Leonid—a crime lord of the Odessa mafia he had formed a business connection with six months ago—and Van Der Saar was in Holland. Tom had maintained relations with a few players but had been subverted by Derek's under-the-counter scheming. Now, with their enemies on the doorstep, Connor knew they had to start building relationships.

As if reading his thoughts, Luke piped up, "What have we got to offer these gypsies anyway?"

"Hughie Birtle's family run a fair all over the north every summer. It was particularly popular around Warrington and Liverpool, that popular that Harry Ellis took a shine to the idea. So he pays these lunatic scallies to keep sabotaging it—then used his contacts in the media to make out it was the gypsies' fault. Eventually, he used Caris to take an injunction out on the fairs. Because Birtle's family are from Yorkshire the council down there fucked them off. Ellis runs his own now."

132

"How the fuck do you know things like this, but you don't know where these gypsies stay in Leeds?" exclaimed Luke. "Did you know this, Tom?"

"Not until he told me. I'd like to know too."

"Well, I broke into Caris's house, restrained him, fucked his wife while filming it then got her to empty my cum out of her pussy on his face. Convinced her to give me the code to his safe in which I found 160K. Gave her half—not sure what she's done with it—and told him he'd have to work to get it back by supplying me intelligence, or the videos would be shared."

"Meanwhile…back in the real world," said Luke.

"I told you, Luke, he won't tell you anything he doesn't have to," said Tom, taking a left. "We're not far."

Connor became aware of having a heightened sense of things as the scrapyard came into view. The lack of cars in the makeshift car park became apparent.

The paint on the big, bowed green sign with the white lettering of 'Treeside Scrap Dealers' peeled at the edges. The entrance sat below it with a long, wriggly-tinned building on the right and the yard filled with broken-down cars, chassis, engines and other motor vehicle parts.

Tom parked and cut the engine before saying, "Two things about this Hughie Birtle is that he's big on honour and respect. And the other is he'll negotiate like an Arab."

"Agreed," Connor said. "Let's play it by ear."

They got out and walked through the gates. A dog's bark echoed through the yard and the faint smell of petrol floated.

A bird flew off a tree at the voice, "Good morning, young Ryders, find us all right?"

They turned to see Hughie Birtle's frame filling the last entrance of the wriggly-tin building.

"Google Maps is an amazing thing, Mr Birtle," said Tom.

"Addles the mind all this technology," he replied, tapping his temple. "Anyway, I haven't seen you two since you were *warches*. And I only know of this one," he boomed, gesturing to Luke.

Connor, because he had been a youth when he had last seen the man, had anticipated him being a little less larger than life—if anything, he was more so. Same slacks, pristine white vest, same slicked-back hair except with hints of grey this time. He was able to pencil in some of the details—the bulbous knuckles and two tattoos stood out—two pretty dark-haired women on either shoulder, one wearing a bearskin, the head of which perched on her head, the other veiled with a crystal ball.

As Birtle stepped down towards them, faces began to appear in the windows—Connor counted six and instinctively knew they were not employees of the scrapyard.

He had expected Birtle to address Tom first due to him being the eldest cousin and having always lived in Leeds while holding the family together.

"So this is Gregory's son all grown up, Connor Ryder," said Birtle, holding out his hand.

"Connor Reed, Mr Birtle—I took my mother's name," he replied, clasping the rough hand.

"Ah yes, he did say."

"Knew him well then?" asked Connor.

"I knew him," Birtle replied simply, before shaking Tom's hand. "Thomas, how are you?"

"Cracking on, thank you, Mr Birtle."

"And this must be 'Cool Hand Luke'," he said, shaking his hand.

Connor and Luke smiled hearing the nickname their Grandfather Frank had bestowed on him. Connor kept Luke's other nickname of 'The Aryan'—on account of this bright blonde hair and blue eyes—to himself; estimates of half a million Roma gypsies dying in Hitler's death camps had been reported.

"Now then," said Birtle. "Pardon my French, but what's that cunt of an uncle of yours up to now? Heard you had a bit of a falling out?"

Connor picked up he had not asked what the meeting was regarding.

"He's away with the geese—or the rats," answered Tom.

"I see. I am guessing this meeting is summat abart him?"

Tom continued, "He's been fucked off out of Yorkshire and told not to come back. He's probably not happy."

Birtle raised three fingers in the air, before pressing them together and performing a reverse beckoning. Three men came out of the building and walked towards them. One seemed around ten years younger than Birtle, with his black hair crowning and dark eyes set in a face that could be kind. The other two were much younger—early to mid-twenties— medium height, dark-haired, sinewy and a confident gait. Maybe brothers or cousins.

They stood by Birtle, the older man to his left and the younger pair to his right.

"Since we are now talking business I've brought my chief negotiators out," said Birtle. "This old boy is my brother-in-law, Leander, and these two are Lash and Danior."

Connor spoke. "And now with the numbers being four to three, some would interpret this as an attempt at intimidation. Obviously, no one here though."

Birtle opened his mouth in what Connor thought to be a protest but then smiled. "So, what's brought you boys out to see me?"

"Harry Ellis torpedoed your fairs in and around Liverpool costing you money and I reckon respect," said Tom.

"Didn't think that was common knowledge," said Birtle. "It has taken a few bob off the table, I'll give you that. How did you know it was Harry Ellis? Took a lot of time and money for me to find that out."

"You know better than to expect us to tell you," said Connor, before noticing the eyes of Birtle's companions narrowing.

135

"Aye, I know young 'un. What I don't know is why you have come to see me? From what I have heard, you have friends in Holland, not to mention that darkie from down—"

"What the fuck did you just say?" said Connor, his eyelids refusing to blink. The feet of the men in front of him subtly widened. The eyes of Lash and Danior flickered.

"What?" asked Birtle, in a tone that Connor could not tell was innocence or mock innocence.

"You know full well that 'darkie' is a friend of mine, so don't ever refer to him like that again."

"He's in London. I don't think his hearing is that good," said Birtle, his voice low.

Connor sneered, his anger conflicting with his concern for Tom and Luke's well-being. "A man who lets his friend be slagged off in his presence isn't a man at all."

Birtle smiled as Leander turned to look at him exclaiming, "How the fuck did you know he'd react like that?"

"Cos he's his father's son," said Birtle, holding his palm up.

"Christ, lad," said Leander, looking at Connor. "Known you for five minutes and you're already costing me money."

He pulled out a wad of notes and handed them to Birtle. Connor smiled.

"Relax, lads," said Birtle, gesturing with his left hand— mainly to Lash and Danior but also to Tom and Luke.

Connor spoke—he had wanted to defer to Tom as much as possible but Birtle had asked him the question. "As you say, my friends are far away. We're at war with Ellis and his associates. My family—the ones who count—and I would rather die on our feet than live on our knees pandering to people who don't even live in our White Rose."

"Well, before we negotiate on whatever you wanted to negotiate on, we have a little proposal for you—well, for this young man here," said Birtle, gesturing to Luke, "and Lash here," gesturing to the dark-haired man immediately next to him.

He saw Luke tilt his head, and Connor said, "Something tells me your man is already fully aware of this 'proposal'."

"Everything is above board. He's a boxer and this one is a boxer. It's a bet—nothing sly about it."

"What do you think, Luke?" Connor asked.

He felt pride at the unflinching reply. "I'd fight that lad in his mum's caravan."

"Keep my mam out of it before I rip yer fucking face off, *Gorga*, and we don't live in a caravan," growled Lash.

"Ahh, plastic gypsy, eh," taunted Luke.

Before the young gypsy could reply, Birtle cut in, "Now lads, let's not start the scrapping before money has been discussed."

Tom spoke. "When and how much were you thinking?"

Birtle made a show of pondering before saying, "Cheeky five grand. Week or two's time?"

Connor's heart tremored and he addressed the young gypsy warrior directly. "Lash, do you believe a true fighting man should be prepared to fight whenever?"

Lash's eyes flickered to his uncle before fixing Connor with a stare. "Yes, but I also believe in money."

Luke said, "See, I'd fight ya for a bag of fucking Space Raiders, not even Monster Munch."

Tom spun around to Luke. "Calm yourself."

Connor suddenly recalled the story of the explorer Hernán Cortés in 1509, ordering his men to burn their ships on their arrival in Mexico, forcing himself and them to press on into the unknown.

He looked at Birtle. "I have six grand in the car. A straight go. You can be referee."

The barks of a dog in the distance could be heard answering the one in the scrapyard.

"I'll have a whip around the lads. Can't be promising I can have it here and now—if we were in Leeds it would be a different story. I can—"

"I didn't say you had to have the money now, only if you insist nothing can happen until this fight happens then I want it out the way now, because I—we—don't have time to fuck around. The reason I don't need you to have the money here and now is the same reason I don't have to check how

137

Lash's handwraps are put on if they are wearing them—because my dad once named me a handful of men he said had 'honour', and you were one of them."

No one spoke for a moment.

"A wolf can spot another wolf even if they are pretending to be something else," said Birtle, nodding seemingly with approval. "And I am guessing your father told you about my preferred business practices?"

"Yeh, he mentioned it."

However, Connor had expected himself to have to fight.

"Well, I guess there's only one question: whether this young man is ready to fight now?"

"I told you, Mr Birtle," replied Luke. "Lions don't set times for straighteners, do they?"

18

As the fresh air cooled his skin and lungs, Bruce admired the beauty of the Albanian town of Berat. He was stood on a bridge over the gentle Osum River, the white houses with red roofs highlighted against the backdrop of the green patchwork hill.

Over the course of decades on the sharp end of special operations all over the world, he had developed within him a tactical awareness so instinctive he could enjoy new sceneries at the same time. Of course, he expected the attractiveness of the town—the Japanese tourist polls rated it the most beautiful European town. As such, tourists were in abundance and he could blend in.

He cut through the streets before beginning the ascent on the rough-cut stone path to Berat castle. His knee had been reconstructed by the best a couple of years back, and though it seldom caused pain, it whispered he would no longer be capable of running to the castle like a gazelle as he would have been even a few years ago.

Bruce had contacts all over the world, whether directly or through intermediaries. Through a covert mission Connor and Ciara had conducted in Ukraine, he was able to pass on intelligence to and establish a relationship with Chen Zhao, the head of Interpol.

However, in a country where the organised crime factions were as powerful as the Mafia Shqiptare, Bruce resisted using any sort of official channels. Instead, he sought activists or, as in this instance, activist journalists.

Adriana Cruz had both Italian and Albanian parentage, and as such dual citizenship. Researching her, he had been impressed.

A study into southern Italy's 'Ndrangheta mafia had ascertained they had turned over forty-four billion pounds sterling last year—more than the Deutsche Bank and McDonald's combined. Journalists who spoke out against them too vehemently had suffered fatal accidents—a correlation that had not prevented Adriana from doing so.

As he reached the top, he spotted her by the pitted cannon that overlooked a hamlet laying in a shallow valley.

She leant on the grey-white wall on her folded arms. The sunglasses and sparse make-up could not hide her rare allure. Her jet-black hair fell into swirls around her shoulders. The green of her willowy top was so dark it could be mistaken for black at a distance, contrasting with the blue jeans and grey trainers.

He took a few moments to scan for watchers before approaching to within her eye line. She turned to face him and removed her glasses.

For a second, he questioned if she wore contact lenses as the amber of her eyes leapt out at him. They stared at him with a hint of curiosity.

"Mrs Cruz," he said, holding out his hand.

Hers slipped into his. "You've done your homework. Usually I get asked if it is Miss or Mrs."

Her English seemed perfect, feathered with an Italian accent. She released his hand.

Bruce said nothing.

"I am impressed with your choice of meeting place."

"The internet is a useful tool," he answered.

"And you have useful friends, so useful my editor insisted I meet you. No telling me who you are, what you want, no—just 'Adriana, you go'," she said, clicking her fingers.

"You must trust him."

"If he accepted money to set up my death, he could have been a rich man long ago. I trust that he trusts you. But I need to know what you want?"

Bruce had never met or spoken with her editor—Ciara's editor had.

"I need information on the Mafia Shqiptare and by proxy the 'Ndrangheta too."

She looked at him for a moment before answering, "You do not seem like a journalist. You are too—confident."

140

"What did your editor say I was?"

"He did not say—maybe he doesn't even know."

"Our aims are pointing at the same target, Mrs Cruz. We just use different weapons."

"What are our aims? And what are the nature of our weapons?"

"Your aims are both personal and altruistic—you want to expose and bring to justice the organisation that had your husband murdered and which has murdered other innocents. I want to prevent an attack on my country. Yours—initiated or at least compounded by your husband's murder—is to fight organised crime in Italy and beyond."

She stood silent for a few moments. "My claims he was murdered are normally shrugged off as the paranoias of a grieving wife."

"An avid recreational tennis player, barely forty years of age, falling dead of a heart attack while proceeding with a legal suit against members of the 'Ndrangheta seems a strange coincidence."

Her eyes flashed with a pleasant surprise, before returning to their hypnotic stare. "He was no athlete and drank too much good wine and ate too much good food—it showed—Orso is what I called him in private."

"Bear," said Bruce simply.

"Yes," she replied quietly. "The case collapsed. My husband left me with money—I studied journalism and here I am. So, yes, that is my motive and weapon, as blunt as it may be. Your weapon?"

"Diametrically opposite to yours."

"You are the same but with a different hat."

"A murderer and a heart surgeon both wield blades to cut a person. It's their intentions that separate them."

She looked away for a second before looking back. "Do you have a wife Mr…"

"McQuillan, no—never—which is maybe why I have lived past your husband's age."

He did not flinch and saw her first smile. "A risky joke to say you want my help."

"A calculated one. Like you say—I do my research," he said. "Will you help me?"

"Yes."

Connor opened the boot and slid his training bag to the edge. He had thought it would be himself having to fight.

"How did you know there'd be a fight? Watching *Snatch*?" asked Luke.

"My dad told me he had to do it when he first had dealings with Hughie. Guess who he had to fight."

"Hughie?"

"No, the geezer that was next to him, Leander Burton."

"Who won?"

"He wouldn't tell me—just said, 'It was a good fight'."

Connor began rooting in the bag and pulled out a pair of trainers, a pair of blue and white shorts with the emblem of their old boxing club, Leeds Reaper ABC, on them, and a white T-shirt with 'Manos De Piedra—Roberto Duran' emblazoned on it. He handed them to Luke along with a gumshield in the packet.

Tom frowned. "You have a fresh gumshield?"

"Better to have it and not need it and all that," said Connor, before turning to Luke with the kit. "Put these on; hopefully some of my fighting prowess will absorb into you."

"Best not wear them then," Luke quipped.

The three laughed, a small release of tension.

Birtle sauntered up to them. "Now then, Mr Ryders and Mr Reed. I scrounged the cash."

With that he opened an envelope—Connor held his tongue in mentioning a wad of crisp twenties and fifties did not correlate with him 'scrounging' it together. Connor delved into the bag again, lifted the base of it and produced a zip bag. He opened it below Birtle's face to show a similar wad.

"Do we need to count?"

"I don't think so," said Connor, "but I need somewhere to wrap his hands and mould his gumshield."

"The first doorway. We'll be waiting around the corner," he said, before walking off.

Connor, Tom and Luke entered the door to a cramped recreational room made up of a tattered three-piece and single piece sofa, a box television, dartboard, girlie poster and a kitchen top with a kettle amid the cups.

After a few minutes, Luke had the mouth guard moulded to his teeth and sat as Connor wrapped his hands—a skill in itself. As the first of the three 'X's' were made between Luke's fingers Connor said, "Listen, Luke, I know you know more about this style of boxing than me, but just be careful where you're stepping and your surroundings—it's not a ring, it's a scrapyard which that lad has been in probably hundreds of times. And there are no rounds, so watch your economy."

"I will, and don't worry, I know not to shoot my bolt."

The young boxer banged his fists into his palms, looked at Connor and said, "They're good, let's get this done."

Connor felt more love and admiration for his younger cousin than he ever remembered feeling before. To accept a bare-knuckle match against a gypsy in front of his blood-baying kin, without so much as a flinch, was a scorching mark of character.

They walked outside and Connor felt his nerves bite upon hearing the crowd. As they rounded the corner the throng parted to reveal Lash, bare-chested in tracksuit bottoms and trainers, shadow boxing. Connor noted how technical and smooth the punches and movements seemed.

He bit his tongue so as not to displace his anxiety by throwing up advice all over Luke.

Birtle raised a hand which quietened the loose circle. As he beckoned the combatants to the centre, Connor quietly said to Luke, "Feints and your jab."

The gypsy leader began, "All right, lads, let's have a clean fight. No hitting on the break, no hitting when a man is down, and woes betide ye if ye bite. The fight is over when one man *gives best* or can't continue. Understand?"

Both nodded.

"If you want to shake hands, lads, do it now."

Connor felt a stab of nerve-edged pride as they did so—
only men can do this.

The unexpected quietness washing over the crowd
reminded Connor of the Japanese crowds at MMA events.

Lash came out with his hands open and away from his
face. Luke's were closer and in loose fists.

The gypsy began the way Connor had wanted Luke to—
with feints of both hand and foot. His cousin's movements
were so subtle it was as if he was not moving.

Which made the next sequence more of a shock. Luke
aggressively faked a jab to the body only to fire it with rapier
speed into Lash's barely turning cheek.

The Romany stumbled with the mask of surprise
mirroring what Connor felt.

The shout of "Get in on him, Lash" cut through.

Fair one—thought Connor—*that's the advice I'd give him.*

Lash's expression suggested he was ready to do so and
then he was hit. Within two seconds, Luke had feinted the jab,
and cut loose with a left hook to the body, right hook on the
cheek before a left uppercut tipped Lash onto his back.

As Birtle counted, Luke looked at Connor, who said,
"Pretend you haven't dropped him—back to your feints and
jab."

He received a nod back as Lash resembled a surfer
climbing back on his board in open water. Connor had not
wanted his cousin to make the mistake of throwing big single
punches without set-up in pursuit of a knockout.

He could see the dilemma in Lash's eyes—to stay on the
outside with someone who had hit him so easily with the jab
could be a slow crucifixion, but to close the distance invited
the risk of being knocked out.

As Lash tucked his chin to resemble a bull, Connor
warned Luke, "He's going to rush you."

The gypsy's head movement began erratic, exaggerated
and quick—ducks, weaves, sideways from the waist as he
pressed forward. Luke, holding his fists closer and chin down,
stepped around him on tight angles.

The gypsy had success with body shots, and a shot skimmed Luke's head.

One of the crowd exhorted, "*Jel* now, Lash, give it to 'im."

Luke began to fire short punches back which Connor liked, but began to hold his feet—which he did not.

"Slide around him and pick your shots, Luke."

The words must have registered with Lash who clasped Luke around the back of the neck—a wrestling 'collar tie'—and punched both head and body. Connor had a brief vision of the first fight between Duran and Leonard, with Lash resembling the marauding Panamanian. The crowd circle got tighter.

However, Luke—using the web between his thumb and forefinger—uppercutted the gripping hand off him, stepped around and thundered in a right shovel hook.

The crack of the nose hushed the crowd as a bloody Lash skittered backwards—the crowd circle widening.

Luke almost sprinted after his prey—catching his foot on a half-buried brick. He fell on his hands and knees.

His cat-like reflexes allowed him to ride the right-handed blow, but his brow split open.

Birtle scooped a bloodthirsty Lash against his chest and pulled him away. The crowd voiced their derision—with respect Connor noticed—and Hughie bellowed, "Not one of my breed is going to win a fight smacking his fallen opponent."

The crowd settled, and Connor glanced anxiously at the blood cascading down his cousin's eye.

Hughie continued, "Given the injury and how it was caused by an illegal blow, I will have to declare this young man the winner by disqualification."

The collective sound of shock and disappointment slamming the crowd could be heard before Luke's voice cut through it. The words sent a bolt of familial pride coursing through Connor's veins.

"Fuck that, a fight's a fight. It ends by knockout or surrender. You said yourself. Now, let's get this done."

145

It lasted a micro-second, but Connor caught the expression on Lash's face at Luke's words—disappointment—and knew his cousin was going to win.

"All right then, fight on, boys," shouted Birtle to an approving roar.

Connor noticed something strange about Luke's body position—he had switched his feet to a southpaw but kept his torso twisted in an orthodox stance. Luke threw left jabs which Lash parried.

Connor then understood—due to the appearance of his cousin's upper body position, the gypsy had underestimated his 'safe' distance from the 'power' hand. The chopping right hook baseball-batted off Lash's temple.

Lash staggered into the side of a black and rusted Fiesta and, pinned against it, his fate was sealed. He could offer no defence to the blistering assault that followed. A fusillade of hooks and uppercuts pinged Lash's head like a continuously bounced table tennis ball. He was unconscious before the last three punches crashed into his skull.

Birtle's bear-like arms wrapped around Luke like a vice, wrenching him off the slumping Lash. The gypsies swarmed around Lash, obscuring Connor's view—*please don't be dead*.

He, Luke and Tom stood together, like part of a Spartan phalanx.

Finally, the throng broke up revealing a dazed but conscious Lash. A quietness blew in the air as Connor moved one foot at an angle behind the other—he saw his cousins had matched him as the attention turned on them. Then a voice laced with enthusiasm rose from the crowd, "That is one hard Gorga bastard—he must be a *Diddykai* at least."

The rest laughed, gestured and murmured their agreement. Birtle came forward with a wry smile, the envelope of cash in hand and held it out. "Fine show, young 'Cool Hand'."

"It's like all you Ryders are blessed with a punch like Jack Johnson," exclaimed Leander, stroking his jaw.

Connor spoke. "You may as well keep that money. The business proposition I have for you means a lot more to us than six grand, Mr Birtle."

"We aren't playing that game, a bet is a bet and this belongs to you," Birtle said, pushing it into Connor's hand, "And one more thing, not you, you or you," he said pointing at Connor, Luke and Tom in turn, "are to call me Mr Birtle again—I am Hughie to you."

19

As Andrei drove in the leather-trimmed cockpit of the hired Range Rover, he admired the efficiency of the British motorway system and its drivers. He lamented how bad the driving etiquette was in his native Shqipëri—what Albanians call Albania. Though the university graduate was not too harsh on his country—when the communist era ended in the early nineties, there were only around three thousand cars to their population of three million.

In the time he spent in these prosperous countries, he realised the more one generation strives, the more spoilt the future ones could become. And he had seen that within organised crime—the first Albanians in the UK, despite a weak grasp of the native language, were harder-working and more cunning, which had given the next wave more of an allowance to become undisciplined. However, he was confident he had stemmed the tide for now.

The cultured female—almost conceited—voice of the vehicle's satellite navigation system had guided him onto the A1 heading for the North of England. In his research into the country, he realised though there was no clearly defined border, the consensus was what a gentleman in a pub explained as 'anything above Nottingham is the north, give or take'. The same gentleman had stated, 'They are all Labour up there, can't let go of how they reckon Thatcher fucked 'em. I can sum up the north—more rain, full of Pakistanis, '"Ey up, ducks", and the dirty bastards have gravy on their chips.' It had taken a couple of hours of clarification for Andrei to decipher all this and more.

When Andrei returned to Tirana, he knew Oso Xhelli—his Krye—would question why he chose to travel to the UK to identify this outsider. And Andrei would answer, truthfully, that because of his skills and mastery of English, it could only be himself who tracked this man. He would leave out the part of being excited at the challenge of entering enemy territory to hunt one who had already proven himself of a degree of tactical skill. Andrei knew, that with several of Van Der Saar's side businesses identified for targeting, his men could handle the preliminary salvos in Holland without him.

He had discovered the girl's name, Rayella Scott, and the club she fought for before setting foot in the UK. Last night, after the pub, the Mik had researched the city of Leeds, specifically its criminal demography. He narrowed the parameters to published government and university studies.

Of its nearly 800,000 residents, around eighty per cent were white British with only three per cent being of Pakistani heritage, which puzzled him given the man's remark in the pub. As he dug deeper, he found that the neighbouring city of Bradford had a twenty per cent Pakistani ethnicity with over sixty per cent being white British. He discovered the criminal lines between the two cities blurred, and they even shared an airport.

Deciphering the demography of the criminal fraternity there had been laborious. The drug trade in Bradford seemed roughly split in two between the British-Asians and British-whites, with the Asians having a greater impact at street level and the whites on the club scene, though with significant crossover.

The Asian influence in Leeds seemed substantial but less than Bradford, though a significant British-African-Caribbean element resided around the area of Chapeltown in North Leeds. He could not find any consistency with the reports of the drug trade and gun crime there.

The gypsy community in both cities, though relatively small, seemed to have a disproportionately large hand in the crime there—though disputed by some sources.

He widened the parameters and typed in 'Leeds Organised Crime' + 'Key Figures'.

Articles splattered his screen pertaining to the murder of a Michael Ryder.

The murder of a West Yorkshire gangland figure, Michael Ryder, has sparked outrage and calls for a tougher crackdown on violent underworld gangs.

Ryder, a 47-year-old father of two, was gunned down in The Buxton Arms, Leeds in the early evening. Police are hunting mask-wearing assailants who fled on motorcycles.

The Ryder family was a name that had come up several times on searches, though only deep into the search. A Caucasian crime family with an age range of early twenties to late forties. He could not glean much more information.

McKinley stood by the Liverpool2 container terminal looking and listening out to the dead-of-night sea. He stood between the five, ninety-two-metre-high Megamax cranes that reminded him of fictional Transformers—by day they looked like red and white Autobots, but now looking like sinister Decepticons.

As a child, McKinley remembered being plonked in front of the TV as his parents chased the dragon in the kitchen. The smell of vinegar and burning floating into the living room still clear in his memory. McKinley always favoured the baddies in the cartoons—Megatron, Skeletor, The Shredder—except they all got beaten in the end.

He had been put into temporary foster care a few times and remembered sitting in front of the TV and the look on the nice lady's face when he declared, 'I hope one day Tom eats Jerry and his family'. That was the day he began learning to hide certain aspects of his character—he was an expert by the time he was a teenager. Then came the mastery of the arts of misdirection and subterfuge.

The lads stood off, looking outward while forming a wide perimeter. He had come in contact with them in several ways; a couple from school, a couple he had done jobs with and a couple he had manipulated. One of his favourite tricks was to hook in a dealer he supplied by having a deal stolen and thus creating a debt to himself—a debt they never got out of; the real magic would be to make them not want to— eventually.

The dark boat came rolling close enough for McKinley to make out the wooden containers encased in the red-painted metal frames. He grinned, thinking of the journey the baby horses would have had, the constant rocking and rolling in a box with barely any light or air.

He took out his phone and dialled. It was answered after a single ring.

"Yep."

"That's them. Let's do it," said McKinley.

He heard the rumble of engines starting in the distance before they crept closer and closer. Behind him, an artic lorry—lights off—stopped with a hiss, almost at the exact time the boat came to a halt before him.

The artic's engine died, the two doors opened and three men got out. Within three minutes, the forklift had been dismounted from the HGV. After another eight, the boxes had been transferred from the vessel to the inside of the lorry. McKinley inspected the locks on the boxes for rust before wiping a finger on them and licking it; he had known from his youth that shiny locks, absent of the taste of sea salt, hinted at police tampering for placement of trackers—these were fine.

One of McKinley's men known as 'The Vet' was inside checking on the horses. After a few minutes, he raised a thumb at McKinley.

Dan 'The Docker' Bunting, greeted McKinley at the back of the HGV. McKinley met the husky, bald Bunting, who asked, "Everything tickateeboo?"

"Seems so," he answered, slipping him two chunky envelopes. "One for your crew. And one for you; they don't have to know how much your cut is."

The Docker slipped both into the pockets of his big, thick waxed coat and disappeared back onto the boat. McKinley smiled knowingly—*he'll cut into the crew's envelope too.*

He climbed into his Range Rover, pleased with the new car smell the Romanian Valets had given it and that he had not paid. 'The Vet', whose real name was Neil Bradshaw, got in after him.

The HGV slowly moved off with the Range Rover on an invisible tow behind.

Bradshaw asked with a breath, "You not worried he'll find out?"

"He's away in Ireland at the minute. Trust me, the only way he'll find out is if either you or I tell him, which I am not planning on doing. You?"

Bradshaw scraped his island of hair in different directions to cover the baldness.

"So, there's no one he could send around before ten tomorrow?"

McKinley smirked. "Who's he going to send around? He doesn't trust anyone more than me, remember?"

"Will you be there when the buyers arrive?"

"Nah. You just point out the box, and they take it away. No messing."

McKinley stepped on the brakes hard as the interior was illuminated red.

A Land Rover screamed around the side of the HGV. McKinley's hand shot under the steering column, but before he could prise the pistol from the tape, men in balaclavas had already burst from the Land Rover and a pair of shotguns stared at him like Cobras ready to strike.

One of the shotguns curved around to his side before opening the door.

"If I have to ask you anything more than once then the inside of this lovely motor will be decorated with your brains. Nod if you understand."

McKinley did so. The voice was rough, confident and edged with *Emmerdale*.

"Turn off the ignition and flick the keys out here."

He did so.

"Put your hands on the steering wheel."

McKinley complied. A similar voice sounded on The Vet's side.

"You. Use these to tie his wrists to the wheel. As tight as you can because if you leave any slack, then your kneecap goes bang. You understand me?"

McKinley could make out Bradshaw nodding before he reached over and threaded a pair of black plastic cable ties around McKinley's hands and the steering wheel. The edges bit into his wrists and cut the circulation. One of the hands left the shotgun pointing at him to check the cable ties by ragging on his hands—tight. Then the hand dived into his pockets and pulled out his 'work' phone.

"For fuck's sake, why do you want—"

The side of the barrel banged under his nose, creating smarting tears of pain.

Knowing anything he said would be answered with hurt, he quietly seethed as he watched his crew frogmarched around to the back of the HGV by other balaclavas. Thrown face first onto the ground, they were hogtied before having their pockets emptied.

The balaclava on Bradshaw's side said, "You, move."

Bradshaw got out as instructed and was soon similarly positioned and tied like the others.

He could see the balaclavas begin to peel away, and said, "You may as well kill me now, la, cos ama going to find yah and fuckin' kill youse all."

Instead of hitting him again, the shotgun-wielding man laughed. "It'll be funny thinking of you trying to convince Harry Ellis you weren't the inside man for this heist. Especially as that's what the lads on the deck outside have been told."

"He'd never swallow that, you prick."

"He's swallowed a lot of things, as well you know, McKinley. And there's no honour amongst thieves, and old Harry should know that more than most."

McKinley opened his mouth to speak but the punch to the temple cut the sentence and his consciousness short.

20

Adriana sat across from the Scotsman amid the hum of chatter. Her mindset was alien to her on speaking to a stranger like this; she reminded herself to be on her guard. Usually, the suspicious vigilance—born of necessity—came naturally to her. With this man, she found herself wanting to talk, to share information, wanted him to be an ally. She threw a leash on the thought; true freedom came from not having to rely on anyone.

They sat on wrought-iron and varnished wooden chairs outside the Shtepia e kafes gimi café. The front of the café was made entirely of glass, framed either side by flower baskets.

Unlike other towns this size in Albania, Berat attracted tourism but there were still glances in their direction.

"Why did we walk past the other cafés before this one?" she asked him.

"I'd have had to sit with my back to the door or street in them."

"But it's OK if I have my back to the street?"

"If you want to sit on this side then by all means. But I think I'll be able to deal with potential danger more efficiently than you can."

"Hey! I am tough," she mockingly exclaimed, flexing her arm. She admonished herself—*stop acting like this*.

"I am sure you are."

"So, what did you want to 'glean' from me specifically?"

"Specifically, I wanted to know if there's a real relationship between the Mafia Shqiptare and the 'Ndrangheta?"

"There definitely is."

"What's the nature of it?"

"Why don't you tell me what you know first? At least then this is of mutual benefit."

The Scotsman's gaze did not shift from hers as he sipped his coffee. When he set it down, he said, "The standard, and now verging on antiquated, model of the global drugs trade was that international importers worked separately from its wholesaler and the street gangs. The Albanians have instead forged direct links with the Colombians, and now their supply chains are kept in-house. In essence, they can supply higher-quality drugs at a lower price."

"If I may say so, what is it your concern where the drugs come from?"

"I didn't confirm or deny it was a concern. You asked me to share what I know."

She felt a jolt. "OK. What do you know about 'Ndrangheta?"

"Based out of Calabria. A loose alliance of some one hundred and forty families. Massive amounts of money, some say hundreds of billions, which is distributed amongst these families. Most of my information is countered by other sources. It's been difficult to nail down any sort of consensus regarding them."

"And that is one of their strengths, their relative anonymity. The books and films are 'Sicilian mafia this' and 'Cosa Nostra that', but not 'Ndrangheta."

"What's the relationship between the 'Ndrangheta and Mafia Shqiptare?"

"The 'Ndrangheta hold traditional values more closely than Cosa Nostra. It is for this reason why they consider the Mafia Shqiptare as 'partners' not inferiors. While the Cosa Nostra look down on the Albanians as violent peasants, the 'Ndrangheta like their sense of family and internal discipline."

"What does each specifically get out of their arrangement?"

She sipped her coffee. "I believe that 'Ndrangheta have penetrated most of the financial institutions in the world, to what degree varies, but their skills in money laundering have no equal and they extend that courtesy to the Mafia Shqiptare."

"And with the Albanian mafia taking over the European market there's a lot of money to be laundered."

"Yes, and also the Mafia Shqiptare have greater control of government and law enforcement, more in Albania than even the 'Ndrangheta do in Italy. This is why there are airfields full of Lear Jets in the countryside of Tirana, making drug runs all over Europe, but maybe not in Rome."

"So, the 'Ndrangheta get a greater distribution of their product?"

"Exactly, against the hopes of any law enforcement that isn't corrupt, they have chosen to work together. And that is very bad."

"The MAD principle raising its head in crime," he said, his eyes subtly scanning the background.

She cocked an eyebrow. "MAD principle?"

"Mutually Assured Destruction. It was coined with the idea that nuclear weapons prevented World War III between the Soviet Union and the West. As you say, it is a challenge to confront."

She caught that he used phrases like 'a challenge to be confronted'.

"You mentioned an attack on Scotland. What did you mean?"

"No, I said 'my country'."

"Scotland isn't your country?"

"The United Kingdom is my country."

"Oh, so you didn't vote for independence?"

"I think we should stay on point."

She made an animated pout before asking, "What is this pending attack?"

"The distribution of fentanyl has been on the increase. We've managed to contain it to some extent, but it is an extremely potent and dangerous drug. Evidence of its more powerful cousin—carfentanyl—being synthesised in makeshift laboratories has been uncovered. Whereas fentanyl is much stronger than heroin, carfentanyl—an elephant tranquiliser—is much stronger than fentanyl."

"What does this have to do with the Albanian mafia?"

"Mrs Cruz, there's been creditable intelligence that the Mafia Shqiptare plan on flooding the British Isles with carfentanyl. They fear they will not be able to operate as freely post-BREXIT and are looking to cash in while they can. They might also be aware that the European arrest warrant may cease when the UK leaves the EU, which will allow them to enjoy a crime wave before escaping back. If this is true, there will be chaos. Naturally, I would like to stop this."

"What is your plan?"

"I need to locate the laboratory or laboratories that will be producing carfentanyl in quantities large enough to flood an entire nation. I need to identify the principal figures. And I need to get them to have someone else to blame when their multimillion-euro plan goes up in smoke."

"Who you planning on having them look at?"

"Well, that might turn out to be the best part."

Robert Caris felt the vibration of his phone echo in his heart when he saw it was an unknown number. He was tempted not to answer. His walks in the Calderstones Park on warm days like this were sacred to him, and he did not want them sullied by whatever the call had in store for him.

In the end, he answered it, preferring to know than not.

"Robert Caris speaking."

"We need to meet."

His heart plummeted at the sound of the confident voice. "When?"

"Now."

"I am out walking at the moment."

"I know. You're sweating like Fred West watching an episode of *Ground Force*. There's a bench two hundred yards on your right. Go sit on it."

The call ended, and Caris felt like a deer being stalked by a tiger.

The bench appeared and Caris took his seat. The ground below was littered with the yellow and brown leaves of the umbrella-like trees. He looked left and right for Connor

Reed to appear. Instead, the Yorkshireman slid from behind onto the bench next to him.

"Morning, Robert."

"Are you crazy meeting me in public, in the daytime, like this?"

"Don't fret. I've been watching you for half an hour now, and no one is following you. I like how we share a fondness for the Japanese gardens around here—how they cut those bushes in the shape of a fountain is clever."

"What do you want?" said Caris, with both nerves and irritability.

"Don't get churlish, Robert. Spending your career taking advantage of people only to pout when it happens to you is the height of hypocrisy."

Caris opened his mouth to protest before deciding to repeat the question in a nicer tone. "What do you want from me?"

"First things first, since you have the situational awareness of the solicitor you are, you won't have noticed the brown paper bag with a lunch box by your feet. Reach down and get it."

When Caris complied, Connor continued, "Amid the yoghurt, apple, Monster Munch—because I spoil you, don't I—you'll find what appears to be sandwiches wrapped in tin foil. Open them just enough so you can see what's inside."

Caris opened the lid of the considerable lunch box and carried out Reed's instructions. His heart began to flutter as the stack of fifties was revealed.

"You pulled it off then?"

"You wouldn't be getting paid otherwise. Though I'd have done it for free. The state those baby horses were in makes you want to join the RSPCA."

"They are viewed as commodities, and Ellis won't stop until he's found out who's taken them."

"Let me worry about that."

Caris slid out a note and asked, "Do you mind?"

Reed replied, "Well, it looks a bit suspect but go ahead."

158

The solicitor began to tilt it back and forth, side to side to watch the motion line move. Satisfied, he slid it back into place.

"There's seven grand in total. Keep playing the game and not only will you make your money back, but more besides. Just don't get caught."

"I just want it back and the video of what happened that night deleted."

"And Oscar Pistorius's girlfriend just wanted to have a shit in peace. Stop acting the goat, Robert, you know that video won't ever be getting deleted. You're staying in my pocket until the foreseeable. And don't act the martyr either, you've gained another source of revenue despite the many people you've fucked over."

"I am not naive—I know they'll ascertain it's me eventually and I'll be tortured before they kill me."

"Calm yourself. 'A man who suffers before it is necessary, suffers more than is necessary'—a bit of Seneca for you there, seeing as you know big words like 'ascertain'."

"Then what do you want?"

"Well, you want to start recouping your money as soon as possible, so I suggest you give me something worth buying."

Caris ground his heel. He watched the walkers with envy as they just floated past him without a care. He knew he was over a barrel—he needed that money back. It was cash that McKinley kept at the legal fixer's house for 'a rainy day'— money the drug-dealing enforcer did not want to risk being kept at his own house. If one day he turned up and it was not all there, then Caris really would be in trouble, and if he told Reed whose it really was, he might never see it again.

A thought came to him suddenly.

"Have you ever heard of the Australian Wedge-tail eagle?"

"The ones that can see infrared and ultraviolet, hunt kangaroos and have been known to attack paragliders and parachutes?"

"Yes," said Caris. "Harry Ellis has one."

"Legally?"

"He has a Royal Permission for it."

"No fucking way has the Queen allowed Harry Ellis one of those bastards here. Brits love their cats too much."

"That's why it's only meant to be released under the supervision of a professional falconer in the grounds of Balmoral."

"So, there's an angle outside of his love of birds?"

"I don't know what it is, but the legal paperwork for the bird transportation comes across my desk. And McKinley regularly asks me questions regarding it."

"If he's Ellis's right-hand man, then why would he ask you?"

"I am not sure they are as much of a unit as it outwardly appears."

"What made you come to that conclusion?"

"Certain questions over the years that didn't make sense."

"Why do you think he was asking them?"

"Any question he's asked of itself could be defensible. But there's been many over the years. And McKinley seems to take an interest in that bird."

"Wait," said Connor Reed. "Do you have any direct contact with Ellis?"

"I've met him once in all the years that I've been working for him."

"If you've been working for him."

"What do you mean?" asked Caris, as a weight of realisation descended on his chest cavity.

McKinley sat in Bradshaw's huge conservatory in a vortex of confusion and anger. Ordinarily, he enjoyed a cup of tea while looking out over the stretch of Cheshire farmland.

He had woken up eighteen hours previously with his cheekbone resting hard against the steering wheel. After a few moments, he had regained his equilibrium, followed by his memory. The absence of the HGV laughed mockingly.

It had been found by the police, burnt out in woodland in St Helens. There had been no sign of the horses.

He had received the message—everyone present on the night was to gather at The Vet's isolated country estate and wait until Ellis arrived.

Bradshaw walked in, scraping his hair again.

"When's he going to get here? Why here? He might have decided to get rid of us all."

"One question at a time, kidda," McKinley said. "He shouldn't be too long. This place is out of the way of prying eyes. And he's not going to do anything until he's sure who the grass is."

"Who is the grass? It certainly isn't me. I don't know anyone like that from Manchester, anyway."

"For someone with all sorts of degrees coming out of his arse, you're not the most perceptive of people, are ya? They weren't from Manchester. Those fucking divvies sounded more like Leeds or Bradford way."

One of McKinley's men walked in from the living room, scratching his wrist. "Seen the lights. I think he's here."

"How many lights?"

"Just one motor, boss."

McKinley thought—*decent sign.*

The confusion in McKinley lay in that he did not know how they had been set up. Only he, Ellis and Bradshaw knew all the details.

Why would Ellis have his own men ambushed and his own horses stolen?

Less and less surprised McKinley in life, but he would be shocked if a toff like Bradshaw had the ambition and gall to rip them all off.

"He's on his own, boss," said one of the blokes.

"Fucking go to the door and let him in then."

McKinley heard the kitchen door kiss open and observed the weird scene of everyone stepping back from the door adjoining the kitchen and living room, even though there was plenty of space.

As Ellis stepped into the room, McKinley heard the pattering of rain on the conservatory's roof and windows.

"Any of these lads know exactly what we were picking up?" said Ellis in a low voice. He was directing his question at McKinley and Bradshaw.

The Vet's response burst from him, "I don't even know who they are. I only met them tonight."

The room seemed to contract, and McKinley said, "No, I told none of 'em what was in there. I briefed them last night at the tobacco warehouse and kept their phones. Unless one of 'em had another phone in the vehicle or had some James Bond follow us then I can't see how one of 'em could bubble us."

Ellis turned his head but did not look at the men before addressing them. "Youse can go, lads. And remember, not a word."

Relief creased their faces before they shuffled out. When the kitchen door crept shut, Ellis motioned with his fingers that they should talk in the conservatory.

Seated, Ellis unbuttoned his suit jacket and began, "We're in a bit of a bind, aren't we? The only people who knew all the details of the drop are in this room. Everyone except for The Docker."

McKinley felt like Tom seeing Jerry with his back turned, but he could not bring himself to pounce—too obvious.

"Can't see how he has that sort of influence outside of the docks. We've been using and paying him well for years. I doubt he's been able to source that kind of buyer—we'd have heard."

"Well, you're going to have to look into it. Men can change—maybe he's got himself a bitch who refuses to work, or a bad coke habit, or he's in debt. Desperate men can think up all sorts when staring at sea for days on end. Finding tooled-up street rats with no respect from the old guard would be about as hard as driving up to a group of youths in Croxteth."

"That's the thing. These lads weren't Scousers, not unless the shotgun ordering me about had been a fucking regular at *RADA*."

"What do you mean?"

"That one, and the balaclavas that ambushed the rest of the lads sounded like they were from around Bradford or Leeds way."

Ellis smoothed the lapels of his suit. "Right, first things first—find the leak."

21

Connor stood watching Rayella hit the Thai pads. The huge blue, matted area was currently divided into two classes—the Thai boxing class with the rings on the far side, and the NoGi submission period he was attending on the nearside.

His grappling class had wound up its instructional and drilling, but not yet entered its free rolling phase. He waited until someone had caught his eye and a man of similar age and build to Connor raised his hand in the gesture that meant— *'Want to roll?'* He nodded.

The man was dressed in a black long-sleeved *rash guard* with full-length *black spats*. The garb reminded Connor of a ninja without the mask.

"Where do you want to start, pal?" asked Connor's opponent.

"We'll start standing, seeing as we won't get into Valhalla by *pulling guard*—at least according to the memes floating around."

Connor knew the idea that guard pullers were pussies was a myth—essentially you were saying to your opponent you were that confident you would give them the advantage of gravity. However, he did not want to develop the habit so that he was not tempted to do it in a street fight—sitting on your arse means being vulnerable to pissed-up onlookers kicking your head in.

His opponent smirked. "I like your style. However, the Gods care not about takedowns, only submissions."

They both laughed as the timer rang and they bumped fists. Connor instinctively knew he would not get away with shooting for his opponent's legs so far out in order to take him down. Instead, he engaged in hand fighting. His opponent felt strong as he clasped Connor's neck. The former Marine countered by putting his thumb over the arm and into the collarbone as he gripped the ninja's wrist.

Using the web of his hand, Connor uppercutted the hand off his neck. He flung the wrist away to grip the back of his opponent's neck, pulled his partner forward and shot in for a double leg takedown. He smashed through it like a car through a pedestrian.

He landed in *side control*, and the battle between Connor remaining in top position and securing a choke or joint lock, and his opponent escaping or submitting Connor from the bottom, was hard-fought and lasted nearly the rest of the round.

In the final twenty seconds, Connor took the ninja's back, trapping his arm behind with his leg.

"Sorry, mate," said Connor, before knifing the knuckles of his bent fingers under the jaw to force the choke in.

The ninja tapped with three seconds to go. When the bell sounded Connor noticed a few furtive glances in the pair's direction.

His rolling partner asked, "Fuck me, mate, what's your name and where you from?"

"Well, Cilla, I am from here originally and my name is Connor."

The ninja laughed. "I'm Darren, and I meant, where do you train?"

"All over really. I travel a lot."

"You a purple or brown or what?"

"Never stayed at a club long enough to be graded."

"Mate, I got given my brown after winning in Manchester a few weeks back. You could *sandbag* to fuck for the first few years, eh. You should train under us. The head coach is easy-going on training different places, 'specially if you explained you travel with work. How come you're here tonight?"

"Rayella trains here, and she's family—"

"Oh," said Darren, tilting his head. "You're Connor Reed, then? Sorry, I didn't recognise you."

The buzzer to indicate the start of the next round sounded.

"It's OK, Darren, it's not as if I am Tom Hardy, despite being marginally better-looking."

Connor had five more rolls, only bettered by one of the other brown belts before the third dan, black belt instructor tapped him with a heel hook.

The class finished and Rayella came up to him on the edge of the mat.

"Saw you tapping like a fanny."

"Where the frick have you learnt to speak like this? You're a fourteen-year-old grammar school girl."

She chortled before saying in a mock accent, "On da street. And 'Frick'? You found Jesus?"

The way she could now express herself, which he put down to her hitting adolescence and confidence gained from martial arts, was startling to him at times. He realised he could no longer treat her like a kid.

"You could do with Jesus in your life or you really will end up on the street and, unlike your mum, you don't have the looks to be a successful prostitute."

She gasped in mock outrage. "I am telling."

"No one likes a grass," he said. "Get showered and meet me by reception."

Connor was ready before her. He sat in the reception area and focused on a spot on the wall. He had read that the ability to think clearly required letting 'the sentiment' of the mind settle. He began to review all the possible scenarios that could now occur in the aftermath of Birtle's stealing of the horses. He had told Birtle it would be best if they could steal the horses without speaking or least disguise their voices. However, Connor could tell by his facial expression the gypsy was paying him lip service in agreeing to it. It would not take McKinley more than a minute to work out who was behind it, and Ellis would seek to wipe the Ryders off the face of the earth.

He checked the drafts box of one of the operational e-mail accounts Jaime sometimes used to send him messages. There he found a warning notification regarding the means of encryption his family were using in their 'business' dealings.

He wondered if Bruce McQuillan knew Jaime was helping him like this.

His thoughts were interrupted by Rayella's appearance. "We going, chump?"

As he stood and feinted a backhander, the BJJ instructor came around the corner and said, "You making your presence a regular thing?"

Connor shook the outstretched palm. "As regular as I can. I can only stand this one so much."

"Whatever," said Rayella.

The instructor laughed as they made their way out. Connor had parked around the corner as the car park had been full.

He had been taught to observe 'atmospherics'—the absence of the normal, and the presence of the abnormal—during his time as a Royal Marine. However, it was his training for, and post-operational experience with, McQuillan's Chameleon Project that honed this skill to a remarkable degree. He had noticed the Range Rover with tinted windows when they had walked into the gym, as he had observed the windows being down a couple of inches—he noticed they were now up. His reptilian brain concluded what his rational part tried to disprove—that there was someone in the vehicle who had waited in it for over two hours, and now wound the window up because of the cold.

He felt the slither of a 'dark' fear—he had Rayella with him again.

They turned onto the pavement and the light raindrops were illuminated in the street lamps.

"Why did we walk the long way around when we arrived?"

"Because you needed the exercise," he replied. He did not want to tell her it was a counter-surveillance tactic—he tried to protect her as much as he could from that world.

He heard the engine of the Range Rover start up.

"Listen to me, Rayella," he said urgently. "When I say, we drop our bags and sprint behind that lamp post next to the stone bin. Don't look around, just tell me you understand."

She looked at him wide-eyed but with a firm voice said, "I understand."

The Range Rover screeched before the rev count roared.

"Sprint!"

Bags dumped, they dashed forward. The Range Rover gained on them like a stampeding elephant. Connor snatched Rayella around the guardsman of a lamp post. The Range Rover swerved but clipped the stone bin, careening off backwards into the railings on the same side.

"Rayella, sit on that wall and look down the road for any emergency services coming. Don't look back at me until I shout to you. Understand?"

He expected her to be in shock but instead heard the same steady voice say, "Yeh, all right."

He bolted for the Range Rover driver's door, opening it from the side with an outstretched hand through the fabric of his sleeve.

"Cunt," he said, on seeing the barely conscious Kevin Kellings, looking like he was having a nightmare on the pillow of his airbag.

Connor made his decision within seconds—his brain being able to compress reasoning into this time span. Kellings was barely lucid and although there were no witnesses as yet, he would not have time to extract any clear answers from him once passers-by came. Connor again used his sleeve to open the vehicle's back door and sat behind Kellings. He reached forward, clasped his hands over the Geordie gangster's mouth and pinched his nose—*cheers, Vagner Rocha.*

At first, the behemoth barely responded. Within a few seconds, Connor's arms were rigid with the electric current of effort as Kellings's thrashing made the Range Rover look like a Transformer having a fit. His fingers desperately tried to prise off the hands choking him like an octopus.

Connor's determined eyes locked with Kellings's pleading ones in the rear-view. He burst into giggles while tightening his grip. His mirth morphed into maniacal laughter as Kellings descended towards death. Finally, the fight drained from the Newcastle crime lord and he stilled. Connor kept the hold on a while longer before accepting he was dead.

Easier when Tony Soprano did it—he thought as he let Kellings's head fall into the steering wheel's airbag.

He got out and his heart fell as he was confronted with Rayella standing, open-mouthed.

After a few long moments he asked, "How long?"

"The car was rattling. I didn't know what was happening," she said, her voice barely tremoring.

"It's all right."

"I'll never tell," she said.

She had been through a great deal in her young life, and Connor had been there for her. His heart welled, not only at her unflinching loyalty but also the realisation he had made her an accessory to murder. Still, for her to tell the truth would mean her testifying against him—*that would fuck her up even more.*

A car purred around the corner before slowing. The driver must have believed Connor and Rayella were the previous occupants because it did not stop.

"OK, there are no CCTV cameras around here. Let's go."

They picked up their bags and walked away. He scanned for onlookers but could not see any—because the man who had witnessed the entire scene was skilled in the art of concealment.

22

Connor became aware that the eyes of the men in his family were on him.

The Buxton Arms had been temporarily closed, so they met in the cramped back office of the Dancing Bear lap dancing club. Tom and Connor sat on the same side of the tidy desk. The large flat screen sat within Connor and Tom's view, flickering images from a multitude of security cameras. Directly in front of Connor, amid the flowery wallpaper and above the heads of the sombre-looking Luke, Lee, Charlie and Ryan, there was a frame filled with a collage of Polaroid pictures showing the various dancers having fun.

Connor saw Charlie's hand vibrating and said to him, "Charlie. You all right?"

"Just keep thinking that if I'd have put my foot down with our Curtis wanting to get those guns, then he wouldn't have got shot."

Ryan spoke. "Hindsight is a wonderful thing, lad."

Tom said, "We all made mistakes—everyone in this room has. We learn from them and move on as a family."

"I don't know, I just think—"

"Hey," said Connor, snapping Charlie's attention on him. "Self-pity is for fucking losers. And we've still got to get through this. Understand?"

Charlie nodded contritely. "Yeh."

Luke, with his eye freshly stitched, added, "Since it's just us here, I take it everyone knows Kevin Kellings was found dead last night?"

There were sounds of affirmation.

"Down where Rayella trains MMA, wasn't it, Connor?" asked Tom, looking at him.

Connor looked his elder cousin straight in the eye and said, "From what I've heard, the police aren't sure why he was down here but suspect he asphyxiated on his own airbag after a minor crash."

There were a few moments of silence before Tom broke it with, "I see. Terrible accident. Shame."

He gave Connor a look which said, *I won't ever press it. But I know.*

"What's happened then?" asked Connor.

"One of our launderers in Harrogate has been roughed up and threatened. He's fucked off to India for a few weeks but hasn't left any, wotcha call it, relief in place. He's not our main launderer but it isn't good," said Tom. "The kids on the estate in Seacroft chased off a couple of coppers. The police had screamed down cos a TV licencing guy got properly filled in on the doorstep of one of the houses. The hood rats torched the cop car and plastered it all over YouTube. Now my contact in West Yorkshire Police is going spare, saying if they knew we'd lost our grip on the area, they'd have sent three cars."

"Have we lost our grip?" asked Connor.

"It's harder than ever to control 'em. Almost any scrote can get a shooter. These kids are hard to track down. They just surf on mates' sofas, and cos they're barely out of school they have fuck all to lose—no family, house, business, nothing," Tom said. "I have taken my eye off the ball with everything that's been going on though."

"Nah, you've prioritised the best you could, given the circumstances," said Connor, knowing it was Charlie and Curtis's usual tasking to enforce the estates.

"That's not the worst," said Tom. "Some scrotes on mopeds tried to burn down the animal rescue centre our Michelle manages. Stupid fuckers used diesel instead of petrol, or else it might have gone up. I think it's too much of a coincidence."

"What the fuck are we going to do to this bastard Ellis?" asked Lee. "We can't just stand by and get picked off. Just as well the girls can't get off that cruise."

"You see, I don't know how much is Ellis and how much is McKinley," said Connor.

"What do you mean? McKinley is Ellis's soldier, tells him what to do," said Ryan.

171

"In the main, that's right, or used to be, but I think he might have been pulling strings—he's had things on the side going on in a big way, for a long time. I don't know to what extent."

No one spoke at the inference. A soft knock sounded on the door.

Tom called out, "Yeh?"

A female voice swirled through the door, "It's me."

"Yeh, come in, love."

The door opened to reveal a girl Connor thought almost cartoonish in her attractiveness. Her chocolate eyes were framed by a caramel complexion, blonde highlighted, curly brown hair and eyebrows that contoured them perfectly. Her frame resembled a stretched hourglass covered in a white, sleeveless shirt and jeans.

"Hi," she said simply.

"Cara, this is my cousin Connor. The only one you haven't met."

Connor looked at Tom and then back at Cara with a frown. "What you talking about, Tom? There's nothing wrong with her."

He stood and held out his hand. She took it with a smile of straight, white teeth and said, "There's plenty wrong with me, or I wouldn't have a set of gangsters in my back office, would I?"

Connor's eyebrows rose. "A fan of saying it like it is, eh?"

"Makes things easier in the long run."

He sat with an agreeing nod.

"What's up?" asked Tom.

"One of the girls has rung in sick. Could you pass me the blue book on the side? I need to get cover."

As Tom reached for it, Luke exclaimed, "Wait. There was a book full of strippers' numbers just sat there all this time?"

Cara replied, "Glad to see this sad time hasn't got in the way of what's important in life. As it better not have yours, Thomas."

Connor noticed Charlie did not join in with the ribald laughter.

Cara left after expressing her condolences and squeezing Tom's hand briefly.

"Fuck me, Tom, you've done well there," said his uncle, Lee.

"Standard." Tom said.

Connor announced, "I want us all to ditch these Encro phones now." Referring to the secondary phones they used to encrypt all Voice over IP (VoIP) conversations before transmitting them over a closed loop network.

Tom asked, "How come?"

"They might not be as secure as we first thought," he replied, before looking at Charlie. "Can you set up a *PGP* server for us and any point of contacts we rely on? I'll pay whatever costs."

Charlie said, "Yeh, I can do that. Take a day or two."

"Cool," replied Connor, before turning to Tom. "How do you want to play it from here with our Merseyside problem?"

Tom said, "It's clear now they are working off whatever information Derek 'as been feeding them; the only businesses that have been hit are the ones he knew about—the ones I kept from him haven't been touched."

"What's the plan of attack then?"

"We haven't got a bead on McKinley yet, but I have a few names and know the regular hang out of his crew. We can start hitting them back."

"Fucking nice one," exclaimed Luke. "Not just for Michael and Curtis, but I reckon Stratton will be happy too."

"Has Stratton been in touch, Tom?"

Tom made eye contact with him. "Nah, he hasn't."

"Funny that," replied Connor.

"Why's that a problem?" asked Charlie, nervously.

"Nothing," said Connor. "Probably just Murphy's Law. You know what that is, don't you?"

Charlie shrugged. "Whatever can go wrong will go wrong?"

"That's right," replied Connor. "And have you ever heard of Cole's Law?"

Charlie frowned before slowly shaking his head. "I think so, but I can't remember."

"It's finely shredded raw cabbage with a salad dressing."

Laughter ensued and even Charlie smirked, which gladdened Connor.

Kathryn Bainbridge grimaced while reading the report in her office. Deaths from carfentanyl had soared to 373 in the last weeks alone. These centred in and around the major cities of Glasgow, Newcastle, Hull, Manchester, Birmingham and London. And she knew this was just the beginning.

Her phone rang, and recognising the number she answered with, "I take it you're reading what I am reading?"

"I am," replied Bruce McQuillan.

"Drug dealers generally don't want their customers to die. But these animals won't care if it's a short-term thing," she said, pinching her nose. "And this will hit the papers tomorrow. The police seem to have more leaks than the Iraqi Navy."

"Will heighten awareness," came the reply.

"You and I know an addict will risk death for a fix."

His voice struck over her anxiety. "Opioids hit the street in batches. We can't do anything about this current one now, but we are afforded a little time until the next one."

Ciara liked the faint scent of polished wood that permeated the Kendo dojo.

The oak was interspersed with light cream walls. Lights resembling honey drops hung at symmetrical intervals.

Weeks ago, she had been in Japan to produce a piece on the devastation caused by a typhoon that had hit Tokyo. As always, when visiting countries to gather information on the topic of her articles, she would collate information on the 'pattern of life' with regards to organised crime.

She had packed as much as she could into her visit including—because of her low-key fascination with how to kill with blades—visiting one of the most prodigious Kendo dojos in Japan. She had sat on the bench, mesmerised by the blend of speed and precision in the fighting practice.

Eventually, the Sensei approached her and so began her immersion in the art for her final few weeks there.

Now, she had been told by Bruce to attend a Kendo class just outside the large town of St Helens. It had been a women-only class taken by a Japanese lady who looked to Ciara to be approaching sixty years old. Ciara found the lesson to be technically absorbing without being nearly as strenuous as those she had attended in Tokyo.

The class broke up, and she removed her mask—*Kendo Men*—and saw Connor appear at the far end of the hall. The Sensei walked briskly towards him, and Ciara thought she was going to admonish him for his presence. Instead, she saw a shake of hands and then the instructor laugh.

Ciara approached him once the Sensei had walked away. "My, you do get around."

"It's not like that. Her original trade in Japan was as a Geisha, and I hired her a few months ago over a weekend."

Because of the blasé manner of how he spoke, before she could stop herself, she asked, "Really?"

His replying laughter pissed her off and amused her in equal measure.

"So, how do you really know her?"

"Never met her before in my life. Bruce told me to come and meet you here. He's given Mrs Miyagi the heads-up."

"Do you enjoy these inflammatory remarks?"

"Who, me? I've got a coloured TV at home."

She shook her head and said, "What did you say to make her laugh?"

"Something about you all looking like the most dangerous beekeepers in the world. To be honest, you looked all right to say it was your first lesson."

175

"It isn't. I did a kind of crash course when I was out in Japan."

"No way. And Bruce happened to know the owner of a Kendo club near Liverpool, eh."

"Is there anyone that man doesn't know? Anyway, what's up?"

"He just told me to meet you, that's all. Said there was a side room." He pointed.

She saw him turn and gesture to the Sensei down the corridor for permission to use it. She nodded. He took off his shoes and Ciara followed him over to it.

Inside was a white-matted area. Behind the thin veil stretched over the window was an outline of an oak tree. She could make out two birds chattering on one of the branches.

"Sorry to hear about what happened to your uncle."

"Thanks."

"How's Rayella?"

"She's sharp with a lot of energy within her. If she can keep it focused and not burn herself out, she'll become terrifying."

She sensed his protectiveness of the girl, but also something she had never seen with him before—fear.

"Has something happened?"

"She's brushed twice now with my world. But I can't just stop seeing her."

"For your own sake or hers?"

"Both."

"Why hers?"

"There's no one else around her who understands her like I do."

"In what way?"

His eyes flickered. "To be honest, I suppose you could empathise with her the most—what with you having a pussy."

She hid her sense of frustration with, "An amazing one."

"For a round-eye maybe, but it's not a patch on Mrs Miyagi's," he said straight-faced. "How did your meeting go?"

176

"My meeting with the esteemed Mr Ellis seemed to go well."

"How did he come across?"

"Personable, endearing almost."

"If you weren't privy to what's going on, what would be your measure of him?"

"I'd have presumed he was now a legitimate businessman. I wouldn't get the sense he's apologetic about his past. Why do you ask?"

"Because I'll need a meeting with him soon."

Andrei Faja looked over the rolling green countryside and felt the sun and breeze on his face. In the far distance lay the town he knew to be Kendal. The view in front contrasted to the one immediately behind him—the farmyard barns had been converted into an amphetamine production factory.

He heard Marty McKinley walk up behind him sooner than the man realised.

"I can still smell the ammonia. It is faint but there," he said, as the wiry man stepped closer.

"You must have the nose of a shark to smell that, la," said McKinley. "The first batch went out a couple of weeks back and has been mega. Fiends can't get enough."

He's trying to curry favour.

"If I can smell it, maybe a policeman can. There's due to be millions produced by this operation."

"If a policeman is up here, it's because he's suspicious already and he'll want a look inside regardless."

Andrei turned and looked McKinley in the eyes. "Are you defying me?"

McKinley's eyes widened for a moment, before shaking his head.

Andrei continued, "Follow my instructions, as I say them, when I say them. Then, you will not have to concern yourself with money or respect ever again."

The Liverpudlian gave him a look to convey contriteness. "There is a thorn in my sock at the moment. I have been—"

"Having conflict with the Ryder family in Leeds?"

"Yes," said McKinley, with brows pressing on his eyes. "How do you know?"

"The General who wins a battle makes many calculations in his temple before the battle is fought."

When the quizzical look did not leave McKinley's face, he clarified, "Winners plan ahead. And in planning, you need all the information that is—or could be—relevant to the game."

"I had to take certain steps."

"Does Mr Ellis know you took those steps?"

"No, he doesn't. I told him I didn't know who was behind it."

"And he doesn't suspect?"

McKinley said, "Nah. He thinks, apart from maybe bits and pieces on the side, I would never do something that major without his approval. He uses me to keep his hands clean. He's not the same man any more. Wants to ride off into the straight goer's sunset."

"How long has he wished for this legitimate life?"

"Been pulling away from it slowly for a long time. It's taken ages, but all his orders go through me and everyone in our world knows that. He won't be seen with any underworld figures now his charities are taking off. Wants to be known as a man of the people and all that."

"Good. Once the first cycle of carfentanyl hits the major cities, your National Crime Agency will tear itself apart looking for this and the other factories. If he suspects your hand in this, it will be a problem to solve."

"What about my Yorkshire problem? If I keep using my guys, then Ellis will eventually hear about it."

"And if you keep using your guys, more may end up dead."

A flicker of hesitation before, "What do you mean?"

"A gentleman named Kevin Kellings attempted to murder Connor Reed, did he not?"

Andrei could see McKinley open his mouth before closing it again. He knew he was trying to work out how Andrei knew and whether to lie.

Andrei had had a clear view of the incident despite his distance as he sat in the rental vehicle. He had been impressed by both Connor Reed's thwarting of the ambush and—though he did not actually witness it—his ruthless murder of the assailant.

McKinley replied, "Kellings had an axe to grind with the man, anyway. I just threw petrol on the flames with a cash incentive."

"It is clear now you cannot send ordinary hoodlums after that man. I may have to take care of this. Do not make decisions in this matter without consulting me first."

Howling pierced the air, punctuated by clunks and yelps. Yells in Croatian followed, and a crazed German Shepherd bolted from around the corner. The dog chased its tail into a tornado.

"Fuck's sake," exclaimed McKinley. "One of the barrels was leaking amphetamine. I told the bloke to keep a better handle on him."

The Croatian mercenaries and another man cornered and, after a struggle, subdued the dog by taping its mouth and legs.

"Which one is the handler?"

"Kenny, my nephew, that's his dog. I brought them here to—"

The sentence died in the same instant his nephew and the dog did.

Andrei held the silenced pistol he had just used underneath McKinley's jaw. "Do I need to emphasise my point regarding consulting me first?"

McKinley's jaw took a moment to unclench before shaking his head. "It's perfectly clear."

23

Connor knocked and felt the sense of nostalgia he always did on entering the familiar street in Guiseley. He remembered first knocking on the door a decade ago when he was seventeen years old on receipt of his first car—a silver Golf. He had passed his driving test that day and immediately called on his best friend for a ride—"*Now we can go wherever we want,*" they said at the time.

Back then, when the pretty, busty brunette in her mid-thirties had first answered the door, Connor's thoughts instantly centred on what she would be like in bed. Now was very different; Ann Scott, though maybe not like a mum to him, was certainly worthy of favourite auntie status.

Ann opened the door and a smile leapt onto her face. "Connor! Come here, buggerlugs."

She embraced him as she always did. Despite the platonic nature of their relationship, he enjoyed the pressing of her tits into his chest. He sometimes wondered if she knew. She loosened her embrace to grasp his arms and looked at him. "Rayella says you dropped her off but never came in. You better have a good reason."

Connor had shot away after dropping Rayella off the night he had murdered Kevin Kellings. He had needed to get things in order quickly and knew if he had stepped inside the house he would have been there at least an hour, being fed and watered. He had not seen Mr or Mrs Scott for a while.

"I heard a damsel in distress with my super hearing. I was rushing around trying to find a telephone box so I could change. They are rarer and rarer nowadays."

She put on an amused frown. "If you don't come in to at least say hi again, I'll have my kryptonite handy." She laughed at her own joke.

"Come on then, let me in, the neighbours are going to talk."

Connor walked into the familiar living room to see Paul Scott sat in his usual chair. Though just over fifty years old, Connor could see Liam's features on his greying father's face.

"Now then, Connor lad, what was that the other night? Shooting off like that?"

He pulled on the armchair's rests for momentum to get up to greet him.

"I was running late for a meeting. You know I would never pass up an opportunity to see the pair of you," he said, then pointed to *The Guardian* on the small table by the armchair. "Staying strong with those newspapers, Paul. Most people now get their news from their phones."

"Most people get most things from their bloody phones. Might as well be cyborgs."

Connor had heard a billionaire technology entrepreneur say something similar on a podcast.

"Is Rayella upstairs?"

"Nah, she's only just gone and taken Dekkers for a run. Then she's off to the pictures with her friend."

Connor felt a bolt of anxiety at her whereabouts before quelling it—*don't be a slave to your emotions*. Dekkers was Rayella's feisty Jack Russell.

"Been a while since I've heard it called the pictures. What film she off to see?"

"I dunno, something to do with shooting and scrapping, I suspect. She should have been the Royal Marine, let alone our Liam, God rest his soul."

Ann came in with a tray of cups and biscuits, to Connor's relief. Paul often fell into melancholy regarding his deceased son. He had taken it about as stoically as any father could—indeed he'd had a short military career himself—but the loss of a son was not something that would disappear.

It heartened Connor to see Oaty Hobnobs and Florentines, as last time Ann had asked him what his favourites were and had obviously bought and saved them.

"Thanks for these, Ann."

They sat, Connor and Ann into the comfort of the sofa, and Paul into his armchair, as he turned the television volume down.

"How's Rayella getting on at school and around here?" asked Connor.

"Much better now, thankfully. Getting her head down at school and seems to have a good circle of friends. I think a lot of it's to do with her doing those martial arts. I've got the article about her going over to Holland—she looked a right *Bobby Dazzler* in the pictures," said Ann.

"Aye, kicking the fuck out of other girls seems to have done more than those counsellors."

"Paul. Language!"

Connor always enjoyed Paul getting any sort of telling-off from Ann.

"Well, that's one of the reasons I've come over. Are you taking Rayella away next week for her summer holidays?"

"Of course. It's Egypt for a week. Heaven knows what we're going to do for the rest of the time."

"I was watching a documentary, and those pyramids," began Paul, "they still don't know how they moved those blocks of stone—six million tonnes. Some say they wet the sand and rolled them on tree trunks. Some say underground boats. None of 'em know though. And they can't understand how they got it all so precise—like nowadays we have the technology, but this was meant to be over four and a half thousand years ago."

"Some say it's a lost civilisation," said Connor.

"You going to tell me it's aliens now?" answered Paul mockingly.

"I think Connor was about to tell us something about Rayella," interjected Ann. "Not to argue with Paul Scott, the Egyptionist after one documentary."

Paul mumbled, "Egyptologist actually."

"Go ahead, Connor," said Ann.

"Well, when she's back, there's an opportunity for her to train down south for a few weeks with George Follet. He's

182

a mixed martial arts legend and I know she'll be thrilled to go."

Connor caught the furtive look between them. Over two years ago Rayella had been sexually assaulted by a politician—now dead—visiting her school.

"I'll be down there, but it's in Wandsworth. Doesn't she have an auntie down there?"

"Yes, my sister, Teresa," Ann replied. "Works from home now too. Doing some sort of healthy food supplement business—"

"Talking about pyramids, that's what that malarkey is," said Paul, interjecting.

"Maybe you ought to think about being a bit healthier," said Ann.

Connor quickly said, "Well, that's her lodgings, isn't it?"

Another look between them, and a subtle nod from Paul to her.

"I'll call Teresa. Rayella will be excited to see her and London. Suppose Paul walking Dekkers will help him to be healthier."

Connor hid his relief.

Bruce had only been to the Albanian capital of Tirana a handful of times. He had a spectacular view of the city from the vantage point on his apartment balcony.

He mused over the incongruity looking at a crane above a dilapidated high-rise, set against the far backdrop of a dusky mountain range.

As his eyes observed the nuances of the city, he began to consolidate his thoughts for a plan of attack.

Jaime had supplied him with a digital intelligence package, and he had studied it on the bus journey from Berat to Tirana.

Bruce knew it was not prudent for him to be 'on the ground' but with both Connor and Ciara in the UK, he had to put in the groundwork himself.

Not that he did not welcome it. The bureaucracy of navigating the UK security services landscape as an official member had more complications than when he solely ran The Chameleon Project.

That said, The Project now lay mostly dormant in comparison to its 'War on Terrorism' heyday. Though its remit was to help combat organised crime that the judicial system could not reach, that mission had inevitably been expanded post-9/11 and 7/7.

He still had agents he could call upon if needed, but they were mostly in the employ of highly lucrative private security contracts which would look suspicious if dropped on a whim.

He knew he was lucky in that his two preferred agents could move freely—mostly. This was the first time Connor could not travel. Bruce knew to allow Connor access to Jaime to win an organised crime war would set a dangerous precedent.

However, the former Marine had never asked for help in dealing with matters regarding his family's operations, and Bruce liked and respected that. And all he had asked for on this occasion was to be given time so he could sort it out himself.

Bruce checked his watch. His appointment with a local contact was not due for another few hours, so he decided to take a second tour of the city.

Harry Ellis looked out onto his vast lawn and tried to conjure the feeling he felt when he had first bought the huge house. The five-bedroom detached house off Sandfield Park Estate was a far cry from the cramped, though well-built, two-bedroom council house in Norris Green. Though rough when he was a teenager a certain decency now reigned even among the local youths.

He did not kid himself. He knew he had been born in a place and time where it had been ripe to make money as a gangster—so long as you had the imagination, daring, ruthlessness and smarts.

However, to last in the game took discipline. When the dance era exploded in the late eighties and early nineties, Ellis had penniless boxers turn to door work to supplement their income. Several morphed into millionaires on gaining control of the club's drug supply either by taxing 'house' dealers or dealing themselves.

The final part of the saga would be their transformation into drug addicts—steroids and coke—as the late nights and stress took their toll. They would invariably lose everything.

Ever since Ellis embarked on this lifestyle he had looked towards a legitimate end.

The doorbell rang. One of the advantages of being openly gay was women felt comfortable accepting the invite to your home.

He opened the door to a suited Ciara. For a moment, she reminded him of a more statuesque and attractive Annie Lennox.

"How are we, Mr Ellis?" she asked.

"I am grand," he replied. "We have time. Would you like a cup of tea?"

"Coffee, if that's OK. Have you locked the Dobermans away?"

"Very funny," he said, stepping back into the house. "I have a coffee machine. What would you like?"

"I'll have it white, no sugar."

She whistled as she entered and walked down the hallway. "It's true what they say about you lot…you do have great taste when it comes to your interior decorating. And by 'you lot' I obviously mean Scouse businessmen."

He hid a smile. "Is there anything you want to ask me? To get 'it' out of the way, as it were?"

"And be accused of being a salacious journalist? I'll defer, thank you."

They walked into the kitchen. He had been involved in the refurbishment of the house on his purchase of it. He had the oak joists stained and varnished. A raised round table, guarded by leather-backed bar stools, sat in the centre. To the left of it was a 65" flatscreen; a little large for the ambience of the room but suitable for picking out the details of a person transmitted from the various CCTV cameras around his property. On his own, he always had the security screen on, but with company such as now, he left it on terrestrial television. *Coronation Street* flickered on low volume.

"And you didn't disappoint with the décor of the kitchen."

"Thanks."

He turned and busied himself with the pod coffee machine—he liked the speed and convenience of it. It hummed before giving a frothy gurgle. When they both had their coffees in hand, he said, "I read a few of your articles online—I was impressed, and I think I am past thinking of you as sensationalist."

"So, I have carte blanche to ask you whatever I want?"

He raised his eyebrows. "Up to me if I answer, isn't it?"

She sipped her coffee. "This is great."

"You can get a lot of great coffees in Liverpool—if you know where to look."

"All right, you don't seem to have even a hint of lavender about you, but I've heard you're openly gay?"

"You must know being camp and being homosexual aren't necessarily mutually exclusive."

"Of course. I feel like I am probing now—no pun intended—so I am happy to speak off the record."

"OK."

"This is for my own curiosity. You can pat me down if you like."

"For what reason? You want to see if I get a hard-on or something?"

He knew what she was inferring but the more you could get them to reach the more you knew about them.

"No. I believe certain people open up more with the knowledge they are off the record and not being recorded."

"People who have allegedly gained financially through criminal enterprises, you mean?"

She opened her fingers. "Well, that is one subcategory, yes."

"I don't have to check for wires. We can drift into the hypothetical when it's called for."

"So, then," she said. "Do you ever find it difficult to exert your authority over certain business figures due to your sexuality?"

"No," he replied.

"Why is that? There's no prejudice within those circles?"

"Oh, there is, more than anywhere else, but two things overcome it. They are the knowledge of what you're capable of—of what you're capable of doing to them, and for them. Being a good gangster—which I won't confirm or deny I am or have been—isn't just about putting the frighteners on people. A good gangster makes the right people rich—that's really how you protect yourself."

"Can you give any examples? Hypothetically?"

"All right, so back in the late eighties, early nineties the dance scene takes off, and with it Ecstasy—or maybe it was the other way around. Anyway, where in the world do you think had the most potential to make money?"

"London?"

He gave her a derisive smile. "Think further afield."

"Oh," she said. "Ibiza."

"Yes."

"When did you first go over there?"

"I was there from the beginning—nineteen eighty-seven—Year Zero."

"Really?" she said, seemingly with genuine interest. "What was it like back then?"

"Well, up until then the island was still a party island but it was rock, pop, funk and that—huge bands and singers but it wasn't like what came in the late eighties. I don't know why it happened, but Ibiza was where acid house first became popular. A few London DJs came over and took it back with them. All of a sudden, illegal raves spread like wildfire—the Second Summer of Love."

"How were you involved at this time?"

"I had a small security firm. I wasn't as well-established back then, but there was so many popping up there was enough work. And naturally, my firm would be the go-to for any…I'd guess you might call it LGBT nights…easy night's work—there's a lot less aggro at those types of events, I mean in that it's rare anyone physically kicks off. And everyone is high on Ecstasy anyway. Started to get a name for myself— and there was a property boom which I took advantage of, but by the time the early nineties came around, I wanted bigger."

"And how did that come about?"

"Well, the arse was always going to fall out of it here. Any time guys like us are making money that big and that easily—and not paying tax on it, the government doesn't like it. So there are two ways they went about it. Raids, using snitches, coppers going undercover—laughable, as you could tell them a mile off, as they'd always be the uncomfortable-looking duo drinking pints in white open-collar shirts and tweed jackets—everyone else would be in baggy clothes as it got so hot in there. The raids got naughty though—there was no CCTV back then—so planting evidence was easier. They'd just drop a bag of Es on the floor near to whoever they had identified as the ringleader and say the individual had dropped them. They'd be arrested, along with others. Seen it happen more than once."

"No camera phones either," stated Ciara.

He shook his head, and said, "The police's authority wasn't as questioned back then. The general public watched shows like *The Bill* and had a rosy image of them."

"What was the second tactic?"

"The government began their scare tactics about Ecstasy. How it could kill you. Look, I accept nowadays there can be loads of shit cut into them. But back then it wasn't like that. The danger was getting dehydrated from dancing for hours then keeling over. Every rave I was at, or ran, had loads of water and Lucozade on tap. We even had ice pops."

"I thought you could die from drinking too much."

"See, that's a bit of a distortion. There was a girl from down south, had her first pill not long after she turned eighteen. She drank something like seven litres of water—while sat at home with her friends. They didn't mention that at first—instead made out it was from a contaminated batch and began scaremongering—like circulating a photograph with all sorts of tubes coming out of her face. It worked too cos back then dying from drugs was seen as something that happened to black kids in the inner cities or poor white people in these deprived mining towns Thatcher had ripped the soul out of—but this girl was middle class, so everyone was up in arms about it. Turns out she literally poisoned herself with too much water. I forget the term."

"Hyponatraemia is when the sodium content in your blood gets low. And I think water intoxication is something to do with your body's electrolytes."

"Not just a pretty face."

"A lot of things besides," she said, sipping her coffee. "What happened then? I am intrigued about your rise to owning this huge house."

"So," said Ellis, warming into it despite himself. "I decided to focus on Ibiza. I always loved the white island anyway and had contacts there, but there was a problem."

"And what was that?"

"The drugs trade was controlled by this Spanish terrorist group who didn't like outsiders trying to muscle in."

"Oh, ETA."

"Yes. They're not around any more but they were serious people back then—shooting, bombing and kidnapping. I may have been in the same restaurant at the time Jordi Asenio was shot dead."

"Who was he?"

"A retired footballer turned nightclub owner—he was involved in smuggling ciggies and what not. It was for cosying up to some politician that went against ETA—they wanted independence in the Basque—"

The doorbell rang, and he stiffened—he was not expecting anyone, and people usually called ahead. Despite his company he reached for the remote and flicked to the security cameras.

Ciara's eyes briefly widened as her heart rate quickened. Derek Ryder—with a hideous Kanji on his forehead—was stood just behind a sinewy man in a football shirt.

She had only met Connor's uncle once but knew he would remember her.

He would tell Ellis she was Connor's girlfriend—his presumption—and the game would be challenged.

Then she saw the look on Ellis's face—*maybe he doesn't want whoever they are to see her in here with him.*

"Where is your bathroom?"

"Down the hall. Third door on your left."

"Thank you."

They both got up and parted in the hall. Ciara walked slowly before creeping back to the corner of the corridor. She removed the audio bug disguised as an earring before setting it down by the corner. Ellis answered the door to a voice saying, "We've got to speak to you."

She began down the corridor towards the bathroom door and hoped Ellis got rid of them soon.

24

Rayella sat in the thrum of Connor's new Blue Lexus LC. It had that new car smell she liked.

The music lifted her and she asked over it, "Who sings this?"

"Imagine Dragons," he answered, before turning the volume down. "OK. Tell me about this motorway we are on?"

"It's the M1. It connects Leeds to London. It's 193 miles long. The main cities on the way are Sheffield, Nottingham, Leicester, Northampton and Luton."

"All right. The M6?"

"The longest continuous motorway in the UK and one of the busiest. Runs from Rugby up passed Carlisle into Gretna. Major cities include Stoke-on-Trent, Liverpool, Manchester, Preston, Lancaster and Carlisle."

"Good."

"Why are you getting me to learn stuff like this?"

"When I was taught geography at school, they taught me stuff like igneous rock formations—something to do with magma—and how the capital of the US was Washington and not New York. But I can't remember ever being taught about my own city, or the motorway system of my own country. It might be different now."

"I can't remember being taught it. Maybe it'll come later?"

"Maybe. What I am saying is, you've only got so much time and energy in one day—well, your life—so, use it to learn things that are going to be useful to you. Do you know what the Zulu principle is?"

"No."

"It's based on this book by Jim Slater, that if you study a subject for a hundred hours, you'll become more expert in the subject than ninety-nine point nine, nine per cent of people.

But I reckon you only need three to become better informed than eighty per cent at least."

"I thought you said to take in everything because you don't know when it's going to be useful. Like you must have learnt about the orchestra and it became useful that night we went out."

"I knew a little bit. When Raymond told me who we were eating with, I went outside to make a call but instead used the Peg System to memorise some main points to impress the girl sat beside me."

Rayella laughed. "Pity you weren't staying in Amsterdam."

"Yeah, pity."

"How does the Peg System work then?"

"You have mental pictures that are shaped like numbers in your head. You can come up with your own but my one-to-ten are the Eiffel Tower, a swan, a magnet, a yacht sail, Captain Hook's hook, a quaver, a boomerang, a fat lady, a street light, and a bat and ball."

"How do you peg them?"

"The first thing I wanted to remember was chamber orchestras were smaller than symphony orchestras. So, I imagined the Eiffel Tower tipped on its side, but one end was really narrow—small—that led to a chamber, while the other end was massive blowing out musical notes—a symphony. Then I pegged what a concerto was, so I pictured Monique— the woman beside me—sat on a pile of money, playing the violin on her own at first, with an orchestra of swans following her. You get it? People memorise stories and daft scenes in their heads better."

"Why don't they teach it at school?"

Connor answered, "It's only really for short-term memory. If you want it to go into your long term you have to recall it at intervals. That's why before mobiles or smartphones people could memorise telephone numbers they can still recall now."

Rayella didn't speak for a moment as she realised that she felt lucky to have him as a mentor. She increased the volume of the music a little. "What's this?"

"'Gimme Shelter' by the Rolling Stones. One of the few songs I don't get bored of."

They listened until it finished before Rayella said, "This trip down to my auntie's was to get me out of the way, wasn't it? I asked my coach about George Follet, said 'he's an old school legend'. I YouTubed him—he's amazing. You haven't got me private sessions with him."

"This was to get you out of the way. But I have got you sessions with him. You'll also attend his class."

"Must have cost a bomb."

She watched Connor stroke his jaw and say, "It wasn't cheap."

"Why did you want me out the way? I wouldn't say anything to the police or anyone."

He felt a thump of disappointment in his chest.

"Rayella, I've never been worried about that. There's some bad men I have to deal with, and until I do, I'd feel better if you were here."

"What makes me safer down here? It's not even two hundred miles from Leeds, remember."

"You'll be watched over."

"By who? My auntie isn't that hard, Connor—she's a southerner, remember."

He laughed—she liked making him laugh. He said, "You'll be watched over by a southerner who definitely is hard."

"Who is he? And what's his name?"

"He's a good friend of mine—and he was a good friend to your brother. His name is Louis."

Ellis stifled his anger at McKinley's and Derek Ryder's presence on his doorstep. These painstaking years of careful cultivation of a legitimate persona could be undone by a click of a phone's camera. Leave them on the doorstep and there would be more chance of that happening, let them in and Ciara might overhear.

"Go around the back and sit and wait for me."

McKinley frowned before doing so.

Ellis walked back into the corridor and called out, "Ciara, we're going to have to cut our meeting short. There's something I have to attend to."

The bathroom door crept open and she stepped out.

"Awww, I was enjoying the history lesson."

As she walked towards him she caught him looking at the earring. If he picked it up and began to inspect it, he would spot the tiny wire nestled within the groove inside.

"That's my earring," said Ciara, touching her lobe. "Didn't even realise it fell out."

"Luckily I have eagle eyes."

As he leant down she said, "Be careful with it, be more than your life's worth."

He smirked. "I'll let you pick it up then."

She scooped it up, stood and said, "Another time then."

"Of course. I'll walk you to the door."

Rayella looked through the car window at the tall buildings. At ground level they comprised various shops constructed in white, sandy stone. Above, in reddish brick, lay six storeys of windows punctuated by balconies with glass tables and wrought-iron chairs.

"What is this place called, Connor?"

"Chelsea."

"No way—it's nice but I thought it would look posher."

"Reality TV only shows what they want you to see."

As they drove past a crowd of caramel-skinned people vying to get into a Mosque, with a sizeable amount of the males wearing what appeared to be white skull caps, she asked, "What are those hats the men wear called?"

"In Urdu it's called a 'Topi', in Arabic a 'Tāqiyā'. They wear it to stop their hair getting in the way when they touch their forehead to the ground during Salah."

"What's Salah?"

"Prayer. You've seen them all on their prayer mats."

"Oh yeah," she replied. "How come they have to take their shoes off?"

"Because in the back there's a big fuck-off bouncy castle they all jump on after they've worshipped," he said. "We're here now."

Connor parked outside a building with floor-to-ceiling windows. Inside, people on treadmills, rowing machines, and step climbers with earphones in, watched various screens or looked at their phones. He tapped his own phone, put it to his ear and said, "We're here," and after a pause, "No worries. Take your time."

After he put his phone away, Rayella asked, "Who was that?"

"My Oppo."

"What's an Oppo?"

"It's a military thing. Short for 'opposite number' but you use it for a friend you can trust."

"Can't you trust all your friends?"

"Your friends or your mates, whatever you want to call them, can mean different things to you. I have mates I can spend time with, and have the best times, but I wouldn't ask them for help."

"Then why would you be friends with them?"

"Like I said, they might be entertaining—no point in cutting your nose off to spite your face."

"What if they ask you for help, though?"

"If it's for one-offs you should, but do it without the expectation of getting anything back because you'll end up disappointed, and that leads to resentment. But don't let anyone leech off you—it's not good for you, and not good for them."

"Do you have any examples, oh wise one?"

They smiled at one another, before he answered, "You'll know men who have lived with their parents all their lives. Their mums will have cooked, cleaned up after them, charged them minimal rent—and they'll tell themselves they are good

195

mothers. They're not, they have just emasculated their sons—and their sons will have to walk around for the rest of their lives never having a chance to become the men they might have been—men who could take care of themselves and others."

"So it's all women's fault then, is it?" she said, with a teasing haughtiness.

He pressed his lips together, and then said, "It's the human attraction to comfort that's the enemy."

He gestured to the gym patrons behind the glass. "Well, look at them *doylems*, driving here to stroll away on a treadmill, and paying to do it too. They're the sorts of people who'll tell everyone—over a cup of tea with two sugars and a dunkable—they go to the gym three times a week and can't understand why they still look the same."

"They might not like walking in the rain. Or they might see their friends in there."

"Then walk with your hood up to church—in addition to Jesus, they have tea and biscuits there too."

A tall, handsome black man appeared out of the entrance. Her heart rate quickened as Connor alighted from the car—she had not even seen what he had done. Realisation cooled her as she watched the two men perform a handclasp embrace.

Connor turned and beckoned her out of the car.

"Rayella, this is Louis Allen. He'll be making sure you're safe down here."

"I haven't seen you since you were bare tiny."

Rayella frowned and Connor answered, "I think it was on Medals Day after Afghanistan. The first one, obviously."

She sensed his awkwardness—the second had been when her brother Liam had been blown up.

"I remember you now. My mum said something like, 'Isn't he a strapping young man'. I don't think my dad was too happy with her saying that."

They laughed before Louis said, "Right, Rayella, this is a burner phone. It's got two numbers in there—mine under 'L' and one of my guys under 'Uber'. Now, when you want to go out, you tell your auntie you're getting an Uber, but it'll be my guy who'll ferry you about. All right?"

She nodded before turning to Connor, "Where are you going to be?"

"I told you," Connor said, thumping against his chest. "I'll be winning zee war."

25

Ellis stood angry but expectant in front of the pair.

"What is so important you felt the need to come to my house—in broad daylight at that?"

"I thought you'd need to know. Connor Reed had been seen at the gym close to where Kevin Kellings died."

Ellis blinked before saying, "So you are saying Reed killed him? Why?"

McKinley replied. "You said if I saw an opportunity that negated the blowback on us, I should take it."

"You paid Kellings to kill Reed?"

"No. I gave him money to put himself up for a few days, before giving him the green light to give Reed a working over. Never told him to kill him."

"Would he suspect your hand in this?"

McKinley turned to Derek who nodded.

This man might be more trouble than he was worth. Ellis had anticipated that Connor and Thomas Ryder would capitulate and come scurrying to the negotiating table once McKinley began to hit their businesses. He also thought whoever had killed Michael Ryder and hospitalised the younger cousin may have done him a favour—weakening their hand and bringing them to the negotiating table.

Ellis's sole portal into the underworld was McKinley—a continually updating encyclopaedia of the UK criminal underworld, and he had not even had a sniff yet of who had done it.

He never wanted Derek Ryder back at the helm in Yorkshire—the man was weak, and could never hope to see the numbers his nephews could rake in. All Ellis had wanted was a kick up, and now he was wondering if this was all worth it.

Still, he could not voice this while Derek Ryder stood before him.

"Any word on who killed your brother, Derek?"

"No. They'll just think it's you."

"If I was going to take that course of action, I'd have told you."

McKinley spoke. "What do you want me to do?"

"I'll think about it and let you know," he said, before pointing at him. "Don't ever come to the house again."

Bruce watched as Eliza Rexha's enthusiasm permeated through the group. He was part of this collective of eleven who had purchased this Albanian cooking class online.

They were stood in the sunshine of Pazari I Ri square in Tirana. A glass ceiling hooded the bustling market to their left, bristling with an assortment of brightly coloured foods.

The sounds of haggling to the left, of conversation of the café patrons to the right, and the chains of the bicycles weaving around the pedestrians filled the air.

Eliza's handsome face was lined and framed by a black bob hairstyle smudged with grey. Her glasses either highlighted her kind, brown eyes or obscured them, depending on what angle to the sun she faced.

Though laced with a northern Albanian accent, her English was clear. "Many of you have lost the taste of home cooking—you are in lives that is rush, rush and rush. If we get fat, it is with good food—we remain strong."

The flexing of her arm elicited chuckles but Bruce got that impression in observing her frame.

She continued, "Like the great pyramids, great food needs good foundations. And that means the best ingredients. I will show you have to pick the best."

For the next hour, Bruce and the rest of the group were shown how to check the food for ripeness—more than once she picked up a piece, observed it before putting it back, shaking her head. The market stall owners must have been used to this as their annoyance seemed mild. She taught them what to look for; potatoes should have a little dirt on them, root vegetables should be heavy, with the skins smooth, and red meat should be bright and should spring back when pressed.

After she had finished her presentation, she announced, "Now follow me. We are going to a sacred place."

They followed her like a gaggle of geese for about half a kilometre through the streets. Bruce admired the lack of uniformity in the buildings; a yellow house with a red roof sat in the shadows of high-rise flats, then there were two-tone buildings of beige and rustic brown. Bruce had engaged in counter-surveillance for decades, and now it was second-nature.

Finally, they came to a café with chairs of all sorts of shapes and sizes. She led them through a side door, into a kitchen Bruce thought to be surprisingly large, impersonal and organised. It was almost entirely covered with metallic surfaces and was divided in two by a white plastic chain.

Three kitchen staff—a man and two women—worked on one side to feed the patrons inside and outside the café. The other side was a mirror image, and the group began setting out the ingredients as per her instructions.

For the next two hours they cooked under her cajolement, scorn, praise and jokes. Bruce could tell by the atmosphere everyone was enjoying the experience.

Eliza snuck around him and looked down at his Tavë Kosi—the unofficial national dish of Albania, a casserole made up of lamb, yoghurt and rice amongst other ingredients. She dipped a spoon in and tasted. Her face expressed a confused approval.

"Are you a chef?"

"No, I have just spent a long time cooking for myself."

"What a selfish man, your cooking should be appreciated by others," she said, giving him a wide-eyed look. "You have a dessert to make—*Fillimi i mbarë është gjysma e punës.*"

"What does that mean?"

"I think the English translation is 'Well begun is only half done'."

Half an hour later, on her inspection and tasting his Toptha Çokollate—chocolate nuggets—he felt vaguely self-conscious under her unabashed praise.

After they had all finished, Eliza gave them a summary of her one-day course, thanking and exhorting them on the importance of real cuisine. She finished with, "And now you may eat your dishes in the tables provided in my café—use the trays over there. All I ask is you post a review on Trip Advisor—a truthful one, of course. If you didn't like the course then wait until you leave this place to post!"

Everyone laughed before scooping up their plates and making their way through the second kitchen and into the café.

"Can you stay one moment?" she said to Bruce.

"She wants you to work here," teased one of the course members as he left.

When they were alone, she turned to him and said, "Adriana didn't tell me you could cook."

"Adriana doesn't know I can."

Eliza said quietly, "If she doesn't know that, then what else does she not know?"

"There's no reason why you should trust me, Miss Rexha. But if you want justice for your dead son, then I am the best chance you have."

Derek watched the distant lights of a car crawling up the night hillside. He sat passenger to McKinley's driving. They were on the M6 motorway, not long past Preston with the view fading into a scenic patchwork of dark.

He liked sitting at the height the rental van afforded them. He said to the smartly dressed McKinley, "What is it you said we were doing? A drop-off?"

McKinley took a can of Coke—one of four—from the inbuilt cooler between them before answering, "It's not just a drop-off, it's a meet and greet."

"What do you mean? Who?"

McKinley sipped the can and said, "He's a serious player from Albania. And I am not talking about fame-hungry faces down south. He's a proper fuckin' gangster."

"Why are you bringing me along?"

"Cos it's you he wants a meet and greet with."

Derek opened his mouth to speak but instead had a coughing fit.

"Fuck's sake, you sound like an old docker."

Derek got control of himself. "Why does he want to speak with me?"

"Cos the quicker we can get you back running things up there, then the quicker we can restore the natural order of things, la."

Derek watched the motorway lights illuminate McKinley's face at intervals. "I thought we said no outsiders? Who knows how far this Albanian will go."

"This isn't an outsider, he'll be our boss now."

Derek felt a cold penny between his skull and brain. "What do you mean he's going to be our boss? Ellis is your boss. And he's my partner—or he will be again."

McKinley's laugh sprayed a little of his beverage he had raised to his lips to drink. "You don't honestly still believe that, soft lad."

Derek's forehead pressed on his eyes. "Of course he fucking is, you've said so yersen."

"Harry Ellis is a fucking lightning rod. All he wants is a legitimate life, all cosy in that palace of his. You saw how fucking shit-up he looked when we turned up on 'is doorstep. He keeps me on cos he's scared of repercussions of his criminal past coming back to haunt him—old vendettas. Pays me to mark 'is cards, but he only knows what I tell him."

The van slipped off at the junction signposted for Kendal. After a short time Derek asked, "So you're saying you're the boss?"

"I don't put that label on myself. You give yourself a title then everyone—from seriously naughty men to hoodrats with fuck all to lose—wants to take it from you."

The van carved onto a country road and McKinley dimmed the lights. Derek noticed how bright the moon and stars were. They bumped along for a while before Derek asked, "Who's this Albanian fella then? I mean, exactly?"

McKinley let out a derisive laugh. "You could pass this bloke on the street and think he's a bank manager—you'd never know."

The van rumbled over a ditch and in the depression beyond lay a massive farm complex.

"What's his name?"

"Andrei Faja."

Ciara thought how quintessentially English this small North Yorkshire market town was. Ellis had contacted her and asked if she wanted to meet at the Dales' Birds of Prey Rescue Centre in Settle. She had researched as much as she could— the centre catered for injured wild birds but also neglected and displaced domesticated ones. They were either released back into the wild, stayed at the centre, or a suitable foster home was found.

In her agent training, it had been impressed on her the importance of regularly switching vehicles. She had rented a Toyota Rav 4x4 and manoeuvred it first up a cobbled side street before following the signs for the centre, down a road surrounded in woodland.

The sunshine peeked in and around the trees. Fallen, golden leaves edged the tarmac. She had the view to herself as the centre was not currently open to the public on a Monday.

The woodland opened up to reveal a large, cylindrical building that looked to Ciara like a giant thatched basket. The centre's name was emblazoned on an artistic sign, complete with the pictures of various birds.

She parked and began to walk to the entrance. She sometimes did not appreciate how polluted London's air could be until she came to places like this. She saw Ellis a split second before his whistle dived into her ear.

"Ciara, over here."

He was stood in an opening in the fence to the left of the building. His hiking boots and all-weather trousers were similar to hers.

She walked up to greet him. "This is a prodigious place. If you don't mind me asking, what gives you the golden pass?"

"Being the chief donor to the place would do that."

"Birds of Prey? Really?"

"Yeh. The old man had pigeons back in the day, and my love of birds—the feathered kind—grew from being a nipper. Shall we take a walk?"

"Of course."

Beyond the fence, a footpath led across an open field. Half a kilometre away was a lake to the left and more thatched buildings.

"Why aren't the huts closer?"

"This is the area where the falconers train the birds. And it's nice to have a walk."

"You're right. It's nice to get out of the city. A place for you to decompress, I would think."

"Most of the time I would agree, but this has become stressful now it's got larger. There are not many places that look after the birds like we do. Construction of a second in the Peak District has seen some financial difficulties, but I'll find a way."

Ciara could hear the bird calls long before they reached the huts. Inside each was a bird of prey. She looked around and said, "You'll have to educate me on a few of these."

"Which are the ones you know?"

She gestured to a bad-tempered looking bird with a blue-grey back, barred white underparts, and a black head. "Well, I know this one is a Peregrine falcon."

"What about the two in the hut next to it?" He pointed to a pair that looked similar to the first but had black backs and rustic orange bellies.

Ciara shook her head. "Not sure."

"They're also Peregrine falcons. They are a sub-species from Indonesia."

"How did you manage to get them?"

"I went there for a holiday. Saw them both cooped up in a pen in their version of a falconry. Threw the owner a bit of money and had them brought back here."

"I would never have guessed you'd have this much affection for them."

"We can look after them better here."

"I am sure you do look after them, but this is essentially a visitor centre, isn't it? One could argue you're keeping these birds captive for people's entertainment when they'd be best served in the wild."

Ellis gave an amused snort. "None of these birds were taken from their natural habitat. Many have been sick or injured, and we try to rehabilitate them. We assess them to see if they are fit to be returned to the wild. Most are, even if it means transporting them back to the country they were injured in."

"Wait. You transport them in from wherever they get injured and then back again?"

"Yes."

"Must be expensive."

"What else am I going to spend my money on?"

She said, "Yachts, cars, evenings out, restaurants, bars and the like."

"I have been around people who chase after those things—and they'll be chasing those things forever. I've been around plenty of criminal millionaires who are on anti-depressives. I mean, I like nice things—you've seen my house—but they don't feed the soul."

"And these birds of prey do?"

"Yes."

They walked around the enclosures and Ciara could not help being impressed by Ellis's knowledge and quiet enthusiasm.

"Any particular favourites?"

"I'll have to whisper in case the other birds hear."

She smirked before whispering, "Let's hear it."

"I'll show you. Follow me."

He led her around a path that curved away from the other enclosures.

While they walked, she asked, "What causes the eyes on some of them to flash, or appear to?"

"Eagles have eyelids that close during sleep. For blinking, they also have an inner eyelid called a nictitating membrane. Every three or four seconds, it slides across the eye from front to back, wiping dirt and dust from the cornea."

Rounding the corner revealed an angry-looking dark brown bird with its feathers shaded in beige. Larger than any of the others, it looked to Ciara to be around a metre in length.

"What the heck is that?"

"That, my dear, is an Australian Wedge-tailed eagle."

"It looks the size of a small car. What does it eat? Crocodiles?"

He laughed. "Well, not quite, although they have been known to go for kangaroos and paragliders."

"What's the story with this one then?"

"With you being a journalist, I am sure you've heard about that bastard in Victoria poisoning well over a hundred of these fine specimens."

"Yes, I have. A hundred and thirty-seven were found dead, if I remember correctly."

"You have. But it should have been a hundred and thirty-eight if this one wasn't such a hardy bitch."

"She?"

"Yes. Female Wedge-tails are generally a little larger than the males."

"How many others survived?"

"She was the only one who ingested the poison and lived."

"Why was she brought back here?"

The eagle let out her wings, and Ciara was astonished at the span of them—looked to be 9ft from tip to tip.

"Shall we take her out for a stretch?"

"We? You mean the falconer you'll call over is going to take her out?"

Ellis disappeared around the enclosure, reappearing with a heavy, leather glove that looked like it came from an age when the gentry used to take part in jousts.

"You're a falconer?"

"I wouldn't call myself that. Being a falconer means a lot more than this part—the fun part. They clean the enclosures, maintain their health, sort out their nutrition. I just help train my favourites so I can fly them."

"Aren't the other birds going to get jealous when you walk past them with her?"

"There's another open space this way."

After a short walk, the trees gave way to a vast clearing. A tree stump with a flat top of moss jutted from the ground close by.

Ciara felt cool pleasure whirl in her stomach as the eagle took flight. She bolted off Ellis's gloved hand, and Ciara could feel the airbrushes created by her wings. When high above them, the flapping ceased and the eagle soared majestically.

"How are they able to still fly for so long without flapping their wings?"

"Because of the expanse of their wings they can ride columns of rising warm air. When you see them at that height flapping their wings, they have hit cooler air and are raising themselves back into a warmer air column."

"Well, if all this is a show to convince me you're a charitable, bird-loving man of the community, then you've certainly gone to town on your preparation."

She saw a wry grin on his face before he asked, "What is it you really want to ask me?"

"Well, you've been candid about your previous life, I suppose I would want to know what's made you 'go straight'—shunning the criminal lifestyle, so to speak."

"Let's call it more of a pulling away. And it wasn't just one thing."

"All right."

"Everyone with any sense knows this life generally ends one of two ways—long prison sentences or death, or at least maimed by a rival. It doesn't matter how much you look after

207

people, how fair you are, you're always alone, because you never know who's going to grass you up—if it's between you and a lengthy prison sentence, they'll give you up—understandably so."

"Does that fact depress you?"

Ellis gave a resigned shrug. "I try and not let any romantic notions of honour amongst thieves settle in my soul. I think there was a bit of that post-war, with a lot of them being veterans. All underworld codes of honour were ripped up when the drugs scene caught fire."

"Was there a straw that broke the camel's back?"

"Yeh," Ellis replied, his eyes seemingly fixed on the Wedge-tail. "There was another gangster that I admired and respected—a contemporary like. He seemed to have it all figured out. You heard of that saying, 'It's better to be a warrior in the garden, than a gardener at war?'"

"Yes."

"Well, he epitomised that—took over his city by maiming some of its most dangerous characters. After it all settled down, he began to build the right relationships, distribute the money out fairly, looking after his community—and when the Triads tried to muscle in, it was those relationships and support that helped him defeat them. And do you know what happened to that man?"

Ciara answered, "Moved gracefully into legitimate enterprises, then into politics, began to lose his way, his ego got out of control and now he's a shadow of himself, lost in a sea of drink and drugs?"

The Wedge-tail began its descent towards Ellis who held out his gloved hand firm, and said, "That may have happened if he had been afforded the opportunity. Instead, he was set up and murdered. That's when I knew that no matter how well you play the game, if you're in it long enough, you'll lose."

Ciara felt an expansion in her diaphragm; she admonished herself for not seeing it earlier. "Who was he?"

The eagle swooped down before rearing back with flapping wings. She floated down before landing on his hand as she zipped her wings in. Ellis produced a piece of red meat and the raptor wolfed it in three swallows.

"His name was Greg Ryder. One of the 'good sorts' as they would say down south. When I heard he was murdered, I thought that was my cue to retire."

When the boxes arrived, Levi Jansen never asked what was in them and he never looked; he simply took the manifest and bid whoever the mule was a pleasant journey back. As the manager of the Haarlem transportation depot, he oversaw the loading of the containers onto the trucks designated for other European cities.

Only he, Lucas, Peter and Ruben were present at this hour past ten o'clock in the evening; the daytime staff of the hangar could number almost thirty workers.

Their voices bounced off the paint-peeling walls of the loading bay amid the smell of oil and petrol. It was Peter's turn to keep watch outside as they loaded the cargo—not that in the four years of doing this had any law enforcement come sniffing around. He knew who was ultimately responsible for these shipments that had made him comfortably well-off. And knew the police tended to turn a blind eye to the operations of Raymond Van Der Saar, especially when there were other targets in an ethnically diverse town such as Haarlem.

They struggled the green containers onto the pallets and Ruben used the forklift to load them.

Levi thought he heard a noise outside. He motioned for Ruben and Lucas to quieten.

"Peter," he called out after a moment.

He walked towards the entrance when there was no response. Shock punched his chest as Peter appeared with a strange man's hand clamped around his mouth and a pistol pressed to his head. Three other men, stocky, with dark hair and darker eyes appeared, levelling pistols at him and his men.

"Get on your knees, now," said the man restraining Peter—the accent Albanian.

Slowly, he and the others complied.

The three other gunmen stood behind them. Levi felt like prey.

The man spoke again. "I want you to give a message to Mr Van Der Saar."

Levi fought the nerves trying to choke him. "I have never had direct contact with him."

The man forced Peter on his knees to mirror the others and nodded his seeming understanding. "Not directly then."

He jutted his chin to the gunmen, and Peter, Ruben and Lucas's throats were cut. His struggles to stand came to nought under a restraining hand.

The metallic thud smashed his consciousness into dark pieces.

26

Bruce sat nursing his salep drink; its consistency reminded him of pudding his *maw* had made him as a child. Indeed, there were similarities to his mother back then and the Eliza Rexha who sat across from him now.

The same kind eyes.

They were sat in the living room on the floor above the café's kitchen. There was a gas fire manufactured to look like a coal one off to the side. Bruce doubted it would ever need to be turned on during the daytime given the heat rising. The tiled floors matched the peach sofas they nestled in. He noticed a picture of a handsome youth with dark eyes and hair in a graduation gown. There were other smaller pictures dotted around of the same boy at various stages of his life— infancy, a seaside picture, a Christmas one as a younger teenager.

"Who taught you to cook?" Eliza asked him.

"Various books and more recently the internet."

She tutted. "I wished it to be your grandmother maybe."

"Sorry to disappoint."

"Why are you here, Mr…"

"Call me Bruce."

"OK, Bruce, why?"

"So we can help one another."

Her eyes were fixed on his as she sipped her own salep before asking, "How can we do that?"

"I know you have already taken great risk to infiltrate the Mafia Shqiptare here."

She gave a sneering laugh. "I cook their food whenever they have one of their 'special parties'. I am kept in the kitchen, so I would not use the word 'infiltrate'."

"Who attends these parties?"

She stared at him, her eyes narrowing before returning to normal. "Politicians, people high, high up in Tirana's police force—they talk about how corruption has improved in Albania, but I think it only hides itself better."

"Can you identify them? If I showed you pictures?"

"I know most of them already."

"I need their names."

She sipped and said, "What are you going to do?"

"I need to know who to target."

"You speak very confident Englishman."

"I am a Scotsman."

Her eyes seemed to fade off at a point on the wall for a few moments. "You know why I help you?"

"You believe they murdered your son."

"Adriana told you?"

"No. The graduation picture is over ten years old. I can see the date in the corner of it, but there are no other pictures of the boy—no wedding, or any other family occasion pictures."

"Are you a detective?"

"Some may say that."

She looked pensively at the picture before saying, "I was so proud of him. His father was a criminal, it is true—always away, maybe with his work or in prison—but every single teacher of my son told me the same, the same, the same—that his brain was a gift. And he used that gift by becoming top of his class at university in Tirana."

"Where is his father?"

"He died in shooting with the police in Lazarat. We were never married."

Bruce was aware of the small village in Southern Albania, once considered 'the cannabis capital of Europe' as, under mafia control, it used to produce nine hundred tonnes of marijuana per year. Over half a decade ago, eight hundred police officers were assigned to the area to crack down on the flagrant flouting of the rules. They eventually gained control after five days of fighting the heavily armed residents.

"There is one thing I never tell Adriana. Shortly after my son's disappearance, I receive money each month—and this payment has grown larger over the years. It was how I have been able to set up my café."

"Whose account is the money coming from?"

"The bank says it's from lots of different accounts each time."

"I see," replied Bruce, looking at the photograph again. "So you're saying there's a possibility he's alive?"

She exhaled and closed her eyes. "Maybe, maybe. But maybe I am a fool. Why would I be sent money?"

"Maybe he got caught up in the same elements his father did, and this is their honour—their Besa—to you?"

"Then why the different accounts? And why does it increase every year?"

"I can look into these accounts. Will you help me?"

She drew in a breath. "Yes."

Ellis walked around the enclosures with a feathering of melancholy. He walked from bird to bird, feeding them and reflecting.

The sun decayed in the face of the moon in the light blue sky. The smell of feathers, wood chippings and the 'grown ons'—pieces of turkey and chicken several weeks old—permeated.

Yesterday, he had shown Ciara Robson around. It had been during this he realised he needed to completely divorce himself from any criminality. He had enough in legitimate enterprises to cushion the financial hit. Getting out now would be a couple of years before he had originally planned, but he realised his heart was not in it any more—had not been for a long time. He had the sports centre, vehicle wrapping centre, shares in various restaurants and clubs, and the jewel being this bird sanctuary.

The murder of Greg Ryder had been a catalyst for Ellis to escape but he had not pinpointed it until Ciara had asked him. He had had a relationship of distant but mutual respect with the Leeds Godfather. Not that it was just Leeds the Ryder family controlled but the West Yorkshire Urban Area—

known back then as the West Yorkshire Built Up Area. Ellis liked his style—a more cultured version of Latin America's criminal modus operandi of 'plata o plomo'—silver or lead—he knew Ryder would bring real or potential enemies into the fold by cultivating business relationships, enhancing their revenue streams. Ellis realised the cleverness of this even though large percentages of potential revenue got sacrificed—it was a long-term game, and no money could be spent by a dead man.

And that was what shocked Ellis when he died, and now thinking about it—he realised it was his time to go—this life was not the life where you had one foot in and one foot out.

He walked around the track, away from the other birds, towards Medusa—the name he gave the Wedge-tail.

A cold mist swirled around his heart on being confronted by the empty enclosure. His eyes scanned all corners of the cage despite there being nothing that could have obscured an eagle of that size.

He felt the metallic prod of a pistol muzzle against the crevice where the back of the neck met the skull.

"Don't move, Harry," said the voice. It came from behind him, and his guess of its owner narrowed to two.

"Tom or Connor?"

The muzzle eased off.

"Turn around."

Harry did so to meet the blue eyes of Connor Reed.

"Where is she?"

"Sedated. Deciding what to do with her. I suspect the usual fences might struggle to offload an eagle—still, where there's a will there's a way."

"What do you want?"

"I want to know why you had my father killed."

Ellis felt a chill roll through his spinal column.

"I didn't—why would I?"

"Mahon was a corrupt copper Caris found for you and my despicable cunt of an uncle to throw the investigation's scent that you and he had my dad murdered."

Ellis met his eyes. "Even you don't believe that."

"Why do you say that?"

"Because we wouldn't be having this conversation, would we."

Connor Reed's face remained expressionless for a moment. Then he spoke. "Then I wonder how many other things he has actioned in your name."

Ellis tried to ask 'Who?' but instead the word "McKinley" came out.

"How long have you known?"

Ellis exhaled and said, truthfully, "Just then, maybe."

"You had my cousin shot."

"No, I didn't."

"The part where I get confused is where McKinley insists on one of my cousins sucking the other's cock while it's filmed for your sexual gratification, and when they refused, Curtis being shot."

Ellis's forehead pushed down on his eyebrows. "You think something like that would turn me on?"

"Don't make out there're not men like you who'd get off on the power of doing something like that."

Ellis said, "You have a point there. But I didn't order anyone to do that."

"Suppose you're going to say you didn't OK the hit on my Uncle Michael?"

"I didn't."

"What did you order?"

Ellis took a breath. "For your businesses to be hit. If that didn't bring you to the table, then for beatings to be meted out. Only then would I have gone the route of topping you."

"So you didn't have Kevin Kellings attempt to kill me?"

"Come on," he replied, with sincere annoyance. "The money I have at my disposal and the length of time I've been in this game, you think I'd pay that meathead Geordie to off you?"

"Not for nothing, but we told McKinley we'd be open to business negotiations. Just not the monthly kick-up you, or maybe he, had been getting under Derek."

"What was the kick-up?"

When Connor told him, he exclaimed, "The fucking slag. I saw not even a third of that."

"If McKinley's been actioning false orders in your name then surely he no longer warrants your loyalty."

"He warrants me verifying—he's worked with me a long time. What sort of a man would I be if I just took your word for it?"

"You have a week. Then I want McKinley," said the Yorkshireman, lowering the pistol. "The eagle is behind this enclosure. It's been sedated. I did my research on the dosage needed. I'm glad we've managed to come to an arrangement. I wouldn't have taken any pleasure in burning this place down."

27

It surprised Derek both how faint the smell of chemicals was and how corporate-looking the drug factory was. The metallic inside of this barn complex looked almost space age. The appearance of the 'chemists' heightened the feeling of professionalism, as they all wore what looked to Derek like the proper protective clothing of goggles, masks, coats to the knees and gloves.

Derek had been in several drug factories in his time, but they never looked like this; usually the walls had paint flaking off, the stench of acetone and anhydrous ammonia choked you, the workers would have maybe a mask and gloves over their T-shirts and jeans. Then again, none of them had armed guards wandering outside as this one did.

"Who are these people?" Derek asked McKinley.

McKinley simply tapped his nose and said, "Come on, he'll be waiting."

The Liverpudlian led him on the walkway denoted by two yellow lines that weaved around the colossal steel vats, horizontal cylinders with pistons underneath shielded by glass, carrousel-type working surfaces that revolved around the perimeter of the room, punctuated by emergency stop buttons and other levers.

The track narrowed into a darkened corridor before opening out into a similarly sized darkened room. The first thing he noticed was the glass vat—around four times the size of a standard bath in width, length and height—against one side of the room. There was a forklift not far behind it.

Still, the room was sparser, making the room appear bigger, with a few pallets with blue drums on top of them scattered around the perimeter.

In the centre stood a man, motionless amongst three leather-backed, wooden chairs. One half of him was surrounded by the dark of the room, the other coloured in the moonlight peering through the narrow windows just beneath the ceiling.

The sound of Derek's and McKinley's footsteps as they approached was booming to the former Yorkshire crime lord's ears. As they got closer, Derek grew more apprehensive. It was not the physicality—Derek dwarfed him in both size and build. And the hairstyle verged on foppish—almost.

It was the eyes—not the expression around the eyes, but the actual pupils themselves seemed to reach right into Derek's face.

Now almost within reaching distance, the man held out his hand but did not stretch it out, meaning Derek had to step into his personal space. The grip felt strong, despite the softness of the palm.

Attempting to look into his eyes reminded Derek of being a child looking at the sun—he could only do it for a second or so. The scar on his forehead seemed to burn under the strange Albanian's gaze.

"Mr Ryder, happy to see you here."

"Likewise, Mr Faja."

"Please, take a seat."

The voice seemed warm enough but Faja had not insisted Derek use his first name. They all took a seat, McKinley to Derek's left with Faja in front of him.

"Mr Ryder, you were head of the controlling criminal faction in and around West Yorkshire, were you not?"

The man had superb English. The tone of the question could just as well have been put to him by a prosecution barrister.

"Yeh, I was."

"I have been doing research on the city of Leeds. Before I did, I did not realise the true potential of the city for people like us."

"Yeh, there's plenty of people that come from all over. Loads of students and business types—"

Faja cut straight across him. "It has the most diverse economy of all UK main cities and has the fastest rate of private sector job growth of any UK city—did you know that?"

Derek gave a shrug. "It's grown over the years, that's true."

Faja did not acknowledge his response. "The largest legal and financial centre outside London. Thirty national and international banks. In the city alone, there is a workforce of one point four million people and an economy worth more than fifty-five billion pound sterling."

The Albanian's hands became a little more animated as he imparted this information. Derek felt a sense of inadequacy—a feeling he felt receded in his brother Greg's death but had returned with a vengeance over the past months.

He scrambled for a response—anything to convince this man he was worth working with.

"I know that the council has been putting a lot of money into it. Summat to do with making it a European capital of the North."

"A twenty-four-hour European city is the aim. What do you know of the Leeds City Region Enterprise Zone?"

Derek fought the urge to squirm. "Dunno, is it a new scheme?"

"No. It promotes development across four sites along the A63 east of Leeds."

Derek attempted to steel-line his voice. "What's this all about then?"

"What this is about, is that the city is full of opportunities—and in your years in charge, you did not execute those opportunities."

Derek frowned. "How was I meant to take advantage of the things you're talking about? I don't have connections in banking or the local council."

As soon as it came out of his mouth Derek knew he had made a mistake. He spluttered, "I mean, there's certain people I know and can lean on—"

"Do not insult my intelligence. I have done my research. You think small, and that is why your operation was small.

There is the West Yorkshire Urban Area—the cities of Leeds, Bradford and Wakefield, and the large towns of Huddersfield and Halifax. It is all for the taking. There is just one element stopping us."

"Yeah?"

"Your family."

"You mean the men in my family?"

"No—I mean your family. You see, when the men get massacred, which they will, the women will scream for justice and people in the media will listen."

Derek felt a chill run up his spine. "I can't run Leeds without allies in the area."

"You could not run the West Yorkshire Urban Area even when you had your family behind you—not effectively. Now, everything you know, I need to know. I do not wish for a war to drag out and attract unnecessary attention."

"What do you mean, everything I know?"

"Everything. Where they all live. Their businesses. Their money laundering. Their allies. Personalities. Any external relationships they might have. We will be here a while. I will have coffee made. You will drink and answer my questions, one by one."

"I aren't daft—if I tell you everything, I lose control. All I want is to get back my place as the gaffer of Leeds. Then we can work out some sort of mutual arrangement. Ask your man here—I am a reasonable person."

"Mr Ryder, men often rationalise their weakness. You've chosen to say, 'I am reasonable'. However, you knelt to the whims of others and became their slave."

"I aren't nobody's slave."

"You're worse—you paid your masters."

The shot of indignation caused him to rise. "I aren't having—"

His words were cut short as a shooting pain in his spine rattled his whole body. His felt like a bonbon being rattled in a glass jar. The floor flew up and hit him in the face. As he lay, his entire body went into an excruciating cramp. Despite all this, Derek was lucid, and so when he saw McKinley stood over him with what looked like a toy gun with wires leading into his neck, it registered he had been tasered.

The pair handcuffed his ankles and wrists before he could regain his composure. Faja then barked in a foreign language and out of the shadow came three large and well-built dark men. They seized him before effortlessly hauling him over to the forklift. Faja climbed into the seat and gunned the engine.

They placed him on the forks, holding him in place. Then the metallic fingers lifted him high into the air with a speed that surprised him. He stopped moving—falling at this height would risk broken bones or even death if he landed on his head. The fork-truck carried him over to the vat, and the stench of whatever acid was in there became stronger.

"When you go in, it will not furiously burn—instead, you will barely feel it. The itching will come eventually—then more and more until at the point where you think it's driving you mad, the burning will replace it. I have been told it's the eyes that feel it first, then it is like sunburn over your entire body. Soon after they beg for death—knowing the horror living would bring. Maybe you'll tell me everything before you reach those stages."

Derek hooked his arms around the forks as hard as he could—Faja only had a few metres in which to reverse and accelerate.

However, his heart pounded with a start as the steel claws began to tilt forward. He felt himself slide and reached out towards the back of the forks for anything to grip. The forks suddenly dropped, then rose, then dropped. He fell—legs hitting the edge of the tank before plunging into the cold liquid.

He surfaced and his breath came out in short, sharp, shallow bursts. With his feet on the floor, he had to angle his chin up a little to prevent whatever he was in going into his mouth. He already knew trying to escape was useless—the edges were too high. McKinley, Faja and the other men's eyes sliced through the glass at him.

After a few moments, he realised he was in water—maybe with a dye in it. The water was cold but no more unpleasant than that. A scare tactic—of course they needed a point man. Faja must know he could not use his Albanian goons in the Yorkshire capital and expect a profit. When the questions began, he would give them bits of the truth, bits of disinformation, and they'd pull him out and, in a few days, sit him back on the throne.

Why hasn't he asked me any questions yet?

Then the itching began.

McKinley fought the urge to avert his eyes from the caricature of horror that constituted Derek Ryder's floating remains. The room felt eerily quiet now the screaming and splashing had ceased. The body—now without clothes—was a piece of molten flesh, and the skin had begun to peel away from the rib cage, revealing bone. Ryder's face was upturned and free of the acid—the expression etched on it seemed similar to being awoken from a nightmare.

Derek had sung from the very first question asked and seemed to welcome the speed at which they came. Eventually, he passed out from the pain—by then the cold Albanian had an avalanche of intelligence on the Ryder family.

"I must return to Europe. You will follow my instructions."

"What do you want me to do?" he asked.

"We'll make them bleed from the bottom up—we'll first begin with their businesses. Disrupt them—but try not to take lives unless in self-defence."

"I thought the plan was to just take over?"

"That's not the most effective strategy. That family has strong leadership, has contacts and knows the area—it is best to make a husky pull the sledge, rather than killing them and pulling it yourself."

McKinley kept his disappointment off his face.

"Consider it done."

The warm evening air felt pleasant on McQuillan's face. He sat with his back to the wall outside a side-street bar in Rome. The handful of other patrons talked and laughed quietly amongst themselves. Above their heads stood a traffic stop sign covered in various advertisement stickers.

He took the first sip of his beer, with the cold, crisp liquid bathing his tongue. He took a few moments to hold the wolves of thought at bay and appreciate the moment. His security phone vibrated, and the Yorkshire brogue spoke when he answered.

"It's me."

"Are you OK?"

"Fine," answered Connor. The duress procedure was updated every so often, but currently if the Yorkshireman had answered, "Yes," that would mean he was under duress.

"Go on."

"My friend in Amsterdam wants me over there. Several parts of his operations have been attacked. Needs me to do some cleaning of his problems in exchange for him looking after some assets of mine over here. Thought I'd let you know in case you had anything coming up for me."

Bruce took a moment before saying, "Do what you have to do. You can use our asset. Anything else?"

"No."

The call ended. Van Der Saar's request to have Connor assassinate Albanian gangsters in Holland aligned with his own aims anyway. However, Bruce would now have to reshuffle personnel.

He spotted Adriana at a distance of sixty metres, walking up the cobbled street. He had always admired Italian women's seemingly effortless sense of style; she wore a cream shirt, rolled at the sleeves over a white blouse, her dark jeans gave way to tan shoes that matched her handbag. She—as with many Italian women—walked with an understated elegance.

Finally, she reached him as he stood. She placed her hands lightly on his upper arms and elevated herself for the

223

customary European cheek kisses. It had surprised him as this was only their second meeting.

"Why did you want me to walk this particular way?"

"So I could see if you were being followed."

She blinked. "You are a professional."

"I try."

"Only try?"

"I am being endearingly modest."

"Do all Scotsmen sound like you?"

He smiled. "Do all Italian women sound like you?"

"Ahh, your point is noted," she said, returning it but with teeth.

"I've booked one of the rooftop tables. What would you like to drink?"

Soon, both were sat with an Aperol Spritz—an Italian cocktail of Aperol, soda and Prosecco—overlooking the rooftops of Rome. St. Peter's Basilica formed the centrepiece as the sun's mist disappeared behind the dark blue buildings.

The angles and curves of Adriana's face were highlighted by the soft dim lights.

"So, what have you brought me here for?" she said, in a tone that hinted at flirtatious.

"I have a plan, but I need your help."

"OK," she said, straightening up.

"A series of…incidences will occur in the not so distant future. People will speculate as to who is responsible for them. If I can point you in a certain direction, and you were to follow, it could be advantageous to both our aims."

"You'll have to do better than that, Bruce. Trust should be mutual in a partnership, should it not?"

He looked at her for a few moments. "A war between the Mafia Shqiptare and the 'Ndrangheta."

"Why would they fight? They are allies, I have told you that."

"They could be given a reason to."

"I am interested in justice—not simply animals killing one another. Besides, death is accepted within their circles."

Bruce sipped at the refreshing Spritz before looking Adriana in her coffee eyes. "Our definition of justice differs, but sometimes the only way to make the king rats appear is to jab at the nest—then they're vulnerable to prosecution."

Her stare matched his own. "Evidence may appear linking bosses to crimes?"

Bruce turned his hand over to show his palm. "If one were to find it and ensure it ended up under the correct set of eyes."

She cocked her head to the side. "Surely if 'incidents' were to happen, then the parties involved—or that were meant to be involved—would simply contact one another for clarification?"

"People in those circles have to lie."

"Maybe in yours too?"

"It's the intention behind an untruth that's important. Would you consider it noble for a soldier present at his comrade's agonising death, to return back home and describe in explicit detail that death to the deceased family? Or have him simply say their son, brother, father had slipped away peacefully?"

"Do they not have official death reports?"

Bruce said, "For the purposes of the argument."

"I take your point."

"Are you in?"

She looked at him intently before saying, "It is my work to report on significant events within the Italian and Albanian criminal circles—and to report on what I find."

"All right. You'll receive the 'tip-offs' through various different means."

"Without being a 'glass is half empty' woman, I do not believe this plan will work."

"I do not require for you to believe in it, I need you to follow through—because if you do, I will reach the people who murdered your husband."

"You must be really good."

Bruce ran his hand over his stubble. "I have good people around me."

225

28

Connor sat in a red, velvet-backed chair in quiet contemplation. He could hear the faint Dutch voices outside his room in the hotel corridor.

He remembered a conversation he once had with a former assassin who was nearing his sixtieth birthday. He'd told Connor, "If I was a footballer, I would be happier with a couple of tap-ins than a spectacular goal that makes everyone 'ooh and ahh'—it is the result that counts, not how it was achieved. It is the same in the profession of contract killing. Young men like the idea of ingenuity—long-range sniper rifles, cyanide in the tea, death by an electrified keyboard. I have killed more men in my jeans and T-shirt by walking up behind them and shooting them in the back than most of these young men could ever kill with their suits, sunglasses and fancy methods."

Connor agreed, and yet here he was, about to attempt a 'fancy method'. He had often contemplated how much of an asset Jaime—Bruce's tech guy—was, as having him in your corner saved so much time, energy and money that Connor knew he was worth many times more to Bruce than himself. As soon as Connor set foot in Amsterdam, Jaime already knew where the members of the Albanian mafia who were hitting Van Der Saar were located.

The Peralta Plaza lay just over two kilometres away from the Amsterdam airport, which was not ideal given the CCTV in operation everywhere. He was not keen on the hotel uniform, even though the top hat that came with it might save him from being identified by the cameras—*better to be dressed as Uncle Rich Pennybags for an hour than Norman Stanley Fletcher for decades*.

He smiled as he recalled watching *Porridge* as a lad with his Uncle Michael—he enjoyed those times. He remembered the first boxing match he watched that truly excited him was the first fight between Marco Antonio Barrera and Erik

Morales; remembered how animated his Uncle Michael got, jumping up and shadow boxing while stating, 'Either of them pair would kill Naseem Hamed', and 'Fuckin' animals, those Mexicans, pair of them can box but they just want to punch the fuck outta each other'. He snapped himself out of his reverie and attempted to clear his mind.

In the relative quiet of the room, his conscience began to gnaw at him. He had recently admitted to himself hurting evil men was his greatest source of fun and pleasure—not long ago he had chained a Ukrainian child killer to the back of a Land Rover before dragging him at speed for miles. Going through with the act had meant turning his back on his best chance of a normal life with a woman he adored, and despite that, he had laughed all the way through it.

This would be different—the men he was about to kill were gangsters, sure. However, so were the men in his own family. These Albanians were on another level in terms of how far they would go but that was due to the criminal culture over there.

He countered these thoughts—*they are killers. They do not contribute anything positive to society. You're doing the world a favour wiping them out. Your family don't hurt 'civilians' or even law enforcement. No one is off-limits to these animals.*

His phone rang and he answered it.

The voice on the other end of the line said, "It's time."

Andrei avoided the long, horizontal moving walkway that the other commuters of the Amsterdam airport seemed eager to use—it inhibited freedom of movement.

He fitted his Bluetooth earpiece and took out his phone, found Veli's WhatsApp icon and pressed 'Call'.

It failed to go through. Andrei had told Veli if he and the men were not connected to Wi-Fi then to switch to their own phone's internet signal.

He would have to risk calling despite it being a less secure means of communication.

He made his way outside and flagged down a taxi. After giving directions to the driver, he made the call—no answer.

Andrei ran through the possible scenarios but all he could do was wait until he got to the hotel to ascertain the situation—no sense in repeatedly calling like an insecure woman to her lover. The taxi freed itself onto the highway.

After a time the hotel came into view, the taxi slowing into the treacle of converging street traffic.

His earpiece rang and Andrei clicked Answer.

"Just seen the missed call, boss. Signal isn't the best here."

"Why do you not have internet connectivity?"

"Can't connect to Wi-Fi, can't connect to my 4G. None of us can."

"You've all tried?"

"Yes. We are all here waiting for you."

Andrei's heart rate increased. "What do you mean you are all here waiting for me?"

"Here in my room like you messaged."

"What do you mean messaged? I never messaged. Besides, I thought you did not have Wi-Fi?"

Andrei could now see the hotel in the distance.

"Your text message—it's your number—came through though."

"Veli, I didn't send any—"

"Hold on, boss, there's a knock at the door. Egzon, go see who that is. Apologies, what were you saying?"

"Veli! Do not let him open that door."

Connor stood for what seemed like an eternity at the door. He found himself tilting his head away from the corridor camera even though Jaime had assured him he had managed to insert a pre-recorded overlap for the next ten minutes.

The Gods were on his side so far—no other guests in the corridor.

The door clicked open to reveal a large, dark-haired, olive-skinned man. A shout came from the room and the man turned his head for a split second.

Connor's suppressed pistol clacked, spraying blood, bone and brain matter back at him. As the body toppled, Connor's hand shot into his pocket and grasped the grenade. He flicked off the steel transit clip—having removed the pin prior—and threw it inside while slamming the door on the chaotic chorus of Albanian voices. The three seconds seemed like ten, but the thudding explosion reverberated through the walls and floor.

He kicked open the door and poked his head around as far as he dared to check no one was in a fit state to level a weapon at him. Seeing this was the case, he entered, as the corridor came alive with people. With deft movement, he shot each man in the room in the head before holstering his weapon beneath his hotel blazer. He took out a packet of baby wipes from his pocket and removed blood from his face—the darkness of the blazer camouflaged the rest. Then he noticed the phone in the hand of one of the Albanians—it was still connected to a call.

The explosion rained glass from the shattered window. The driver slowed to a halt as did the vehicles in front. Andrei threw a fistful of Euros at him, before alighting, snatching his bag from the back seat and running towards the hotel.

"Veli? Veli? Can you hear—"

A voice in English interrupted him. "Can you speak English?"

Andrei took a few moments to reply. "I take it Veli is not available to speak?"

"If by Veli you mean the original owner of this phone then no. Seeing as you pair used to be friends, I am looking forward to arranging for you both to meet."

Andrei cupped his hand over the earpiece so he could hear above the screaming guests pouring out of the hotel like ants from a water-soaked nest.

The call disconnected.

Connor had connected the victim's phone to his Bluetooth earpiece upon the exchange with whoever was on the other end. As he had joined the rushing throng of guests crowding into the corridors, it had taken him a moment to decipher that the sounds of a frightened and animated crowd were coming through his earpiece, and not just around him—*the voice is close by.*

The call ended, and he joined the herd in their stampede down the stairs. An image of Nakatomi Plaza briefly came to him—*relax, folks, it's not even Christmas.*

He began to consider his options—he was armed with a silenced pistol, but the voice might know what he looked like since they had attempted to shadow him on his previous Amsterdam visit. He pulled his hat further down over his forehead.

He spilt out with the rest into the hotel lobby—no law enforcement yet. The security and hotel staff simply pointed to the exit with one hand while making the 'hurry up' motion with the other. Connor took up a position at the foot of the stairs and mirrored them. His eyes began scanning for dark-haired fighting-aged males—particularly ones trying to get into the hotel.

After a moment, he thought he spotted him—a dark-haired man, more white than olive, looking at the exit anxiously with a holdall at his side. Could be he was a man separated from his family—but why would he have exited without them? Maybe he left them and now can't get back in? Left with a holdall?

Connor's hand slid into his pocket and clicked the Call button—*come on, answer, you prick.*

He did not answer but he did not need to—the man outside looked at him briefly but it was enough. What Connor did not know was if the man knew he had been *pinged.*

The man picked up his holdall and began to walk away. Connor began to move too—*I'll kill him now and have done with it.*

As he walked to the entrance something in his mind gnawed at him. He quickly dismissed it—more was lost by indecision than wrong decision.

He could not risk losing him by searching for an alternative exit. So, he briskly walked out into the shoal of people flowing around stationary vehicles. Catching a glimpse of his target as it disappeared around the corner, he sped into a jog—he could shoot him in the spine and pretend to attend to him in the confusion.

The reptilian part of his brain told him to peer around the corner instead of rounding it at speed. Like he had after he threw the grenade into the room. He did so and saw it—the man in urgent conversation with three police officers.

Connor jerked his head back, before sprinting on another shot of adrenaline. Others were running so he did not look out of place. There was no sense in attempting to ditch the uniform—it would have his DNA on it, and even though he had covered his fingertips in silicone caulk and had the serial number burnt off, he did not want to needlessly leave the murder weapon for the police.

The rental car stood in the hotel car park. He rounded the corner in full flight and bundled straight into a policeman with a startled look on his face. The law enforcement officer barely had time for his hand to form a halt sign when Connor's fist smashed into his jaw, snapping his head around and leaving him unconsciousness.

He did not look back, fearful he would now have several camera phones pointed at his back, ready to catch a snap or recording of his face.

He need not have worried—seemingly in their concern to abandon the hotel, people appeared to pay no heed to the police officer or himself.

Connor reached the white Citroen C4 Cactus—his SOPs dictated he had changed the registration plate two days ago to match a vehicle from another rental company in Rotterdam. He got in and took the hat off.

Gunning the engine, the traffic around the hotel had mercifully freed itself enough to allow him a clear route out onto the main roads.

He cursed—*I might have wiped out six of them, but that copper has seen my face.*

29

Rayella looked around the dojo in awe. The sunlight from the windows formed pools of warmth on the floor. There were portraits of mixed martial arts legends around. Her eyes were drawn to a logo in the centre of one of the white mats—some kind of Japanese markings encircled in red.

Towards the back of the hall, the man she knew as George Follet sparred with a man twice his size. She had arrived early to the Youths Shoot Boxing class, so sat and watched.

George kept the black-bearded man at bay with a variety of rapid, punishing kicks to the legs and solar plexus. Seemingly frustrated, the opponent bolted forward only to find his left leg snatched up and his other foot being swept out by George's right foot.

Rayella felt a flutter in her stomach at seeing the bigger man topple. She remembered something Connor had said once—*"There's a reason why there aren't open weight matches in wrestling like there are in jiu-jitsu."*

But here George was. Not only had he taken him down, but he was on top. Rayella could not quite see how but, by some magic trick, he was now latched onto the beast-like man's back with his arm in bold relief as it crushed the lower part of the man's face. As a defending arm came up, George's other arm zipped underneath like a ratchet around his thick neck—the man tapped his submission.

George began explaining to him where he could improve. She caught something about telegraphing and that giving up position just because he was in pain was him being a *'Morris Minor'*. She would have to ask Connor what that was.

Some youths began to trickle into the dojo, before stepping onto the mat and beginning various warm-up routines. They parted as George walked through them—and she stood up to greet him.

He held out his hand. "It's nice to meet you, Rayella."

"Thank you…I mean…you too, Mr Follet."

"You can call me George—I don't need students to call me Mister, or Sensei, or bow or anything like that to show respect. The way I want you to show respect to me is by arriving on time, giving me your full concentration as I teach, and full effort in general—understand?"

"Yes, Mister…yes, George."

"I know of your Muay Thai credentials. Connor said you've been dipping your toe into grappling?"

"I have."

"Well, after today you'll realise why you need to dive and stay under forever. You're obviously a hard, talented girl—and you've chosen a superb martial art for striking—but you're incomplete, and therefore vulnerable. You're smart, so you'll know this in your brain but not in this," he said, lightly punching her in the chest. He continued, "Get your kit on and get warmed up."

Within five minutes, she was rotating her joints before lightly shadow boxing.

George called them to sit in a circle around him and announced, "A highly respected Brazilian jiu-jitsu professor stated these rules: number one—be the guy on top. Number two—when on top stay on top. Three—when on the bottom, have a guard you shall not pass. And number four—Don't forget rule number one. And that's a BJJ professor, not catch wrestling that I was blooded with. Some of you have been too willing to sit on your arse and play from there, and it stops today. You play guard when your opponent puts you there. Just because you watch these submission-only grappling events where they do that and think it's cool, don't be thinking it automatically translates to the street or a mixed martial arts fight—because why?"

"Because people can hit you in those," answered one of the girls.

"Exactamundo—they can punch and kick yer fackin' swede in. Now, I am not saying there's not a place for pulling guard and attacking the legs, but don't make it your 'go-to'."

For the next half hour, the class drilled the techniques that George showed—how to cause pain to get the opponent to shift, how to keep the pressure on, and the use of cranks.

Rayella had been paired with a brunette girl of similar age and build named Ida.

Rayella had asked her, "Where you from?"

"Denmark. You?"

"Yorkshire."

She and Ida hit it off, and Rayella found herself completely immersed in what she was being taught. She loved the atmosphere of the place.

George yelled, "MMA gloves on. Shoot boxing rounds."

Rayella's adrenaline spiked but she was adept at channelling it now. However, her wrestling and grappling were rudimentary—*I'll just sprawl.*

Ida met her with a toothy grin and the round began. Rayella's opponent flicked out snappy kicks that though did not hurt, kept Rayella at a distance.

The Muay Thai fighter tightened her defence and began to press more forcefully behind feints. Ida looked uncomfortable under the heavy low kicks and punches. Rayella caught her in clasped hands around the neck—a Muay Thai plum—but her knee strike was caught. She found herself unceremoniously dumped as Ida's sweeping foot took out Rayella's balancing one.

The Leeds girl wrapped her right leg around the Dane's right leg in a half guard. She prevented Ida's torso closing the space with her 'knee shield'. Rayella looked to shoot her arm under her opponent's so she could escape.

However, Ida's right hand whipped back and caught the toes of Rayella's right foot, before her other hand slid over then under the ankle, before grasping her own wrist.

The toe hold forced Rayella onto her side in a futile attempt to escape the threat of a break. Pinned mercilessly, the pain hammered her ankle and her hand hammered the mat.

Rayella endured four more six-minute rounds with various other girls. Taken down in every single round— sometimes just once and in others several times—she quickly realised it was not just Ida, but all the girls, who grappled her into a pool of pain. Unlike the Brazilian jiu-jitsu classes she had attended, these girls were trying to hurt her before submitting her—shins driven into her shins and pressed into her face, elbows forced into the soft part of her body like the crevice between her clavicle and shoulder. At times they pulled on her head in a way she thought her spine was going to break.

"Time," yelled George. "That'll do ya."

Rayella felt bruised, spent and elated.

George walked over and said, "Facking 'orrible, isn't it?"

She nodded and he continued, "The last girl had you in a crank and a lot would have tapped to it. Now two things happen when someone has been put through the ringer like that—one is they never come back—that's most people. The second is they stay and develop this superpower of fighting."

Rayella already knew she would be staying.

Andrei drove the cliff-side road admiring the view of Tirana below; the distant green hills, valleys and lakes simmering into the blend of trees and homes, until finally opening up to the city.

His mind calculated his chances of surviving his meeting with Oso Xhelli. He had given his assurance the men would be able to conduct probing attacks against Van Der Saar in his absence from the UK.

Andrei could not understand how the assassin managed to obtain his number and clone it to send that text. Surely, he would need access to, and knowledge of, high-tech cyber systems.

Getting his men to break protocol to trap themselves in the same room had been the key to the Yorkshire killer's ambush.

Oso—whether he killed him or not—would expect answers, and Andrei did not have them. He could simply not go—though on the surface, being estranged from his family and with enough money to make a fresh start in another country, it was a viable option.

He dismissed the pipe dream—Oso's reach extended globally, and a life looking over one's shoulder was no life at all.

He swung the car onto a minor road heading into the hills before picking up a long, meandering track leading to Oso's villa.

After a time, the trees on either side created a dark tunnel against the sunlight.

He slowed to a halt before the wrought-iron gate. Various concealed cameras stared at him from different angles. He wound down the window so the camera on top of the intercom had an unobstructed view of him. The gate opened.

The estate held three white buildings in a U-shaped formation—two guest houses to the left and right, with the main domain at the back. They all faced towards a water feature located precisely level to the walkways to the buildings. Forestry crept in close to the estate from the rear-left, with a view of Tirana over to the right.

Andrei got out and smelled the faint fragrance of moisture and flowers in the air.

He knew that although the house to the right was reserved for guests, the one to the left held at least six of Oso's security team at any one time—including the valet who took his car keys with a subtle bow.

As Andrei stepped on the walkway to make towards the house, he imagined the mutineers of pirate ships being made to 'walk the plank'—though they were reputed to be made to do it blindfolded, and his eyes were wide open and scanning.

A member of the security team met him at the entrance and said, "He's in his study, Faja."

The polished wood stairway led up before curving back on itself to the upper floor. A painting of a man and a woman, both in traditional headdresses, dancing together, greeted him at the top.

He made his way down the lantern-lit corridor and into the study. The fire warmed and lit the art, desk, dark blue and gold patterned carpets, and landscape paintings.

The Shqiptare crime lord peered up from his letter-writing. Black and grey chest hair peered out from his opened shirt and rolled-up sleeves. Andrei noticed he had changed his watch to something equally as cheap as his last watch, recalling his Krye's words of "I need it to tell the time—that is all."

Oso stood and came around to embrace him.

"Andrei, I am so glad you are safe."

Andrei hid his surprise. "Thank you."

The older man released him, gesturing him to sit in the mahogany armchair across the mahogany desk.

Oso's chest rose and fell before he spoke. "A challenge faces us, Andrei—maybe the deadliest we have ever faced."

As the younger man heard a drawer being opened, he braced. However, his Krye pulled out an envelope and handed it to him.

"This was sent by a messenger to my gate."

Andrei opened it to find a letter written in Italian, but his eyes were drawn first to the print of a rotting leaf smeared with blood. He speed-read the Italian prose.

Il peccato di molti è stato lavato via dal sangue di pochi. Con l'equilibrio ristabilito tra le nostre organizzazioni, ti imploriamo contro gli errori.

"'The sin of the many has been washed by the blood of the few. With the balance restored between our organisations, we implore you against misdeed'," he recited. "I do not understand."

"I do not either. A war council will now be called."

The younger man's brain began its calculations before asking, "I would ensure this is not fraudulent, Krye Xhelli."

"That is one of their symbols. Besides, the men you left in Holland were warriors and professionals—Van Der Saar

239

could not have out-fought them on his own—to kill them all with a grenade inside a hotel and then for the assassin to escape…there's only so many organisations capable of it, or who dare to cross us."

"I am just cautioning you against eliminating all other possibilities. We know a war with the 'Ndrangheta has the potential to destroy us—even in victory, we would suffer. Can we not reach out?"

"To do so would show weakness. I will not act recklessly—but I cannot let this pass."

Andrei allowed his frown to show. "What motive could they have? Many of our businesses are intertwined?"

"As you know, there have been many fallouts in local regions in Europe at lower and mid-level. Profits have always smoothed relations but maybe they have decided on showing their dominance."

Andrei refrained from telling Oso who the assassin was—if the old man believed it to be a strike out of nowhere by an organisation like the 'Ndrangheta, and not a criminal from the North of England, then Andrei would not immediately correct him.

Oso continued, "How was your visit to England?"

Does he know?—mused Andrei.

"I have reiterated our expectations to our associates in the capital. We are on schedule with our production in the north. There's a proxy war that may be a threat to our interests there."

The most powerful man in the Albanian mafia leant back on his chair and said, "You're right, a war with our Calabria friends will be costly for as long as it lasts. You need to return to the UK to ensure our investment is secure. Do not let there be any room for reprisals, Andrei. Take whatever men you need."

"I will not take men away from you here at this dangerous time. I can use our affiliate organisation over there to get what we need done."

"You are a smart man, Andrei. As you wish."

Rayella floated down the chipped painted stairs of the dojo on a cloud of dopamine. Ida walked beside her. "So, I will see you the day after tomorrow?"

"Yes. I am looking forward to it—kinda."

Ida laughed and said, in a surprisingly accurate parody of George's accent, "Yer hav' to be the fackin' nail before you can be the hammer."

Rayella laughed too. They parted on the street, and Rayella checked her phone and found a message.

Turn left when you exit and head down the street. I am in the green Audi. L.

'L' meant Louis.

Rayella headed towards the corner and saw the front end of a dark green Audi Quattro TT a hundred metres down the road.

She heard a zooming engine behind her. She spun around to see a white van screech to a halt beside her. Burly men bomb burst from it.

She dodged their clutching hands the best she could but there was no escape. She fought with an adrenaline-fuelled ferociousness despite the fatigue from her training session. The hands snatched a grip of her arms before her feet left the floor and a rough hand clamped over her nose and mouth. The man holding her fell on top of her but did not move. She heard a voice she recognised as Louis's.

"You two, pick that sack of shit up off her now."

She took a draught of breath with the relief of the heavy body being lifted off her.

Louis stood facing the three men—two holding up another, unconscious—with a pistol pointed at them.

"Now, I am going to let you off this time. I can tell by your faces you know who I am—just like I know who you are. If I pull this trigger then we're at war, and I don't want that—

but you ever lay a hand on her again, I'll turn south London into the Helmand province."

The two men exchanged a look before bundling their colleague into the back. As they made into the van, Rayella felt Louis manoeuvre her behind him.

Her would-be kidnappers' vehicle drove off.

"You know what they say, don't ya, girl?" asked Louis.

Rayella felt her pulse and breathing return to normal, "What do they say?"

"It's nice to be wanted," he replied. "Unless it's by Hellbanianz."

30

Harry Ellis sat in his office at the vehicle wrapping centre. The air conditioning whirred as he sipped his coffee. The clock provoked him—McKinley was now seven minutes late and he was always early. Indeed, McKinley had never taken more than a few hours to come and meet him, but yesterday, when Ellis had requested a conversation, McKinley told him it would have to be today.

Finally, he heard the click of the external door and then McKinley strode in.

He flopped into the seat opposite. "You wanted to see me?"

His demeanour conveyed a nonchalance Ellis did not like.

"What moves have you been making without my knowledge, let alone consent?"

There were a few moments' silence before McKinley answered with, "Fuck me, it's taken you long enough. What finally made you twig?"

Ellis stared at him. "A little birdie."

"I see," said McKinley, cracking his fingers. "What are you wanting, then?"

"What have you been up to, specifically?"

"That's my business, Harry—it has been for a long time. You get it, the police—and everyone else—still think it's you, don't they. They can't believe you want to be a straight shooter, and they're fucked off you're this multimillionaire businessman swanning around the 'pool' with this and that charity bigging you up, la. To be honest, I couldn't understand why you were importing those horses on the sly—then I found out. You needed loose cash to pay for another bird sanctuary, quick time. Anyway, they snag me then it'll be all 'he told me to do it, Guv', you get me?"

Ellis fought the urge to smash McKinley to pieces right there and then. One, McKinley might have been armed—Ellis had stopped 'carrying' long ago, he knew too many gangsters doing time because of a forgotten about gun found after a tip-off. Two, he did not know if he could stop himself going too far.

"So, you're a grass as well as a snake."

"I am what I need to be."

Ellis clenched his fist tight before releasing it.

"Did you order Greg Ryder's murder?"

McKinley leered. "I noticed you stopped pressing so hard for the killer after those fat monthly envelopes began making their way into Caris's hands and then into your bank account."

"I stopped pressing after you told me even his brother Derek said—"

Ellis paused as it dawned on him—Derek had his brother killed.

"Ahh, the penny's dropped. That's one of the reasons why the family was kept under the cosh. I told that fucking idiot he had to fork out for both you and me. You, for protection that he would never get, and me, to keep my mouth shut. And the fucking divvy did…for years."

"Where is he now?"

"He's gone. Dissolved, I should say."

"You killed him?"

"Nah, mate. You're looking at me a certain way, but I am not the villain you want to be worried about. Someone much scarier than me is going to be staying up 'ere—a bit like when in *Batman Begins*, Scarecrow tells Carmine Falcone that big, bad Ra's al Ghul is on his way—although this Albanian has already been up here. And it was him who took care of Derek Ryder. Fucking nasty how, too."

"You're dying to tell me."

"Acid…fucking horrible. Really slow."

"Let me guess, this Albanian is one of these Hellbanianz 'head-the-balls' for backup, should I choose to kick off, or decided to end our partnership."

"Nah, Harry. He's from the old country, and we both know you've too much to lose to be kicking off gangster-style like it's the old days. Besides, the blokes are loyal to me. Now, I am not going to hold your feet to the fire if you want to let everyone know we're no longer a partnership—it's not like I need the wages any more, and I reckon there's a few piranhas with long memories who might want a bite, Harry, with me out of the way."

"I'll take my chances," he replied. "Why is this Albanian up here?"

"Ahh, can't tell, can I? This isn't a Bond film."

"I know one man who'll love knowing you were the one who killed Greg Ryder."

For the first time since he sat down, McKinley's mask of arrogance briefly dropped.

"Who told you it was me?"

"There's no way that fuckhead had the minerals to pull the trigger on his own brother—he'll have got you to do it."

McKinley sneered. "You're sort of right—it was me that didn't trust him to do it, so I offered. And, as for Connor Reed, the man's a dead man anyway."

"Is that what you said when you sent Kellings after him?"

"Nah. Kellings had a bee in his bonnet anyway, and there was no downside to giving him a few readies as an extra incentive and telling him it would be a favour to Harry Ellis. How he fucked that up, we'll never know."

As Ciara walked through Tirana International Airport Nënë Tereza, she wondered whether, in the grand scheme of things, the way she looked helped or hindered her. She could think of several instances where, in both her work as an agent and a journalist, her short, silvery-blonde hair, emerald eyes and figure had helped her to charm or distract. However, she also stood out, and she could feel the glances in her direction.

Though the airports of some European cities were more extensive, this one appeared substantial, modern and professional though a little more relaxed. The security checks were more rapid, despite the long check-in queues.

The design of the outer and inner buildings sloped outwards like square glass bowls.

She exited into the Albanian sunshine, and passed the yellow taxis and the cascading foundation, down the steps and into the car park. The dark blue Land Rover sat where she had been told it would be. The spare tyre fixed to the rear had a stretched cover with caricature paw prints on it.

Ciara checked the inside before getting into the passenger side. The lady in the driver seat turned to her and offered her hand.

"Gëzohem që të takova, I am Eliza."

The lady smoothed her black bob, dashed with grey, behind her ear. Sunglasses shaded eyes that Ciara knew to be brown.

Ciara took the older woman's hand and said, "Good to meet you, too. And of course, I am Ciara."

"Have you been to Albania before," asked Eliza quizzically as she turned the ignition over.

"No. But I always brush up on useful phrases before I arrive."

As Eliza pulled away from the airport she said, "I thought he would have sent a man."

"He sends the person best suited to the task."

"I picked you up as many of the taxi drivers act as their eyes and ears."

Ciara was already aware of this. "My visit isn't secretive, quite the opposite. The reason is, but not the visit itself."

"What is this cover?"

"I have reached out to members of government in this city for interviews regarding the EU not opening formal dialogue with Albania. I'll insinuate I want to make a case that the country should be considered for membership."

"You must understand the government has its informants to these people—they control everything. And these people might not wish for Albania to become part of the European Union as their corruption will have extra eyes looking. They might not be happy with the picture you wish to paint."

Ciara said, "That is good. Then they might seek me out."

"And that is a good thing?"

"Best way to get to know them."

Ellis lay on his soft bed, staring at the ceiling. The 3D ceiling design of a forest canopy had been worth the expense at times like these. His brain had been in a whirr in the immediate aftermath of his meeting with McKinley the previous day. That he misinterpreted McKinley for years stuck in his mind like a barb—judgement of character had been a strength of his for decades, but failed him with the one person with whom he shared his most sensitive information. His mind began to ease when he realised this might have been the best possible outcome; he could not have one foot in and one foot out—he needed to make a clean break and this was it.

He reached for his phone and within a couple of minutes had an Uber driver on the way to his address.

The young bodybuilder, who frequented one of the gyms he owned, had been a welcome distraction. It had been fun, but now he resented his privacy being encroached. Ellis elbowed the muscular, tattoo-sleeved arm until the blonde cracked open his blurry eyes.

"Time for you to get going," said Ellis.

The young man palm heeled his eyes, and swung out of the bed. Ellis fought the urge to look at his arse as not to tempt himself—he had things to be getting on with. Instead, he got up and donned his luxury cotton gown.

He turned around to watch the slim-fit jeans being pulled onto thick legs before a deep plunge T-shirt stretched over the balloon-like chest.

When the expectant eyes met his, Ellis checked his phone and said, "An Uber will be outside in a minute. I'll see you to the door."

With the house to himself again, he made his way to the kitchen.

He stiffened momentarily on walking in. Connor Reed stared at him over the top of Ellis's favourite coffee mug and said, "Good taste. Coffee, I mean. I think if I were gay the noise that lad was making would put me off my stroke."

Ellis's diaphragm cooled with the knowledge the Yorkshireman must have been in his house all night.

"How did you get in here?"

"It wasn't easy. You haven't half forked out on the security systems. I won't go into specifics—retain a bit of mystery, so to speak."

It took Ellis a few moments to find his words. "You staying for breakfast?"

"That's very nice of you, Harry. What were you thinking?"

"I was going to do a fry-up."

"Please. No tomatoes. No hash browns or toast. Watching my figure."

After a short time, they both sat facing one another, eating. Harry expected the question earlier than it came, as Connor polished off the mushrooms before asking, "So, what do you have for me?"

"McKinley. He's been orchestrating his own criminal enterprise in my name for years."

Connor put his knife and fork on his empty plate, and took a sip of his coffee. "You know, a cynical man might suggest you're trying to pass the buck so I don't kill you in your own house."

The statement shot adrenaline into Ellis's system.

"Alexa, play recording under 'McKinley'."

Connor sat quietly listening to Ellis's last conversation with McKinley.

When it finished, Reed said, "Where is he now?"

Ellis raised his hands to indicate he was not going for any type of weapon in his pocket, before retrieving a business card from his vehicle wrapping service.

"On the back of the card is the link to the vehicle tracker along with the username and password."

"You had his car bugged?"

"McKinley—for tax and for appearances purposes—is on my books with the vehicle wrapping centre as a salesman. The M4 he drives around in is registered as a company car, and as such has a tracker fitted. I genuinely forgot to tell him. When you log on you should see the route history for the last thirty days."

Connor looked at the card before giving a subtle nod. "Right then. Unless you're lying, I don't see why you and I would meet again."

31

As Connor rode the Speed Triple along the country road he kicked himself for not having gotten his motorcycle licence sooner. The burr of the engine beneath him, the wind in his face and the hint of danger in taking it to a high speed made car travel seem sterile.

The sun shone and the wind was but a breeze—his friend John Foley had informed him that in cold, wet weather he would be all right if he wore the right gear, but it could turn into an ordeal on longer rides.

Tom—forever concerned about his family—had warned him over the phone to "take it steady". Connor felt a mild hint of guilt sometimes—Tom was the real leader of the family, the one who kept it together while Derek had been seemingly intent on fucking it all up. He had been the one who had established relationships with both the meek and mighty in their world, and with straight goers. Connor did not dismiss his own contribution—he had been responsible for the creation of criminal business contacts in Holland and Ukraine. However, it had been Tom who formed alliances with various managers of independent trucking companies, and had facilitated those imports to happen on the scale they did.

Connor slowed and purred the bike into the Raven Crest's gravel car park. Luke, who had been sipping a Budweiser, put it down and came over to greet him as he parked and dismounted.

"Makes you look cool as fuck that. Grandad would have been proud."

Connor removed his helmet. "Look? I am cooler than the other side of the pillow."

Luke laughed, and Connor continued, "I'll tell you what doesn't make you cool is you drinking."

Luke frowned. "It's only a beer."

"On its own, I'd agree. But you've been drinking a lot, not to mention the risk you took in Thailand. And there are the other instances of ill judgement."

"Different people have a different—"

"Shut the fuck up and listen," said Connor, clasping his hand around the back of his younger cousin's neck. "Not only do I love you like mad but I don't even think you realise your potential, otherwise you wouldn't be retarding it like you are doing. Not only are you involved in a sport that no one with a substantial career gets out of without some type of damage, but you're in this world—our uncle has been shot dead and our cousin nearly killed. You don't get to just turn up when you feel like it. You have to be sharp all the time—for both things, for yourself and this family and the people who rely on us. Do you understand?"

Luke slowly met his eyes. "I understand."

"Good. Lecture over. Let's go in."

He noticed Luke left the bottle as they entered. The narrow bar stretched and curved around the length of two living rooms with the intimate seating arrangements close to it. The soft lighting shone off the chrome beer taps in front of smiling bar staff. The Ryder clan sat together in an alcove at the far end. Connor glanced at the wallpaper surrounding them, depicting patrons of a theatre in the upper tiers looking down.

He caught sight of Curtis. He was glad he was there, but Connor could see the discomfort—and it reminded him why he had to deal with McKinley.

Seeing the group down to six weighted his heart—with Luke stood with him, there sat Charlie, Curtis, Tom, and his uncles Lee and Ryan.

They rose to greet him, and began the familial hugs. When he got to Curtis, he said, "Pity you can't rap, you could have milked it."

Curtis laughed.

They sat on the red-cushioned seating curved in a semi-circle around a thick wooden table. Connor sat by the twins

251

on the left, then it was Ryan with Tom and Luke, with Lee facing him.

The dark-haired waitress, around her late thirties and in great shape, wearing vertically striped leggings, came and took their order. As she sauntered away, Ryan exclaimed, "Look at the arse on it."

Luke frowned. "Eh? Bet she has a face like fire-damaged Lego under all that make-up."

Ryan's expression mirrored Luke's. "It's called doggy style, something I thought you'd be into after seeing that old bird with a face like a Rhino's kneecap hanging off ya the other night."

Connor held his hand over his face as laughter bubbled in his belly and around his family. After the waitress returned and left them with their drinks, he asked Tom, "How are the Dutch operators working out?"

"The first couple of days were full on with sorting them out—giving them full lists of the girls' routines, habits, personalities and all kinds. Stood over a map of Leeds all morning telling them about the different areas. But since then I haven't heard a peep and the girls haven't noticed anything."

Tom was referring to the professional security team sent by Raymond Van Der Saar to watch over the Ryder women. This had been in exchange for Connor's assassination of the Albanian team in the Amsterdam hotel.

"Where they holed up?"

"They are using the mansion as a base."

His conservative but shrewd cousin had procured a mansion in the affluent Alwoodley area of Leeds, around twenty minutes from where they were now sat. He had begun to develop a select client list who paid a 'fee' running into the thousands of pounds to attend the nights of hedonistic debauchery Tom put on every month or so. High-quality drugs were left out in a back room that had a balcony overlooking a meadow, for anyone wanting to indulge. There were several bedrooms, some to fuck in and others to sleep in.

"When can we start smashing these mad Scousers up?" asked Luke.

"Sun Tzu said a protracted war doesn't benefit anyone," mused Connor. "But he also stated, 'If you know your enemy and know yourself you don't need to fear the result of a hundred battles'."

"I have a list of Ellis's businesses," said Tom. "We can start smacking them tonight."

Connor replied, "It's not Ellis. It's McKinley. Has been for years. Ellis kept him on the books as a sort of portal into that world and to mark his cards regarding any reprisals that might look to catch up with him. Apparently, he's been legitimate—ish—for years."

Luke's words put into words the confusion on the rest of their faces. "How's that? I thought those Arab horses the gypsies stole were illegal imports?"

"Caris said that was an enterprise that gave him ready cash without going back into drug dealing. The money would go into one of Caris's launderers and he'd pass it on to McKinley to pass to Ellis. Even in supposedly legitimate business transactions wheels can still be greased with loose cash. I'm not saying he's clean, but it's McKinley who handles all the criminal enterprises."

Ryan asked, "Why did he give Ellis all the praise—make out he was the King of Liverpool? Wouldn't he have wanted that cred for himself?"

"Because if he ever had his collar felt and was looking at serious prison time, he'd pin it all on him. Ellis is still the 'one that got away' for the NCA and Merseyside Police."

"Who's told you all this?"

"Various sources."

"So, you're saying McKinley controls the muscle in Liverpool, not Ellis? So, the businesses we've identified don't even belong to the person we need to be going after?" asked Ryan.

"Yeh. I think he deals mostly in cash too, but I am not sure what he's using it for. I'd guess he's paid a lot of the right people—people who will back him up in a fight."

Charlie said, "Yeh, there were a load of 'em that day they snagged Curtis and me."

"It gets worse than that. McKinley has formed a link with the Albanian mafia—and I mean the one back in that country not the gangsters down in London, although they are affiliated."

Ryan murmured, "For fuck's sake."

Connor ignored him and asked, "What do you think we should do, Tom?"

A few moments of silence passed before Tom replied, "We can't beat them head-on. It's harder to cut your teeth as a gangster in Liverpool than it is in Leeds, and McKinley has more soldiers than we do. And everything Derek knew, they will know. The only advantage we have is we're a family—we can co-ordinate better, our security is tighter. It'll have to be urban guerrilla warfare. We can't stay at our houses. We'll take cash and do bed and breakfasts."

When they nodded as a collective, Tom continued, "Nights out or any type of socialising that isn't to do with collecting intelligence will have to stop. And we need to reach out to everyone who is our ally. I have some contacts dotted around that me and my dad will go see. Curtis and Charlie, speak to our local ones. Luke, go see Hughie Birtle and let him know what's happening."

Tom looked at Connor, and Connor understood what Tom was trying to say—'*I'll lead the family, but I won't tell you what to do.*'

Connor added, "I have some moves I can make."

No one spoke for a few moments, until Ryan said, "Can't we do these conferences in the middle of, or after, we eat. I am fucking starving."

32

Ciara almost respected the Albanian minister's admiration for her figure for its blatancy. They sat opposite one another on plush, peach seats across a small coffee table with a matt black surface stood between them like an inert guard dog. A jug of ice water and two glasses sat on it. Behind them stood the Albanian flag—red with a silhouetted black double-headed eagle in the centre.

"I thank you for this interview, Mr Fico. I understand your ministry is particularly busy, especially at this time."

Dimples appeared as he smiled. The forty-six-year-old, with his jet-black, gelled hair and shadowed chin, reminded Ciara of an American 1950s advertising executive. The yellow and blue striped tie stood in a weird contrast to the Khaki suit.

"Do not be troubled. I wouldn't be much of a Minister for Europe and Foreign Affairs if I refused to engage with the media of European countries."

"Still. I am guessing you have vast requests for interviews and so have to be selective in whom you choose, so I thank you."

Fico leaned forward, and Ciara kept stoically smiling as he tapped her knee with the back of his fingers. "It is a pleasure, Miss Robson."

"Mr Fico—"

"Please, call me Bledi."

"OK. Bledi, Albania has been recognised as a 'potential candidate country' for the EU since 2000, and here we are two decades later and still not a member—frustrating, is it not?"

He clasped his hands. "Yes, of course. Albania has made continuing strides, but certain officials of the European Union government see fit to keep moving the line of achievement."

"Moving the goalposts, as we say in the United Kingdom."

"Ah, yes, moving the goalposts."

"During my interviews, I like to play devil's advocate—even if I have to reach. However, Albania had received 1.2 billion Euros in aid as an 'Instrument of Pre-accession Assistance', as it is titled, surely an indication of the seriousness of their intent?"

"Then why aren't we?"

"The last I was aware, is that they set reasonably sounding pre-conditions—reforms to your justice system, a new electoral law, open trials for corrupt judges, greater respect for the Greek minority and...there was something else, to drop the ambitions for a 'greater Albania'."

Ciara hid her smile at the predicted reaction. Fico raised his voice and seemingly forgot his charm offensive. "The EU acts as if it is Albania's parent. We can thrive with or without them. Those areas are populated with Albanian blood. The Treaty of London is still an insult to Albanians—half our land and people left outside our present borders. It is not us wishing to annex land that is not ours but for our people to be once more reunited. Perhaps you are too young to remember how the German people rejoiced at the collapse of the Berlin Wall—but the EU want to deny us that same justice."

Ciara sipped her water and asked, "Are you saying this is an ambition Albania would prioritise over entry into the EU?"

"We understand the meaning of compromise but that is different from the word capitulation."

A smooth politician—thought Ciara.

"If I may, Bledi, can I venture into a topic not directly related to international politics—although I will understand if you need permission from someone."

"I need no such permission." Fico bristled.

Ciara had only ever met a few men whom she considered had control of their male ego.

"Indeed, I did not think that was the case." She smiled again. "It is refreshing to talk to a politician whose every phrase is not scripted like some robot."

"Only men of fear have their words controlled."

Ciara agreed with the sentiment despite the minister speaking them more out of boast than wisdom.

"It is to do with the reputed organised crime element within Albania."

She watched him stiffen before thawing back into a relaxed posture. "Every nation on earth has organised crime of some type."

"With all due respect, Bledi, not all have the reputation for ruthlessness combined with global reach as does the Mafia Shqiptare."

The politician leant back. "I think some of the more dishonourable types like to fictionalise the idea of an Albanian criminal empire. That they have headquarters in the major cities here with evil hands reaching all over the world—this is ridiculous. If English criminals commit crime in other countries, are they an evil empire too?"

"But, Bledi, this isn't just the media. Interpol has reported findings to the fact, as well as other law enforcement agencies."

"Interpol claims to be the world police when in fact it is a European agency, no matter what the nationality of the puppet they put in power."

"Do you think that perception may have been a reason why this latest delay has occurred?"

"Who knows what goes on in the French president's mind. But this reputation Albania has of having organised crime is not a new one, so why delay at the last moment? Since you are to play devil's advocate, as you say."

She replied, "He might be misguided. Everyone I have spoken to here—members of the public, police—all express the sentiments you do. Unless I am approached by the said members of this supposed crime organisation then I will not be reporting there is one. And as a freelance journalist I will ensure the plight of your country to join the EU will be heard by many different outlets."

She thought she saw a flicker in his eyes at her words.

"Then I look forward to reading your articles, Ciara."

Oso kept his wariness of Eralda Mancuso, also known by her nickname of 'I Kuq'—*Red,* off his face. If the 'Ndrangheta decided to murder him, he suspected they would approach her for the task. Though an accepted and one of the most important members of the Mafia Shqiptare, she had blood ties to the Calabrese criminal organisation. He decided to keep the message he had received from the 'Ndrangheta in the wake of the Amsterdam assassinations to himself and out of the conversation.

Her dark hair, shaved on the right side, tumbled down to the left before being pinned away from her eyes. A black blouse covered her arms, with a grey chequered skirt coming past the knees—Oso suspected she had her assassin's blade strapped to her inner thigh.

He asked, "How are operations in Puglia progressing?"

Oso had wanted the heel of Italy's 'boot' to be one of his outposts—a step off into the EU; as such, the Mafia Shqiptare had guaranteed safe passage and housing to those 'chosen'. Forming a business relationship with the 'Ndrangheta—Italy's shadowy and massively influential mafia based in the 'toe' of Italy's boot—had been laborious but lucrative. Red, a dual citizen through her Albanian father and her Calabrese mother, had been his chief liaison for the operation.

"You now have eight families settled in the region who understand their debt to yourself, Krye. Our counterparts over there are satisfied with the proceedings—sometimes a personal visit can quell problems before they even arise. Maybe Mr Faja should take note."

Eralda's distaste for Andrei had not been subtle. Unlike his Mik—whose face never gave anything away—I Kuq's Italian passion made her a little easier to read. Oso encouraged the rivalry while giving the outward appearance of his disapproval of it.

"I am glad to hear this. Just because I do not wish for a corrupt European Union to dictate to my country does not mean I do not wish to take advantage of what they have to offer."

"That is why you are the Krye," she said. "You see and exploit opportunities."

Oso clasped his palms together. "There has been an opportunity that has appeared in our city. I will need your assistance in exploiting it."

"Tell me what you need," she answered resolutely.

"Firstly, I need a troublesome rook removing from the board."

Louis looked around the huge restaurant. He knew the outcome of the upcoming meeting could make or break the empire no one had envisioned him being able to create. He had deliberately chosen the furthest corner of The Paris Clarence so if it was an ambush, the assassin would have to make his way back through a sea of people, including two of his own men sat by the door, to escape. They were two killers who just looked like a couple of white-collar workers, and that was how Louis liked his close protection.

That said, some of the most dangerous people in his crew looked childlike, complete with effeminate voices. However, it was because of this, along with their penchant for oversized jackets, hoodies and geometrically patterned haircuts that meant he could not use them in these settings.

The glittering gold stripes popping off the red carpet matched the lighting above which bounced off the wooden walls and the velvet red, orange and black seats. The open kitchen provided a stark contrast with its steel blue layout and white-dressed kitchen staff.

Even taking this meeting had been an act of will. He had always kept money as the master focus of his criminal endeavours. Everything to do with it—from the flow of investment into an asset, to the re-investment of the profits of that asset into another, and round and round it went. Financially, the wisest decision would be to lift his protective wing off Rayella.

259

Professionals who lost sight of the overall intent in his game ended up either broke, beaten, tortured, imprisoned or killed—or all five.

He knew what had enabled him to rise and consolidate so much control over south-east London crime culture. It was not just one thing but a blend.

Louis's Irish-Nigerian father Dermont—a former pro boxer—married his Nigerian wife Emilohi and raised Louis in Little Lagos—the Nigerian Yorubas of Peckham in south London. He could not remember much from his time with his parents. He recalled loud arguments and occasional flashes of domestic violence with both initiating it but thought them generally happy.

His father liked a drink on a weekend, and he liked to smoke when he had been drinking. More than once he had come down the stairs in the morning to find his dad passed out on the sofa with an ashtray beside him. If it was not cigarettes, it was occasionally cannabis—strange when their house would be spotless but stank of weed.

A well-built man—a similar age to himself—entered, wearing a tan suede coat over a black knitted sweater and smart jeans.

The grey eyes seemed to take in the room as he approached. Louis stood and towered over the man whom he must have outweighed by a couple of stone.

"You wanting to check me over?"

"Nah, it's OK, Arben," replied Louis, holding out his hand. "If you're going to try and kill me, it would be the old motorcycle assassin when I step outside. And I don't think the police would have turned you into an informant just yet. Why? Are you wanting to pat me down?"

Arben shook his head and Louis's hand—strong grip.

They sat. A waitress came over, both men declined food and ordered coffee.

"Can I ask you a question?"

Louis replied, "Sure."

"If three geezers owed you money. One owed you five thousand, one owed you twenty thousand and another fifty thousand, and didn't pay—then it would reach a point when you'd have to get nasty, yeh?"

Louis nodded, and Arben continued, "Then which one would you chop up?"

Louis replied immediately, "The one owing five thousand."

Arben gave him an expression of approval. "Most would say the fifty-thousand-pound man."

"A dead man can't pay it back."

"So, you are focused on the real. But I knew that already. I reckon you are target number one for the Metropol'. All these well-paid jobs—special needs tutors, social workers, youth offending teams, prison warders all depend on black lads failing."

"You've been swotting up on me and now are appealing to my sense of injustice."

"It is an injustice when I see black street urchins, some in their twenties looking like fourteen, go into prison before coming out looking healthier than they go in—all those regular meals and pumping iron. Not your employees though—they all seem well fed."

"Well, in our thing you don't need a CV, and it isn't prejudiced. But I'm not here to discuss social inequality. Be rude, what you really wanting?"

Arben tucked his jaw in for a second, and said, "First thing is to know why a black G from London would protect a young girl on behalf of a white G from up north. Then I find out you were in the forces together."

"You see, if you had done your research, you'd know I wouldn't let any young girl be kidnapped by Albanian gangsters—I am like the black Liam Neeson that way."

"Even though you know a street war with us would cost you a lot of pounds as well as the lives of your soldiers?"

"Yes, even then, Bossman. Because I know you know it would cost you just as much—in time and money."

"Maybe. Or maybe I'd risk it—take over your turf, gain back that money and more in a year. And there will always be fresh soldiers when there's money to be made."

Louis said, "I know you're bare ruthless, Arben. That's why you're in charge and poor Enver has been away with the geese and not heard from. Not that I am sorry—Enver was an insecure little bitch and a slave to social media, ya get me? But you don't want it to come all on top for yourself this early, and that's why you came to see me. What I don't understand is why you're after my man in the first place?"

The British-Albanian looked at him for a few moments and said, "We all take orders from someone."

Louis shook his head. "I don't."

"Yeah, you do. If whoever supplies you wanted something doing, you'd do it."

Louis thought for a moment. "Fair enough."

"This guy is from the old country. I've been around loads of bad men—killers—but nothing like this. He's strange—he could sit in any boardroom of this city in the day, then kill someone in a back alley at night. Everything is like pure logic to him."

"Why you telling me this?"

"Cos nothing you're going to say is going to stop me solving this problem."

"I hear you."

Arben sipped his coffee. "This is my offer to you. I'll agree the girl is not to be touched. But Connor Reed—he is proving to be a pain. If you get in my way in dealing with him then I will declare war on your Southwark Union Gang."

"Have you opened a line of communication with my man?"

"I told you. It's above me and not an option."

"Then how come you're allowed to make this offer to me?"

"Because I have my orders, but I still run my crew here and it's up to me how to execute them."

Louis kept a blank expression on his face. Connor was more than a 'criminal acquaintance'—he was his Oppo, but their friendship was forged from war—military and street—as well as a liking for one another as people. And Louis knew

Connor to be a man of honour, despite how nasty he could be.

That said, Louis had a responsibility for a multimillion-pound business that well over a hundred people made money off, including soldiers, dealers, distributors, enforcers and mules. It was not just himself he would be putting at risk for his friendship, it would be all of them.

"This is my counter-offer. The SUG will not roll up in your yard if you give me your word none of his 'civilian' family or friends be targeted, cos that is when you'll see me switch."

The man stared at him for a few moments before responding, "Safe."

"Notice I said 'my organisation', I didn't say myself on my own."

"I don't understand how someone like you would latch yourself to a man destined to lose."

Louis smirked. "A man who sticks by his friends only when the going is good is a 'fair-weather friend', innit, like one of those glory supporter football fans. Besides, I wouldn't be too sure on the result, ya get me."

"Why is that?"

"All I'll say is the man is way more capable than you'd ever think. You're here negotiating with me because of the little army am in charge of, but I don't like going outside my own manor—I'll do it if I have to, but I like being a homebird, ya get me. But it doesn't faze him going into someone else's gaff—their hometown, city or country where they feel safe—and dealing with 'em there—even really, really naughty people. You into nature shows?"

Arben frowned for a moment. "Some are all right."

"I watched this clip on the internet where it showed these jaguars in Brazil, diving in the rivers after these caimans—like alligators and crocodiles but different somehow—dragging them onto the bank and eating the bastards. When I think about it, he's a bit like that. So it might be you who's bitten off more than he can chew—no pun intended." Louis sipped his coffee. "Now, do I have your word—your Besa."

The man smiled for the first time. "You have my Besa."

Bledi Fico still felt a warmth of pleasure every time his massive and suited bodyguard/chauffeur opened the door of the silver Bentley Continental GT. It was not the comfort of the ride, the performance of the vehicle or an admiration for the engineering—it was the symbolism of the power he possessed. Why else would both the Mafia Shqiptare and the back-channel financiers of the European Union court him?

The journey from his office on Dëshmorët e Kombit Boulevard to his home in the affluent hillside suburbs took nearly an hour. The night sky had clawed in and the street lights danced past.

His bodyguard's French nationality had raised eyebrows not only amongst his political peers but also with his mafia associates, who insisted they could protect him better for a fraction of the price. He told both groups his bilingual security officer was an asset when conducting business in Brussels and therefore worth the taxpayer expenditure. In truth, the hulking Fabrice cost the politician not one Lek, as he was the point of contact between him and certain officials within the EU.

He claimed the expense back anyway.

Bledi knew the dangers of the game he now played. However, old man Xhelli's influence, though near-absolute in Tirana, petered out into ripples away from their native Shqipëri. The Eurocrats would get their way eventually, so why should someone else profit? Xhelli's desire of an Ethnic Albania was a fantasy—a dream Bledi indulged him and publicly supported, as he had with the journalist that he would have loved to make his whore.

Finally they escaped the urban district and the Bentley hit his favourite part of the journey—the final fifteen-minute rural stretch into hills. Usually, they had the road to themselves at this time of night, but the distant vehicle lights of one of his few neighbours followed.

He meditated on the size and luxury of the Swiss home he would eventually live in once he had signed off on the reforms necessary for Shqipëri's absorption into the EU and received his windfall.

The Bentley began to slow when still over three kilometres away.

"What is wrong, Fabrice?" he called out in English—the language they shared.

"I do not comprends—understand—I fill up the fuel before you leave office."

The Continental juddered to an embarrassing halt. Seething anger blighted Bledi's relief, as whomever the neighbour driving behind was would naturally provide assistance but also dine out on the laughter the story would elicit upon retellings long afterwards. He would leave Fabrice in the car to guard, more as a punishment than a necessity, as he took the inevitable lift to his home. He would call one of the departmental lackeys to deliver the fuel as Fabrice waited.

The lights behind arrived fast—very fast. Bledi turned around and cursed, snatching his eyes away as the truck scalded them with full beams.

None of my neighbours own a truck.

The adrenaline shot his insides a few seconds before a giant's fist hit his body with a crushing, bone-snapping force. He barely registered the rain of glass.

Shock warded off the pain that circled like a pack of wolves.

A few moments of crushed stillness before he saw it pass the window. A nightmare of black—of leather and a motorcycle helmet.

The shocking cold swooshed in with the wrenching open of the left door.

The visor flicked up confirming what the figure had hinted—a woman.

She spoke in Albanian. "You should have asked your friends in Brussels for a bodyguard of a higher quality, one that would at least notice a slowly leaking fuel tank. That he didn't know his seatbelt had been tampered with is more forgivable. He left this beautiful car through the windscreen and his life upon impact."

The black icicles of her fingers evaporated his shock and stabbed his entire body with pain as they dragged him out by his lapels. His soul released agonised sobs as his body hit the asphalt.

She removed her helmet to reveal a sculpted face, with one side of her head shaven. The hair and eyes were as black as her leather.

"I didn't trust the seatbelt with a collision like this," she said with a wolfish smile. "You know, Bledi, there is a special place in hell for traitors."

The second helmet smash took his consciousness.

The sixth his life.

Connor drove the M6 following the tracker north. The black Mitsubishi Evo Tom gave him was a little conspicuous, but he needed a car with speed. He loved the black and silver interior and could feel the power of the vehicle beneath him.

A number he recognised as one of Louis's appeared on the dashboard through the encrypted phone. Connor had heard one of the reasons it had taken so long for law enforcement to ensnare Liverpool's infamous drug czar, Curtis Warren, was he never noted anything down; dates, names, figures, addresses, both e-mail or physical, numbers of any kind including account and telephone. Connor, lacking the photographic memory Warren must have had, used the 'Peg System' and the 'number-character-story' system to compensate.

Connor answered with, "Eey up."

"Wha-gwan."

"How did that thing go?"

"Good news and bad news. Which first?"

"Bad news—finish on a high and all that."

"When these Albanians go for you, I can't use the SUG to protect you."

Connor took a breath. "All right, rude boy, tell me the good news."

"This geezer has given me his honour—his Besa—that Rayella and any non-combatants in your friend and family circles aren't going to be touched. That was my price for a deal."

Connor's heart felt an expanse of gratefulness before he tempered it. "You believe him? That Besa thing is something the real Albanian mafia hold dear. Some of those Hellbanianz lads are descended from Kosovans who came over during that war."

"Nah, fam, he's a proper Gee. I knew about him before he took over, and you can tell after five minutes of talking to him."

"*Robocop it*," said Connor.

"I am not doing that, bruv. I am just saying I believe him. Funny you should say that about the old country mafia. Arben said he's working on orders—says a geezer "as come over from the old country' and is like a criminal version of *Rain Man*, except less autistic and more *The Terminator*."

"Who is he then?"

"He wouldn't tell me a name."

"If an Albanian high up in the real mafia is sniffing around Leeds, then that alone is bad news. The river of money running through here is only going to get larger. The government has OK'd millions for this City Region Enterprise Zone, and there're loads of other developments kicking off."

"Well, by the sounds of it, this cat will know that."

Connor knew it was irresponsible to take the Dutch security off his family, despite the deal Arben and Louis made.

"Are you OK to keep a watch over Rayella?"

"She'll have tight security while I am away."

Connor's stomach tightened. He did not like Louis being away while his lads were meant to be looking after Rayella—out of sight and of mind.

"Going anywhere nice?"

Louis laughed. "Fucking no, mate. I am going to a place that's full of backward inbreds and grim as fuck."

Connor's forehead creased. "Where?"

"Coming up to Leeds, aren't I."

"How come?"

"To give you a hand, you mong-child."

"You said—"

"I said I couldn't use the SUG. I told him that didn't include me."

Connor felt a flower of gratitude bloom in his chest. "Can't get you involved in—"

"Shut the fuck up, fam, you always go through this. Unlike your family, as good as they are, none of 'em have military operational experience like I do. Am coming up—end of story."

Connor hoped he would say that. "It'll be like Riggs and Murtagh"

"Nah, it'll be like Billy Ho and Sidney Deane."

"It'll be like Schultz and Django."

"This could go on all day," said Louis. "What you up to now?"

"Following a lead."

"Safe. I'll be up this evening."

"I'll send you the address."

The call clicked off, and Connor reached for the screen of his phone and tapped it.

It rang a few times before Caris's weary voice answered. "Yes?"

"Do this for me, and your debt is paid—you have my word on it."

"Why should I believe you?"

"Because I didn't need to say that to get you to comply, you nugget."

Caris asked resignedly, "What do you want me to do?"

Connor laid out his instructions concisely and made Caris repeat them to him before ending the call.

He looked at the tracker page as it refreshed. It showed McKinley heading towards Kendal.

33

The ceiling lighting above doused the entire bar in a red hue. Ciara sat on a stool, looking at the mural artwork of Ernest Hemingway next to the quotation of 'An intelligent man is sometimes forced to be drunk to spend time with his fools'.

She sipped the milky raki, enjoying the aniseed and fruit flavour. A bottle of water stood on her left in response to her request to dilute the forty-per cent alcohol. She avoided eye contact with the men dotted around the bar. They were all smartly dressed. With quiet music playing, voices did not have to be raised to be heard.

Her stretch jeans ended at her brown ankle boots. Dressing for function and fashion as a female agent had been more challenging for her than her male counterparts— Connor almost always wore footwear he could run and fight in, whereas ankle boots were the best she could do on this occasion. Her green leather jacket fell over her cream shirt.

Ciara had first spotted her follower hours ago when leaving the Supreme Court of the Republic of Albania after a dignitary gave her a tour of it. She waited for the gap to appear amidst the yellow taxis and cyclists before crossing the road into a park criss-crossed with footpaths. In carrying out a counter-surveillance technique of doubling back on herself, Ciara spotted her—a tanned woman, with her head shaven on its right side, and the rest of the jet-black hair pinned back. She had been wearing a black jacket and white jeans.

Now the woman sat in the far corner behind Ciara in an air of fierce attractiveness and a change of attire. Her smoky mascara highlighted large coffee eyes. The hair—the blackness of which Ciara used the word 'noirette' for their owners—fell past the left shoulder before curving inward at the bottom to seemingly draw attention to the ample cleavage which the tight, ash dress opened to reveal. The dress showed her muscled, shapely legs from her mid-thigh, ending with white, strappy shoes. Grooves of muscle etched the forearms.

Surprising to Ciara was neither she nor the girl had been approached by any of the men yet.

After a time, the raven-haired woman stood and approached the bar. Ciara remained nonchalant as the girl, who appeared to be in her late twenties, stood closer to her than was necessary—her perfume smelling faint and exquisite.

She ordered in Albanian before turning to Ciara and saying in English, "Is it your first time drinking raki?"

Ciara met her gaze. "Yes, first time."

A beguiling smile lit up the noirette's face. "You have made good choice in asking for a bottle of water."

"I thought it sensible." Ciara smiled back.

The bartender gave the woman what Ciara knew to be a Gorani Sok—a fruity, fermented drink with a low alcohol content. The bartender did not ask—nor did the woman offer—any payment.

She turned to Ciara and raised her glass. "Gezuar."

Ciara clinked her glass with hers. "Gezuar."

The woman asked, "First time in Tirana?"

"First time in Albania."

"We are complicated but friendly," said the noirette as she lightly touched Ciara's forearm with her fingertips. "My name is Eralda."

Ciara instantly understood—*she thinks I am a lesbian*. This had happened a few times in Ciara's life—she could see how her short hair combined with an uncommonly muscular feminine physique would hint at 'Butch'. In her agent's training, she had been taught, amongst other things, how lesbian and heterosexual flirting could differ. One had been that lesbian displays of attraction could be subtler; a series of exchanged 'hooks'—eye contact, a returned smile, a specific compliment.

"My name is Ciara."

"Sarah?"

"No—'See-air-rah'. I think my father might have been driving a car model of that name, although mine is spelt differently."

"It's a beautiful name."

"So is yours."

"Are you alone?"

"I am." Ciara said. "Here with work."

"Are you wishing to be left alone?"

Oohh—thought Ciara—*you took a risk there. What if I said yes?*

"You're not going to rob me, are you?" she said playfully instead.

The noirette laughed like a song, before saying, "None of your possessions, no."

"Then I'll be glad of your company."

Eralda pulled up a stool and sat close. "So what brings you to Tirana?"

"I am a freelance journalist. Boring stuff really— investigating the challenges Albania is having in respect to its potential membership into the EU."

Eralda sipped her Gorani Sok. "I do not think it is boring at all. Who have you been interviewing?"

Ciara sighed. "Just various government officials."

Eralda feigned a yawn. "The same people who have their words prepared before you even speak to them, yes?"

Ciara said. "They are politicians, after all."

Eralda lightly placed her hand on Ciara's forearm. "Not everyone here wants us to join those criminals in Brussels, maybe just the criminals you have interviewed. I hope you don't restrict your questions to only those kinds of people."

"I want to interview a cross section, but my Albanian is pidgin at best, and I do not have access to all the differing societal classes. And I want to paint a broad and accurate picture of what's going on here."

"Pidgin?"

"I mean, my Albanian isn't very good."

"If you are serious about wanting to report what is really happening, I can help you."

"I would like that very much."

Ciara held eye contact before Eralda reached over and gently turned the lapel of Ciara's jacket out. "I really like the way you dress."

Ciara let her fingertips stroke Eralda's before saying, "I like to think all my garments look good on me."

Ciara checked the size of Eralda's hands as was her habit before admonishing herself for doing so—*she's a woman and it's a myth anyway—sort of.*

Eralda pursed her lips. "Why don't you let me show you some of the sights of Tirana."

"I would like that."

Darkness had long descended on the old market town of Kendal as Connor alighted from the black Evo. It lay around the back of a small desolate car park outside a Judo club, and he lifted the boot and grabbed one of two daysacks—the green role, not the black role.

Hours earlier, the tracker had begun to lead him up a narrow, long, winding country road and he knew he had to withdraw. He did not know what McKinley would be doing up there but taking his Evo up in broad daylight would be begging to get caught. He headed through the quiet streets instead, before skirting around the town. One of the pubs had a quiz night, and Connor lamented on how before the advent of smartphones, two men could argue all night about something that could be now resolved with a few taps of a screen.

Eventually, the town petered out behind him along with the streetlamps. He climbed a fence before melding into the edge of woodland. There, he rummaged through his daysack, pulling out his 'old school' *DPM* trousers, combat jacket and a pair of *pussers* boots.

Earlier, as he waited for darkness to fall, he had completed a map study of the route from where he now stood to the point where McKinley's tracker had halted. He remembered cringingly how, back in his Royal Marine career, some lads—*shit blokes*—used to just set a waypoint on their GPS and trundle off. However, maps could be dated or inaccurate—they could show features like dense woodland when only a smattering of trees would be present. Fortunately, this woodland housed tall trees and dense vegetation.

He had incorporated Naismith's rule—fifteen minutes for every kilometre of horizontal distance, plus ten minutes for every hundred metres of ascent—into his map study, as well as navigation checks and pauses to listen for any potential patrols of any kind. In doing so, he estimated the near four-kilometre patrol ought to take around an hour and a half. He allowed himself a couple of hours for the actual reconnaissance.

He fought the urge to don any warm kit against the chill that had befallen the meadow, remembering an adage of his past military career—*Be bold, set off cold. Or start redders, and then be threaders.*

He removed the lid of the green plastic box of a similar size to a tin of blusher. Inside, on one side lay three colours—black, green and brown—of the almost clay-like camouflage paint, with a mirror on the other.

"Fuck's sake," he whispered—he always hated putting it on, knowing the rigmarole of taking it all off, even with the baby wipes he had. It reminded him of the British Military mantra of—*"Civies would pay thousands for this"*—often spouted by sergeants taking charge of shooting ranges—civvies might not if they knew they could not go on their weekend leave until the rifle was spotlessly clean.

Still, he applied the 'cam cream' liberally with his fingers, breaking up the features of his face and ensuring no flesh patches were on display. He would have covered his hands too but the dexterity the gloves provided by Jaime meant he did not have to.

He still got a kick out of the night-vision glasses the cyber genius had provided him, which essentially looked like standard glasses albeit thicker and heavier; and they truly did make night into day without giving off any glare. Back in the Marines, the night vision looked like one half of a pair of binoculars strapped to the helmet, that required the turning and tightening of various knobs to fit correctly over the eye and to focus them. How Jaime got hold of various gadgets he provided Connor with only he and maybe Bruce knew.

The only weapons he possessed were the commando dagger strapped to the inside of his left forearm, and a Taser in a pouch strapped to his combat belt. Though he had access to a few armouries in the UK through his status as a Chameleon Project agent, and could also obtain firearms through various underworld contacts, Connor refused to get into the habit of carrying. His father had done prison time for possession of a gun that was not even his.

The leaves crackled in the dark wind, and frost glinted off the ground. The cold air felt cleansing to his lungs, and he realised he had not spent any sustained time outdoors since leaving the Marines. Not that he enjoyed it back then—the terrain and climate of the Brecon Beacons in Wales or the Munroes of Scotland, the weight of a small person cutting into his trapezius through Bergen straps, and the sleep deprivation of the soldiering routine throughout a week-long exercise made it only enjoyable to masochists—*or Mountain Leaders*, he thought grimly.

The terrain flattened out half a kilometre from the target and, after a time, began to descend.

Through the trees on the high ground he saw it—the side of some sort of farmhouse complex. Out of his daysack he grabbed his 'Head and shoulders'—a jungle hat with long strips of DPM clothing stitched throughout it to break up the outline of his head and shoulders. Wearing it always evoked the image to Connor of a Rasta with green dreadlocks.

Next, he pointed his laser range finder at the building— 178 M flashed up. After that, he took a few pictures with a 'First-photon Image Intensifier' camera that could take photos in the pitch black.

He saved them under the GPS position along with the distance. He chose his memo app and whispered a few observations.

He slid back into the forest. In both the Marines and his *FIWAF* training under Finnish Special Forces instructors, he had been taught the reconnaissance technique of 'Petalling'—

observing and noting in one position before covertly moving to another spot to carry out the same routine from another angle. It had proved time-consuming on his Junior Command course to become a corporal; instead of picture taking, detailed sketches were made, and instead of voice notes, observations were written before being collated into a patrol report—*this should be a piece of piss. Apart from the torture and likely death if caught bit,* he mused.

He stalked up to higher ground. He spotted a pair of armed sentries wandering about. After a few moments, he ID'd the weapons to be AK47s. He could make out the bulges in the thick black, bubble jacket even from the distance he was observing at—89 M.

The dog bark pierced the night.

"Fuck," Connor whispered. Dogs, he knew, had 300 million receptors in their noses in comparison to the six million humans had, and the part of their brain responsible for analysing these scents was forty times greater than their human counterparts. The agent knew that even if he had spent a week in the field, whatever dog it was could easily detect him at this distance. His curse almost choked him when he saw another man wheel around the corner with a monster of a German Shepard on a lead—only the Beagle, Basset Hound and Blood Hound had a better sense of smell, and none of them could savage a man like an Alsatian could.

The dog pulled its owner to the edge of the fence line. Mercifully, though the man craned his head and presumably squinted his eyes, he did not seem to don any night vision on his person or scope on his weapon. Connor began receding slowly back, deeper into the tree line. He kept his green gaze on the scene even though he had confidence the men could not see him in the cloudy darkness.

His heart pumped as he observed the man reach down for the collar, before exploding in adrenaline as the unleashed Alsatian leapt the fence. Connor turned and ran as hard as he could.

The vicious barks got louder and louder, vibrating his primal brain with fear.

He did not kid himself that he could outrun the dog, but he needed as much distance between dealing with the dog and men who would come sooner or later.

The barks now seemed to swirl around his legs as he unclipped the pouch.

He spun around to see the saliva flying off the leaping wolf-like fangs.

The prongs shot into the dog with an electric crackle. The animal dropped in a strange convulsing stiffness. Connor suppressed a giggle, as the dog's eyes bulged out and its tongue hung out, giving the appearance of demented laughing.

He removed the prongs and began running again. His hope was that the animal lived—if it did not die, it would eventually wander back after the shock wore off. Connor knew from experience that the beast would not be capable of running down and savaging anyone for a few hours.

If it did die, the situation could get complicated.

34

Ciara and Eralda drew stares walking to, and when they were in, the bars they visited. Despite being only a touch taller, the Italian-Albanian's frame made Ciara feel almost masculine in comparison. Not that it bothered her. She realised in her late teens she did not seem to feel the same hang-ups regarding her appearance as did other women; not that she did not care, but she had an awareness of her attractiveness without it meaning the be all and end all to her.

Eralda turned out to be great fun and Ciara allowed herself to enjoy her company. In every bar, the staff seemed to treat Eralda with an inordinate amount of respect—and she never paid for any drinks. When Ciara had asked her about this, Eralda replied, "I am a member of an organisation here that supports the people."

She had been amusingly evasive when Ciara pressed her— "Maybe after a few more drinks."

During the evening, Eralda became increasingly tactile, touching her on the forearm, hand and knee. And Ciara's body was responding to it.

Ciara feigned mild surprise at Eralda's offer that she could sleep at hers. She accepted, nonetheless.

The black converted Mercedes pulled up outside the quiet bar. Eralda opened the back door for her, and Ciara felt the light stroke on her backside as she bent down to get in.

As soon as they were both in, the car set off and a blind surrounded the glass between the driver's compartment and themselves. Ciara turned to face her, stroking the soft cheek with the back of her fingers before gripping Eralda's jaw and drawing her into an open-mouthed kiss.

The Italian-Albanian responded enthusiastically. It felt strange—softer than a man's kiss—with the heady perfume adding to the thrill, as their tongues met. Ciara interlaced her fingers with Eralda's as they crept up her leg and pressed her hand against her stretch jeans-clad pussy, as Eralda moaned into her mouth.

If she wants the image she has of me, she can have it—thought Ciara, before releasing her hands, reaching under and drawing up the hem of the dress. Her fingers danced on the inside of the thighs, before they were squeezed together, trapping her hand before opening more fully. Ciara stroked her thumb around the silk mesh patch, before hooking it to one side and delving her fingers into the hot, wet pussy.

Eralda buried her face into Ciara's neck, biting, kissing and whimpering in Italian.

The car slowed and Eralda whispered, "Fermare, fermare. I mean, stop, stop, stop."

Ciara gripped her jaw again—harder this time. "We'll stop when I say."

She pressed her pussy-juice stained fingers into Eralda's sucking mouth.

The car halted, and Eralda's hands smoothed her dress back into position, before opening the door.

They got out onto a downward slope. The big, white houses, with their large windows, and grey slate roofs were separated by great, green clouds of trees. The sounds of crickets bathed under the soft amber streetlights.

With the pressing of a key fob, the shiny, black gates drew back like curtains.

Eralda led her up the stone stairs to the side entrance of the luxury villa. Yellow lights reflected off a turquoise Jacuzzi to the right.

"Wow, you must be successful at whatever you do," said Ciara.

"Thank you," she said. "Would you like to swim?"

"Maybe another time."

Eralda opened her door into a huge kitchen, with a grey-blue marble table as a centrepiece.

"Would you like coffee—or English tea? I have some."

Ciara stepped towards her and said, "Don't be acting the coy virgin now. I didn't accept your invite for drinks, or swimming or anything else except bedding you. Now stop wasting time and take me to your bedroom."

Ciara watched her lips part and eyes dilate, before turning slowly and leading her by the hand up the spiral stairs. As Eralda's backside swayed, Ciara mused that she may not have to feign enjoying it. She logged into her memory the layout of the house, items and any security apparatus.

Eralda turned the brass handle to a wood carved door and opened it into a large bedroom. The walk-in wardrobe stood to the left, along with a large mirror in front of a sit-down table. On the right, a door of frosted glass presumably led to the bathroom and shower. The bed looked huge—Emperor size—with the pink and beige duvet rising up out of the velvet, tuffet frame.

As Eralda turned to face her, Ciara brushed passed her and sat on the frame.

"Take your clothes off, slowly."

The noirette blinked a couple of times before reaching up behind her neck and untying her dress. It fell to reveal a physique of hard muscle and sensual curves. Her breasts stood high and proud. The black patch of her pussy hair was visible beneath the white gauze of her black trimmed knickers.

Ciara stood and began to undress while looking into Eralda's dark eyes; she looked at Ciara with as much hunger as any man had.

"Come here," Ciara commanded.

Eralda woodenly complied until Ciara said, "Stop."

When Eralda did so, Ciara said, gesturing with her fingers, "Give me a twirl—slowly."

She placed her hands on Eralda's hips, halting her as she faced away. She drew her back onto her, slid her hands around—one cupping her tits, feeling the hard nipples under her palm and the other gripping her pussy with delving fingers.

"You're soaking."

"Yes," Eralda croaked.

"You're mine now, you dirty bitch," Ciara whispered, her teeth lightly pressed into the top of her ear.

The Albanian-Italian's moan intensified into a gasp as Ciara snatched her head back by the hair. She marched her over to the bed, positioning her on all fours with her arse raised up and legs explicitly splayed. Kneeling behind her, she gripped and exposed Eralda's pussy and arsehole.

Been a long time since I've done this—mused Ciara—*better do a good job. I need her exhausted before me.*

At one a.m., McKinley fought to control the elation in his veins as the M62 motorway lights zipped by. He passed Stotts Farm, remembering his 'arl fella before he became an addict taking him up to Huddersfield for a collection, and telling him that the government had offered the farmer millions to move but the stubborn bastard refused, so they built it around him. He believed the story until a few years ago, when Ellis set him straight—there was some sort of fault under the earth.

McKinley would have been happy to keep Ellis as his lightning rod for a few more years—indeed, he had been surprised the ruse had lasted this long. However, he had rinsed Ellis of as much as he could, knowledge-wise, and had steadily forged the loyalty of criminal connections that once had an allegiance to the elder crime lord. They could all see what was happening anyway—Harry Ellis was a legitimate businessman still trying to hold on to his name, still dipping his toe in when it suited him, and when guys want to go kosher, that was when the plod turned them into grasses.

Now McKinley would take his place as the boss of Liverpool—the Prince of the city after tonight. He could not believe the opportunity he had been afforded in this time of change; all the Ryder men in the one spot along with the gypsies who had stolen the horses.

They thought they could use Caris to broker a deal for the horses; expecting him to make the journey up the M62 to some shitty scrapyard in Halifax. Their naivety in thinking Caris would not tell him—despite the high five-figure broker fee the Ryder's were offering—was laughable.

McKinley had grinned listening to the sly Caris's recording of Connor Reed's salesman tactics: "*If this goes well, we'll be using you regularly*", and "*We're only going to get bigger, which means more coin in your pocket*".

McKinley felt a tinge of pride at how his legal fixer had played the divvy Yorkshireman. First, he stated his reluctance due to his fear of McKinley's discovery of his helping his enemies, and if there was likely to be any violence at the site.

"*How would he ever find out? I am not going to tell him, and neither are you*", and "*No one is going tooled up*", had been the soothing ripostes.

McKinley did not know who they were selling the horses to, but they would just have to be collateral. Although not apparent to anyone looking, he now drove the rear vehicle of a convoy with three other nondescript cars that held twelve lads. He knew them all; they were all solid and all killers—the same men who had shot up Michael Ryder. Still, to lessen the risk of one of them informing on him after the fact, he had given the cash and the instructions to one of them, who divvied out both to the rest of the men.

He had been tempted to ask the Albanian for shooters—if they got caught, they would be less likely to grass. However, he would not be able to control them.

As the convoy peeled off the M62 onto the A672, McKinley could feel his excitement build as it had when embarking on any major 'job'. The difference now was the excitement of his own power, not the danger. He was a boss now, and bosses did not get their hands dirty—it was like what the old man said in that film *The Layer Cake*—"*you take shit from day one, rise up, and one day you forget what shit even tastes like*", or something like that.

Still, he wanted to be there—wanted to see the shot-up bodies of Connor, Tom and all the rest, as well as those dirty gypsies.

All the lads were armed with silenced pistols—although the scrapyard was out the way, multiple guns going off on any other night than bonfire night would have people looking out their windows and the police zooming down. Even if they escaped before they got there, they would have their chopper out—'*pigs do fly, they are called police helicopters*', had been his dad's joke.

The sat nav told him the target lay four minutes away, and that meant they would be stopping in three and a half minutes. The plan was to park in and around the residential streets a couple of hundred metres away before making the rest of the way on foot.

The tips of his fingers and toes began to tingle as the cars slowed before turning off into streets and parking up. He followed suit, parking further along, fighting the urge to join them as they got out—*you're a General now, not a soldier.*

As they disappeared, his fingers began drumming on the steering wheel—*a General oversees the battle, you're just sat here like a spoon.*

Opening the door, he walked out in the eerie silence of the crisp dark. He kept his head down as he broke into a jog before slowing back into a walk—*people remember joggers at this time of night.*

A nervous ball of energy ballooned in his stomach as he took the dark side street leading up to the scrapyard, and he ran. He had looked at Google Maps while planning this and knew it was near.

It briefly narrowed into a snicket before opening out again into some young woodland skirting an expanse of wasteland.

His men must have been still in it—he had told them not to cross the open ground in case it alerted their prey to an ambush; not that they could escape, the yard only had one entrance and exit, and he gazed at it now.

He crept forward and knelt. He could see the row of Portakabins, and one of them had the lights on—this would be easy. Finally, the guys appeared and crept up to the wall of the entrance with their pistols out.

He could not remember the last time he had felt such excitement.

Their shadows followed the men through the gate as they made their way to the lit Portakabin.

A whoosh of shock dived into McKinley's mouth, as the men silently collapsed beside their shadows. His heart pounded in his ears as men appeared like ghosts around the fallen.

A concoction of fear and anger injected itself into the shock in his veins as the half silhouette of Connor Reed appeared amongst the men and tilted his head back—*the cunt's laughing.*

McKinley remained transfixed, watching Reed use his foot to lift the heads of those who had collapsed on their faces. Reed then opened his arms with his palms in the air in a gesture of annoyance, and it dawned on McKinley—*he expected me to be there.* The Yorkshireman put something around his eyes—glasses it looked like.

The Liverpudlian's mouth fell open as it seemed Reed's head snapped up to look right at him. McKinley exploded to his feet as Reed began sprinting at him, before he ran on jelly legs back through the snicket.

Adrenaline pressed its cold fuel into his legs although time seemed to be slowing. He hit the street where his car stood poised, and stuffed his awkward fingers into his pocket, grasping his keys.

The fob bleeped open the car door, and McKinley dived in, his key slotting into the ignition on the second attempt. He took off down the street just as Connor Reed burst out of an opening between two houses on the left side of the road in front of him.

His pursuer's wolf-like grin morphed into a laugh and sent a burning blade searing through his ego.

35

Ciara sat on the floor of her hotel room in full splits. Bare legged, her cream blouse wrapped around her torso, and her 'fighting' trainers on her feet—her training necessitated she be aware of potential intruders, especially when on assignment.

Using her 'work' phone she dialled the memorised number. It rang once before being answered by a digitalised voice: "Are you OK?"

"I am fine," answered Ciara, meaning "*I am not under duress*".

"What do you need?" asked Jaime Rangel.

"I've activated SIM card clone number 32657A. Patch me its live tracker to my phone, please."

"I will activate it. Anything else?"

"No, thank you."

A cab from 'City Taxi'—Albania has no Ubers—had picked her up from Eralda's villa early in the morning. She would have said goodbye but knew the Tirana native would not be roused from her deep sleep for at least another few hours—Ciara knew, because she had stuck the patch of gamma-hydroxybutyrate and gamma-butyrolactone onto Eralda's back once she had fallen asleep and did not peel it off until the full ten-minute absorption time had expired. From there, Ciara had—after dabbing her fingers in the tub of silicone caulk disguised as lip palm—spent over two hours of intelligence gathering before taking Eralda's phone to give Jaime the SIM card details.

She had left a note with the phone number of her 'normal' phone.

Ciara had known who Eralda 'I Kuq' Mancuso was the moment she spotted her following her that day. The Mafia Shqiptare hit woman provoked fear not only throughout the city but received respect amongst the members of Italy's 'Ndrangheta. Ciara's confidence grew when the assassin had introduced herself—if she had wanted to kill or capture her,

284

Ciara would not have seen her face—she would have simply been picked up by a corrupt policeman or surveilled back to her hotel. And Ciara did not kid herself—though they were both killers, Eralda's body count dwarfed her own.

Though Eralda would have been given orders to befriend and subvert Ciara to a narrative, there had been no doubt in her mind the lesbian had genuinely desired her.

Ciara—though firmly a man-eater—had enjoyed the night too. It had not been her first time with a woman—but it had been the first with an ardent lesbian. At first, she had felt faintly ridiculous when assuming 'scissors' position, but after a time she lost herself as they both came.

Bruce had confirmed he shared Ciara's own suspicions the Mafia Shqiptare would not want Albania to become a member of the EU. Requisites of membership would include a crackdown on corruption and an adherence to EU law. Though Interpol had offices in Tirana, the mafia here could still subvert the judicial system to a degree.

To her mind, Ciara could think of two ways they could use her to influence the European authorities that Albania was not ready for membership: one would be to influence her to write an article detailing why it would not be, and the other would be to kill her. The latter would be the course of action she would have chosen if she led the mafia in Tirana. She replaced the image of a fly in a Venus trap with a rat eating itself out of a snake's stomach.

The ring of her phone—her 'normal' one—interrupted the sobering thought. She recognised the number but feigned ignorance upon answering, "Hello."

"Hello, Ciara."

"Didn't expect for you to call so soon," she replied, edging in a flirtatious tone. "You seemed so peaceful sleeping, I did not want to wake you."

"Well, I do not know how long you will be in our beautiful country and besides, I do not like to play games."

"Neither do I."

"Can I kidnap you for tomorrow?"

"As much as I might like that, this is supposed to be a journalistic mission."

"Do not be troubled. I have people you can meet—I remember our conversations."

"Who am I to meet?"

"Ahh, he is a local businessman and community leader—he knows the people and they know him. I have told him about you, and he is kind enough to offer an audience to you."

"How do you know him?"

Ciara could guess but had to fully take on the persona of being strictly a journalist in search of the truth.

"I work for him from time to time."

"You see, we never discussed what it is you do?"

"We can talk when we see one another again. I'll send a driver."

Ciara was not sure if Eralda would already know which hotel she would be in. The standard practice—as per her Chameleon Project agent training—when on assignment was to book into a hotel under her real name but not stay there; instead, she stayed at another underneath an alias, that way she would escape any 'name flagging' checks made. However, she might have been ID'd as to staying here.

"I am going to go over to Skanderbeg Square in the morning. I can meet you there?"

"Yes, of course."

Connor heard the steps behind him and turned to see Tom.

"Who was it?" asked Tom.

"McKinley," Connor replied, dragging his phone out of his pocket and dialling Caris's number. When it cut to voicemail he spun to his cousin as he took his jacket and gloves off. "Get rid of those bodies ASAP. Rinse the entire killing zone with the cola. If I was McKinley, I'd ring the police and send them straight to the scrapyard, and that's bad news. I am going to have to blast it down the M62. I'll explain later. Take these and burn them with yours. If I get pulled for speeding they might put two and two together and test them for propellant."

With that, he gave Tom his jacket and gloves, who broke into a sprint.

Connor did the same in the opposite direction and after just over a minute found his car. The Evo's speed pressed him back into his seat. He ran through the likely scenarios. He would probably catch McKinley—Connor knew it unlikely McKinley would be a better driver than himself at speed, and the two to three-minute head start would not be enough. He could not run him off the road or shoot him—the M62 still had vehicles on it even at this time of night, as well as being peppered with cameras including ANPR (Automatic Number Plate Recognition)—*and I am not Vin Diesel.*

Connor—putting himself in McKinley's mind—anticipated he would head to Caris's for answers. He would get them too—someone like McKinley would be able to tell immediately if someone like Caris was lying—unlike the courtroom, the threat of violence would act as truth serum.

Connor dialled Caris again through the Bluetooth connection—no answer.

He thought about something he said to Tom before he had driven off. He tapped in the three-digit number as he slowed the Evo.

McKinley burned down the motorway both in speed and inside of himself. He needed to look in Caris's eyes and ask him if he knew. The fixer had been going through a rough time of it lately, he guessed—his sexy piece of a wife had not been on the scene.

McKinley gripped the steering wheel tighter. Instead of underestimating Reed, he should have questioned why he would contact his fixer. Should have questioned why Caris recorded it from the off—he could not record every call; it would be hanging tackle should the CPS ever get hold of them.

A thought flew into his head—call the police and send them to the scrap yard. He reached for his phone before retracting his arm—he had not brought a disposal phone; there would be a major investigation, and they would track it. Once they had their claws in, they would not give up—he could throw them Ellis, but he would go down too, and as a grass. He thought about a payphone, but quickly dismissed the idea—it would be too hard to find one and he had no coins.

Reed might try and warn the lawyer, but McKinley remembered Caris's mantra regarding contacting him—'*Only Batman and ladies of the night work past ten o'clock. I am in bed with the phones off.*'

He knew now Reed would not be dumb enough to chase him into Liverpool and it was not as if the Yorkshireman would be shooting him from car to car on the M62. Suddenly, he wondered why he was risking the attention of the traffic police and slowed.

After an hour, he curved into and through the residential area leading up to Caris's home. He turned the corner and saw the flashing blue of a police light.

Two coppers were perched on his legal fixer's step as the dressing gown clad Caris appeared to be remonstrating with them.

"Fuck," whispered McKinley. It was a one-way street and he could not reverse, or at least not without looking suspicious.

He set the car trundling up the road. The police turned to briefly look at him, but his gaze focused on Caris's face—and that was when McKinley knew he had betrayed him.

36

The sun peered through the buildings overlooking Skanderbeg Square, reflecting its warmth across the vast flooring of multi-coloured stone tiles. Even this early in the morning, people walked Tirana's main plaza. Ciara had read the square had been named after an Albanian nobleman and military commander who led a twenty-five-year rebellion against the Ottoman Empire.

The entire square totalled around forty square metres, and many buildings of historical and cultural significance rested on its perimeter. She stood admiring the eleven-metre grand Skanderbeg monument before her; on four layers of white, block stone sat the proud, bearded, jut-chinned, sword wielding Skanderbeg in the saddle of a majestic horse.

"Do you know much about Skanderbeg?" said the man's voice.

She turned her head to look at him—around sixty, long grey hair with flecks of white as with his flowing moustache. He had the physique of a farmer who ate heartily, encased in a white shirt, black leather jacket and jeans.

"I know some. He was a major factor in grinding the Ottoman Empire's expansion to a halt. Had a massive influence in fifteenth-century European history."

The man nodded. "His real name was Gjergj Kastrioti. Did you know he rose through the ranks of service to the Ottoman sultan for twenty years before deserting them at the Battle of Niš?"

"Yes. I also know originally he was sent to the Ottomans as a hostage, not voluntarily."

"Sent, not taken," said the man, stroking his moustache. "A common practice amongst various cultures at the time to ensure alliances did not break."

"I thank you for the history lesson, Mister…?"

"Mister Xhelli."

"Do your friends get to call you Oso?"

The corner of his mouth twitched. "I do not have many friends left, but to answer your real question, yes—my name is Oso Xhelli."

"Should I be afraid?"

"Why would you be afraid?"

"I am thorough in my research on entering a city, Mr Xhelli. A man like you might not appreciate the presence of a foreign journalist."

"I appreciate anyone who attempts to educate the uneducated. A person with an open mind, not a pre-determined story."

Ciara made a show of looking around. "I am a little surprised. I thought you would be accompanied by burly men in suits and sunglasses."

"How powerless is a man who cannot walk freely in his own city?"

"Powerful men attract powerful enemies."

"This is true."

"Then I guess you aren't entirely alone—maybe your security watches over you from a distance."

Ciara did not elaborate but if she had, she would have told him of her suspicions of sniper overwatch in one of the buildings as well as some of the wandering pedestrians being members of his security team.

He replied, "She said you were smart. I can see that now."

"Eralda," she replied rhetorically. "I must say, Mr Xhelli, your English is perfect. I realise around half of Albanians can speak it, but nowhere near the fluency you do. Especially an Albanian man as mature as yourself."

He smiled. "You are correct. Not many my age can speak it this well. However, with the fall of communism, the elected Democratic Party contracted a woman from England as an interpreter. Her mother and father had escaped to London during the communist repression. They returned when it fell. And I, wanting to improve, bought lessons from her for five years."

Ciara tilted her head. "Just lessons?"

He laughed. "No. Not just lessons. However, my mastery of the language helped in business, as it is now."

"Impressive."

"Shall we take a walk?"

"As long as a walk doesn't turn into a car ride. Or down dark alleys or bar basements and so on and so forth."

"Park Rinia is half a kilometre from here. The streets are all on the surface and we walk past the Resurrection of Christ Orthodox Cathedral. Would I have you murdered in the sight of God?"

At that, he pressed his palms together and bowed his head sagely. She gave a small, though genuine laugh, before saying, "Do you mind if I ask you questions during our walk?"

"You can ask me anything."

"I assume a recorder is out of the question?"

"You assume correctly," he said, before gesturing towards their direction of travel. "Shall we?"

They set off and Ciara began, "May I ask—because I have never been given a definitive answer—what religion is your...ahem...organisation made up of."

"The majority claim to be Muslims, but not solely. We have our own code of ethics that supersede religion. As a discerning journalist you'll know Albania is a secular state with no official religion—that socialist puppet Hoxha took a lot of pride in declaring Albania the world's first atheist nation. Various media and law enforcement agencies like to cast us in a dark shadow of helping terrorists."

Ciara knew about the divisive communist politician Enver Hoxha who served as Head of State from 1944 to 1984. Many praised his efforts in rebuilding post-war Albania while many criticised the various political repressions he brought about.

"You deny your organisation has ever dealt with Muslim fundamentalists?"

"Do you deny members of the newspapers you sell your articles to may be liars, cheats, abusers?"

"No. But I haven't seen it and, more importantly, I do not instruct them to be liars, cheats or abusers."

They walked towards Taivani, a huge, white, terraced restaurant and multi-functional recreation complex that looked to Ciara like a Bond villain's den. It was also known as the Taiwan Centre due its shape resembling the island. The fountains sprayed high before falling into the aqua green of the huge water feature.

"My aim is the empowerment of my organisation. That is the overriding objective—I must be able to delegate as it is the only way to ensure manoeuvrability. The price is I do not have full control of everyone."

"What would you say to those who say the existence of your organisation promotes misery?"

"A flawed and simplified view of the world."

"Is this going to be a speech on nihilism?"

"Not at all." Oso chuckled. "The opposite. The most important thing in a man's life—a man or woman's life—is a sense of purpose. And if families like mine did not exist then entire judicial and law enforcement structures would not exist—and those people employed within them. If there were no sickness, they'd be no doctors, nurses, medical researchers, health ministers. No war, then no military—no soldiers, sailors, pilots, defence ministers, or innovations. There cannot be a yin without a yang."

"So, you're comfortable being on the side of the malevolent?"

"That depends. We employ hundreds and thousands of people—where the government has shunned them, we have not. And, young lady, I have lived many more years than you, been through wars and seen my country kept down by the boot of communism on its throat. The West now try to dictate we be denied the rights to land stolen from us."

"May I ask, Mr Xhelli, why you have taken the time to meet me—taken the effort to have one of your…ahem…employees strike up a friendship with me. I am a freelance journalist, not a CNN news anchor."

"No, but you are one of the more influential journalists. I understand attempts to manipulate you would be futile. But please, you cannot expect a balanced view if all you ever interview or converse with are government officials who want a European Parliament career after holding National office. And they would betray their homeland for European Union money."

"Do you have an example of that?"

"Their capitulation, allowing the thievery of our nation's lands and the people who live in them."

"You are talking about the notion of Greater Albania?"

Anger edged his voice. "Ethnic Albania, Miss Robson. It isn't a desire for expansion, but a desire to see our homeland complete once more."

"I understand," said Ciara. "What now then?"

"I will be in touch."

"I guess I won't be seeing Eralda again now."

Oso said, "Knowing her the way I do, I think you'll be seeing as much of her as you like."

"Should I be concerned?"

"Why?"

"Because she is on your payroll, and she doesn't strike me as a secretary-type."

Oso smoothed his moustache. "She is half Italian—their jealously can be like fire."

"I don't think that would be the case, it was just the one night."

He chuckled. "That woman has been trained to identify her targets quickly and to achieve her objective quickly and efficiently."

Connor watched his old friend approach, and smiled—the market town of Kendal, Cumbria, was a far cry from Louis's south-east London. Connor suggested his friend park closer and wear a baseball cap—a black guy would be memorable to potential after-the-fact witnesses.

They had met yesterday, and Connor had taken him to the ranges so they could zero their weapons.

Louis, dressed in dark clothes and a cap, with a large canvas duffel bag on his shoulder, vaulted the fence in front of Connor with an athleticism the Yorkshireman envied.

He greeted his friend with a, "Just like old times, G."

They hand clasped embraced and Connor replied, "Except instead of armed robbery, we're going to kill everyone in there who even looks at us wrong."

"Awwww, even the little white lab coats up there, fam? A bit harsh, no?"

"Don't feel too sorry for them. From what I've heard they're pumping out carfentanyl and etizolam. One tranquillises elephants and one's called the 'Blue Plague'."

"Heard from who?"

"A little birdie."

Louis said, "Some might say we're hypocrites."

"Good-quality cocaine, Es and puff is the spice of life for a disciplined man. That shit up there is poison—and you know it is," said Connor.

"While we're on the subject. Someone told us that zee Germans back in zee war, laced chocolate with speed—mad ting."

"A bit like how Haribo must be laced with something," said Connor, thinking of the 'morale in a bag' for most soldiers. "Anyway, think anyone saw you come in?"

"Nah, mate, kept away from the street lights and didn't smile."

"Got that one in before me, eh."

"Could tell you were thinking it."

Connor swung his daysack around and set it on the ground as Louis did the same with the duffel bag. He took out two Heckler & Koch G36Cs and their suppressors. He had been tempted to go with the Heckler & Koch UMPs but decided although they had planned for close engagements, the G36C offered a little more range should it be required.

"What's in that?" asked Louis, referring to the hardened plastic, rectangular carrying case around three feet long in the duffel bag.

"Didn't you have a look?"

"No, fam, old habits from me being a *younger* on the streets—you don't look in packages you're transporting."

Connor opened the case to reveal a Remington MSR (Modular Sniper Rifle) custom sniper rifle with a suppressor sat detached in a separate slot.

"Where did you get hold of that?" asked Louis.

"Fell off a lorry," answered Connor. A Ukrainian contact of his had procured it for him. He continued, "The magazine is filled with subsonic rounds—with the suppressor it sounds like an air rifle. Hopefully, I can slot everyone outside before they know what's going on."

"I didn't see that beast yesterday. You zeroed it?"

"Of course I have. What do you think I am?"

"All right, keep your hair on. How you going to patrol up? A Heckler in one hand and the sniper rifle in the other?"

"Nah, this is a specially designed daysack. It won't affect the zeroing."

With that, Connor opened the daysack, and placed the rifle inside the polymer mould before slinging it over his back.

"I don't know where you get this stuff."

"The gypsies, isn't it."

"Fuck off."

Connor laughed, but he did not want to tell his friend somehow Jaime had obtained the daysack for him.

They had zeroed the Heckler and Kochs the previous day at a gun range near Otley; Hughie Birtle had some kind of arrangement with the owners and Connor had not asked.

"You got a bead on McKinley?" asked Louis as they fitted the suppressors.

"Yeh, he can wait for now. He can't call in favours as the lads we've mown down will have heavy connections and they'll be gunning for him."

"Or maybe us cos McKinley will tell them it was a meet and greet and you ambushed them all."

"He might say that. He still has to go around the houses, so we have time," said Connor, before handing Louis the box of Cam Cream. "Here, put that on."

"Here we go," said Louis before he began to apply it. Every British infantry recruit was taught the 'Seven Ss' in their Camouflage and Concealment training: Shape, Shine, Shadow, Silhouette, Sound, Spacing and Sudden Movement. Even soldiers of darker ethnic hues had to apply cam cream to break up the features and take away the shine.

"These fell off a lorry too?" murmured Louis rhetorically, as he donned the night-vision glasses and the earpiece which allowed communication between the pair up to around thirty metres away. They fastened their webbing, and Louis nodded.

Connor said, "I know you have a soft spot for dogs, but I can't afford to taser them this time."

"I get it, but you know there's a special place in hell for people who kill dogs."

"I know, but Barbara Woodhouse died back in the eighties, so I am out of ideas. You?"

"Who's Barbara Woodhouse?"

"She was like a supernanny for dogs," Connor said.

"You should have brought those Dutch boys here, they could have topped them and our consciences would be clear."

"An individual—or a couple of individuals—can have a benefit over the masses as he is more easily manoeuvrable."

"Who said that? Sun Tzu?"

"Musashi—greatest Jap swordsman who ever lived—or serial killer, depending on your view."

"The sword maker in *Kill Bill*?"

"No," exclaimed Connor. "He was an actual person who died in 1645. Anyway, prepare to move."

They checked the pouches of the webbing were fastened correctly, the magazines in their rifles were secure and the firing mode selector on the correct setting: safe.

Connor moved first, zigzagging as he sprinted the first ten metres before slowing into a patrolling pace. Louis then did the same.

This felt strangely familiar to Connor, especially with Louis by his side. He hedged his bets whoever stood guard over the factory would not suspect his previous visit.

Connor whispered, "Push deeper into the right of the wood. Then we can start petalling around the back."

"Roger," came back the reply in his earpiece.

Eventually, they cut through, passed the three o'clock position where Connor had been compromised previously. The terrain began to steeply ascend, the wood denser. They sank back to the left until they stopped and observed from a one o'clock position. The vast wriggly-tin roofs were dotted with vented chimneys and other outlets. Armed sentries—two static and five wandering—patrolled the fenced perimeter.

They knelt, ten metres apart, and observed. Finally, Connor said, "I count seven."

"Same, AKs."

They continued to observe for half an hour before Connor spoke. "Close in on me."

Louis did so and Connor said, "I am going to struggle slotting them all before at least one can give a shout. The pair at the front are in mutual view of the other. We can't wait all night for a shift change, and McKinley probably doesn't have the tactical sense to do a regular rotation."

"Agreed. No point in me cotchin' around here. I'll creep down as far as comms between us go and we'll kill them together. You take the one on the left."

"Sounds like a plan. Closer the better—those G36Cs don't have much range on them."

"I know. I was there at the zeroing, remember."

Connor looked at him. "Put your 'Head and shoulders' on."

"What? Now?"

"Yeah. I wanted to see what you look like with green Bob Marley Dreads."

Louis tutted. "Cretin. When I am in position, I'll call it with a 'One, Two, Three, Execute'."

The Londoner then slid off into the vegetation.

Connor swung his daysack off and set up the MSR and fitted the suppressor. He took up a prone position and began to test and adjust his position. He had a flashback to the last time he had killed with a sniper rifle, and he felt the corners of his mouth curve up.

Two bodyguards who accepted money to protect a paedophile politician had met their deaths through the sights of a stolen L115A3 sniper rifle—he remembered the thrill he felt as the .338 rounds tore through one's face and the other's chest. Even more the delight he felt in torturing the MP and how he set him on fire.

It had been Rayella who had been the catalyst, and it occurred to him she was the person he most cared about. And it had been Louis he had turned to when he needed her to be watched over.

His thoughts were broken by Louis's voice in his earpiece. "I am in position."

"Acknowledged."

He positioned the crosshairs on the dark-haired man's jaw—no need for aiming off to compensate due to the short range and lack of wind.

"One…Two…Three…Execute."

The round punched a hole of blood and bone through the sentry's lower mandible. The way he fell stiff convinced Connor he had caught the medulla oblongata, freezing the post-death nerve twitches. He looked up from his scope to see Louis's victim similarly fall.

Connor spoke. "I'll make my way to you."

He collapsed the MSR back into the daysack, checked the magazine of his G36C was fitted correctly, and webbing pouches were fastened securely and began to make his way down.

He waded through the thick vegetation, being careful not to disturb the canopy above.

"Two of the sentries are walking down the right-hand side. If they loop the corner, they're going to see their mates' corpses."

"How much time do we have?"

"About twenty seconds."

Fuck—Connor's reptilian brain snapped on.

"I am still on the high ground—I'll get into position in time. Take out the front one on my mark. I'll take out the rear."

"At that distance?" said Louis, referring to the G36C's effective range.

"We don't have a choice," said Connor, already fighting through the thicket aided by adrenaline.

"Roger."

Connor bit his anxiety down by fighting harder against the saplings and undergrowth.

"Ten seconds."

He broke through to a clear view of the compound and spotted the two walking down. Taking up a standing, supported position against a narrow tree, he tracked the crosshairs a half finger to the left side of the rear sentry's face.

"Three, two, one, execute."

Connor expelled his breath and squeezed the trigger. The top part of the head came off like a bloodied Frisbee. Louis's target had fallen on his face and remained still. However, his victim lay convulsing on the floor.

Connor barely held a belly chuckle. "Look at the breakdancer go!"

Louis replied, "You ever thought about seeing a counsellor, Connor?"

"No," he replied, meaning it. "I am inbound on your location in *figures few*."

He linked with Louis in less than three minutes and said, "Has he finished auditioning for the new *Step Up* film?"

Louis grinned. "Yeh, he got the part."

"All right, I think we've been saved by the wind where the dogs are concerned, but they'll go banzai when we get in."

A cool, nervous excitement began feathering his stomach. The three core principles of room and compound clearing were speed, surprise and violence of action—and that would be the MO once they were inside.

They 'covered and moved' up to the perimeter fence under the soundless night sky. They instinctively switched to hand signals, and Connor gestured for the pair they had last shot, to be pulled back around the corner with the other two corpses.

Louis shook his head when Connor motioned he covered while Louis dragged them. Connor gestured Louis was stronger, who silently laughed his agreement and took a grip of the pair. When he had finished, he shook his head at Connor's insinuation of whipping him.

They took up parallel positions facing down the side of the compound.

The barks punched Connor's heart rate up twenty beats—now it would go 'noisy'.

Three German shepherds careered around the corner like starving Dire Wolves. Connor had steeled himself to what he had to do the day previously, knowing Louis's reluctance to harm any animal. Three clacks of his G36C snapped the barks into death mews.

Shouts went up like flares, and Connor and Louis took up firing positions behind cover—Louis behind a steel skip and he a metallic housing for a giant inert extractor fan.

Connor unlatched his pouch and thrust his hand in, taking out one of the L109A1 HE Fragmentation grenades.

"Louis," he shouted, receiving a nod from his battle partner on showing him the grenade.

He stripped the transit clip off the throat, pulled the pin, waited a second and launched it at the far corner just as three men skidded around it.

Connor, though knowing its effective radius to be fifteen metres, and he had thrown it at least double that, still took cover as did Louis. Even so, he could observe the effect through the steel mesh of the housing.

The dust volcano picked up and tore apart the three in a blood mist.

He bit down a belly laugh before hissing to Louis, "Shoot the lights on the right."

Connor did the same to the few on his left before saying, "Prepare to move."

They went through the usual routine, and Connor moved off first.

A part of his brain screamed at him, spinning him around. Four armed men raced around the corner, mirroring their colleagues' pre-explosion.

"Contact rear!" he screamed, firing and hitting the front gunman in the throat. The steel 'wasps' hissed passed his ears as the others fired back.

They had made a tactical error—seeing their targets in the open, they became 'target fixated' at the expense of their own protection. In addition to his operational experience in the Royal Marines, Connor had spent hundreds of hours on the various secret firing ranges he had access to as one of McQuillan's agents. He developed the habit of practising with his heart rate elevated by a succession of burpees to 'train how you fight' in replicating the dump of adrenaline of actual combat. Other methods included the firing of 'simunition' in team on team when there were other agents present, the painful impact of which bruised the ego as well as the body but drilled in the importance of self-protection combined with correct shot selection and accuracy. Louis himself—though not the shot Connor was—had been battle-hardened in Afghanistan and various street altercations.

With no immediate cover available both he and Louis dropped into a kneeling position. Their rounds shredded the remaining three before Louis fell with a, "Arrrhhhffuucccckkkk."

37

Connor rushed over, seeing the bloody tears in the back of his *Oppo*'s DPM trousers. As he began to reach for his Med Pack, Louis's words interrupted him, "Nah, man, fuck that, it's a bit of shrapnel. Fucking kills—let's kill all these now including any fucking dogs."

Connor's tongue pushed into the side of his mouth as Louis stood and said, "Let's use that opening as an entry point. I'll go point, and you protect the rear…no pun intended."

Louis latched his hand on Connor's webbing as they moved from the skip to a door. They took up position on either side.

After hand signals, Connor booted the door to reveal a staircase into darkness. They flicked their glasses on and Connor said, "You cover this so a grenade doesn't bounce down after us. I'll look for an entry point."

He floated down the stairs. As he turned the corner his night vision became dimmer; they worked by drawing in any surrounding ambient light which became less the further he went down, the sounds of clanging, hissing and machining getting louder.

"Connor, we get back now. Four vehicles speeding up. Looks like some type of *QRF* to me."

The Yorkshireman reversed with his G36C still pointed down the corridor. He joined Louis to see the four Range Rovers speeding up to their location.

"Let's withdraw back where we came from."

"Hang on," said Louis. He went over to a corpse laying on its back, pressed his thumb on the eyeball—a dead check—before rolling the body on its front. He took out a grenade and armed it, before carefully placing it under the shoulder.

They covered and moved back to the treeline and disappeared into it.

"Let's smash it to the original position. I'll set up there," said Connor.

They picked up the path Louis had previously cut through and fought their way back.

Looking on the compound they could see armed men dismount from the vehicles.

After a minute, Connor said, "I count twelve."

"Seen."

"I'll take as many as I can."

"Fuck me," said Louis, "This is Kendal, but it looks like a scene from *Call of Duty*. Why the coppers haven't been up here? I know there's hardly anyone about but there must be a village not far. Grenades and gunfire can't be something they hear every day up here."

The men fanned out in formation and patrolled up to the perimeter.

"Not sure," said Connor, as he finished setting up the MSR, and lay behind it. "Maybe they were told there was to be some building works. Maybe they've been paid off. These lads look more professional than the ones we've just rinsed."

Louis nodded while looking through his weapon's scope. "Looks like they're doing 'dead checks' with one covering."

"Let's hope they don't know the 'anti booby-trap' drill, eh. Either way, I am going to start shooting when it goes off."

He was referring to how they were taught during their pre-deployment to Afghanistan; if a suspected enemy corpse was lying on its front, then one man would grip his webbing straps or clothing, lay on top of the enemy before rolling him a few degrees to one side so if there were an explosive underneath, the soldiers would be largely protected by the enemy's body.

Connor focused in on the man who appeared to be giving the orders—tall, black-haired, impressive chest rig. Connor then looked at the others' body language in relation to him and it confirmed his thoughts.

As if reading his mind, Louis said, "That one at the rear, centre, who looks like an extra from *Predator*, I reckon is the gaffer."

"That's what I thought," replied Connor, swilling saliva around his gums as they got closer to the booby-trapped corpse. "They'll probably spray those seven-six-two rounds at us once they've ascertained our general direction."

"Why do you use big words like 'ascertained' when 'guessed' would do?"

"Because I am smart as well as hard—the thinking woman's bit of rough," he replied, testing and adjusting his position.

One of the men approached the body-covered grenade. Connor stifled a giggle, when one of the men reached out with his foot before kneeling and grabbing the cadaver by its shoulder.

His life incinerated in an explosion of RDX, metal shards, bone and blood. A second later, Connor had shot the commander in the face. The rest scattered for cover, but some were still exposed, seemingly not knowing where the shot had come from and disorientated by the grenade going off.

Connor shot three more—one more in the face, another in the chest, and one in his exposed knee. The rest concealed themselves more fully, so the former Royal Marine sniper used the remainder of the ten round .338 Lapua magazine to disable the vehicles the best he could—two engine blocks and two tyres. Shots were fired back but way off the two friends' location.

"Let's speed cover-and-move back. I know we need to create distance as quick as possible as I don't want us falling at the last hurdle by running into a second QRF unawares."

"Roger that. I'll be like a blend of Usain Bolt and Andy McChad."

Hissing rounds began to disturb the vegetation around thirty metres away.

Connor said, "Let's make like a black man after getting a bird pregnant and split."

"Don't be like that, mate. I'll make an honest woman of Rayella if the condom splits. Just two years until she's legal."

Connor straightened the smile on his face. "Prepare to move."

Andrei sat in the back of the Vendi Special sipping an English tea. The young waitress eyed him furtively and he could see her nervousness. He found social interaction hard and it had marked him out as a child. He had wanted to be close to people and had approached it like any other puzzle that needed to be solved; he had trained himself to observe people's faces for emotional 'cues' and work out the best ways to respond. Eventually, people stated he was 'charming', and although being spontaneously 'funny' had always eluded him, he had observed and memorised some 'high percentage' jokes.

The waitress approached him, clasping her hands. "Mr Tinaj says he will be ten minutes, Mr Faja."

"Did you make this?"

"Yes, sir."

"It is excellent. They tell me you can only get a nice cup of tea in the north of this country, but you might be the exception."

They displayed smiles at the same time; though his was of paternal warmth—despite his young age—while hers was of relief and gratitude.

"Thank you, Mr Faja."

"Take a seat."

She complied, her nerves back again.

"What is your name?"

"Vlora."

"Nice name, nice place," he said, referring to the Albanian municipality of the same name.

"Thank you."

"So, you are a universiy student, yes?"

"How did you know? … Sorry, yes, I am."

"You do not have to be sorry. There is a large handbag tucked into one of the shelves behind the bar, with something inside keeping it upright. I am guessing it is a textbook."

"Yes, Mr Faja, well, not just a textbook, but yes."

"I think you are taking a degree in business."

Her mouth opened a little, before replying, "Yes, yes, I am."

"Business school is good—it helps shorten your learning curve. Do you know what made McDonald's so popular?"

She answered, "Because their food is the fastest and most addictive?"

"In part, but also they were the first—fast-food restaurant at least—to find a way to replicate their business model to the point where a McDonald's cheeseburger tastes the same the world over. And there are more of them than any other fast-food restaurant in the world. "

"I wouldn't want to run a business like McDonald's. Whatever business I decide to go into I want it to be good for people. And not so large I cannot influence it."

Her face turned into a mask of contriteness and fear, seemingly at the realisation she might have caused offence.

Andrei shook his head reassuringly. "You remind me of someone back home who would feel the same way."

"Who is that?"

"It is not important. But it is good you are thinking like this already. Do you know what made Apple so successful?"

She shrugged. "They had the most cutting-edge technology?"

"That's the perception. But other companies were ahead of Apple in some areas of the technology stakes. The reason was, or is, because they were very clear about what they stood for—constant innovation to create beautifully designed, simple to use and user-friendly products. That is what you have to do—with that, you come to see me, OK?"

He produced a card and as she took it, he said, "Can you name a country that doesn't have a McDonald's?"

She opened her hands. "Our homeland. They have Kolonat, the McDonald's imposter!"

They laughed, as the door opened and Arben Tinaj walked in. Vlora excused herself and returned to the bar. Andrei saw Arben's eyes flick to her before setting themselves back at him. As he approached, Andrei admired how he dressed—dark blue corduroy trousers, dark aqua green shirt and a woollen shirt jacket—a little flashy but businesslike, and not the 'gangster' black leather jacket look.

"I got here as quickly as I could," Arben said in Albanian with a watered down *Gheg dialect.*

"Do not be troubled," Andrei replied in the same tongue.

"How can I help you?"

"Do you have business relationships with men of our ancestors in the North of England?"

"Yes, I do."

"My Krye, in anticipation on the borders being tightened post-BREXIT, insisted I find a way to make a lucrative score before that happens. I have formed an alliance with a gentleman from Liverpool. Their distribution networks throughout the United Kingdom are still the most extensive. After many, painstaking months we located a suitable site and built a substantial underground pharmaceutical factory."

"Why didn't you come to us, sir?"

"I could not risk using Hellbanianz while you were drawing attention to yourselves as you were. Now it is under your leadership I feel more confident with bringing you in on certain things."

"Trust is built over time."

"Precisely."

"What can I do for you?"

"There was an assault on this compound two nights ago. Thankfully, they did not penetrate the factory, as I had posted a security element on standby nearby. However, they killed twelve men in total."

Arben frowned. "Why hasn't this been in the news?"

"The security detail was made up of Eastern Europeans who had crept into the country from Ireland. They were given strict instructions not to tell a soul, and were paid a substantial amount into off-shore accounts. There will be no trace of their bodies either."

"No trace? In these times?"

"No trace."

"So they used silencers? Both the attackers and your security?"

"That's correct. Although a grenade went off, the area is very sparse and the few residents nearby have been told there is fast building work going on for an ecological test site. They have all been very well compensated."

"OK. Has this friend of yours made any progress since this has occurred?"

"He doesn't have the human resources to do so—the nucleus of his men was ambushed and killed four nights ago."

Arben gave a subtle nod. "Do you have any suspects?"

Andrei sipped his tea and said, "There is a crime family at odds with my ally—they are from the county of West Yorkshire. It seems I have underestimated them—in particular a man named Connor Reed."

Arben's forehead creased. "He's the one who paralysed Rashid Kumar after he'd already bit a hole in his face."

"Who was Rashid Kumar?"

"A nasty man from Birmingham. His boss, Waseem Khan, was murdered not long afterwards at the hands of his cousin, Thomas Ryder."

Andrei scratched his chin. "Plenty of gangsters are capable of ruthless acts and murder. This Connor Reed has formed links in the Ukraine and Holland. He also has military experience."

As far as Andrei's sources could tell, he had made the trip to Ukraine alone—which struck him as audacious. The more stories he heard, the more he pondered the possibility of a backer. However, though the British law enforcement agencies allowed criminal informants a long leash, they kept them on one—this man had apparently murdered several people both in the UK and on the continent.

"What would you have me do?"

"I have a target package of businesses, both legitimate and criminal. I want you to take your best soldiers and hit them as hard as you can."

"Sir, I cannot hit the civilians in the family."

"Because you made an agreement with the leader of the Southwark Union Gang there would be no family or civilians."

Arben's mouth opened briefly and Andrei continued, "Do not be troubled. I delegated to you because of a trust in your judgement. You were correct to make that deal. Hellbanianz are not an asset to my organisation if you are embroiled in needless street wars. But I need that family taken care of now."

"It'll be done."

38

Bruce sat in the log cabin and looked out onto the vast lake.

Joe Waldron had been a friend of Bruce's since 'P-Company' back in the eighties and owned the area of land. He had gotten out of the Army at the rank of Regimental Sergeant-Major and went on to form a highly successful security company. Waldron was often away and had given Bruce all the security codes to allow full access to his property and land whenever he chose.

Bruce took advantage of the offer at times like these— times he needed to think.

He reached over to his laptop and flicked it on. He typed in various codes before a black box appeared with an audio line through the centre. The digitalised voice stated, "Secure link commencing now."

Ciara's face appeared.

"How are you?"

"Fine. You?"—she was not under duress.

"I am fine. What's your status?"

"Oso Xhelli made contact with me when I was supposed to be meeting Eralda in Skanderbeg Square."

"For what purpose?"

"I think he wanted to get a measure of me, with the view to introducing me to people he knows. If he wanted me dead, I'd be dead. He knows I have a profile amongst newspaper editors, so I've discounted a desire to pimp me out. I think he wants to subvert me to the cause."

"And what is that cause?"

"Generally, it's the resistance to government types and especially outside agencies dictating to Albania."

"He knows once they join the EU, agencies like Interpol and especially the Italian ROS will be given access and cooperation."

Bruce was referring to the elite operations section of the Italian Carabinieri specialising in high-risk anti-mafia actions.

310

"I guessed—but played the open-minded journalist, which of course I am. But specifically, he expressed his dislike towards the EU's stance on disallowing unification of parts of Kosovo, Serbia, Montenegro and Greece into 'Ethnic Albania'—he sharply corrected me when I referred to it as 'Greater Albania'."

"I would surmise it was an attempt at a smokescreen. Oso Xhelli is too shrewd a man not to realise it wouldn't happen."

"I am not too sure. I could be wrong, but I sensed it was a genuine ambition. It was me who brought it up, not him."

"All right," said Bruce. "Jaime will be sending you an updated intelligence package he's been working on—read it thoroughly and commit it to memory—but I can give you the highlights now."

"OK."

"Much of it is what we already know. It is definitely a mafia—it has all the hallmarks of sophistication, a clan structure—family is a requisite, but they put biological inclusivity above marriage—"

"Why? Isn't a meritocracy the way to run a successful business?"

"It is a meritocracy, but bloodlines ensure silence. Members of the Albanian mafia—the real one—never inform, never talk outside the 'family' about business, not even in personal conversations, because they know their entire family is on the line if they do."

"That is a convincing reason to keep one's mouth shut."

"Aye, and they have an ancient code of honour."

"The Kanun," she said.

"Yes, tell me what you know about it."

"I found it in a brochure that was on sale in newspaper kiosks in the country. Passed down by word of mouth for centuries until a medieval Prince back in the fifteenth century codified it. And in the nineteenth century it was written down. Helps govern all aspects of life—the economic organisation of the household, hospitality, brotherhood, clan, boundaries, work, marriage and so on. It's more prevalent in the north of Albania."

"Correct. And Oso's clan is originally from the northern tribes."

"Just how powerful is Oso Xhelli? I know he's one of the main bosses—"

"He's the most commanding of Mafia Shqiptare chiefs, which makes him one of the most influential crime figures on the planet. He's made a series of intelligent moves throughout his career, one being that he supported the *UCK* when the Kosovan War broke out, so now he has a small army in addition to his mafia. A talented linguist, he also speaks Serbo-Croat, which helps his dealings with Bulgaria, Romania and Albania. However, all of this could potentially make him vulnerable—the lightning rod, so to speak."

"Funny you should say that. He approached me without any protection in sight."

"In sight is the operative phrase. I am guessing a stab-proof vest maybe, and a sniper overwatch. Or perhaps he's inclined to take the odd risk—almost every man holds the perception of his freedom dear."

"I got that impression. I have been invited to a function."

"When?"

"Saturday night."

A dawn of possibility rose in McQuillan's mind.

"As you are aware, Eliza Rexha is now the chief caterer for them."

There was a moment's pause, before she asked, "Why is she an insider for you?"

"She's convinced they had her son killed."

"She'll be at this function?"

"It's more than likely."

"What's the plan, boss?"

"I'll speak to Jaime and we'll work up a tactical package between the three of us."

"You know," began Ciara, "Eralda seems to be quite taken with me. Maybe that could be used to our advantage."

Bruce sensed the tone in her voice and did not deem it prudent to ask for clarification.

"I'll factor it in. Anything else for me?"

She shook her head, and they terminated the call. Bruce sat staring at the screen before peering out over the lake.

Ever since a bullet to the knee had forced him out of active field duties and into a more coordinating role, he had always felt a pang of unease when sending his agents into precarious situations. He had developed a better handle on it as time in the role went by—they were not being forced, he had prepared and supported them the best he could, and he had risked his own life and liberty for nearly three decades.

Still, Ciara would be soon walking into a nest of vipers on a mission he had orchestrated. He also knew his feelings—though still present—would not be as acute if he was sending Connor into the fray. And he admitted to himself it was in part due to their differing genders—an old-fashioned cognition maybe, but it was in there. More so was the fact that Connor came from a criminal dynasty—he had an instinctual understanding of how other outlaws thought.

The more Bruce delved into the Mafia Shqiptare, the more impressed, and concerned, he became. Jaime had sent him evidence that a security company in Tirana had purchased various ultra-high-tech alarm and security systems from the US, Germany and the UK—but he could not trace any of the installations. That was when it occurred to Bruce they were being reverse engineered with the purpose of learning how to defeat them.

Similarly, the more he discovered regarding the 'Ndrangheta, the more he realised they and the Mafia Shqiptare were now the two most potent global dragons of criminal enterprise.

As he watched the wind skim the water into waves, he began to construct a plan.

Connor knocked on the hotel door. He could hear shuffling inside and tilted his head down so only the stolen porter hat was visible to the peephole, not his face. The door crept open and Connor rammed his shoulder through it knocking Caris back onto the floor.

Whipping out the Glock 17 he backheeled the door shut. Caris began scooting before Connor said, "Stop."

When Caris did so, he removed the hat and continued, "I am not here to shoot you. Besides, if I was, how's that going to save your life, you div?"

Caris's breathing settled a little, and the fear on his face simmered into anger.

"You...you fucked my life. He knows. He was there—outside my house in the middle of the night. The only reason he didn't kill me was—"

"Was because the police were there, who I called with a red herring."

Caris just stared for a few moments before retorting, "You probably only saved me so you could continue to use me."

Connor put the pistol into his waistband. "How do you work that out? Now McKinley suspects you, you're not exactly spy-worthy any more."

He gestured for Caris to sit on the bed and he complied while asking, "Then why you here?"

Connor reached into his jacket and extracted a heavy envelope before tossing it to him.

"There's all your money back plus interest. It'll help you move around a bit until I sort this out."

Caris stared at it before mumbling, "Thanks."

"I said I'd give it you back."

"How long do you think it'll take?"

"Soon."

Connor left the room and made his way out of the hotel to the Speed Triple. He checked his phone; three missed calls from Tom and a message:

Curtis has somehow managed to snag M. He's got him at one of the disused warehouses—not the posh end one, another one in the south-

east corner of the industrial estate near to the rec where we played as kids. Spoke to him directly on the phone to make sure it's kosher. Heading there now with Luke and Charlie in the van.

Connor reread the message before attempting to call Tom back. It went to voicemail. So did Charlie's and Luke's.

It did not sound right.

Louis had gone back to London and Connor could not think of anyone else to call to help. He took out his phone and opened Google Maps and flicked to satellite view, before zooming in on the warehouse he thought it was.

After a minute, he jumped on the Speed Triple and roared off, not knowing how much time he had.

39

Tom stood looking at the green warehouse Fire Exit door from five feet away. He, Charlie and Luke had purposely parked half a kilometre away and made their way through the trees skirting the path in and around the warehouse itself on its left-hand side. Luke and Charlie now stood on the other side of the building.

Tom felt the phone vibrate in his pocket—that was the cue. He ran up, smashing his boot through it. Though he had told himself, Charlie and Luke it could be an ambush, his brain still half-expected to see Curtis, and McKinley. Instead, there were several olive-skinned men with his cousin who was tied to a chair in the centre.

His peripheral vision caught the reaching hand from behind. He took a step back and dragged the sleeve of the stumbling man before ramming his pistol into his back.

"He has a gun to my back," barked the man.

The men were now turned towards him, all but one with pistols in hand.

"Right, this is what's going to happen," said Tom. "I am going to leave with my cousin, and we'll sort this out later."

"No, my friend. No one is going anywhere," said the grey-eyed, suited man without the pistol. "This is a Mexican stand-off, yes?"

Tom scoured the corners of his mind for a solution. An icy shock bolted down his spine as a metallic clink tapped the back of his head,

"Drop your gun, bitch."

Ciara felt her back press into the red-stitched passenger seat of the black Lamborghini Huracán Evo Spyder as it flicked into sport mode. Her body vibrated with the loud, intoxicating engine noise. She wore a fabric shirt and trousers resembling washed-out denim. Her fur-lined ankle boots had barely a heel to them and her hair was swept behind one of her studded ears.

Grooves in Eralda's forearms appeared as she gripped the steering wheel, her teeth bared in a wolfish smile. The green, yellow and orange scenery whipped by in a blur under the assassin's skilful handling. The sun began to dip on the horizon and Ciara imagined them catching it.

"I had to take a long course with a professional instructor to be able to handle this," she called out over the engine.

She wore a black pressed wool dress with the gap revealing her cleavage. Her hair was scraped into a ponytail flowing high behind her head and the shaven section on display. Her rectangular sunglasses reminded Ciara of the black patches used to shroud Special Forces personnel's eyes in photographs.

"I am impressed," Ciara called back.

Within seconds the road narrowed, and the machine's engine melted into a growl as it slowed.

"It will be slow for a while. These roads are not designed for supercars."

"So, we can talk before we get there."

"Of course."

"My next question could be considered personal."

"You can ask anything you like. It doesn't mean I have to answer it."

Ciara smoothed her trousers. "Is being of dual citizenships a benefit or a hindrance to your profession?"

Eralda took a moment to answer. "Being of both Albanian and Italian descent has its benefits—I can travel and conduct business meetings more easily between the two. Italian and Albanian organisations are respectful of one another—but that respect needs to be watered like a flower, and things must not be lost in translation."

She manoeuvred the Spyder along the narrowing cliff edge road with a nerveless deftness.

"What are the drawbacks? Nothing in life is all sunshine and roses."

After another few moments of nothing but the sound of the engine, Ciara purred, "It's OK, baby, it's early days and I am a journalist. One day in time."

She thought she saw the raven-headed woman's shoulders drop a little before she began to speak. "If you work for two businesses then both may begin to question where your loyalties lie when negotiating between the two."

"A smart girl like yourself might find a way to make it work to your advantage."

Eralda turned momentarily towards Ciara and said, "How do you think I have been able to afford my car?"

"It is a very nice car. You must be very successful," said Ciara, briefly feathering Eralda's forearm with the back of her fingers, who answered, "However, in these organisations it is not just about how successful a person is—it is about something they cannot control—their birth, their bloodline."

Ciara took a moment to answer before saying, "History is full of men and women who affected change."

"Some have died trying, too."

"And most have died of some horrible disease or old age having led a miserable life of unfulfilled potential."

"You are wise as well as beautiful," answered Eralda, reaching over and dragging her fingernails along the inside of Ciara's thigh.

In the distance, Ciara could make out isolated lights on the hillside. As they got closer, she could make out they belonged to a large estate with three distinct buildings separated by a water feature.

"I'd have thought Mr Xhelli might have opted for something less extravagant being a man of the people. Though he didn't seem a fan of Enver Hoxha."

Eralda laughed with mirth before saying, "Liking, maybe no, but benefitting, yes. Hoxha may have been seen as some tough and pure communist revolutionary but half of his cabinet came from the same northern Albanian clan. Believe me, nothing in Albania happens without at least the blessing of the real people who hold the real power here."

"Mr Xhelli's clan?"

"That I cannot say. But it would have been before his time."

"So, when the man Hoxha shared power with for forty years apparently committed suicide and was then denounced as a traitor with his entire clan arrested and imprisoned, this would have been because it would have been in the best interests of certain northern clans?"

Eralda said, "Mehmet Ismail Shehu died in 1981—I was not there, and I could not tell an outsider. But you are an intelligent woman. However, Oso is a man of the people—the house at the back is for himself and his family. The two either side facing one another are for members of his clan, though all houses contain upper floors with guest rooms."

"Which one is mine?"

"I am not sure—he will tell you."

Over the brow of the bend, Ciara could see the white stone car park and an array of luxury and supercars.

"Wow," she exclaimed. "You'd have thought this was Dubai. Now I wonder if I am dressed for the occasion."

Eralda chuckled. "It is a cliché, but you cannot buy style. Give a person money with no sense of dress, and you will not believe how ridiculous they can make themselves look."

"Who is going to be there?"

"Various powerful people—but relax, you are there as my guest."

"About that," said Ciara. "Will anyone there be aware of the nature of our relationship?"

"Some may suspect. But no one will dare ask you about this so do not be troubled."

Finally, the Huracán reached the showroom of a car park. The fireflies danced in the lights of the overhead lamps Ciara suspected housed security cameras.

Eralda parked, and they got out. As they approached, the black iron wall parted, sliding into the marble pillars. The stone eagles on top looked down, and Ciara noticed their red pupils following them inside.

She gestured to them. "Very…ahem…original."

"Oso likes to mix the traditional with the modern."

She could see now that stone foot squares crossed the huge aquatic feature like a crucifix; they were dry and appeared perfectly level with the water. As they stepped on them to reach Oso's home, she could not see the bottom and mused on just how deep it went.

Silhouettes shadowed the windows of the buildings to her flanks though she feigned not to notice. Through the windows of the house in front she could make out men and women talking to one another, some with drinks and others smoking.

The large dark wood doors had a glass window covering the expanse of it in the shape double-headed eagle—a representation of the sovereign state of Albania. The craniums separated with the opening of the entrance, even before they had knocked.

A huge, dark-haired man squeezed into a Tuxedo held up his palm.

"Please excuse, Miss Mancuso, I search Miss Robson here."

Ciara could not decipher the rapidly spoken Albanian, but she recognised the acid in Eralda's voice.

The man bowed in a surreal meekness that put Ciara in mind of a foot soldier being scolded by his evil Queen.

Eralda turned to Ciara. "There is a side room. I will search you. OK?"

Ciara nodded. "OK."

The side room walls were covered in shelves of books with a small table with a thick, sparkling glass ashtray.

"I apologise for this, Ciara," Eralda said, seemingly sincere.

"It's OK. I know I am privileged to even be here. And we haven't known one another long at all."

Eralda nodded. "Please open your handbag."

Ciara felt a rush of relief—that morning she had spent a few moments debating whether to take her commando dagger—a gift—with her. She had surmised she could have explained it away as personal protection before dismissing the idea—personal protection for a journalist might consist of a Taser to stun, not a knife to kill. In the end, she left the Taser also, so as not to be asked questions of why she felt the need to bring it to a party.

As Eralda checked the sparse contents of her small handbag, she asked, "Where is your phone?"

Ciara looked at her. "I didn't think you'd have appreciated me bringing it."

Eralda's forehead creased briefly before replying, "You are a smart girl."

She snapped the handbag closed and said, "You must remove your clothes."

Ciara did so while holding eye contact all the way through, seeing Eralda's lips purse. When she had stripped bare, the black-haired woman made a motion for Ciara to twirl around, and she complied.

"I am satisfied."

"Well, not yet—maybe later," said Ciara with a wink.

Eralda's lips curved upwards.

When Ciara had dressed, they exited. As they stepped into the vast hallway, despite the furtiveness of glances everyone gave her and Eralda, they collectively left no doubt she was an outsider—and she suspected only Eralda's presence prevented stares.

The general dress code seemed to be cocktail dresses for the women and suits for the men. Within this was a spectrum; while most of the women were dressed demurely, one or two, to Ciara's eyes, proved Eralda's theory on fashion taste and money. One lady had a sheer black sarong over a dress comprising an array of bright colours, another a glittering gold dress and matching jacket with maroon lapels. There were not any outlandish clothes amongst the men, although some wore their suits more successfully than others.

The mansion impressed Ciara; more in its thoughtful décor than size. She once thought 3D flooring to be a gaudy invention, but the sharp detail in this open space made a part of her brain feel like she really was about to cross the sky. It juxtaposed the rest of the old-fashioned hallway made of wood, crystal chandeliers, traditional art pieces and deftly colour-coordinated flowers.

There were four polished wood stairways—two on either side—curving up to the first floor before turning back in on themselves to reach the second. A person looking down could see most of the ground floor if they peered over the balcony; however, the opposite was not the case.

The guests parted to reveal Oso strolling through. He greeted her with, "I am glad you could come, Miss Robson."

"I am glad to be here."

"You relax and enjoy yourself. Your room is one of the best I have to offer."

"A room?"

"Yes. You are my guest."

"Are all these people your guests?"

"All these people," he said, throwing his hand back, "apart from a few exceptions—want something from me, whereas I want something from you."

"Which is?"

"For you to attend, which you have. I have special entertainment later, after dinner. My caterer is magnificent."

Tom had Luke and Charlie repeat the plan a few times prior to setting off for the warehouse. Luke would loudly 'Knock-a-door-run' into the woodland along with Charlie. Tom would kick the door in from the opposite side. If things were kosher, Tom would immediately call and tell them to come back. If he had not called within two minutes, Luke was to call Connor and refrain from being a hero.

He counted six, the one immediately in front, the one behind him, and the four around the twins. Those he could see wore gold chains, fur-lined hoods, balaclavas or skull masks and baseball caps—and all but one armed with what he recognised as Stribog SR9 semi-automatic carbines. The one without a gun looked different to the rest—collared shirt, smart trousers, polished shoes and a good watch. The man, about his own age, barked a command in a foreign language—

one of the men unsheathed a huge machete and ran through the door Luke had knocked on—*fucking better have done what you've been told this time.*

That there were no sounds of a scuffle was encouraging. The faint sound of traffic dampened the silence.

After a time, the man issued another command, this time to the man behind him. Tom felt the barrel of the gun leave his head and the sound of feet running away.

"I have seen you once before," said Tom. "London, wasn't it? Orphan, or Aven—"

"Arben Tinaj," answered the man.

"Aahh, that's right, I thought you were the King now? Why you doing the heavy lifting? Seems a bad policy?"

Arben grimaced. "Why are you here? I thought you were the Jon Snow now?"

"I am not Top Dog, I am a General maybe, but not the King."

"That would be your cousin, Connor?"

"Yeh."

"Well, he's not here doing the 'heavy lifting', and I am disappointed. He is the one we want."

"So, you were behind the murder of my Uncle Michael?"

"I have only just been sent here."

Tom caught the hint of a grimace—*you weren't meant to give that away.* "A Mexican stand-off as you say."

"I wouldn't want my man killed, but if I let you go, we're dead anyway."

A desperate sadness swirled around Tom. He knew Curtis's life ended here—he rattled through his options. He could shoot the man he had a grip of through his spine and take his chances at shooting as many as possible—which he would be lucky to get one before he went down in a hail of bullets. And even without the two outside—running out on his family would never be an option, he would rather die, and he was going to.

When the serenity of a decision made came over him and as his trigger finger tightened, it flew through the door—a human head.

Tom felt the man in front stiffen, and the room quietened. The doorway darkened and the shapes of two men filled it. The one at the front, he realised, was the man who must have been holding a pistol against his head earlier.

The man behind was Connor.

40

Ciara divorced herself from the pleasure of the attention she received. First, it had been Ramiz Suxho, the Kryetar—'Underboss'—who had hogged her for a time—his presence had been a surprise, as Jaime's target package suggested he might be out of town.

Finally, he left her, and no sooner had she finished conversing with one person than another would vie for her consideration. Finally, when another man came up to speak, his eyes flicked behind Ciara before turning about foot—Eralda stood behind her.

Oso stood on one of the stairs and silence fell over the crowd.

He began to orate in Albanian and Ciara could see the nods of agreement, then murmurings followed by laughter. She marvelled at his ability to control the throng of people. They began to shift to one end of the large room before exiting.

Eralda whispered, "Now we will eat."

They were the last two to file into the vast dining room. The walls were a light turquoise trimmed with white patterned frames. Ciara admired the flickering fires seemingly within picture frames high on the walls. The light grey-cream seating curved around the occupants, along two rows of three tables that held eight.

Eralda sat across from her, and the other six were made up of four men and two women. Ciara recognised the women as financiers for the Mafia Shqiptare.

With everyone seated, Oso stood to say some words that again Ciara could not decipher apart from the last two — Eliza Rexha. The caterer appeared at the sound of applause.

She smiled humbly and gave a shy wave. Anyone could see she was nervous, although their presumption of the reason would be incorrect.

Arben held his hand up to steady his men's nerves as Connor Reed used Esat as cover to enter the room. Though he couldn't see it, he surmised the former Commando now held Esat's own Stribog into his back, as he gripped the scruff of his hoodie in a tight bunch. Esat's glassy eyes would not focus on him.

Arben asked, "What did you do to him?"

"My cousin gave him a factory reset with a punch," he answered. "As for the headless one, I wouldn't let someone I love drive a fast car on the motorway without at least taking some lessons first—maybe you should adopt the same policy with your men and their weapons."

As if to emphasise the point, the cousin he knew to be Luke together with Charlie Ryder dragged in the headless corpse, and Luke had the dead man's Glock 19 in his hand.

Arben stared at the seemingly unruffled Yorkshireman. "It takes time to change."

"Time no one in this room might have if we fuck up these negotiations."

They stared at one another before Arben broke the silence. "You think we can negotiate now you have killed one of my men?"

"I think you're a businessman. Besides, you sent him out with a machete to chop up my cousins. Can't cry just because he failed."

"I am not the one you need to negotiate with."

"I know that. I just need a meeting with him."

"You think killing him will solve your problems?"

"No, I do not."

"Then why do you want to see him?"

"To make him a business proposition."

"You don't understand—that organisation—even more than ours—is all about honour and vengeance—"

"I know all that. But I also know some things about him you don't."

"Then you should know he contacts me, not the other way around."

"All I need is a picture of some kind. I can track him myself."

"Track 'im off a picture? You some kind of James Bond in disguise?"

"A working-class version maybe."

"What makes you think I have a picture of him?"

"Because you're a smart motherfucker…apologies, I can't say it in Samuel L Jackson."

"Let's just say that is true. You said I was a businessman—what's your proposition?"

"We'll cut you in on the product I get from Ukraine. That way you're less reliant on your suppliers from the old country—they won't be able to dictate to you as much."

"They dictate because they are prepared to slaughter our relatives back in 'the old country', as you say."

"Nah, he won't. He knows if he does he'll get—"

"Why do you keep talking about him as if he's the boss of all this? He has his boss too."

"Leave that to me."

"This man might be in Albania—"

"I don't care where he is. I need to meet him. If you have a name, that would be great, a picture even better. We both know of one another, and what we're both about, and so you know my word counts. I know that if you declare war on us my family wouldn't be able to hold off Hellbanianz, but I know you want your independence. I am offering this to you. I just need a few days."

Arben stared at him for a long moment. "I will give you forty-eight hours. One condition."

"Go on."

"I want confirmation from Louis Allen if you fail, the restriction on the civilians in your family is lifted and the SUG will still honour the ceasefire."

Arben saw the brief narrowing of the eyes before Connor asked, "Do you have his name and a clear picture?"

"I have several pictures and the name I have been given—that's not to say it's his real name."

The eyes flicked to his cousin Tom. Arben could not see the elder Ryder's expression.

After a few moments, Connor said, "I agree to your terms."

"Good, call him now," insisted Arben.

The Yorkshireman gave a replying nod and said, "I'll have to video call him."

"Why?"

"Because he'll want to see I am not under duress."

"OK."

The Yorkshireman let go of the collar and fished his phone out of his pocket and dialled the number.

There were several attempts.

The strong answering voice made as if Louis Allen was in the room. "Fuck me, Del Boy, I'd have given you a call back. I am driving."

"It's urgent. Me and our Albanian friend have come to an agreement. I have two days to square something away for him. If not, they recommence proceedings against my family, and that includes the civilians in it."

"Nah, mate. I aren't fuckin' agreeing to that."

"You have to—I've got this. This is the only way it gets resolved."

"Fuck that, mate, show me your surroundings."

"They have guns. We have guns," said Connor, panning the phone screen around so Louis could see.

The phone exclaimed, "What the fuck is that, man? A human head?"

"Yeh. I was messing around with it and it just came off."

Their laughter, bemusement and irritation jolted Arben. Connor continued, "Listen, this isn't a negotiation. I've made a decision, and I need you to sign off on it."

Time drew out before the phone said, "Fine."

Arben called out, "I want to hear you say it fully."

"If my man here fucks up his end of the bargain, you get to declare war on his family including the civvies, and the SUG won't retaliate."

328

Arben nodded, his heart beating hard and Connor ended the call.

"Name and pictures."

"His name is Andrei Faja. I have the pictures on my phone. How do you want them sending?"

"Do you have Snapchat?"

"Snapchat?"

"Yes. I am not giving you my phone number."

Within two minutes Arben had sent them. Connor looked up from his phone. "I expected him to be older. He looks not that much older than us."

"Men in his position are usually older than he."

Connor said, "I'll be in touch. Could you untie my cousin now?"

"He stays with me."

"You think I am going to let my wounded cousin stay with you? Especially after I've topped one of your men."

"And you think I am going to just let you all walk free after some agreement you could easily go back on—you could simply relocate your family or protect them better. I need insurance."

"Then I'll take one of your men then."

"If that's what you want."

Charlie Ryder said to him, "Listen. Take me instead. My brother is still susceptible to sepsis, and you won't want to listen to him moaning all the time, believe me."

Several eyes flicked towards the other twin. Arben nodded. "All right. I'll take you."

Connor stared at him for a long moment. "And on second thoughts, you can keep your men."

Curtis didn't speak and Arben said, "OK, he goes free," before gesturing to one of his men to untie him.

Connor said, with his hand on Charlie's shoulder, "Don't touch my cousin. Charlie won't try to escape. Do what you have to do from a security standpoint but other than that—"

"Charlie here will be treated like my own family for the next two days—he won't want to come home. But if you don't come through with your promise, he will come back to Leeds—in a body bag."

He saw Connor take a breath and say, "Pick a number between one and five."

Arben stared for a moment. "Four."

Connor's foot back-rolled the severed head before sliding underneath and hoisting it in the air. He performed four kick-ups with it, blood flicking like from tension-released paint brush bristles. As the dead face dropped on the floor, it reminded Arben of one of the pig's heads in the butchers' shop.

With that Connor tilted his head to Luke, Tom and Curtis, who followed him out under Arben's floaty gaze.

Ciara loved the food. She had begun with the Qifqi—balls of rice, egg, cheese and herbs that rolled delicious spikes on her tongue. Next was frogs' legs, which had been a first for her— she felt the texture and taste to be somewhere in between fish and chicken and enjoyed it more than she thought. Stuffed peppers—one with cheese and another with meat.

Eralda's foot touched hers and she asked, "I see you've not eaten all your dishes—you leave part of it?"

"I visited Japan and learnt the teaching of Hara hachi bu."

"What is that?"

"Roughly translated it means *Eat until you are eighty per cent full.* The Okinawans eat like this."

"Oh, so you want to live forever?"

"Maybe not, but I want to stave off old age as long as possible."

"What does 'stave off' mean?"

"Delay."

"So you are enjoying the food?"

"Absolutely."

As she looked around, she thought of Connor poking fun at a copy of 'The Last Supper' by Leonardo Da Vinci in an Amsterdam coffee shop—"*OK, lads, let's put all the seats on the same side of the table*".

She leaned forward and asked Eralda, "Who are these people as a collective—as a group?"

The Italian-Albanian smiled. "I know what collective means. They are all business associates of Oso. The lifeblood of this empire."

"So—no friends or family outside of the business?"

"He likes to keep the two separate."

Ciara found the admission heartening. Her internal dialogue simmered throughout much of the evening. She had been thorough, as always, regarding the files on Oso's clan structure and associates. However, not even Jaime had been able to complete it. This had reminded Ciara of something she had been taught during her agent training—"*The way to defeat futuristic technology is to go back to the past*". If you abstained from the use of phone and e-mail, and instead relayed your messages in person, it made life hard for tech wizards like Jaime to keep track. The dialect differences between different clans meant even other Albanians could struggle to decipher certain words and phrases. And this wrapped in a rigidly adhered-to Omerta meant even though Ciara recognised most of the faces, she did not know them all and therefore had to trust they were all part of it. She had to steel herself with the knowledge that despite how charming Oso and his guests were, they were running an organisation of global reach involved in murder, human trafficking, drugs, arms smuggling, blackmail, corruption and racketeering.

As Oso stood the volume lowered. He spoke in Albanian that swirled murmurings amongst the guests before they all stood.

"What's happening?" asked Ciara.

"This is now the time for the entertainment."

"What is it—strippers, cocaine, cigars and whisky?"

"No, not quite."

They stood and Eralda steered her with a light touch of her hand on the small of her back. The ensemble flowed through the mansion down some spiral stairs. The deeper they went, the more oxygen expanded in her diaphragm.

Finally, they pooled in the bottom of the vast stairwell outside a heavy oak and black iron door, framed by a white marble arch.

He said a few words in Albanian, then caught Ciara's eye and as if reading her mind, he said in English, "I said no one has ever been down here. It has been completed now and I feel ready to share this."

He unlocked the door with keys that looked out of a film about dragons and fair maidens. Ciara's stomach exploded in petals of adrenaline as she heard them—the roars of big cats.

So this was his plan all along—she thought—*to feed me to the lions as everyone watches.*

41

Connor lay on the bed in one of the Heathrow hotels. He was unable to settle despite the cloud-like comfort of the bed. He reminded himself the difference between a genius and a fool was whether he was successful or not—except this time, he had gambled with the lives of his loved ones.

He remembered the icy look on Tom's face as they left Charlie. All he could do was to exude an air of serene confidence—which he did not fully feel—and had shot off on the Speed Triple.

He thought about praying, wondering if he was a hypocrite for doing so. His idea of God was the belief in cause and effect—a level of physics no human could understand.

He decided it was worth a try. He began to murmur the prayer before stopping himself—*you can at least get on your knees, you lazy bastard.*

He knelt beside the bed and felt faintly ridiculous as he clasped his hands—*what the fuck do you care? No one is watching.*

"God, I know this is cheeky since this is the first time I've prayed for a long time and it's to ask you for something. I am not asking you to solve my problem for me, just…just…give me the means to sort it out myself. It's not for myself—it's for my family. If I have to die then I will. I know I am a bad bastard, but these Albanians are worse."

His phone rang.

Ciara calmed herself as they began to file into a small amphitheatre. The dark green leather seating elevated and circled the audience around an octagon made of reinforced glass. Inside prowled a huge lion, the black-beige mane running right down the torso to its stomach, and so thick it gave the impression of short legs.

As Ciara sat the beast looked right at her—the amber eyes momentarily paralysing her.

From the floor a glass divider shot up, enclosing the lion in one side of the enclosure.

Eralda leaned against her and whispered, "Do you know what kind of lion that is?"

Ciara shrugged. "An African lion?"

"No, my sweet. That is a Barbary lion—they are, the phrase is, regionally extinct. It survives only in captivity."

"Is it usual for them to be that big and the mane that vast?"

"Yes, they are originally from the Atlas Mountains in the north of Africa—much colder."

"What is this? A circus?"

Eralda laughed with mirth. "Not quite."

An aperture opened on the far side. Six men appeared pulling a massive, black steel, roaring box. When they finally reached the octagon, a partition in the glass, the exact size of the front of the box, was slid back and the box pressed against it before being opened. A colossal tiger leapt out before thudding into the glass walls with its clawed catcher mitt-like paws.

Eralda whispered, "That is a Siberian tiger. It is still wild."

Ciara looked around at the crowd—not one had a look of discontentment on their faces—just the opposite.

She was aware some would consider her a hypocrite—she was not a vegan, and though she did go to the extra expense of buying hunted meat, her rare cheat meal was the biggest, juiciest cheeseburger she could get from London street vendors.

However, the obvious pre-emptive pleasure these people were taking steeled her with anger.

"How often does this happen?"

"This is the first time. Although he has more than a few animals since this is his opening night."

"Opening night? What will this be?"

"You know how these rich and powerful men get bored. Some people will pay good money to recreate Rome."

The glass divider slowly came down, compressing the chattering crowd to an anticipatory hush.

Ciara's jaw slackened as the tiger leapt over the partition when it was still the height of two men. The lion exploded up to meet it. A tornado of insane roars ensued, amid clawed strikes and upper body wrestling. The tiger gripped the black mane with its claws and fangs before rolling its opponent onto its back. Ciara, despite her loathing of what was happening, could not help thinking of how much it resembled a NoGi jiu-jitsu match with strikes.

Their terrifying roars echoed around as they exchanged killer swipes, bites and throws.

After a time, the relentless pace seemed to be wearing on the lion, whose mane now began to look less like a protective crown and more a cumbersome hindrance, as the tiger began to grip it before 'pulling guard' and using its hind legs to claw the stomach. Both animals showed the signs of battle, but the Barbary's face bled from deeply clawed grooves, and on its hide appeared patches of claret.

It began looking for an escape, thudding its pleading paws against the glass. The throng roared and Ciara felt her hatred towards all of them boil within her.

The lion's attempts to defend itself became feebler as the amped tiger repeatedly took its back to sink its teeth into its furred neck, before ragging it.

It pinned its black and beige cousin by its throat, pinning its front paws with its own, before deeply slicing the undercarriage with its hind claws.

The Amur stopped clawing as the life ebbed out of the lion, despite keeping its jaws clamped to its throat. Finally, it reared up before releasing the dead lion.

The crowd's screams washed Ciara with sadness, anger and conviction.

"Excuse Eralda, where is the ladies' room?"

Oso's eyes flicked over to Eralda 'I Kuq' Mancuso, as the journalist got up, either to use the ladies' room or to calm herself—sometimes the stomachs of more 'civilised' people did not find such displays palatable.

Though it pleased him to see the gleam in Eralda's eyes he had never fully trusted her. Although her actions had helped make his clan millions—her status maybe only matched by Ramiz—her bloodline was impure. However, her familial links to the 'Ndrangheta had helped his clan become the most influential in the Shqiptare.

He thought it strange how she and Andrei had never gotten on. They were brother and sister, albeit half.

It amused him they did not know.

They shared the same father—his cousin on his father's side. Oso did not kid himself; if Nako had been alive, it would have been him ruling the clan. Before he had gone to Lazarat he presented details to Oso of his two bastard children and asked for them both to be watched over. It was as if his cousin knew he was going to die. Indeed, Oso and Nako had been keenly aware eight hundred armed police officers were about to descend on 'the cannabis capital of Europe'. He remembered the conversation.

Nako had said, "I will go down there to command our men. They must not think we have abandoned them."

"Nako, victory is impossible. There are hundreds of armed police on the way—they will overwhelm you with sheer numbers."

"I did not say I was going down there for victory. I am going down there to uphold the Besa we have to our men."

"Sorry, of course. I will come with you."

"No, you will not. You will stay, and one day it will be you who leads our clan."

"You cannot know this."

"I do. It has been said to me—do not be troubled."

After a moment he had asked, "Are you going there to die, Nako?"

"I am accepting of the probability."

Another silence for a few moments. "Is there anything I can do for you?"

"There is," said Nako, pulling out a leather-bound folder. "These are two of my children—they have different mothers—they are both grown. I want you to watch over them, Oso. And when the time comes, bring them in."

"That will be difficult if their mothers are not part of our clan."

"You are the smart one—you will find a way once you are in power. I believe in you—that is why I am going to Lazarat and not you."

And he had managed to have them brought in—indeed Oso had not even known who Andrei's mother had been, all his Mik would tell him was that she died while he had been young. In a fantastic stroke of luck, one of the girls from the clan had run away years before to Italy—Oso discovered she had died on a transit back to Albania; and so she became Andrei's 'mother', and thus ensured his full acceptance within the clan.

Eralda had not been so lucky—her mother was very much known also as the mother of a formidable 'Ndrangheta underboss. Her dual bloodline had been both a blessing and a curse. Oso had always been wary of Eralda's loyalties.

The roars of two African lions drew his attention back to the octagon. Amid the noise of the crowd he could hear bets the amount of the yearly wages of three good men in some of Albania's poorer villages.

A feeling of confidence welled within him. After this, they would open their coffers even wider. He needed access to their money if he were to challenge the 'Ndrangheta.

He remembered what Eralda had said, and she was correct—the ability to see the opportunities in seemingly perilous situations was a strength. If he could lead the Mafia Shqiptare to defeat the 'Ndrangheta, not only would almost all of Europe's cocaine trade belong to his men, but he would ensure, one way or another, that the money laundering expertise would be transferred from Calabria to Tirana.

He looked around at these people who controlled vast wealth and resources, caught in a primal frenzy, and smiled—*we are all beasts by our nature.*

337

Eliza Rexha's heart would not stop reminding her of the terrifying scenarios that could follow. She tried to concentrate on the after-service cleaning. Hygiene was something she had always been scrupulous on. After a time, it had occurred to her how silly she was being—ensuring the utensils and cooking equipment was so free of bacteria they would not harm the people she wanted to die anyway. She had dismissed her staff twenty minutes ago, insisting she could finish off the remaining bits herself.

Her nerves had been jangling all night at the thought of anyone going near the basket.

Eliza hung up the stainless-steel spatula before jumping with a start. "*Zot!*—I didn't even hear you."

The woman with short, silvery-blonde hair stood before her. The emerald eyes met hers and she asked, "Where are they?"

Eliza pointed to the bottom shelf underneath the worktop. "They're in the large handbag."

The broad-shouldered woman walked over to it and knelt, before lifting the cover and looking in the bag—the bag full of grenades, a pistol, an urban webbing belt and magazines.

Eliza's heart shot into her throat, choking her warning cough—Eralda Mancuso had entered seemingly from nowhere; Eliza had heard her referred to as 'I Kuq'—*Red,* due to the blood she spilt.

Ciara stood, and the two women faced one another.

"What are you doing?" I Kuq asked the English woman.

Ciara looked at Eralda with a smile that was not returned. She would have rather been caught by anyone else in the house other than her—Oso even.

"I wanted to thank the chef personally," said Ciara.

"Then what are you doing knelt underneath the kitchen surface?"

"Excuse me?" she replied, feigning anger. "She was showing me the ingredients she uses."

"Show me."

"Look yourself, we're not starting off with you following me around and demanding I jump through hoops."

She saw a flicker in the eyes before Eralda walked over.

When they were close, the blonde killer said to the dark-haired assassin, "Why did you follow me?"

Eralda's eyes engaged to answer, and that was when Ciara punched her hard in the jaw.

The snapping of the Italian-Albanian's head had not been from Ciara's punch—it had been from her razor edge instincts in riding the blow.

Still, the connection was solid and Eralda fell, skidding on the floor.

"Lock the doors," Ciara hissed at Eliza. The chef responded immediately.

As Ciara descended on Eralda, she saw a kaleidoscope of emotions in her eyes flicker within seconds; shock, fear, anger then hate.

Ciara thanked providence the guests were transfixed by whatever spectacle they now watched in the belly of the estate.

Eralda used her feet from her laying position to tip one of the work tables between them. The stainless-steel rain of utensils, chopping boards, pans—and knives—crashed to the floor.

Ciara's negotiating of the metallic litter allowed the assassin to get back to her feet, just as she stepped towards her.

Both threw strikes so swift and precise that an onlooker would have thought them choreographed if not for the sounds and the resultant marks on both their faces.

There were no wild screams or shrieks from either woman—only the sounds of their exertions.

In Ciara's peripheral vision she saw Eliza slide around the perimeter to reach and close the far door.

Eralda's speed surprised Ciara, and she realised she was finding the fight more difficult than she imagined. However, she felt the stronger and more powerful.

The Italian-Albanian's forehead smashed against her cheek like a battering ram, with the surprise and force leaving her momentarily disorientated.

She stepped back, and catching the bloodlust in her pursuer's eyes, took advantage. Snatching the wrist of her attacker's striking arm she whipped through a modified *ippon seoi nage*—shoulder throw—pile-driving her bodyweight through the impact of the landing.

The noirette's eyes bugged out in pained shock before swiftly returning to beacons of determination. She tucked her head into the muscular Brit's shoulder before reaching with her untrapped arm.

"Knife," shouted Eliza.

Ciara reacted instantly, switching her attention to Eralda's stabbing hand. The mafia hitwoman passed it to her other hand, scoring pain down Ciara's ribs.

Her desperate attempts to keep her opponent pinned while getting control of the blade was akin to trying to grip wet soap and being cut every time you failed.

Though the Italian-Albanian killer had not yet managed to stab her, the slices had blood-soaked Ciara's torso. Her concentration kept at bay thoughts of death.

Finally, she snatched the wrist holding the blade and straightened it out. Her head whipped into the pretty face like a smashing bowling ball, over and over—*this is how you headbutt, you fucking witch.*

She stopped, long after the body beneath her stilled and the knife released.

She turned and saw the slack-jawed and glassy-eyed Eliza staring at her.

"Eliza."

The older woman remained catatonic.

She stood to full height and walked over.

"Eliza!" Her voice snapped the caterer's attention on her. "Stay here. Don't move. I'll come back in not less than

340

four minutes and we can leave together. If I am not back in four minutes then leave on your own and I'll make my own way out. If someone comes in here before four minutes have elapsed, then tell them I killed her. OK?"

"Yes."

"Repeat what I have said."

"Stay for four minutes. You will come back and we will leave together. If you are not back, then I will leave on my own. If anyone comes before you are back, then I tell them you killed this witch."

"Maybe not call her a witch."

"Yes."

Ciara walked over to the sink, wrung out a flannel and quickly wiped the blood from her face. She did not have time to assess, let alone dress, her wounds.

And she could not estimate how long until she bled out.

She turned to Eliza, pointed at the clock on the wall and said, "Four minutes, starting from now."

42

Oso observed the crowd as it screamed in bloodlust. It had been a grand display, as the three ferocious cats fought in the same enclosure as the dead Barbary lion. Oso knew why the Amur tiger had easily defeated the Barbary—it was not because it was outmatched—it was because it had never known the harshness of the wild as the Siberian had.

The two African lions were a different story—they furiously harried the tiger to exhaustion. As they now tore it apart, Oso looked up to focus on the individual reactions.

His brow furrowed as he noted now both Ciara's and Eralda's absence. He cursed—he had been so enamoured with the spectacle he had not been mindful of his surroundings and thus did not know how long Eralda had been gone.

He turned to Ramiz and asked, "Did you see Eralda leave?"

His Kryetar shook his head. "I was too focused on the amazing show before us."

The journalist at least had been gone too long—he stood and began to make his way to the door.

That same door opened in time with his widening eyes and mouth—a grenade came sailing through.

He dropped to the floor with a scream of, "*Ulu!*"—Get down!

His thumbs jammed in his ears, saving his hearing, but the guests did not stand a chance. They were shredded by the scalding shrapnel that sliced his fingers and scraped blood-grooves on the top of his head.

He looked up only to see another one flying, this one to the far end. Even through his thumbs he could hear the screams stop.

He could feel the dripping blood sobbing from his lacerated hands and head. His bones had been rattled to the point he did not trust them to support his frame.

That treacherous, murderess cunt. My own blood.

342

He decided playing dead was his best strategy. He stared into the wide dead eyes of Ramiz.

His ability was being tested as he heard futile gunfire being returned by the clacks of a silenced weapon.

Then more clacks.

Then the clacks got closer.

And finally, "Won't you look at me, Oso?"

The English voice stunned him.

He lifted his head with as much dignity as he could muster. He saw the claret slices intersecting on her body.

"You?"

"Yes."

He nodded. "Is she dead?"

"Yes."

"At least she was not helping you."

"Well, not yet, but she will be. In her own way."

"You will not escape. I can see your strength leaving you. My security—"

"Your internal security—the wandering sentries—they are dead, as are the men in here. Your external security won't have heard or felt these grenades due to the superb soundproofing, and because this hideous place is deep underground—rather like hell."

"You stupid bitch. They monitor the security cameras. They will be here any moment. I would—"

"Taking a while, aren't they?"

"What have you done?"

Her bared, blood-grooved teeth kicked him in the stomach. "I like you not knowing. Now this was not ever meant to be personal—until you made me sit through that revolting spectacle of animal cruelty."

"You think killing me is going to change anything? All you will do is speed the process of ascension."

"I am counting on it," she replied, squeezing the trigger.

43

Andrei sat on the balcony of the Parisian hotel bar nursing a black coffee while assessing his options. The gold lights of the Eiffel Tower had a hypnotic effect against the backdrop of the sky's layering of black, purple, and dark blue. He allowed himself to enjoy the moment as it might be the last sunset he witnessed.

He had an evening flight back to Tirana booked.

If he boarded it now, he could not be sure if he would be walking into an organisation craving his leadership or baying for his death. However, not to board it would be a confirmation to the suspicions that at least some in the organisation must have.

The apparent massacre of Oso, Ramiz and some of the most politically and financially influential people in Albania, and the fire razing the Krye's home to the ground, would cast suspicion on him by his absence. The bodies had not been identified yet, although two were unaccounted for. The last people to leave were the kitchen staff, although Andrei found it strange the head chef had stayed behind a full hour after her staff had left. He thought of his mother—his real one. She ran a restaurant in Tirana and every time he visited the capital, he would make sure to observe her from afar. The one thing he could not allow was the clan discovering who she was. For one, he would be excommunicated and probably killed, and two, she would be in danger too.

A voice bolted him out of his thoughts. "Gorgeous view, eh."

Andrei looked up, already knowing what he was going to see—Connor Reed. He was dressed in a white shirt, blue three-piece suit and red tie. He carried a small, leather man-bag in his left hand, and held a glass of the cocktail French Connection in his right.

"It certainly is."

Reed took a seat next to him without asking and said, "You know, I was reading about this conman from the Czech Republic—well, back then I think it was Austria-Hungary—who, in the twenties, convinced a group of metal dealers the government couldn't maintain the tower and was going to scrap it. Said he was overseeing the sale. Anyway, cut a long story short, he convinced one of these businessmen to impart a massive sum as a bribe—he fucked off back to Austria, and this bloke was so embarrassed he didn't call the police."

Andrei nodded. "Victor Lustig, a very clever man."

"Can't have been that clever—he eventually died in prison."

"Subjective," replied the Albanian. "What are you doing here? To kill me?"

"Don't be silly, we wouldn't be talking like this, would we? And I wouldn't have bothered getting myself a drink."

"Do you like that drink?"

"Yes, it's on a par with Margot Robbie's bathwater. Now, can we dispense with the small talk, seeing as it's not your strong suit?"

"Yes."

"You're in a bind now. It's one of those make or break moments for you."

"How so?"

Reed showed him his hand before putting the bag on his knees and opening it. He pulled out two folders and set them on Andrei's table.

He touched one and said, "This is a folder with all the mock-up evidence that shows Eralda Mancuso was responsible for the mass assassination at Mr Xhelli's residence."

He paused to take a sip of his drink before touching the second folder. "In box number two, is mock-up evidence you orchestrated the killings—not only that, you used your own mother—your real one—to do so. There is security footage of her being the last one to leave the compound before the explosion hit."

Andrei could feel his heartbeat on his eardrums.

"Oh my—look at your face—you didn't know she had become chief caterer."

After a moment, Reed began laughing and snatched words out of the air between gulps of it. "You trying to protect your mum…by keeping your distance…making her think you were dead…was the thing that brought her into the fold. The irony."

"I am glad it amuses you."

"Don't be like that, you'd be laughing too if you were in my shoes—in fact you probably wouldn't be."

"Who are you?"

"You know who I am."

"No, you're something more than a criminal from the North of England. You killed six of my men and escaped, you have these…documents…tracked me here. Are you a law enforcement informant?"

"Don't be a spaz, it doesn't suit you. It would have to be a pretty lax law enforcement agency to turn a blind eye to me killing people."

"Then what?"

"Put it this way, justice and the judicial system aren't mutually exclusive—the gap has to be filled by some entity."

"A vigilante group?"

"If you like, mate."

"We are not mates."

"I know. You autistics find it hard to make any— something to do with a lack of vasopressin which helps males to bond."

"You think I have autism?"

"No," said Connor. "Besides, I don't like labels. Hopefully the extreme logic will make this an easy decision."

"Eralda Mancuso was the half-sister of someone very high in another organisation. He will not believe this 'evidence'."

"Salvatore Mancuso, an underboss in Calabria."

It irked Andrei how much this Connor Reed knew. He said, "Then you are aware this could lead to a war that will cost money and lives."

"There's a story of a warlord who finally united the Mongol tribes. When faced with the task of conquering China, he confessed to his wife his doubts of his ability to achieve such a huge undertaking. Do you know what she said?"

Andrei shook his head. He had never heard the story. "No."

"She said, 'Your name is Genghis Khan, not Genghis Khan't'."

"That did not happen."

"Fuck's sake, Rain Man, it's a joke. I just mean, you have to have a 'growth mindset' regarding these things, as well you know. I am sure you'll figure it out to your advantage."

Andrei did know this was true and said, "I sense this isn't a case of simply choosing between the two."

"See, that's that big brain working. You're right—there are stipulations."

"Tell me."

"I want a financial compensation package met after your…interference in my family's affairs."

"The financial damage of your attacking of our pharmaceutical factory will exceed any reasonable request of restitution."

"How do you work that out? The assault had to be curtailed before I even got in?"

"The mercenaries you killed cost a lot of money. And I discontinued operations with the knowledge we had been compromised."

"Fair enough," said Connor, "but the proportionality of loss—if that's a phrase—is far greater our end. And not for nothing, but it was your fault in backing the wrong horse in McKinley, which brings us to my second stipulation—"

"And you assassinated six of my men—men of our clans."

"No. Eralda Mancuso assassinated six of your men, at least that's what the narrative can be, or you assassinated them, since you were there. It's up to you."

Andrei knew for sure not only did he have the weaker hand, but that Reed knew that he knew. He asked, "Do you

347

know the reason Oso invited those particular people to his home?"

"To squeeze them for money in the war against your Calabrian cousins."

"It is a war I wish to avoid. Given the reasons for it are false."

"You want to avoid it because you believe you can't win," said Connor Reed, sipping his drink.

"This would seem reasonable given their vast wealth and a large number of our donors now lie dead."

"A smart guy like you will be familiar with the Soviet-Afghan and Vietnam wars."

"Russia and America were superpowers that invaded, not the other way around."

"Listen, you need this war, and to win. The folks back home are going to want vengeance, and if you fail to give it to them, they are going to get more suspicious than they already are. However," said Reed splaying his fingers, "if you pull off a victory, then you become a demigod, and most importantly you can protect your mother. And I'll be helping you."

Andrei picked up his cup but saw it empty. "I understand why you—or the people you work for—would want a war between us and Calabria. But why do you wish to help me?"

Reed put one ankle over the other and said, "You defeating them, rather than them defeating you, will cause more damage to you both as a collective. There's always going to be mass organised crime, but our Italian friends are beginning to form a monopoly, which isn't cricket, old sport."

"Isn't cricket?"

"It's a term the posh people in England say," said Reed. "Be that as it may, I told you there're stipulations."

"What are they?"

"If and when you become Krye, I want you to sit down with Van Der Saar."

"Anything else?"

"Yes, and this is the most important."

44

McKinley laughed, seeing the blonde twin tied up.

"You again. One of the divvy Kray wannabes of Yorkshire."

Arben Tinaj stood at the opposite wall of the dank farmhouse shed, with three of his men who wore balaclavas. McKinley had with him three of his own, all tooled up, as per the agreement—he would not be meeting anyone again without armed backup for a long time.

In the past two days, several of the men whom McKinley could have called upon for assistance had been arrested. Luckily for him, a police informant of his had advised him several weeks ago to ditch his Encro phone, and that seemed to have saved him from the copper bracelet. However, his pool of manpower was further reduced adding to his anxiety.

Still, his nerves calmed seeing the young Ryder tied up because if Arben truly wanted to kill him, he would have probably had them ambushed leaving the car, such was the desolate nature of the location.

The Hellbanianz leader said, "He is for you. I want you to remember this gift. But he must be used to get the others out into the open. Andrei wants this matter ended once and for all so we can all make money again."

"Don't you be worrying about that, la," replied McKinley. Though he did not have to feign gratefulness, he knew why Arben had given him his kidnap victim and the assignment of killing the remaining members of the Ryder family—*so it's my responsibility and my head should it fail.*

Still, he looked forward to torturing this kid—he would have the little cunt raped on film. Then take one of his ears off—*fuck it, the pair of 'em off.*

"What now then?" he asked.

"Have you brought a van like I asked? Untraceable to yourself?"

"Yeh," he answered truthfully. He had one of the lads buy it for cash at a used car dealer in Ellesmere.

"Then take him and—"

Arben's words were cut short by a can clanking into the room. The door slammed shut.

"Get the door!" shouted Arben at McKinley, who froze for a moment. He rushed over to grab the handle before yanking it in futility. The cylinder burst forth hissing gas into the small room. He clamped a sleeved hand over his mouth. Arben could not have betrayed him as he and his men were being gassed too.

The blurring of his vision coincided with the hollowing of his legs. He sank to his knees before his survival instinct shot adrenaline to his arm so it could reach for his gun. Its responsiveness ebbed before it got there, and he passed out.

McKinley's unconsciousness gave way to an interplay between reality and dreams.

"He looks like he's coming around."

"Give him the shot. I don't want this to be taking all day," said another, familiar voice.

He felt a sharp pinpoint of pain in his arm before a rush in his veins catapulted him back into the room. His heart rate boomed as his brain desperately attempted to unscramble the scene before him.

Naked, he was rope-bound to a wooden chair. The Ryder men stood in a semi-circle around him. The gaps between them allowed him to see the bodies of his lads, slumped against the wall, wearing bibs of blood.

He could not contain his shaking, which was mirrored in his voice when he asked, "Where's Arben?"

"He's outside. Fair play to him, allowing himself to be gassed out so you and your men didn't start shooting him and us," said Tom.

McKinley felt the freeze of fear pool in his stomach as the pitiless eyes stared back at him.

"You know, Marty," said Connor, centre left. "Throughout this whole thing, I've had a healthy amount of respect for you. Even though you killed my old man and—"

"I didn't kill 'im," he cried out. "It was Der—"

The back of Connor's right hand smacked the rest of the sentence out of his face.

"Don't fucking interrupt me again. Where was I? Yes, even with you killing my dad and uncle, and shooting my cousin, I respected you as a tactician. That's before I found out you was a grass."

"What the fuck? You never told me that," exclaimed Tom in Connor's direction.

McKinley's voice burst forth. "That's cos it isn't—"

He screamed as Connor snatched his ear in a crushing grip before tearing it from his head with several agonising yanks.

"Charlie, how you feeling now?"

"OK to say it's the first time I've been gassed. Seems to be out of my system now."

"Good, go out to the bike," said Connor, throwing him some keys. "There's a first aid kit in the left saddlebag. I don't want this fucker bleeding out."

"OK," replied Charlie, sprinting off.

Connor looked at McKinley, despite talking to Tom. "Caris told me yesterday. He also told me the gun Uncle Ryan bought and my dad got nicked for was from a Scouser named Brian Etim—who our little friend here worked for. When our dads got pulled over it was because this creature tipped off the coppers. And that's how my dad ended up doing a stretch in Armley."

McKinley fought to control his bladder. The blood dripped down his shoulder and onto his chest. He shivered as he heard the squeak of rodents.

Charlie came back and within a minute McKinley had a pad pressed hard against his head with the bandage holding it in place, wrapped tightly around his forehead.

"There we go. We don't want you dying, do we," said Connor, and McKinley's heart leapt. Maybe they were going to let him go—use him, obviously, but—

"Yet," said Connor, and McKinley's heart fell into a bath of fear.

"What…what do you want?"

"Well, we were thinking about what to do with you. I was all for just slitting your throat until the revelation about you being a rat. Then it hit us," said Connor, speaking to the Ryder men. "Let's take him over."

As the ropes were cut releasing him, McKinley attempted to escape, only to have Luke Ryder's punch suck the wind out of him. The hands gripped him before marching him into a small windowless room made of stone, as he fought for breath. They forced him face down before yanking his wrists back and his ankles up. He felt and heard the fast clicks of the handcuffs snap around to secure each wrist to its opposite ankle—he had been hogtied. He fell on one side and began to awkwardly shuffle around.

He faced them as they watched from the door.

"Please, I'll do anything. I'll give you anything. Just, please."

He saw Connor clamp his palm over his face as his body vibrated.

"Why the fuck are you laughing? Please," McKinley begged.

"Anyway," began Connor, "like I was saying. It just hit us. Uncle Mike had a thing for quirky pets. When he got out of the nick, he bought these three little critters."

He reached around the corner before revealing a cage with three white-furred, red-eyed rats. McKinley began to shuffle back before bursting into tears. "Please. What the fuck are you going to do with them? Please."

"Be quiet, you little cunt, you're putting me off my story. Yeh, well, none of us fancy looking after them now he's gone, and so we thought—with you being the King Rat, you could. Now they haven't been fed for a couple of days. Watered, but not fed. We're going to leave them in here with you a few days or so. Don't worry about disturbing anyone should you want to scream—as you know, there's no one for miles around."

"Just kill me. Please, just shoot me."

Connor replied, "The longer vengeance is drawn out, the more satisfying it is."

The door was shut before the steel hatch drew back. The three rats were dropped in. They began to scratch at the door before darting around. McKinley's wet-teared roars banished them back when they moved closer. Their red eyes looked at him, before nudging forward again.

The thought slivered into his brain that Connor Reed might have already killed him, and he had awoken in hell.

The following is a chapter of Quentin Black's follow-up novel—

Counterpart

Carlo Andaloro sat at the end of the Italian bar, enraptured with the football game while still fully aware of his surroundings. His attire consisted of light blue shirt and the white chinos that wrapped around his strong, compact physique.

The scene of the patrons, mostly men, transfixed by the enormous flat-screen, reminded him of a painting he had seen of *Inti Raymi*—an Inca ceremony where they begged the Sun God Inti for the return of the sun. He rubbed his fingertips on his shaved head, and wondered if Juventus's manager would be held in the same reverence as Inti Raymi if his team won the Champions League trophy.

Indeed, it hadn't just been South America he had

travelled to in the last two years since he left the French Foreign Legion, but Europe and Asia too.

He had enjoyed the initial few months of unemployment, until a lack of purpose began to settle on his soul. That and his system being deprived of the adrenaline it had been used to since childhood.

Fortunately, a man from his past reached out to make use of his substantial skill set.

An incident in his childhood inclined him to be aggressive and adventurous, and being born in Reggio Calabria combined to forge a youth who had seen more action and danger—and learnt more about human nature—than most humans ever would.

He raised his hand to one of the men behind the bar—who Andaloro guessed to be the manager, given how he directed the other staff.

"Yes, sir?" the man asked.

"A Campari," said Andaloro, referring to the bright red bitter that included orange peel, bergamot, rhubarb, ginseng and herbs.

"On its own?"

"Yes."

The bar manager reached up to the hanging shelves above them.

"Who owns this place?"

"I do," said the man, with a smile that died as soon as it appeared. "Well, I mostly do."

"Husband-and-wife team?"

He shook his head, "No."

"I guess nights like this are stressful."

The owner nodded. "In more ways than one. Here's your drink."

Italian passions rose throughout the bar as it became apparent that Juventus's chances of winning fell further with another opposition goal, putting them 3-1 down.

Andaloro did not mind the tension crackling in the air; a life without danger and action beat a slow, monotonous slide into the coffin.

He thought about the owner's words—*"In more ways than one"*—being such a busy city bar, the prospect of a brawl was to be expected.

After another ten minutes, the bar's collective eyes switched to two patrons' raised voices, squaring up to one another. Andaloro smiled at the posturing peacocks. Though their demeanours were meant to indicate 'I want to fight', Andaloro knew the real intent behind the gesticulating was, 'I am trying to scare you into backing down, because I want to avoid a fight if I can'. Even as a youth, a person touching him in any manner at all aggressively would trigger him to attack.

The doors crashed open, twisting the crowd to face them like a shoal of fish.

Five men. Three were in their early to mid-twenties, wearing dark jackets, designer facial hair and masks of snarling aggression. A man in his early thirties, with cropped hair, had a shotgun tilted back against his shoulder. He barked, "No one move. We are not here for your possessions. Stand completely still and no one gets hurt."

The man behind him—fifties, the lack of sharpness of his jaw indicating his love of good food had caught a slowing metabolism, and who bore a thatch of grey hair—stood by the door, watching the scene without speaking.

Andaloro knew *what* they were without knowing *who* they were—*Società foggiana*, a relatively young, organised crime group by Italian standards, being around thirty years old, and considered perhaps the most brutal, if not sophisticated.

Andaloro's demeanour betrayed no sign of the

adrenaline bleeding into his veins. It would be in these first few moments that they would be most vulnerable. He admonished himself—this had nothing to do with him. They were here for their protection money—their *Pizzo*. The landlord was probably late paying and this was the Società foggiana's way of convincing him to be on time.

Andaloro knew the template for low-level mafia extortion very well: indebt the owner with an impossibly high interest rate, smash up his business and beat him when the payments were late. Then, at the point of his greatest desperation, offer to wipe his debt in exchange for a controlling share in his business. Use his good reputation and honest face to launder money through it.

And Andaloro did not have an issue with this—everyone got fucked by someone, eventually.

"Everyone stand back," said the mouthpiece, casually bringing the shotgun to bear on the crowd at waist level.

When they did so, he commanded to one of the men, "Ferrucio, go and turn this shit off now."

Andaloro breathed out through his nose at hearing one call the other by his name—*Idiota del cazzo*.

Ferrucio marched menacingly towards the bar, pistol raised. He would have to pass around Andaloro. When the mafioso stepped within two metres of his space, the former legionnaire turned on his stool and said in their native Italian, "Do not turn the television off. I am watching this game."

The comment momentarily rooted Ferrucio and splashed a mask of confusion on him. His face then twisted with anger as he began to bring his pistol to bear.

Within a half-second, Andaloro snatched and twisted the gun out of Ferrucio's grasp. His shaven head crushed the mafioso's nose before his victim hit the floor.

Plummeting to his knees, he blasted Shotgunner in the chest. The man tipped backwards, his nerve twitch causing the shotgun to fire into the air.

The crowd dispersed in a screaming panic, as Andaloro sprinted for a square pillar. Knowing the two armed youths would have tracked him, he popped his head out from one side for a split second. He then spun into a crouch on the opposite side, switching the pistol to his left hand and sliding out.

As he anticipated, their pistols were trained on the other side.

He shot both—one in the throat and the other in the face.

He turned to face the entrance, but amid the melee the old man wasn't there. Andaloro shot back behind the pillar, trying to anticipate where he might be.

Satisfied he had left, the former legionnaire skipped over to the nonplussed mafioso lying on his back with his palm cupping his nose. Andaloro snatched a fistful of his black hair and wrenched back his head, before ramming the pistol underneath his jaw and pulling the trigger. A geyser of blood, bone and brain matter spewed out of the top of the head.

The bar now lay empty of its customers.

He ran over to the side of the bar to see the owner and his staff crouched with hands hovering over their heads.

He barked, "Take me to the CCTV room."

They shot him a collective look of fear, and the owner said, "They have been switched off. They made me—since Wednesday. I knew they were coming but did not know when."

Andaloro murmured, "In more ways than one."

"Yes."

He looked down at the staff—the living witnesses—and contemplated his options. If he murdered them, they could not identify him, but the law enforcement pursuit would be relentless in the face of the public outcry.

He would use them another way.

"You," he said to the owner. "Stand up."

When the owner did so, Andaloro pointed to the man he had initially disarmed, and continued, "He went crazy before turning the gun on himself. Repeat it."

"He went crazy before turning the gun on himself."

"If your story to the authorities strays from that you will join him."

Carlo took a napkin from the bar and strolled over to the previous owner of the pistol. He wiped the gun thoroughly before placing it back into his hand.

A skilled and determined investigator could see through the 'mafioso gone crazy before turning the gun on himself' scene he had set. However, with no CCTV and if no one talked, how far would they be willing to go to disprove it?

It was crowded on the path of least resistance.

AUTHOR'S REQUEST

Please leave a review of Northern Wars

As a self-published author, Amazon reviews are vital for me getting my work out as many readers as possible.

By reviewing it means I can continue to write these books for you.

Thank you so much

Quentin Black

Northern Wars Review

GLOSSARY

Advance to Contact—An offensive operation designed to gain or re-establish contact with the enemy.

Blaze—Slang for cannabis.

Bobby Dazzler—Northern English slang for someone special, either through good looks or by simply wearing something fancy.

Bray—to beat up.

Cabbaged—slang for grieving, or tired, or mentally disabled.

Checking—using one's shin to block kicks.

CPS—the Crown Prosecution Service is the principal public prosecuting agency for conducting criminal prosecutions in England and Wales.

Diddykai—Used by Romany gypsies to describe someone of mixed gypsy and Gorga (see below) blood.

Doylem—North of England term for idiot.

DPM—Disruptive Pattern Material is the commonly used name of a camouflage pattern used by the British Armed Forces

Emmerdale—a British soap opera set in the Yorkshire Dales.

Figures Few—Military term for a few minutes.

FIWAF—Fighting In Woods And Forests.

Geggin'in—Scouse slang for joining in on something when not invited.

Gheg dialect—A variety of Albanian spoken in the north of Albania and other Balkan regions.

Gives best—Gypsy slang for 'to quit'.

Gorga—Romany Gypsy slang for non-gypsies.

Guard—a ground grappling position in which one combatant has their back to the ground while attempting to control the other combatant using their legs.

Het Up—slang for upset.

Jel—Gypsy word for 'Go'.

Legends—fully or partially fictionalised biographies used by undercover agents and people placed in witness protection.

Loiner—a term to describe the citizens of Leeds.

NCA—National Crime Agency.

Maw—Scottish slang for Mother.

Oppo—Royal Marine term for a friend within the service. Derives from the term 'opposite number'.

PGP—Pretty Good Privacy (PGP) is an encryption program that provides cryptographic privacy and authentication for data communication.

Pinged—Derived from the sound a World War II submarine detector made when a submarine was identified. In Royal

Marine and Navy parlance, it means to be found out, or 'volunteered'.

Pulling Guard—to voluntarily adopt a sitting or lying position when grappling.

Pussers—often put in front of words to indicate belonging to the Ministry of Defence i.e. pussers gloves are gloves issued from a military store. If a soldier is pussers, it means he abides strictly to military regulations.

QRF—Quick Reaction Force.

RADA—Royal Academy of Dramatic Arts.

Rash Guard—an athletic shirt made of spandex and nylon or polyester.

Robocop (or Robogen)—if a Royal Marine or Navy rating is asked to 'Robocop it', this translates to 'Accept that if what you're saying is found to be untrue, the front of your cranium is to be shaved in such a manner as to resemble RoboCop with his helmet removed'.

Sandbag—a term used in martial arts to denote a practitioner who competes at a skill-bracket deemed less rigorous than their actual level of competitive ability.

Side Control—(often also called **side** mount, cross mount or cross side) is a dominant ground grappling position where the top combatant is lying perpendicularly over the face-up bottom combatant.

Spats—athletic long pants made of spandex and nylon or polyester. Worn by grapplers to prevent rashes and other abrasions.

Stedhead—Steroid abuser.

Von Flue Choke—a choke from side control using the shoulder as a counter to a guillotine choke. Successfully applied by Jason Lee Von Flue in 2006.

Woolyback—to describe someone not from Liverpool, but from surrounding, more rural areas - derives from the days when bales of wool were being shipped through the docks in huge quantities. The handlers would wear leather jackets, to which the wool would stick when heaved onto their backs for transportation.

UÇK—The Kosovo Liberation Army (KLA; Albanian: Ushtria Çlirimtare e Kosovës) – UÇK, was an ethnic-Albanian separatist militia that sought the separation of Kosovo from the Federal Republic of Yugoslavia (FRY) and Serbia during the 1990s.

Warch—slang for child.

ABOUT THE AUTHOR

+ Follow

Follow me on Amazon to be informed of new releases and my latest updates.

Quentin Black is a former Royal Marine corporal with a decade of service in the Corps. This includes an operational tour of Afghanistan and an advisory mission in Iraq.

AUTHOR'S NOTE

Join my exclusive readers clubs for information on new books, deals, and free content in addition my sporadic reviews on certain books, films and TV series I might have enjoyed.

Plus, you'll be immediately sent a **FREE** copy of the novella *An Outlaw's Reprieve*.

Remember, before you groan 'Why do I always have to give my e-mail with these things?!', you can always unsubscribe, and you'll still have a free book. So, just click below on the following link.

Free Book

Any written reviews would be greatly appreciated. If you have spotted a mistake, I would like you to let me know so I can improve reader experience. Either way, contact me on my e-mail below.

Email me

Or you can follow me on social media here:

IN THE CONNOR REED SERIES

The Bootneck

How far would you go for a man who gave you a second chance in life?

Bruce McQuillan leads a black operations unit only known to a handful of men.

A sinister plot involving the Russian Bratva and one of the most powerful men within the British security services threatens to engulf the Isles.

Could a criminal with an impulse for sadism be the only man McQuillan can trust?

When the ruling class commoditise the organs of the desperate, who will stop them?

When Darren O'Reilly's daughter is found murdered with her kidney extracted, he refuses to believe the police's explanation. His quest for the truth reaches the ears of Bruce McQuillan, the leader of the shadowy Chameleon Project.

As a conspiracy of seismic proportions begins to reveal itself, Bruce realizes he needs a man of exceptional skill and ruthlessness.
He needs Connor Reed.

Ares' Thirst

Can one man stop World War Three?

When a British aid worker disappears in the Crimea, the UK Government wants her back—quickly and quietly.

And Machiavellian figures are fuelling the flames of Islamic hatred towards Russia. With 'the dark edge of the world' controlled by some of the most cunning, ruthless and powerful criminals on earth, McQuillan knows he needs to send a wolf amongst the wolves before the match of global war is struck across the rough land of Ukraine.

Northern Wars

The Ryder crime family are now at war...on three fronts.

After ruthlessly dethroning his Uncle, Connor Reed must now defend the family against the circling sharks of rival criminal enterprises.

Meanwhile, Bruce McQuillan, leader of a black operations unit named The Chameleon Project, has learnt that one of the world's most brutal and influential Mafias are targeting the UK pre-BREXIT.

Counterpart

Can Connor Reed survive his deadliest mission yet?

Bruce McQuillan's plan to light the torch of war between two of the world's most powerful and ruthless Mafias has been ignited.

Can his favoured agent, Connor Reed, fan the flames without being engulfed by them?

Especially as a man every bit his equal stands on the other side.

"When there is no enemy within, the enemies outside cannot hurt you."

Reed, a leader within his own outlaw family, delights in an opportunity to punish a thug preying on the vulnerable.

However, with his target high within a rival criminal organisation, can Reed exact retribution without dragging his relatives into a bloody war.

The Puppet Master

For the first time in history, humanity has the capacity to destroy the world.

When a British scientist leads a highly proficient Japanese engineering team in unlocking the secrets to the biosphere's survival, some will stop at nothing to see the fledging technology disappear.

In the Land of the Rising Sun, can Bruce McQuillan protect the new scientific applications from the most powerful entities on earth?

And can his favoured agent Connor Reed defeat the deadliest adversary he has ever faced?

A King's Gambit

Can the Ryder clan defeat a more ruthless organization that dwarfs them in size and finance?

When the **dark hands of a blood feud** between Irish criminal organizations begin to choke civilians, and strategies to halt the evil fail, fear grips law enforcement in the United Kingdom, the Republic of Ireland and continental Europe.

When this war ensnares the Ryder clan, Connor finds with the choice between trusting the skill and mental fortitude of untested family members, along with the motives of his enemy's enemy.

Or the complete **annihilation of his family.**

Made in the USA
Middletown, DE
23 March 2025

73117282R00219